PRAIS

Nora Roberts Land
"Ava's story is witty and charming."
—Barbara Freethy #1 *NYT* bestselling author

Selected by *USA Today* as one of the Best Books of the year alongside Nora Roberts' *Dark Witch* and Julia Quinn's *Sum of all Kisses*.

"If you like Nora Roberts type books, this is a must-read."
—Readers' Favorite

Country Heaven
"If ever there was a contemporary romance that rated a 10 on a scale of 1 to 5 for me, this one is it!"
—The Romance Reviews

"*Country Heaven* made me laugh and cry...I could not stop flipping the pages. I can't wait to read the next book in this series." —Fresh Fiction

Country Heaven Cookbook
"Delicious, simple recipes... Comfort food, at its best."
—Fire Up The Oven Blog

The Bridge to a Better Life
Selected by *USA Today* as one of the Best Books of the Summer.

"Miles offers a story of grief, healing and rediscovered love." —USA Today

"I've read Susan Mallery and Debbie Macomber...but never have I been so moved by the books Ava Miles writes." —Booktalk with Eileen Reviews

The Gate to Everything
"The constant love...bring a sensual, dynamic tension to this appealing story." —Publisher's Weekly

More Praise For Ava

The Chocolate Garden
"On par with Nicholas Sparks' love stories."
—Jennifer's Corner Blog

"A must-read...a bit of fairy magic...a shelf full of happiness." —Fab Fantasy Fiction

The Promise of Rainbows
"This is a story about grace, faith and the power of both..."
—The Book Nympho

French Roast
"Ms. Miles draws from her experience as an apprentice chef...and it shows...I loved {the} authenticity of the food references, and the recipes...looked divine." —BlogCritics

The Holiday Serenade
"This story is all romance, steam, and humor with a touch of the holiday spirit..." —The Book Nympho

The Town Square
"Ms. Miles' words melted into each page until the world receded around me..." —Tome Tender

The Park of Sunset Dreams
"Ava has done it again. I love the whole community of Dare Valley..." —Travel Through The Pages Blog

The Goddess Guides Series
"Miles' series is an **exquisite exploration** of internal discomfort and courage, allowing you to reclaim your divine soul and fully express your womanhood."
—Dr. Shawne Duperon, Project Forgive Founder, Nobel Peace Prize Nominee

"The Goddess Guides are a **world changer**. Well done, Ava." —International Bestseller Kate Perry aka Kathia Zolfaghari, Artist & Activist

Also by Ava Miles

Fiction

The Merriams Series

Wild Irish Rose

The Love Letter Series

Letters Across An Open Sea

Along Waters of Sunshine and Shadow

The Dare Valley Series

Nora Roberts Land

French Roast

The Grand Opening

The Holiday Serenade

The Town Square

The Park of Sunset Dreams

The Perfect Ingredient

The Bridge to a Better Life

The Calendar of New Beginnings

Home Sweet Love

The Moonlight Serenade

The Sky of Endless Blue

Daring Brides

The Dare River Series

Country Heaven

Country Heaven Song Book

Country Heaven Cookbook

The Chocolate Garden

The Chocolate Garden:

A Magical Tale (Children's Book)

Fireflies and Magnolias

The Promise of Rainbows

The Fountain of Infinite Wishes

The Patchwork Quilt of Happiness

Dare Valley Meets Paris Billionaire Mini-Series

The Billionaire's Gamble

The Billionaire's Courtship

The Billionaire's Secret

The Billionaire's Return

The Goddess Guides to Being a Woman

Goddesses Decide

Goddesses Deserve The G's

Goddesses Love Cock

Goddesses Cry and Say Motherfucker

Goddesses Don't Do Drama

Goddesses Are Sexy

Goddesses Eat

Goddesses Are Happy

Goddesses Face Fear

Other Non-Fiction

The Happiness Corner: Reflections So Far

Home Baked Happiness

Wild Irish Rose

The Merriams

Ava Miles

This is a work of fiction. All of the characters, organizations, and events portrayed in this novel are either the products of the author's imagination or are used fictionally.

ISBN-13: 978-1-949092-07-3
www.avamiles.com
Ava Miles

To the magic of life and new beginnings—in all forms.

And to my divine entourage, who makes me laugh so hard when I most need it and pretty much every other time in between.

In the storied history of matchmaking, no two people could have been more ill-suited for the job.

Some would say they were both far too old, although neither would admit it.

He was cantankerous yet sweet, like a tattered old teddy bear who'd seen too many years.

She was a bit loony in a fun Auntie Mame "let's jet off to Paris for the weekend" kind of way.

But Uncle Arthur and Aunt Clara's hearts were in the right place and that was all that mattered.

Or so they told themselves...

The Merriam children *tried* to tell them that they didn't want or need their help.

Like that would do any good with these two.

It was going to be fun to see what kind of matchmaking mischief they cooked up.

Chapter 1

The Wild Irish Rose Inn was the kind of place that called to mind the rolling emerald hills, lush mist, and magical rainbows of Ireland, what with its sweeping two-story structure punctuated by dramatic towers on each end.

Too bad Trevor Merriam was here to buy this place from Becca O'Neill and put it out of commission.

A lot was riding on this deal, and it was Trevor's job as Merriam Oil & Gas' leading deal maker to make sure it happened. The company didn't want the inn, per se, but the land associated with it. According to geothermal imaging, Ms. O'Neill was sitting on a hefty tract of crude oil, which stretched out to the sea and their company's offshore oil field. Drilling was usually easier on land, and after a recent accident in the South China Sea, Trevor's oldest brother, Connor, Chief Executive Officer of Merriam Enterprises, wanted easy—and safe. He was determined to drop their original offshore plans and set up shop where The Wild Irish Rose was currently located.

Connor was so motivated he'd personally called Ms. O'Neill with a generous offer last week, taking care not to tell her why they wanted to buy her land, of course—

people reacted unpredictably to news of oil. Occasionally, land owners even went to their competitors for a better offer.

Not Ms. O'Neill, though. She'd turned Connor down flat.

When his follow-up attempt had failed just as miserably, Connor had turned the job over to Trevor, saying they needed boots on the ground in beautiful County Cork. Besides, no one had a better track record with this kind of work.

Trevor was intrigued by a woman who would turn down thirty million dollars without so much as a by-your-leave. Then again, Irish women had intrigued him with their perspicacity and frank speaking since he'd made his home in Dublin three years ago.

He stepped out of his Land Rover and immediately detected the pleasing rose scent coming from the hedge of pink and white wild roses that flanked the house. They'd be a requirement with the inn's name, he supposed.

Trudging along the gravel path to the periwinkle front door, a perfect match for the aged gray stone, he almost laughed at the quaintness of the scene. He was already looking forward to savoring the inn's award-winning scones. No reason they couldn't conduct business with a little civility.

He knocked on the door and waited. And waited. Of course, he wasn't expected. Connor had thought it best for him to show up unannounced after Ms. O'Neill had hung up so abruptly on him. Twice.

A dog whined behind the door, followed by the angry meow of a cat. Terrific. He wasn't a patient man, so the crank of the old door handle was music to his ears. When he saw the woman who'd opened it, he was struck speechless. And for a man who made his living sweet-talking people, that was something.

God, she was beautiful. Standing there holding an

Irish setter by the collar, the woman who'd answered the door looked like the portrait of an Irish lass. Her shoulder-length, dark brown hair was laced with hints of mahogany, shining as it were from the afternoon sunlight streaming down. Her narrowed eyes were as blue as a calm Irish Sea. Then there were her lips... Lush and red like a ripe pomegranate waiting to be enjoyed.

He wasn't usually the type to be carried away by romantic fancies. That had been the purview of his twin brother, J.T., at one time.

"May I help you?" she asked.

Oh, she had the softest, sexiest Irish lilt too. He'd lived in Dublin for years but still wasn't immune to the charm of a lilt like that.

"Hello," he said, shifting on his feet as a fluffy white cat with eerie green eyes wound around his feet. "Might you be Becca O'Neill?"

She nodded decisively in a way he found compelling. "I am."

"Everything okay, Becca?" a man called from somewhere inside.

"Yes, Cian," she called over her shoulder. "Are you here looking for a room? Normally, we ask guests to call or go through our online process before arriving, but you strike me as a spontaneous sort of fellow."

"I'll take that as a compliment," he said, wishing the cat would stop weaving figure eights through his feet. His expensive suit would be covered in cat hair.

"American, yes?" she asked him with a straightforward look, as if she were taking his measure.

He liked that about the Irish. They sized people up and made up their minds about them. Part of the reason he'd settled in the country was its no-bullshit attitude about everything from life to relationships, a delightful contrast to the legends and lore infusing Irish culture. "Yes, but I live in Dublin."

"It's a nice day for a drive up," she said, leaning against the door, a picture in a blue cotton dress that seemed to cover her like a waterfall. "Having a weekend away then?"

The three-and-a-half-hour drive had been pleasant. He'd counted the numbers of rainbows he'd seen along the way. Four precisely. Although he wouldn't admit that piece of information to his brothers under torture. "A little business, a little fun. The Irish way, you know."

Her mouth pursed like she was holding back a smile, and the dog barked softly as if to admonish Trevor for letting his eyes slip to her lips again. "You're fortunate. We have one room in the main house left if you'd like it. Of course, the bed will be a bit small for you, I think. It's only a full."

He laughed. "I'm used to having my feet hang off most of the beds in Ireland."

This time she laughed at him outright. "Stay in many beds not your own, do you?"

Leaning closer, he ignored the dog barking again softly. "Wouldn't you love to know?"

She slapped him playfully in the chest. "Oh, you're a cheeky one, aren't you? I imagine you do well in Dublin with that kind of charm. Out here in Cork too, I expect. Have you visited our fine county before?"

"Many times," he said, finding himself smiling full out at her. God, he was enjoying himself more than he should. She was as charming as her bed and breakfast. He needed to keep his head in the game, sure, but he'd learned a long time ago that you *could* catch more flies with honey than vinegar, as his Irish-American grandmother, Anna, had been fond of saying. "I hear you have the best scones around, Becca. Perhaps we can check me in and then have a nice visit."

"Oh, you *have* taken on the Irish ways, haven't you? Cian," she called over her shoulder, "could you ask Aileen to bring out a basket of scones for the gentleman? As for the visit, we'll have to see." Was that a wink she gave him? The dog gave a resounding bark, whether to welcome him or warn him off he wasn't sure, and the cat stopped its weaving and stared up at him.

A car backfired in the parking lot suddenly, and she jerked at the sound, jumping back. He was afraid she was going to fall, so he caught her arm. "Just a car," he said.

She was trembling, he realized.

"Don't worry," he felt compelled to say. "I've got you."

Her eyes met his gaze and lingered there. She licked her lips and drew away, and to his amazement, his hand burned as if it had caught fire.

"A guest's car. Of course. How silly of me." She shook herself. "If you're staying with us, you should meet Boru and Hatshep. Come inside."

He knew enough about anatomy to know the dog was Boru and the cat was Hatshep. "Boru after King Brian Boru who drove the Vikings from Ireland?"

"Ah, you've done your research," she said, leading him to a rosewood desk with classic lines set against a massive stone wall that rose from the floor to the second-story ceiling. "Usually only the Irish know him. What about Hatshep? Any guesses?"

Since Trevor always took note of his surroundings, he caught sight of the wiry older gentleman standing by the wide main staircase, watching them. He nodded a greeting, but the man only continued to take his measure. Protective, he thought. Well, who could blame him? While Ireland was built on hospitality, you couldn't count on a guest being completely above board, he supposed.

"Hatshep," he said, rolling the word around on his tongue. Trevor looked around for clues, taking in the tasteful yellow and navy furnishings in what would have been called the great room in older times. There were paintings of people he didn't recognize on the walls—her ancestors, perhaps, the inn had been in the family for hundreds of years—a couple of country landscapes, and a few hunting scenes. Then he saw the cat's collar, decorated with crowns. "Ah...king and queen. Hatshepsut, the famed female ruler of Egypt?"

"Exactly!" she exclaimed, sitting in the chair behind the desk and drawing out a sleek gray laptop. "Oh, it's so nice to meet someone who knows their ancient history."

She was a history buff? Another piece to what looked to be a really interesting puzzle.

"Have you seen her temple in Luxor, Egypt?" she asked, her whole face brightening.

"It was one of the most incredible sights I've ever seen."

"I've always wanted to go." Those lovely blue eyes shuttered, and she looked down, punching her computer keys so hard they clacked. "Unfortunately, running the bed and breakfast doesn't leave much room for holidays. We're technically big enough to be an inn with twenty-odd guest rooms, but I like the other term since it conveys a warmer hospitality."

And Ireland was built on tourism and hospitality. Yet he hadn't become one of the company's lead negotiators without developing a knack for reading people. The regret in her voice indicated she longed to travel. Now this was something he could use. He well knew the value of discovering what someone really wanted—even if it seemed like an impossible dream—and using it to structure a deal they couldn't pass up. If she wanted to travel, the deal he was offering would make that happen, and in a style she might not have imagined. Connor had made this out to be difficult. Trevor was going to have this deal in hand by dinner, if not bedtime.

If he was lucky, perhaps the inn's proprietress would be willing to celebrate with him even.

A delectable buttery scent wafted to him, and an older woman decked out in a blue-and-white floral apron appeared with the basket of scones, the perfectly golden pastries cradled in a white lace doily. They certainly did have hospitality down to an art. The woman's white hair bobbed around her round face, framing a friendly smile. "Here you are. I'm Aileen, by the way. Welcome to The Wild Irish Rose, Mr.—"

He was already reaching for the scones, their scent making his mouth water. "Merriam. Trevor Merriam."

Becca plucked the basket out of his grasp and stood up so quickly her chair scraped on the stone floor. Boru barked sharply, Aileen gasped, and Trevor caught the lurking Cian straightening to his full height.

"How dare you abuse my goodwill as the owner of this establishment," Becca snapped. "I told Connor Merriam, whom I expect is your relation, that I'm not selling this land. Ever. It was rude of him not to respect my wishes. Please leave, Mr. Merriam."

The cat pawed at Trevor's feet as if to punctuate her mistress' ire. "Let's all settle down a minute. You didn't ask for my name before, and I'm sorry learning it distresses you. My brother said he hadn't handled things well—"

"It must be a family trait," Becca said dryly. "Don't make me ask you to leave again, Mr. Merriam."

The charming, approachable innkeeper was gone—the woman he saw before him was pure steel. "I still need a room for the night."

She gave an indignant snort, a sound he normally would have found adorable if she hadn't taken away his scones and wasn't trying to kick him out.

"I'm sure you can find accommodation in town," she said, closing her laptop with a snap. "I hear The Beastly Pig has vacancies."

Given the name, that place didn't bear contemplating.

"You're seriously kicking me out?"

She walked to the front door and opened it, gesturing. "As assuredly as King Boru kicked the Vikings out of Ireland."

Trevor saw no other option than to do as she asked. For now. When he reached her, he leaned in. "Savor your victory because I'll be back."

"You'll be wasting your time," she said, drawing up under his scrutiny.

Her long, graceful neck caught his eye, the skin delicate and welcoming. Goodness, if they weren't at odds, he'd have asked her out to dinner.

"Admit it," he heard himself say in a cajoling tone. "Up until you knew my name, you were liking me as much as I was liking you."

She playfully swatted him again, and Boru gave a short bark. "Up until I knew your name, Mr. Merriam, I was planning on serving you our mouthwatering scones followed by the most delicious venison tenderloin you've ever tasted. You certainly don't want me to tell you what I'd planned for dessert."

His mouth went dry.

She gave a knowing look, indicating he would really have enjoyed "dessert." "But I can assure you that after you leave Cork, all you will recall of our encounter is what you *didn't* enjoy. Including my land, mind you."

"I will think about it," he told her as he stepped onto the stoop. "But now that you've made it a challenge, rest assured I'll be back." He had to see her again, land or no land.

"Don't bother." Then she slammed the door in his face.

As he left, he found himself whistling.

It had been a long while since he'd enjoyed such a challenge, especially with such a woman.

Chapter 2

Becca watched Trevor Merriam saunter down their lane to his car with a gait as easy as a cool summer breeze. And he was *whistling*.

"Goodness, but he was a handsome fella," Aileen said, her hand resting on her ample hip. "I rather liked the look of him until I heard his cursed name."

Since those words echoed the cheeky ones Trevor had given her, Becca ground her teeth. She *had* been liking him—all six foot three inches of him—until she'd learned he was from the family who'd offered millions for her land. In fact, after he'd touched her arm, leaving a trail of fire sparks, she'd thought about asking him to have dinner with her tonight, in her suite, and seeing what might come of it. It wasn't like she had the opportunity to run across men like him every day. This was something to capitalize on, something the Irish in her would call a magical encounter.

After all, it was unusual for her to be so taken with a man. Sure, he was easy on the eyes, and charming enough. More, he'd known about Boru and Hatshepsut, and the cat had liked him. But she encountered scads of people who were handsome and charming, and few had affected her in such a way. He was smart, and she liked a smart man. Too bad he was a Merriam.

"And suggesting he go to The Beastly Pig," Aileen said, starting to laugh. "That was a good one."

She'd invented the name on the spot, trying to insult him while also misdirecting him. She hoped he'd be stumped when he searched for the inn on his phone.

Cian walked over. "He'll be back, that one. I know the kind of man who doesn't take no for an answer."

"He'd be a stook to come back here," she scoffed, even though she rather agreed with him. "I couldn't have been clearer to his brother and now him."

"If he does," Aileen said, patting Boru on the head when he gave a short bark, "we can set the sheep on him."

"You'd think the Merriams would have troubled to do their research, but he didn't seem to know about our new enterprise. Whatever they want our land for, they'll not have it." After combing through the various Merriam holdings online—there were many—Becca was running toward them developing her inn and the land into some kind of seashore luxury hotel.

Aileen gave a rude snort. "Maybe they don't see one hundred and fifty sheep, a dozen alpacas, and sixty angora rabbits as a moving problem."

Becca had watched the rise of the indie dyeing market in Ireland with interest—and envy. She loved everything about yarn, from the colors to the textures to the woolens she could knit them into. Knitting was a passion for her, one that perfectly suited her lifestyle, although finding the perfect yarn online could be challenging. She couldn't feel the texture, couldn't see the way the yarn changed in the light. One day, after a particularly frustrating online shopping session, it had occurred to her that this was something she and Cian and Aileen could do—they had the land, why not buy some animals and produce and dye their own yarn?

The bed and breakfast was the largest of its kind and

one of Ireland's top places to stay, so they had a solid base of guests. Perhaps some of them would care to buy her Irish yarn and woolen goods. They already had a small storefront for crafts and goodies from locals, mostly women in the community. Plus, they could sell their yarn online on their website. Word of mouth brought in business for their bed and breakfast. Why not yarn?

Cian and Aileen had agreed to give it a go, sensing she needed a new challenge. Plus, it would hopefully get her outside more. Every day was a constant battle to walk out of these walls.

Agoraphobia. A big word for what amounted to a small life.

They'd hired some men and women from town who'd been forced to sell their farms due to hefty tax increases to look after the animals and do the shearing. It was early so far, but she knew it was going to be a success. Maybe not as big of a business as the Merriams were used to, what with their oil and gas and their pharmaceuticals and other holdings. But she was proud of their enterprise, and she wasn't going to let a bunch of bullies with more money than sense stand in her way.

"Powerful men like to have their way," Cian said, shifting on his feet as if calling on his old boxing training.

"The Merriams can't take what's mine by law," Becca said, feeling the need to assure him. Cian understood her condition better than anyone. He was the one who'd pried her out of that small, dark closet in Angola where she'd hidden from her parents' murderers. Her parents and Cian had been doctors with Doctors Without Borders in Angola, but he'd left the service to see her settled back in Cork with her grandmother. He'd ushered her into these safe and cherished walls, and she'd never left since.

The Wild Irish Rose was more than her home. It was her sanctuary.

"Your grandmother won't give it a thought in heaven,

Becca, my love, and neither should you," Aileen told her with a brush of her hand on her cheek. "When you came here and fell in love with The Wild Irish Rose and the O'Neill land, she knew you'd be the one who'd keep it going until it could be passed on to your son or daughter."

Aileen had meant it as a comfort, but the words didn't settle easily. Becca still hoped she would have a child to continue the O'Neill tradition of running this bed and breakfast, but the cynical side of her doubted it would happen. What man wanted to be with a woman who couldn't leave her home to go on a simple date?

While her agoraphobia was more manageable than it had been in early years—thank God, the transformer in town had only blown once, causing one of her worst attacks ever—the Merriams' offer had caused a noticeable setback. She hadn't been able to take Boru on a walk since Connor Merriam had called.

She patted her beloved Irish setter, and he rubbed his face against her hand as if he knew she needed the comfort. Cian had gotten the puppy for her at a low moment, hoping it would force her outside. She'd named her dog after the famous Irish king noted for his courage, a courage she very much craved for herself.

When Boru had needed to walk, she'd gritted her teeth and taken him out. That first time she'd barely made it more than a few steps, and by the time she'd closed the door to the outside world, she'd been panting and covered in sweat. Back then, making it past the hedge of wild roses surrounding the sides of the house had felt like a miracle. Every attempt had been agony, but she hadn't given up.

Over time, she'd found a way to focus on Boru and the leash she held tightly in her sweaty hand, and some days she managed to walk a few times around the house. Boru was her champion, always pausing when her feet seemed to turn to clay.

She'd worked remotely with several specialists over the years, but most had suggested drugs—the kind she'd likely have to take for the rest of her life. They had horrible side effects for her, it turned out, and worsened her depression. She'd tried breathing and relaxation techniques, made lists of her fears. Spoken with therapists. Journaled.

The work she'd done had helped, but she still couldn't leave her land. And so she'd focused on making The Wild Irish Rose a microcosm of everything she wanted from the world. She hosted guests from dozens of different countries and decorated the inn as if it were a global bazaar. They had a five-star restaurant and music on the weekends. Local women came to knit with her every month, and she hosted forums with other community business people. Soon they would produce their own yarn. She'd made it work, and she was grateful at how well her life was going despite the affliction that could have crippled her.

But when Trevor had talked about traveling, she'd felt that deep longing in her heart rise again. She wanted to see those places—Hatshepsut's temple in Egypt and the Taj Mahal in India and the Eiffel Tower in France—but knew it was never to be. While her courage was great, she measured it in the number of steps she took outside these treasured walls, not the airline miles people like Trevor Merriam racked up.

Her home was everything to her, *everything*, and she couldn't let the Merriams or anyone else take it away.

"Let's not give it another thought," Becca said, picking Hatshep up off the ground and stroking her fur.

Cian and Aileen shared a familiar look—they thought she was trying to tuck her fear in a back drawer. They weren't wrong.

The couple had fallen in love straightaway after Cian had brought Becca home to Cork. In some ways, they looked after her like parents might, especially now that her grandmother had passed on.

"Well, I think I'll make a pot of tea," she said, heading in the direction of the kitchen. "We can enjoy it with those scones." Thinking of the comical horror on Trevor's face when she'd plucked the basket out of his grasp lightened her mood.

"You might take Boru for a walk instead, my dear," Cian said. "It's a grand day out."

Her stomach clenched. All she wanted to do was surround herself with the four sunny walls of the kitchen.

"Maybe later," she called. "Aileen, why don't we talk about some of the hand-dyeing we want to test this next round?"

The animals had already given them some wonderful wool to work with, what with the spring and early summer shearings. The alpacas were due for another round in a few weeks given their heavy coats.

She and Aileen were still creating a baseline for her dye samples. So far, they'd had some hits and misses, which was expected, but she was pleased with the progress they'd made. The variegated yarn wasn't as distinct as she'd liked, and God knew the speckled ones were too muddy. But the solid shades were as rich as the sources of her inspiration outside her window: the heather covering patches of the cliffs; the mist rising up from the sea; the wild flowers punctuating the hills; and of course, the wild roses growing around the main house.

"I'll grab my notebook," Aileen said, patting Cian as if to assure them both.

"I won't let the Merriams stop my progress," she felt compelled to say. She couldn't let this trigger another long-standing agoraphobic episode.

Again, they shared a look, knowing she wasn't only speaking of the new enterprise. "We know that, love,"

Aileen said in a loving tone, one she could always count on.

Somehow Becca would muster the courage to keep leaving these four walls, even with the Merriams coming for her land.

CHAPTER 3

NORMALLY, TREVOR ENJOYED TALKING TO HIS OLDEST brother, Connor.

Only not when said brother was busting his balls in the run-down bed and breakfast Trevor had been forced to settle for after being kicked out of The Wild Irish Rose.

"This is why I didn't call you yesterday." He'd hoped to buy himself some time, but Connor was so eager to get Becca O'Neill to capitulate that he'd called the next morning, which was the middle of the night for Connor in California. The lack of sleep likely wasn't helping his mood. "I knew you were going to take this badly, but it's just the first pass."

"But how could you leave without upping our offer?" Connor asked, exasperation lacing his voice like the cream lacing Trevor's tepid coffee. "For God's sake, Trev."

He supposed he should be grateful the coffee was drinkable since the scones were hard as bricks and the Irish breakfast sitting in front of him, with its runny eggs and even runnier blood sausages, looked more like an abstract painting than a work of culinary art. Even the porridge at The Stag's Head Inn was goopy.

There were no other vacancies in town. He'd checked

twice. Of course, there was also no Beastly Pig Inn. Score joke one to Becca O'Neill.

"I told you to go to thirty-five million," Connor spat.

"Money alone wasn't going to do it," Trevor told him for the third time. "I was trying to get her to like me." And she had, darn it. Something that had kept him from sleeping as well.

Connor scoffed. "*Like* you? Who cares about liking you?"

If the lady had been anything other than a business interest, Trev would have been concerned with her liking him—and much, much more. My God, she was beautiful and starchy. Maybe it came from having an Irish-American mother and cousins from the South Side of Chicago, but he liked starchy women.

"Trev, have you forgotten the one rule of business?"

Connor didn't expect a response, so Trevor didn't give him one. He lifted his cup of coffee to his lips.

"It's more important to be respected than liked," his brother finished.

Of course, Trevor could have mouthed the words. "We do things differently. Sometimes you have to start off with a soft sell."

"A hard sell usually works for me," his brother fired back.

"Does it? Becca O'Neill hung up on you. Twice."

There was an audible pause.

"Connor, I love you like a brother—"

"I *am* your brother—"

"But you need to get off my back here," he ground out.

Another moment of silence passed before Connor cursed softly. "Sorry, but do I need to remind you of what's at stake here? I'm not going to build another offshore rig."

This time it was Trevor who cursed. Reminders of the accident did that to him. Their first cousin on their mom's side, Corey Weatherby, had been the lead engineer on their deep-water rig off the Makassar Strait. The steel had buckled in the aftershocks of an earthquake, crushing Corey and some of their workers. Trevor tried to tell himself they were lucky the rig hadn't exploded and caused a devastating oil spill, but the human cost of the accident still haunted him. So did the memory of Corey's two young sons crying softly at their father's graveside.

Connor had taken it the hardest since he and Corey had been longtime pals. They'd even gone to the University of Chicago together to be roommates.

Which was why Trevor was going against his better judgment and not telling Connor to drop his pursuit of the O'Neill land and proceed with their original plan to drill offshore.

"I know the stakes and the reasons, Connor," he said softly. "Dammit!"

"Patrick still wants the head job at the new rig, and I won't have another cousin or Merriam employee injured or killed, Trev."

Shit. More guilt. Patrick Weatherby was as tough as Corey, his brother, and Trevor respected his cousin's gumption. A lesser man might have let fear stay him, but Patrick was excited by the new opportunity, whether the rig was offshore, as originally planned, or on land.

Connor was determined to obtain the Irish government's approval to drill on land. But they'd need to convince Becca to make it work. Making matters worse, oil drilling was a notoriously controversial subject in Ireland, something Connor refused to hear. The local community wouldn't be as open to the kinds of community projects Merriam Oil & Gas funded in countries starving for hospitals and schools. Ireland was different, and Trevor only saw an uphill struggle. Plus, he didn't like opening the door to anyone else drilling on Irish land. He'd come to love this country he'd made his home.

There was also the larger issue that Connor had unilaterally decided the company wouldn't pursue new offshore operations. Anywhere in the world. A pretty big damn decision to make without their board of directors, if you asked Trevor, and he was on the board. For now, he was making allowances given Connor's grief and trying to be a good brother and Merriam employee, but he was ripe with moral dilemmas. He almost laughed at himself.

"We're going to drill on land and be the first in Ireland proper to do it," Connor said, his tone brooking no dissent. "Offer her forty million when you go back," he added, "and don't take no for an answer this time."

It came as a relief when the line went dead. Trevor couldn't take Connor's grief and guilt any more than he could his own. Here he was, feeling like shit, when he'd done nothing to cause the earthquake that had killed their cousin and the others. Even if he'd been there, he certainly couldn't have stopped it. Their final risk assessment had shown all that, but it hadn't stopped any of them from feeling responsible for the accident.

The O'Neill land was the best they could hope for in terms of drilling and transport. Did a bed and breakfast owner really need four hundred acres for her guests? Maybe she'd part with some of the land, if not all. It was worth a try. He picked up the phone, thinking it might be better to call than show up in person. She might set the dog on him.

"Becca O'Neill, please," he said when someone answered the phone.

"May I ask who's calling?" a woman asked. Not Becca. Her voice, he'd recognize. This was likely the older woman with the scones.

He winced. "I'm a local contractor interested in speaking to her about a business offer." It wasn't a lie.

There was a pause. "Just a moment."

He tapped his knee as he waited, impatient and not sure why—until he heard her voice. "Hello."

Her lilt seemed to caress the words and did tantalizing things to his skin. Good Lord, he'd never been this turned on by a simple word. "Be honest. You've been thinking about me, haven't you?"

"Mr. Merriam?" Her voice sounded like she'd eaten maggots now, and he laughed.

"Trevor. Look, I have this crazy idea."

"Imagine that."

Dry wit perhaps, but she hadn't hung up. "You gave me the impression that you liked to travel. How would you like me to arrange for you to have a private tour with a noted Egyptologist in Luxor?"

Was her breathing faster suddenly? The very idea turned him on.

"We're talking the Valley of the Kings, Karnak Temple, and Hatshepsut's Temple, of course. I could even arrange with Egyptian Customs to bring your cat in faster without quarantine. You could stay in one of the luxury hotels. At our expense."

"Would I have to trade my soul to Osiris?" she asked.

God of the dead and afterworld. Good one. "No, not at all. I was thinking—"

"I didn't know you could."

He couldn't help but smile. "You have a large spread. How about you sell me two hundred acres, away from your beautiful inn, and I'll give you twenty million? You could travel anywhere, live anywhere, all without giving up everything you've built, Becca." He made sure to use her name now, and he liked the feel of it on his tongue. "What do you say?"

"I'd say you're a tease and a charmer, but I knew that when I first met you."

"See, I told you that you were liking me."

She gave an indelicate snort. "Be that as it may, I'm going to speak slowly so you understand me."

"What? I couldn't keep up you were speaking so fast."

He could have sworn he heard her chuckle. "I wish we'd met under other circumstances."

"Me too. You're still not speaking slowly, Becca. Or perhaps you'd like to do something else that's slow. I can do slow real nice." God, he was outright flirting with her. Over a business deal. Part of him was shocked, but she was remarkable, and he couldn't help himself.

"Goodness, you are cheeky, and while I like the idea of slow, here's mine. No. Deal. Ever."

Damn. He'd been afraid of that.

"Was that too fast for you?" she asked, sauce in her tone.

"No," he said. "Well, I'll have to think up something else then and come round. I want to see you again, Becca." There, he'd said it.

"If you were any other man, I'd love hearing it. Goodbye, Trevor."

She hung up, and he knew the use of his given name was a sign. He was getting to her, although perhaps not in the way he'd hoped. God, didn't he have enough complications?

His phone rang again, and he was disappointed to see it was his younger brother, Flynn, and not Becca calling him back.

"Hey," he said when he answered. "Is there a wave of Merriam insomnia or something? Isn't it four a.m. in the Big Apple?"

"Yes, but I'm in Stockholm."

"Do I want to know why?"

"It's August and beautiful and the days are long," Flynn said with a sigh. "Gorgeous women abound."

Normal Flynn speak. "If you like blondes..." Right

now, Trevor was into brunettes, namely one. Becca O'Neill.

"You're in the mood I expected. I heard Connor just busted your balls. Do you need a Band-Aid?" His brother laughed.

"Like I'd let you get that close to my jewels," Trev said. "What do you want? Is the tech side of the company getting you down? Do you need to get off on torturing me?"

"You wound me. I called to check up on you, Trev. Few people get under your skin like Connor."

Trevor poured himself more coffee. "He gets under everyone's skin. I'd like to say it's because he needs to get laid, but I don't think that would improve anything. Maybe I'll ask Santa to bring him a cute little Mrs. Santa for Christmas. What's new with you?"

"That brings us to the other reason for my call," Flynn said. "Aunt Clara and Uncle Arthur are starting their European tour."

He sloshed his coffee. "Their what?"

At his eightieth birthday party in Dare Valley, Colorado in May, his adopted great-uncle had threatened to visit all of the still-single Merriam children, with Trevor at the top of the list. The reason was terrifying. Uncle Arthur—as they called him—had just married Trevor's Aunt Clara, who'd been estranged from the family until recently. After their success in matching up Trevor's twin, J.T., with Arthur's grandniece, they'd decided to take up matchmaking. Trevor feared Uncle Arthur would pour as much energy into this endeavor as he'd given the newspaper he'd founded and run for decades.

If they were on their way to Europe, he was in trouble.

"You heard me," Flynn said. "I was just talking with J.T., and he said Aunt Clara was talking about a second honeymoon—in Europe."

"Didn't they just finish a honeymoon in Arizona?"

Aunt Clara had talked Uncle Arthur into driving to the Grand Canyon in his new convertible.

"You have to admire the man, don't you? Two honeymoons at eighty. I want to be him when I grow up."

Trevor had told Uncle Arthur as much on occasion, which didn't make him any more eager to be set up by a couple of senior citizens. "I don't want their help finding a woman."

And yet he found himself thinking of Becca O'Neill again. Surely she was the kind of woman King Boru had fought to protect during the Vikings' invasions.

Trevor would have picked up a broadsword to defend her had she been his. Oh, he was talking nonsense. She was a takeover target. But he wanted her to be so much more...

"Well, they're coming your way. Cheer up. Maybe they can help you with the bed and breakfast owner. Connor said she's as tough as nails. I bet him a hundred you couldn't make the deal in a week's time."

He stabbed one of the blood sausages, much like he wanted to stab his brother with the fork. Flynn often initiated side bets on the more interesting business activities. "That seems almost sacrilegious when you think of Corey."

Silence reigned over the line. "You can be such a dick sometimes. Corey would have doubled the bet if he were still with us."

True that.

"You know...you aren't going to want to hear it, but it needs to be said. You and Connor are taking things a little too far here. Quinn too. What happened to Corey wasn't your fault. Heck, it wasn't anyone's fault." Which was the only reason he was here in the first place. Had circumstances been different, he would have told Connor to drop this.

"I was just telling myself that earlier, dammit," Trevor said. "You need to up your bet with Connor. A hundred won't do it, Flynn. She's a challenge."

"And we all know how you love challenges," Flynn said. "I'll increase it to a thousand and give you two weeks."

Two weeks to dance with Becca O'Neill. This might be a bet to lose.

"If I win, I get to bring the new French model I've met to your place in Dublin for the weekend. I've told her about the music scene, and she's intrigued."

"You're a moron," Trev said. "First, your bet is with Connor so I shouldn't have to pay you shit, and second, French models are high-maintenance."

"You think all models are high-maintenance," Flynn said.

For sure. Trevor liked a woman with more substance, one who knew what was important in life and would stand up beside him when the chips were down. Rather like Becca O'Neill.

"Personally, models are great because they're beautiful, have their own careers, and travel a lot. There's a low commitment factor. I like them for all that. That's why I get laid more."

Trevor laughed. "In your dreams..."

"Uncle Arthur and Aunt Clara are going to change your solitary existence, bro. Soon you'll be walking up to your front door whistling at the very thought of seeing your lovely missus inside."

"I'm hanging up now."

"Have fun with Uncle Arthur and Aunt Clara," Flynn said. "Tell them I said hi."

With that threat, his brother hung up. "Moron," he said out loud.

And then it hit him. Maybe it wouldn't be so bad if his aunt and uncle *did* drop in on him. The Wild Irish

Rose had a five-star honeymoon package, he'd seen on the website, with a private cottage on the grounds. If Uncle Arthur and Aunt Clara stayed there, he could visit them. Surely Becca wouldn't throw out a devoted nephew visiting his elderly relatives. He almost laughed. They'd both beat him to death with an umbrella for calling them elderly.

But no one who worked for Becca was going to help him, he expected. Certainly not the older man who'd watched him like a hawk from the stairs. And the one who'd brought him the scones with the sweet smile on her face. Aileen? She had turned as cold as an Irish winter the moment he'd given his name.

He decided to bide his time until his aunt and uncle called. It only took a few hours, he was delighted to discover.

He connected them to FaceTime and settled back in his rickety chair. "Well, hello, you two. You're up early. How's marital bliss?"

"Marital bliss?" Uncle Arthur scoffed, crunching on what Trevor knew to be one of his favorite red hot candies. "At our age? Pull yourself together, Young Trevor."

Aunt Clara socked him, a picture in a white ruffled blouse. Even though he hadn't known her until recently, she looked years younger than her long white hair suggested.

"Our bliss is fine, Trevor," Aunt Clara said. "It's yours we're worried about. I was sorry to hear about your cousin, Corey."

They'd been on their extended road trip/honeymoon when the accident had occurred. "I appreciate that, Aunt. How's everything in Dare Valley?"

"Pretty much the same as it's been since I came here in 1960," Uncle Arthur blustered.

"It's wonderful," Aunt Clara said after giving her new

husband a harsh look. "But we're hankering for another trip."

"You and Hargreaves are, my dear," Uncle Arthur said.

Hargreaves was his aunt's English butler, who was as old as the couple he served. Trevor found him hilarious, what with his formality and dry wit. He always traveled with them. His aunt had said she couldn't do without the man or his Indian food. He served as a cook and chauffeur as well, something Uncle Arthur blustered about constantly.

"We're coming to Dublin to see you, dear," Aunt Clara said. "J.T. said you'd love a visit."

J.T. had told them that? He wasn't sure whether to kill him or kiss him. Time would tell. "I'm not in Dublin right now, Aunt. I'm in the countryside."

"Even better," she said, bouncing in her seat. "I've always wanted to see the Irish countryside. The green hills, the mist, the rainbows—"

"Don't forget the unicorns and leprechauns," Uncle Arthur quipped. "My passport isn't in order."

"Bull," his aunt said. "Hargreaves and I found it in your sock drawer yesterday. Now, Trevor, we won't be in your hair all the time. We know you have work and such. Plus, this will be like a second honeymoon."

"You're supposed to take that after you've been married a while, Clara," his uncle barked.

"But we're old and need to make up for lost time," she said, glaring at him. "Especially after your heart attack. Enough. Trevor, please text me the town you're in, and I'll have Hargreaves look for a charming place for us to stay."

"She texts now," Uncle Arthur said, peering closer at him over the phone. "It's terrifying."

He fought laughter. "I don't want you to have to do any research, Aunt. I know of a bed and breakfast with a really great honeymoon cottage."

And a beautiful owner to boot. Part of his motivation, he realized, was simply to see her, and their presence would give him the excuse.

"I'll send you the information. I'm staying in town because I wanted to be closer to the pub, but I think it will be perfect for you and Uncle Arthur."

She clapped her hands. "How nice! Doesn't that sound nice?"

"If the plane ride over doesn't kill me," his uncle said, all bluster like usual.

"Can you come right away?" Trevor asked. "I shouldn't be here more than a week or so."

"We'll be on the next plane if we can," his aunt said. "Arthur, I won't hear another word."

"Might get trampled if I say more," his uncle said, his lips twitching. "Let the boy go, Clara. You got what you wanted."

His aunt turned. "What *I* wanted? Have you forgotten that this was your idea, you addled old man?"

"Goodbye, Young Trevor," Uncle Arthur said as he leaned forward, ignoring Clara's sputtering, and disconnected them.

Trevor let loose the laughter he'd been fighting. Oh, they were a perfect pair. He wondered if he should feel bad for using them when they planned to come and do their own matchmaking.

Nah.

***

"That was way too easy," Arthur said, studying the phone.

"You're being paranoid," Clara responded, transferring to his lap. "Who wouldn't like a visit from us?"

Arthur decided to let it go. "You need to remember we're only there to have a good time. Not find Trevor a wife."

"But you said—"

"Okay, we might give the countryside a look around for a good woman," he said, thinking it over. "After all, my track record isn't bad here in Dare Valley."

"So you keep saying," Clara said. "This time I'd like to take the lead. However will I catch up to your matchmaking record if I'm not given a handicap?"

"A handicap? Lord Almighty, Clara, I can get you one of those handicap signs for your car."

"The limo? Hargreaves wouldn't appreciate that, and neither would I."

Why the woman insisted on being ushered around in a limo in Dare Valley he'd never understand. This wasn't Manhattan, after all. Hadn't she left her New York City ways behind her? As he looked at the ruffled white blouse she wore, he acknowledged she hadn't. Honestly, she looked so good in it he wasn't going to complain. If there was one thing he wasn't, it was a stupid man.

Clara's phone gave a honk, the horrible sound alert she'd chosen for her texting.

"Must you have that tone, my dear?" he asked, putting his hands over his ears playfully.

She kissed his cheek before hopping off his lap. "I chose it to make you crazy, my love. Have to keep you on your toes now that we're married."

She certainly did that, and he did love it despite his grumbling. He had to keep her on her toes too.

Picking up her phone, she sighed like a girl being asked for her first dance.

"What did he send you?" he barked. "Some picture of a hot Irish guy?"

She laughed. "No, The Wild Irish Rose Inn. Oh, Arthur, it's perfect. We're going to have such a wonderful time there. I know it."

He imagined they would, and besides, seeing Trevor would be nice.

"All right, go ahead and book the honeymoon cottage," he said. Truth be told, he'd do anything to keep that glow about her, and didn't she know it.

She gave him that special soft smile he loved so much. "I'll have Hargreaves prepare everything. We'll leave tomorrow."

He hadn't believed it when she'd said so earlier. "Tomorrow? But that's—"

"Tomorrow," she said dryly, her head buried in her phone. "I can't put my finger on it, but Trevor needs us. Maybe he's more upset about his cousin's death than he's letting on. J.T. said Connor is mad with grief."

Mad with grief? What was this? *Hamlet?*

"After being out of my family's lives for so long, I want to help any way I can."

Oh no, she was developing motherly instincts. *Merriams, look out.* Of course, she could be right about the cousin's death. Something like that would upset anyone. Still... "Trevor needs us like a pair of pants needs a dress."

She leveled him a look, and he shut up.

"We'll go tomorrow."

Chapter 4

Becca couldn't help but smile as she surveyed the older couple standing in front of her on the stone steps of the bed and breakfast. They were by far the oldest honeymooners The Wild Irish Rose had hosted.

An elderly man in a black raincoat was holding an umbrella over their heads, and she knew he must be the butler they'd secured a room for in the main house. His dubious gaze was fixed on Boru, who was bouncing in place by her side. Her dog knew who the special guests were the moment he laid eyes on them. Hatshep was a tougher nut to crack. It took a true treasure of a person to win her loyalty.

The memory of Hatshep making figure eights around a certain unwelcome guest's feet intruded on her consciousness before she could banish it. That he should ask for half her land! The audacity. And yet she hadn't stopped hoping he'd show up at her door with a new offer she could deny. Drat.

"Welcome to The Wild Irish Rose," Becca said, gesturing for the couple to come in out of the rain. "It's a grand treat, having you stay with us. I'm sure you'll have a lovely visit."

"I'm Clara, and this is my beloved husband, Arthur,"

the woman said, shrugging out of her pink raincoat with Arthur's help while the butler closed the umbrella and placed it on the rack for drying. "Hargreaves, our butler."

"Good God, woman, don't say 'our butler,'" Arthur said, taking off his wet spectacles and drying them with a white handkerchief. "He's part of your entourage. I can tie my own shoes and button my cardigan just dandy on my own."

"He's cross from the plane ride," Clara said. "Ignore him. He's usually a lovely conversationalist. On the way here, he was telling me about the last time he visited your fine country."

"Don't tell her how long it's been," Arthur said, his American accent crisp. "If she guesses how old we are, we might not qualify for this honeymooner cottage you're so set on."

The man shot Becca a cheeky grin then, and she fought the urge to laugh out loud. So he was all bluster, like storm clouds that produced no rain showers.

Aileen bustled in with a tray filled with scones and a tea service. "Age wouldn't disqualify you," she said, setting the tray on the side tea table. "In fact, we're downright tickled to see two people finding love at your age. Aren't we, Becca?"

"We are, indeed," she said. "Everything is in readiness at the cottage, Mr. and Mrs. Hale. Mr. Hargreaves, we have a fine room for you with a view of the sea."

"It's Hargreaves only, miss," the man said in a formal English accent. "Any room will be fine. I plan to catch up on my reading and do some bird watching."

"You read and watch birds at home," Arthur said. "Nothing much new there. At least someone else will be doing the cooking. I'm in an Indian-free cooking zone while we're here."

After the grin he gave her, she couldn't resist teasing him. "I'm afraid to burst your bubble, Mr. Hale. We serve Indian food exclusively on Wednesdays."

His mouth twitched. "Clara, we'll have to eat elsewhere on Wednesdays."

"She was kidding, Arthur. Good heavens, most people would be grateful to enjoy Hargreaves' naan bread. He's a master in the kitchen."

"Thank you, madam," the butler said, almost bowing. "Should I see to your things?"

"No, you're on vacation too," Clara said. "He's been with me for decades."

"Few men have their wives bring their butler along on their honeymoon," Arthur said. "I hit the jackpot with this one."

The woman gave him a playful punch as Aileen's laughter spurted out. "You did indeed, and don't you forget it."

"Oh, you two are going to be so much fun to have around," Aileen said. "Anything you need, you just let us know. I'm going to hustle off to call for my husband, Cian. He'll get your baggage squared away."

"Seriously, madam, I can see to the bags," Hargreaves said, looking a bit squeamish.

"Not on your life," Clara said. "Now, let's go see this wonderful cottage. The pictures on the website were amazing, but I know it will be even better in person."

Arthur grabbed a scone off the tray and broke it in half, giving the better portion to his wife, who lifted onto her toes and kissed his weathered cheek. Becca thought it adorable.

"We'll see you later, Hargreaves," Arthur said. "You might check out the deer stalking I saw online. You'd be a prime candidate for lurking in the woods." He delivered that last comment with a delighted bark of a laugh, which made Boru bark as well. Arthur leaned down when Boru came to his side and scratched under the dog's ears, making his tail twitch. "He's a fine dog, I imagine."

"I prefer the cat I see lurking under the sofa over there," Clara said. "Is she a Persian?"

"Yes," Becca said. "Her name is Hatshep, and this one is Boru. They'll leave you in peace if you wish or settle down at your feet if you have a mind for some company."

"Wonderful," Clara said, petting Boru, who nuzzled to her side. "Hargreaves isn't fond of animals, but I've always liked them."

"You don't have to clean up after them," Arthur said. "All right, my bones are aching, and I need to sit after that trip."

"What you need is a good walk," Clara said, "but we'll see to it after we settle in."

Cian appeared, a happy smile on his face. Becca introduced him to the group.

"If you'll take this lovely couple to the cottage, Becca," Cian said, "I'll see this gentleman to his room."

Becca met his gaze. She hadn't been out of the house since Trevor Merriam had appeared two days earlier. The rain had been her excuse for not walking Boru, although they'd all known better. She knew a good prodding when she saw it, but he was right. Perhaps this couple would help give her the push she needed to take the thirty-five steps out to the cottage.

"Wonderful," she said, infusing cheer into her voice. "Arthur and Clara, please follow me. We'll have to get a little wet again if that's all right."

"Contrary to some people's opinions," Arthur said, "I don't melt. Not sure about Clara here."

Becca almost laughed out loud at the Wicked Witch reference to *The Wizard of Oz*. "We'll be fine."

She took them through the house to the back door, stopping to distribute umbrellas.

"The house is beautiful," Clara said, tucking her arm through her husband's after they decided to share an umbrella. "Has it been in your family since it was built?"

"Yes," Becca said, hoping the reminder of her ancestry would bolster her courage. "Six generations back."

Boru gave a bark when she reached for the door latch, as if to reassure her. Her heart didn't pound like this when she opened the front door for guests.

Open the door. All you have to do is take that first step. Then another and another still. You can do it.

She pulled on the door handle, aware she'd stopped breathing but unable to draw breath. Boru nudged her backside, and she stretched her foot out like a ballet dancer might and touched the wet stones of the path outside. *One.*

"Everything all right?" Arthur asked.

She turned her head quickly to meet his gaze and flashed what she hoped was a reassuring smile. "I hate getting wet, is all. Don't mind me." She hated to lie, but she figured God would forgive her a white fib. She didn't share her agoraphobia with anyone, although some in town had likely guessed.

Raising her umbrella, she clutched it as if it were a lifeboat on the *Titanic. Two.*

"You needn't get wet on our account," Clara said.

Part of her craved the reprieve. It would be so easy to give in. To direct them to the cottage without leading them to it. "No, I'd love to show it to you. If it's not too personal of a question, how did you two meet?" She made herself take that third step and then the fourth.

The couple started walking next to her, and Boru nuzzled her clenched hand. She'd forgotten the leash in her anxiety, but he would never leave her side.

"We knew each other when Arthur came to New York City for college and worked at *The New York Times.* He thought I was a brat, and back then, he was much too driven for me. He returned home to Dare Valley to start his own newspaper and got married. I stayed in New

York and did the same. Our spouses passed away, and we reconnected through my nephew. It's been a surprising and wild ride, especially now that this one finally retired. At eighty, no less."

Becca focused on feeling the path under her feet, counting silently. "Eighty? You're pulling my leg. Arthur, you don't look a day past sixty."

He laughed loudly, the sound helping her loosen her grip on the umbrella. "You must not have a lot of old people for guests. Sixty? You made my day, Ms. O'Neill."

"Becca, please," she said, listening to the squish of wet grass under her feet when she took those first couple of steps off the stone path. "One of my ancestors purposefully left the path to the cottage unfinished, hoping to confuse his oftentimes inebriated cousins whom he let live here for free for a spell. They overstayed their welcome, you see."

"I need to do something like that with Hargreaves," Arthur said, laughing.

"Oh, you're too terrible, and I don't know why I love you so," Clara said. "Becca, are those alpacas I see?"

She steeled herself to look away from the ground for a moment and let her gaze travel to their pasture off in the distance. They still looked funny to her, what with their long necks, but she loved them. They were hers, after all, and part of her new plans. "Yes, we have sheep and rabbits as well. We're going to be making some of the finest Irish yarn around pretty soon."

"That sounds wonderful," Clara said. "I love a woman with a head on her shoulders. Arthur, we should get you a good Irish sweater while you're here. He's always complaining about the cold."

"I can make him one, if you'd like," Becca found herself saying. She'd knitted items for special guests before. Although she usually didn't make the offer so soon, something about these two had charmed her. "I love to knit, and I have some new yarn I'd like to try out."

Arthur patted her gently on the back. "I'd love to be your guinea pig."

She finished counting the steps to the cottage and breathed a sigh of relief as she lowered her umbrella and opened the door for them. Boru stayed where he was, knowing better than to walk into the cottage. "Welcome to Honeysuckle Cottage." She stepped inside quickly, the walls of the cottage immediately calming her. "The name was from another ancestor."

"Sounds like your ancestor liked the ladies," Clara said cheekily. "Goodness, Arthur, isn't this the loveliest spot on earth?"

The sitting room was done in creams and gold, and roses and wildflowers spilled out of crystal vases arranged on the antique furniture she'd used to decorate the cottage. "The bedroom is to the right, and over to the left is a lovely little kitchen nook for having a cozy dinner or enjoying a spot of tea.. There's a house phone on the desk in the small office off the bedroom. Please call us for anything you might need. We don't answer after nine, but we're ready to help at seven in the morning. Oh, and there's bottled water and some snacks in the fridge and an electric kettle and some fine Irish teas in the kitchen."

"It sounds delightful," Clara said as Arthur stuck the umbrella in the stand.

Becca watched as he turned around and gave his wife a golden smile.

Oh, to be loved like that, she thought.

"I'll leave you be," she said, joining Boru outside and reopening her umbrella.

"Oh, Becca, I almost forgot," Clara called, leaving her husband's side. "My nephew will be joining us for dinner, so we'll need a table for four tonight if you have it."

Oh, they had family here? Now their honeymoon destination made more sense. She always wondered what drew people to this part of the country, but she figured they'd tell her if they wanted her to know.

"If he's your nephew, I'm sure he'll be wonderful. We'll look forward to meeting him and serving you in the dining room. See you then."

She closed the door and leaned back against it. Boru pressed his nose to her thigh, grounding her. Retracing her steps was never as hard as taking those first ones, she'd discovered. The trick was to look at how far she'd come. If she'd done it once, she could do it again.

She let her gaze follow the dark, wet grass to the rain-splattered stones leading back to the main house. Another thirty-three steps and she'd be back home.

As she took that first step, she felt a tide of courage course through her body. Nothing was going to stop her from walking back to the house. Cian had been right to press her.

Nothing was going to make her hole up in her house for days on end again, not after all the progress she'd made. Certainly not the Merriams' continued offers. She took each step more quickly this time, feeling stronger with each stride.

Yes, it was important to remember how far she'd come.

CHAPTER 5

TREVOR'S TREK TO THE LOCAL PUB HADN'T PRODUCED MUCH useable information about Becca O'Neill. In fact, the townspeople had seemed downright hostile. Sure, their turned-up noses and cold-shoulder disregard wouldn't have felt notable somewhere like New York City, but this was Ireland, the country where almost everyone was friendly. Or so he'd found. Some would say it was a stereotype, but he'd traveled enough to know better. The Irish were some of the most welcoming people he'd ever met, one of the reasons he'd moved to Dublin.

But not here, it seemed, and he had a notion someone had spread the word about who he was and why he was in town. They were closing ranks around Becca O'Neill and making sure he knew what they thought of his plans. And they didn't even know the full scope yet.

One of the barmaids had loose lips, at least, and she'd waxed poetic about how much Becca did for the community, especially with this new venture of hers.

The woman had sheep now? And rabbits and alpacas? He hadn't noticed any animals on his brief visit, and the information wasn't in Connor's file. According to the barmaid, Becca was planning to make and dye her own yarn. He'd spent enough time in Ireland to know its knitwear was rightly famous.

But why raise the animals when it was far easier to buy wool for dyeing from other sources? She liked animals obviously, but sheep? They were a nuisance if you asked him. He hated shooing them out of the road when they crossed in front of his car on country roads. They never listened.

A woman with this herd wasn't going anywhere. And she likely needed all four hundred acres with that kind of herd. He decided to call Connor with an update—it was early morning in California, but Con would be up—and sat on his undersized bed as he tapped his brother's number.

"I hope you have good news for me," Connor said the minute he answered.

"Do you ever say 'yo' or 'hello' when you answer the phone, or is it just me you're cranky with?" Trevor asked.

"I'm too busy to be cranky," Connor said. "Hello, Trevor, how's your day been?"

He snorted. "Like you care. Look, this isn't going to be a quick deal. I discovered Ms. O'Neill's just bought a bunch of sheep and other animals for her own Irish yarn business, which is likely why she turned down my offer to buy only half her land."

"Half? You're already weakening our negotiating position?"

"The inn's been in the family for hundreds of years, Con," he said. "There's no chance she'll sell it all. Also, from the vibe of the pub, I don't think we'll have any allies in town. In fact, I think we could have some problems."

"Music to my ears," he said dryly.

Their operations didn't need community buy-in, but everything seemed to go easier when they had it. "As you know, not everyone believes in oil and gas ventures in Ireland. We'll have to bring more to the table than our usual community outreach. I could talk about how Merriam Enterprises is into renewable energy until I'm blue in the face, and it won't do much to assure these locals." The residents would balk at the idea of their quaint town expanding and changing. He just knew it.

"Thanks for the depressing update. I'm working my ass off with the Irish oil and gas authorities to get them to make an exception and let us drill on land."

"I told you it wouldn't be easy," Trevor said.

"If it were easy, we wouldn't be in this business," Connor said.

"As lead negotiator and board member, this is where I need to ask if you're really sure you want to continue." He had to say it. "We're running into obstacle after obstacle with this one. I've got a bad feeling about it."

"Becca O'Neill is the only real obstacle, and convincing her is your job. Do it! I don't want to hear any more excuses."

That shut him up. Connor never talked to him like that.

"I hear Uncle Arthur and Aunt Clara are visiting. Flynn mentioned you set them up to stay at the O'Neill place. Good thinking."

He took a sip of his cold coffee, hoping to remove the bitterness in his mouth. "I've been known to have a few good ideas over the years. I'm meeting them shortly for dinner. Hopefully Becca won't kick me out. Of course, Aunt Clara might kick me too if she finds out I used her and Uncle Arthur."

"Remind her she's a Merriam and that we need her help," Connor said.

As if. "You call her and tell her that. I know J.T. has fallen for her completely, but I'm still a little scared of her."

"J.T. thinks she might be able to outdrink you," Connor said. "Now that I'd love to see."

Another challenge. No one could outdrink Trevor, except one wisp of a Chinese sailor he'd come across on a trip to Hong Kong. As far as Trevor was concerned, the man had been half-human. "I'll let you know if we have a drinking showdown. I need to run. Hey, maybe take an hour and get a massage. You need some downtime."

He didn't often comment on his brother's working habits. All the Merriams worked hard; it had been bred into them, but Connor was the most driven, and he'd been working almost nonstop since Corey's death.

"You fussing like a mother hen? Make the deal, Trev. We need this one."

No, he thought. Connor needed it. Was this the only way he could help his brother assuage some of the guilt he felt for Corey's death? God help him. He felt like it would be a deal with the devil.

"I always give you my A-game," Trev said. "See you, bro."

"You too," Connor said before hanging up.

Trevor tapped the table, looking for a solution to their problem. Usually their goals were clear and focused, but emotion had bled into this one.

It didn't help that he was attracted to Ms. O'Neill. He walked to the mirror in the run-down bathroom and ran a hand over his jaw. Would shaving a second time be too obvious? Hell, he was being a moron. It wasn't like she'd notice, and even if she did, it would be better if she hadn't. Connor would kick him in the ass if he knew what he was thinking right now.

He settled for slapping on more cologne and walked out to the bedroom again. The cleaning crew hadn't made his bed, and he was beginning to wonder if the owners of this bed and breakfast were in league with the rest of the chilly townspeople. No one could make scones that bad unintentionally, could they? His stomach grumbled. He needed a good meal, or he was going to have to buy some prepared food at the market.

As he left The Stag's Head, he was sure one of the cleaning women gave him a nasty look. That confirmed it.

On his way to The Wild Irish Rose, he called Aunt Clara and arranged to meet her and Uncle Arthur at their cottage for cocktails before dinner. She'd described how to find it on foot from the parking lot, so he parked and strode in that direction, taking in the various greens on the land before him. Until he'd come to Ireland, Trevor had never known there were so many shades of green, everything from the green you'd find in a spring leaf to the steely emerald of Irish moss. The sea was crashing in the distance, the gray-blue waters plowing into the coastline. A large tangerine sun was slowly descending from the sky to the sea. Miles of oil lay under it all, and no one would know it from this scene. He took a moment to enjoy the view. My God, Becca O'Neill really did have a fine stretch of land. If he weren't on the move so much, he'd want a place like this on the coast.

Something wet touched the back of his neck, and he jumped. Turning around, he almost let out a girly scream. A brown alpaca with a tangled brown mess over its big eyes was standing two feet from him, and while he didn't know anything about the breed, it seemed to be smiling at him.

"Shoo," he said to the animal.

He stepped back quickly to avoid another overfriendly lunge, and when he reached his hand out to stop its progress, it licked his palm.

"Stop that!" he cried. "Go away."

It lunged at him again, humming in a way that made his short hairs stand up, so he tried out an Irish phrase in his desperation to move it along. "Feck off."

He heard someone laughing and turned to see the woman who'd brought the scones the other day, Aileen.

Great. He'd probably get kicked out before he made it to the cottage.

"She seems to like the look of you," the woman said. "I remember thinking the same thing until I realized who you were. I'm Aileen. We met the other day."

"I remember," he said, stepping back again as the alpaca tried to rest her head on his shoulder. "This is awkward. Can you call this animal off?"

"She's not a dog," Aileen said, laughing softly. "She seems to be sweet on you." Her expression shifted to a more serious look. "I like to think animals know the true nature of a man. What are you doing here, Trevor Merriam?"

"Yoo-hoo," he heard Aunt Clara call from a distance away. "Trevor, did you get sidelined by the alpaca? Come here and kiss your auntie."

Kiss his auntie? Words he'd never imagined hearing from her. Still, the interruption was welcome. "My aunt and uncle are staying here for their second honeymoon."

"You're the nephew?" She shook her head. "Well, if that isn't a Janey Mack. They're lovely people. Are you really a hardline businessman?"

He lurched out of the way when the damned alpaca tried to put her head on him again. "Yes, of course. I need to go to my aunt, if you'll excuse me. Stop that!"

"Her name is Buttercup," Aileen said. "We'll see you at dinner with your family, Trevor Merriam."

She strode off, and he was left staring at the animal. Its big brown eyes were crinkled at the corners, and from the way its mouth had turned up in a human-like smile, he feared Aileen could be right. Buttercup might have a crush on him.

The animal made a loud humming sound and cocked its head to the side.

"Stop looking at me like that," he said.

"Trevor, stop playing with Buttercup and come here!"

Playing with—

Of all the ideas. He felt that wet nose touch his neck again as he strode off toward the cottage. Dammit! It was following him. Even though he knew it was stupid, he started to run. The alpaca's hooves pounded the ground right behind him. The animal might be ugly, but it had speed. It pulled even with him, and again, he swore it was smiling at him. He dug his heels in and sprinted, huffing and puffing, and for a man who considered himself in good shape, it was embarrassing. Buttercup wasn't the least bit winded.

Uncle Arthur had joined Aunt Clara outside the cottage, and they were both laughing like loons. Terrific. He was never going to live this down. He ducked through the door without stopping to greet them. Let them deal with Buttercup.

"Clara, my dear," his uncle called out, "we can go home now. It appears Trevor won't need our matchmaking efforts. She's a little hairier than I imagined, but I'm sure you two will be very happy."

"Haha," he said dryly.

"I can't wait to tell J.T. about this," Uncle Arthur said, hooting and wiping tears from his eyes.

This story was going to live on in infamy. Trevor knew it. He eyed the alpaca standing in the doorway. It gave a loud hum and then Aunt Clara closed the door awkwardly, which was when he noticed she was holding something in her hand as she continued laughing. A sleek smartphone.

"You were *recording* me?" He slapped his hand to his forehead. "Oh, Jesus."

"Of course, I was taping you! You were being serenaded by an alpaca, and then you ran off like a fraidy-cat." She gave another hearty laugh, and Uncle Arthur joined in. His frown didn't stop either of them.

"Ever since I discovered this smartphone, I keep it handy all the time now to capture such moments."

He crossed his arms. "I need you to delete that."

She slipped the phone inside her navy blouse. Oh, God! Was she sticking it in her bra like he'd seen some older women do in airports? Jesus, could this day get any worse?

"Not on your life," she said. "Now come and kiss your aunt."

"Seriously, Aunt Clara, what do you want?" He'd beg if he had to.

"Clara, take that contraption out of your underwear, for God's sake. When I touch you, I don't want to be touching technology."

She laughed as she crossed to her handbag, perched jauntily on a hardwood side table, and dropped the phone into it. "I have a passcode, so don't even think about trying anything. Also, I have it backed up on that cloud thing."

"She really does," his uncle said, pulling him into a man hug. "Snap out of it. We all have undignified moments in life."

He shot Uncle Arthur a look as he stepped back. "You haven't."

The man only shrugged. "What can I say? I'm a special kind of breed. By the way, why aren't you staying here? This place is wonderful."

He wouldn't feel guilty. They were enjoying themselves, weren't they? "Like I said, I like being closer to the pub, and I wanted to give you two some time alone. It is your honeymoon, after all."

"It's our second," he said, "and for a man who just turned eighty, I don't care if that's boasting."

Aunt Clara came over and hugged Trevor warmly. "He's not boasting. Seriously though, you should stay here. Hargreaves is in the main house, and it sounded like there was plenty of room. Trust me, when Arthur and I want to be alone, you'll know it."

"Yeah, we'll simply leave you," the man said with a

laugh. "We can talk to Becca about it when we go to dinner."

He acted like it was decided, but Trevor was hoping he'd get to talk to Becca alone first. It wouldn't go well if she revealed the ruse to his aunt and uncle. Of course, for all he knew, he'd be kicked out the moment he stepped foot in the restaurant. Aileen would have alerted Becca of his presence by now. His body tightened at the mere thought.

"I like being in town. More women, you know." Too bad the only one who seemed to interest him was right here at the inn.

"But you won't need another now that you've found Buttercup," Uncle Arthur said.

"Your true love," Aunt Clara said, batting her eyelashes in a frighteningly good impersonation of that damn alpaca.

"Of course, people will balk when they first see the two of you going around town," Uncle Arthur continued, "but when you love someone..."

"Okay, you've had your fun," he said.

"Not even close," Aunt Clara said. "Personally, I'm curious how you consummated your relationship. Oh, wait. Arthur, perhaps we should move out of the cottage for Trevor and his love. They'll need plenty of space."

His uncle gave a wicked chuckle.

"I'm going to leave," Trevor protested.

"You and Buttercup need a honeymoon!" Aunt Clara said, laughing again so hard she clutched her waist.

His uncle joined in, and soon they were holding each other up, they were laughing so hard.

"Are you finished yet?" he asked, sitting down on the sofa in the parlor. "I'll read the paper until you get it out of your system."

Aunt Clara giggled one last time, and Uncle Arthur patted her waist as they dialed it back a touch. "Oh, don't be so cross. If you can't laugh at yourself, what's the good of it? How about a drink to remove that sourpuss look?"

"Whiskey. Neat. And no more alpaca jokes."

Uncle Arthur strode over to a side bar and poured a couple of whiskeys. Then he made a martini for Aunt Clara, who continued to giggle.

"My dear, you've lost all control," Arthur said as he handed her the drink.

"I can't seem to help myself," she replied.

Trevor grabbed a tumbler from his uncle and took a healthy swallow of the good Irish whiskey.

"All right, let's start again," Aunt Clara said. "It's good to see you, my boy. J.T. seems to be missing you something awful even though he and Caroline are in their own newlywed bliss."

He knew the feeling. He'd spent the last couple of years fighting for J.T., helping him move on from his disastrous first marriage to a woman who'd rather ruin him than let him leave her. It had been hard to leave his twin behind in Dare Valley, even though he knew his brother was happy and in love.

"You'll have to visit Dare Valley soon," his uncle was saying. "Of course, everyone will be delighted to meet Buttercup."

And so the jokes continued as they told him about their trip to the Grand Canyon. This time he was the one who laughed when his uncle bitched to high heaven about burning his legs on the leather seats in his new convertible courtesy of the hot Southwest sun. He asked for another drink, and although he wouldn't admit it if pressed, he knew he wanted to delay another potential meeting with Buttercup.

After two drinks, Aunt Clara was bouncing on the sofa next to her new husband, gushing about how lucky they were to have reconnected. Uncle Arthur didn't make a joke. In fact, he got downright misty-eyed.

"Everyone is so happy for you both," Trevor said, finishing his drink.

"Let's move along to dinner," Uncle Arthur said. "Back home, I'd be in bed by now."

Trevor laughed. He knew a bald-faced lie when he heard one. It was only seven thirty. "I can take Aunt Clara to dinner if you'd prefer."

Uncle Arthur grumbled the whole way as he stood up and held his hand out to Aunt Clara. "Nope. If she's not with me, I miss her. She's turned me into a sap."

"You've turned me into an even bigger one," Aunt Clara said, taking his hand and laughing as he pulled her off the sofa. "Does this mean I can embroider our bathroom towels back home?"

This time his uncle snorted. "Not on your life. Come on, Hargreaves is probably prostrate with loneliness."

"Tell the truth," his aunt said as she grabbed her purse. "You miss having him around."

"Bah," was the only response she received.

His uncle cracked the door open and peeked out. "No sign of the missus."

"Funny," Trevor said. "Let's go."

They stepped out of the cottage, and Trevor stopped for a moment, awed by the view. Pinks and golds streaked the sky, and he caught the first star winking overhead. By God, it was beautiful.

"Takes your breath away," Uncle Arthur said.

"I've totally fallen in love with this place," Aunt Clara said, resting her head on her husband's shoulder. "We'll have to come here again someday."

If the Merriams took it over, that would be impossible, and Trevor was saddened by the thought.

Uncle Arthur patted her hand. "Let's focus on today, my dear. You never know what may come."

Trevor's thoughts shot to his cousin, Corey, who'd died in the prime of his life, leaving behind a beautiful wife and two kids. As they walked to the house, he firmed his resolve. He didn't care how beautiful the sky looked. He couldn't. He had to help his brother and do his job.

Becca O'Neill *had* to sell this land to him.

CHAPTER 6

"I'VE BEEN LOOKING HIGH AND LOW FOR YOU," AILEEN said, bursting into Becca's office where she sat knitting on the side sofa.

Becca was a bit miffed at first—she'd lost count of her stitches. But all thoughts of the sweater fled when the older woman continued. "Trevor Merriam is the nephew joining Arthur and Clara for dinner tonight."

Her eyes popped clear open, and she dropped her knitting onto the cushion. "I am in me wick." Hadn't he come to mind a time or two while she was knitting?

"No, I caught him on the way to the cottage," Aileen said. "And I'll tell you something else, love. Buttercup is sweet on him."

"What?" she asked, doing a double take. "But she doesn't like anyone. Not even the other alpacas." Hence the animal's predilection for leaving her pen. She'd figured out how to lift the latch on the gate, and Cian hadn't yet discovered a way to keep her inside. Becca had known alpacas were smart, but this was something different.

"I know it!" Aileen said, pulling on her apron for emphasis. "I told that Merriam fellow that animals know the true measure of a person. He insists he's a businessman through and through, but I suspect he has a soft heart. Becca, I think we should change tactics now that his relations are staying with us."

Becca narrowed her eyes. He was putting her in a horrible position, wasn't he? They didn't want a holy show of things. Refusing him a room privately was one thing, but she couldn't very well throw him out of the dining room, especially since Arthur and Clara were so lovely. Good heavens, the sweater she'd started knitting today was for Arthur.

But, oh, to see him again—those big broad shoulders and long limbs, that intense, perceptive gaze. She wanted to touch him and banter with him. Her heart turned over in her chest.

"What do you have in mind?" she asked.

"I say we let him come around all he wants," Aileen said. "You'll tempt more flies with honey. Perhaps even invite him to stay at the inn. His aunt and uncle love this place, and when he sees for himself how grand it is, he'll stop pressuring you to sell. I'm convinced of it."

He should stop pressuring her because she'd told him no, but Aileen had a point. Plus, she didn't want to risk offending or upsetting Arthur and Clara. "I can see your way of things." Plus, she'd get to see him every day...

"Cian won't like it at first," Aileen said, "but I'll work on him, don't you worry."

How many times had she heard her friend say that? "All right, I'll talk to Trevor and see if he's amenable."

"Oh, he'll be amenable, love," Aileen said. "The staff at The Stag's Head have been giving him a right hard time out of loyalty to you. Heck, I hear tell they haven't made his bed, and they've served him runny eggs and scones hard as bricks with his full Irish."

Normally, she'd have felt a little guilty, but the townspeople's defense cheered her.

"Now, let's go look in on him," Aileen said.

They'd almost made it to the dining room when Cian came storming out of it. His ears were red, and he looked in a right state.

"That Merriam lad is sitting in the dining room with Arthur and Clara like he's the king of England," he blurted out. "He's their nephew! I almost punched him in the face when they *introduced* him to me."

Aileen dragged him away from the dining room lest he give in to temptation. "You'll keep your head, Cian O'Shea. Becca and I have a downright good plan brewing, and that would only ruin it. Becca, you go out now and mingle with the guests. I'll speak with Cian and come straightaway."

Cian didn't look any too pleased, but he knew better than to protest. Becca nodded and made her way into the dining room. Sure enough, Trevor was seated in the corner of the room with his back to the wall, bold as brass. Well, he wasn't hiding his association to Arthur and Clara none. A lesser man might have put his back to the room, hoping to go unseen, not like that could happen at her place.

And goodness, he looked fine in his blue suit.

"Arthur, Clara," Becca called out. "I see you brought your nephew with you. And Hargreaves. How good to see you." Was Mr. Merriam going to pretend they hadn't met? She waited for his eyes to meets hers.

Trevor Merriam jerked his chin. "It's good to see you again, Becca. Thank you for making my aunt and uncle's stay so wonderful. I just knew they'd love the honeymoon cottage when I came by to look at the property the other day."

So this was the way of it. "Indeed. How are you liking your stay so far?"

The couple beamed, and Clara reached for Arthur's hand. "It's pure magic here, Becca. Everything we've come across is top-notch."

"Hear, hear," Hargreaves added.

"We're especially fond of your alpaca, Buttercup," Arthur said, biting his lip to keep from laughing. "Trevor has taken a shine to the animal. Haven't you, Trev?"

She still couldn't imagine Buttercup taking a shine to anyone, least of all Trevor, but part of her hoped she would see the lovesick interest Aileen had described. "We also have rabbits, Mr. Merriam. How do you feel about them?"

His beautiful mouth worked like he was fighting a smile, and she wondered what it would feel like to kiss him. "Rabbits make me hungry. How's the rabbit on the menu tonight?"

"We don't eat the rabbits on the property. Or the sheep."

"What about alpacas?" he asked, lifting his whiskey and taking a healthy sip. "Just kidding. Ms. O'Neill, may I have a word? You lovebirds need a surprise, and I'm sure Ms. O'Neill here will be happy to help the cause of true love. Excuse me."

He rose and patted his Aunt Clara with affection—that, at least, seemed real—and proceeded to follow Becca out of the dining room. She was aware of the veiled glares the staff was giving him, and she made sure to smile. As much as she appreciated their support, there was no need for anyone to be rude.

"I was hoping to speak with you as well," she said, gesturing to her office down the hallway. "Imagine my surprise upon learning you were related to these fine people."

"They were coming to visit me in Dublin, but I was here calling on you," he said. "They were eager to join me when I told them about your picturesque establishment."

She wanted to kick him, but she had a new plan to enact. "How are you liking The Stag's Head?" she asked, trying not to smirk.

"It's a real kip of a place," he said, not batting an eye.

So he'd picked up some slang while living in Dublin. "I'm sorry you find it inadequate. Perhaps you'd prefer to stay with us. Your uncle and aunt are here, after all, and they're some of the loveliest people we've ever had. We want to make their stay as enjoyable as possible. Surely they've asked why you're staying elsewhere."

"They might have mentioned it." He regarded her with narrowed eyes. Goodness, it was a shame for him to squint like that. His green eyes were alluring.

"It must have been terrible," she said, almost snorting. "Did you feel no remorse, lying to them?" For she knew they couldn't be part of his scheme. Both displayed a charming lack of artifice.

"I did, actually, and they're still in the dark, this being their honeymoon and all." He tilted his head to the side. "How did you know they weren't in on it?"

She looked down her nose at him. "Because they're good and kind people, honest as the day is long. I can always tell. Clearly, such values have skipped you and your brother's generation."

He had the audacity to laugh. "You're singing a different tune today, Ms. O'Neill."

"They can't help being related to you."

"True enough." His mirth continued. "That's better. For a moment, I thought someone had taken possession of you. If I stay here, do you promise you'll serve me those award-winning scones of yours? I won't move from The Stag's Head if you're planning on luring me here only so you can give me the same abominable treatment."

Ah, now they were talking. She liked to negotiate. "Abominable? How very queer. But to answer your question, yes, you will receive the full five-star treatment. On two conditions. One, you promise not to pressure me into selling while they stay here. And two, you leave when they do. In the same car, if possible."

He rocked back on his heels, a sly smile cresting over his full mouth. "Now we're talking. I won't pressure you while I'm a guest, but you'll hear my final offer *before* I leave, along with all the reasons it's in your best interest to sell your land. You could still sell me a parcel. A hundred acres would leave you plenty for your new animals and such."

"Not even one acre." Pigs would fly. "I'll hear you out, Mr. Merriam, if only out of courtesy, but I won't change my mind. For the entire lot or a parcel."

Oh, she was getting worked up, but not only because of their banter.

"We'll see," he said with the same bravado he'd displayed in the dining room. "There's an offer for everyone, Ms. O'Neill, and trust me, after staying here, I'll know enough about you and this place to make an offer that will give you *everything* you could ever want."

Everything? Her mouth went dry at those words. Long-ignored parts of her body tingled when his piercing green eyes fell to her lips. My, it had been a long time since a real man had looked at her like that and not some jackeen, hoping to score with a country maid, or a philandering husband whose wife didn't understand him.

No, there hadn't been anyone interesting since Sven, the most divine Swede who'd come on holiday to hike the Irish hills and write an article about it for a nature magazine. He'd wanted to see her again, but she'd turned down his invitation to spend the weekend in Stockholm. Twice. Their fragile relationship had crumbled when she'd confessed the truth—she couldn't meet him in Stockholm, or even in Cork. She couldn't leave the inn. Just like her first serious love interest, Sven had balked upon learning the truth. His professions of love had dried up in an instant. He'd flinched and told her she must have a lot going on and that he wished her all the best working it out.

She'd promised herself she'd never open herself to that kind of shame and hurt again.

Trevor cleared his throat, saying, "Tempting, isn't it?"

She let her gaze rest on him. Yes, he was tempting. Maybe fate had brought him to her door on purpose. She couldn't discount the singular attraction she felt for him. With Trevor, she wouldn't hope he'd fall in love with her and stay here forever. That was a stupid and unrealistic dream. No one would ever do that. But she could enjoy some male companionship. She was attracted to him, and he to her. With her first two suitors, she'd been more serious about sex, but she was thirty-four years old and some nights in the dark, she felt like she was withering away from the lack of a good man's touch. She would take this chance fate had given her, even if she questioned the reason Trevor had come to her doorstep.

"One more condition," she said softly.

His eyes seemed to darken to pure emerald at her tone. "Let's hear it."

She took a wild breath. "While you're here, you're not a Merriam and I'm not Ms. O'Neill. I'm just Becca and you're—"

"Trevor," he said, his voice dipping low like the sun on the horizon. "I see where you're going with this. I'm a little surprised."

She found she was breathless. "So am I. It's a first for me." Oh, was that revealing too much? He would use it against her, wouldn't he?

He crossed his arms. "Why me?"

She said the first thing that came to mind. "You knew who Boru and Hatshepsut were. You...traveled to Luxor and likely other exciting places. I've never met anyone like that." Sure, Sven had traveled, but never to the Valley of the Kings. And he had never intrigued her enough for her to set aside her knitting needles mid-row.

His nod was perfunctory. "Is that all?"

She waved a hand. "You're not bad to look at." The scrutiny in his gaze brought blood to her cheeks. "Oh, forget I said anything. Stay at The Stag's Head." What an idiot she'd been. "I have guests waiting."

As she turned, his hand curled around her arm. Slowly. Gently. The heat and power of his touch stopped her in her tracks.

He moved closer and cupped her cheek in a hand as warm as one of her fresh-baked scones. "I don't want to forget it."

She looked up and found herself falling into the myriad green depths of his eyes. Oh, goodness, there was power here, one that resounded in her bones.

"This isn't about putting you off either," she said, a kick of defensiveness rising. "I could order you off my land right now and never take a meeting with you."

He rubbed her cheekbone delicately. "I know that. Just so you know, I'm not interested in you because of the deal either. If I met you in a pub or around town, I'd ask you out."

She'd guessed as much, but it was good of him to say so. Of course, he *wouldn't* meet her out. "Then we're on the same page, as you Americans say."

Nodding, he stroked a finger down to her lips. "I believe we are...Becca."

Oh, the deep baritone way he said her name made her knees weaken. No one had ever said her name quite like that, like it was a rich candy to be savored.

"I'm going to kiss you now," Trevor said, his head descending slowly. "Last call for any objections."

Even now he seemed to be setting the terms, but she couldn't imagine adding any caveats. "Then kiss me," she said simply.

His lips brushed hers, and she closed her eyes, letting herself savor the smell and feel of him. The earthy cologne he wore had notes of sandalwood and pine, and his lips were soft yet insistent as they covered her own. She felt her blood beat faster, like the addition of an Irish drum to an easy medley. It was inviting her to dance, and when his arms came around her, she gave in to the desire and pressed herself to him.

He gave an audible groan, and then his hands were clutching the edges of her blouse, as though he wanted to rip it from her. Desire rushed through her, like a fast storm coming in from the sea, and she found herself fisting her hands in the shirt covering his strong back. His tongue swept across her bottom lip, and that was all the invitation she needed to pull him closer. The music of her body had a strong, insistent beat, and she found herself panting. Her hands crept up between them, needing to touch the muscles of his chest. God, he was beautiful, and she wanted him like a moth flying for the flame.

When he broke the kiss and pressed her head to his chest, she heard the knocking of his heart against his ribs and the urgent intakes of breath. Surrounded as she was by his embrace, she reveled in his warmth and quiet affection as he stroked her hair.

"*Well,*" he said finally, his voice rough.

"Yes, *well,*" she breathed out. If she'd had any remaining doubts, that kiss had dismissed them.

He stood her away from him and gazed down at her. "You're beautiful. I hope you don't mind me saying so."

"I'd like both of us to say what's on our minds. Except when it comes to business."

"I'll keep to our deal. Would you like to take a walk with me after you settle your guests?"

A lance of fear stole through her expectant heart. She glanced out the window. It would be dark out by then. She couldn't walk outside at night because she couldn't see anything around her. Her imagination went wild.

"How about a drink in my personal quarters instead?" she asked. "It's better anyway since I don't want any guests to see us together."

"A *rendezvous* as the French say." The corner of his mouth tipped up. "Even better. I like this new deal we have, Becca."

Since it was the only one they'd ever have, she smiled back at him easily. "Me too. Enjoy your dinner, Trevor. The rabbit is delicious, if you have a mind."

He caught her to him once again and kissed her full on the mouth. "Make sure to send out extra scones with plenty of butter. I haven't had a good meal since I arrived, and I'm hungry."

She was hungry too, she found, and she loved the feeling after being bereft of it for so long. "Don't worry. You'll have plenty to feast on."

His eyes widened a moment before he outright grinned—grinned—at her. She gave in to temptation and rose on her tiptoes to kiss him smack on the lips.

"And so will I," she said as she left him, liking this deal much better too.

CHAPTER 7

SAYING GOODBYE TO THE STAG'S HEAD SHOULD HAVE BEEN the best part of his day after the gruel they'd served him. Who would have imagined that instead it would be Becca O'Neill? The soft hush of her voice inviting him to have an after-dinner drink—that had nearly felled him. And the way she'd said her "private quarters?" Mercy.

Still, before leaving the dinner table and seeing Uncle Arthur and Aunt Clara off, he'd pocketed two of her mouthwatering scones. They'd been delighted, though not surprised, to learn he'd be joining them at the inn.

As Trevor drove back to The Wild Irish Rose after collecting his things, he discovered he was speeding in his haste to return. He dialed it back when he saw his brother J.T. calling. He hit the speakerphone.

"Hey!"

"You're dating a *llama*? Is this what happens when I get married and abandon you? I'm sending a doctor right away to examine your head."

Aunt Clara hadn't waited a moment. "It's an *alpaca*, and her name is Buttercup. Don't judge. How's Caroline?"

His brother laughed. "Oh, no. You're not getting off that easy. Did the owner set that animal after you or something? Connor says you're having trouble closing the deal, and Flynn is bragging he's going to win his bet."

After his side deal with Becca tonight, Trevor had a feeling Flynn was right. Oddly, he wasn't upset about the prospect of losing. "I'll get it closed."

"You always do. Aunt Clara says their honeymoon cottage is incredible and that Caroline and I should come visit. Maybe we can pick up the slack after she and Uncle Arthur leave. If you're finding llamas attractive, you might need an intervention."

As much as he'd love to see his brother, having more family underfoot wouldn't help. "I'll be back in Dublin soon if you want to pop over. Of course, I can come your way."

"No, fair is fair. You spent months with me in Dare Valley. Caroline hasn't been to Ireland, so she's game. She'd love to meet your llama girlfriend."

He dug into his pocket for a scone. "Alpaca, you philistine."

"Whatever," J.T. said. "Hey. I also wanted to give you a heads-up. Mom called Corey's wife, and she's flying out to visit them in Chicago. Uncle Liam is worried about her and the kids. Thought Mom might be a stabilizing influence."

Grief thickened in his chest at the thought of Olivia and those two great boys. "I'm glad she's going then," Trevor said. "Connor is really torn up about it. I've never seen him this emotional over a deal."

"It's understandable," J.T. said. "Well, I'll let you get back to your sweetheart. I noticed she's a hummer, not a screamer."

Trevor chuckled despite the thickness in his throat. "Yeah, yeah. Laugh it up now. I don't want you to hurt Buttercup's feelings when we're ready to meet each other's families."

His brother was laughing so hard he was probably crying. Damn but he loved his twin. "All right. Have fun," J.T. choked out.

"Right," he said dryly. "Tell Caroline hello and give my best to the peeps in Dare Valley."

"You got it," his brother said. "Talk to you later."

As he continued on toward the inn, Trevor gnawed on the second scone he'd taken. Connor might be emotional about this situation, but he needn't be. Compartmentalizing had always been one of his skills. Besides, it comforted him to hear his mother was stepping in to handle things. Assumpta Weatherby Merriam was a force to be reckoned with—she always knew instinctively when one of her kids needed cheering up or a kick in the pants. He loved her like crazy, and if he had more time, he would have called her, but he caught sight of the turnoff to the inn.

As he pulled back into the parking lot for The Wild Irish Rose, he felt excited again. Grabbing his overnight bag from the back seat, he headed to the main house.

Aileen was waiting for him at the door. "Good evening, Mr. Merriam. Becca asked me to show you to your room. Then I'm to take you to her."

Since the woman was smiling, he relaxed even more. He hadn't thought Becca would change her tune, but he'd learned never to get too cocky with women—another life lesson from his mother.

"Thanks, Aileen," he said, aware of Hatshep weaving around his ankles. Dammit, he was going to have more cat hair on his pant legs. The stuff just wouldn't brush off completely, and he was damned if he was going to buy one of those pet rollers. Talk about leaving your Man Card at home.

"She likes you," Aileen said as they walked up the wide wooden staircase.

He didn't comment, taking in the array of paintings on the walls. J.T. and Caroline would get a kick out of them, being art people and all. Just like downstairs, there was a mix of portraits and landscapes, and Trevor wondered again if the portraits were of O'Neill relations.

As they walked down the hallway, Trevor noted a few interesting items. A set of Russian stacking dolls. A lacquer box from Russia depicting the frog prince. A few Moroccan mirrors and lamps. A hand-painted Asian silk fan. So Becca didn't just long to travel to Egypt. Although they shouldn't have belonged together, they'd been arranged and paired in a bold, eye-catching way. His apartment in Dublin was pretty minimalistic, which suited his travel schedule. Situated in an old warehouse, he loved the brick and had loads of family photos around, but little else. J.T. had jokingly bought him a classy nude for his birthday one year, and it hung in his den. Most of his visitors found it pretty funny. But this...

The Wild Irish Rose was more than a bed and breakfast. It was an oasis, everywhere he looked.

Aileen stopped in front of a gold door and turned the antique doorknob. "Becca thought you might be comfortable in the Oisin and Niamh room since there's a sitting area where you can work. If you have any questions about the house or need anything else, you let us know. Now that things are squared away with you and Becca, we'll make you feel more welcomed."

Squared away, eh? He wondered how much the older woman knew. Something told him there were few secrets between her and the proprietor. "Thank you, Aileen. What prompted all the names for the rooms?"

"Becca thought guests might enjoy learning more about Irish folklore and the like, so she renamed all the rooms in the main house. The honeymoon cottage was the only name she preserved since it was a longstanding name in the family."

Of course she had. He thought it a lovely touch. As he ventured into his room, Aileen stayed in the doorway. The décor was a bold and rich marriage of golds and reds, and the four-poster king bed with the canopy was going to feel like heaven compared to the full bed he'd slept in at The Stag's Head. This was a different room than the one she'd first mentioned when he'd come to her door, and it lifted his spirits that she'd seen to his comfort in such a way. He noted the small sitting room off to the right, a soft lamp illuminating it. There was a bottle of whiskey on the side table with a note alongside a plate of scones.

"You left me more scones," he commented as he crossed the room and picked up the note.

Enjoy your stay, it merely said. He wondered if it was Becca's writing.

"You're a darling, Aileen."

"It was Becca's idea," she said, following him. "She saw you pocket two scones after dinner."

So Ms. O'Neill didn't miss anything. "What can I say? I was hungry."

She laughed. "We'll make sure you're well fed here."

He was glad to hear it. "I've heard of Oisin and Niamh, but I don't remember much other than they were star-crossed lovers."

"We have a lot of myths about star-crossed lovers in this country," she said, leaning her head against the doorframe. "This one is especially sad. Oisin was the son of a great man, like many of the heroes are, and he and his fellow warriors came across this beautiful woman—"

"And she was more beautiful than any woman they'd ever seen," he said, flashing her a smile and grabbing a scone. God, he loved the Irish for their storytelling. They could spout off folklore at a moment's notice, like they were the Irish Mythic Britannica encyclopedia or something.

"She was indeed," Aileen said, her voice taking on a hushed tone. "The other men were afraid of her, coming out of the sea on a white horse such as she did."

"But not Oisin," Trevor said, polishing off the scone and grabbing another.

"No, he wasn't. In fact, they fell instantly in love and spent the next days together. People marveled at how inseparable they were, and their love grew stronger, until one day Niamh told Oisin she was bound to return to her land and her people in Tír na nÓg."

Trevor nodded. "The land of the fairies and gods." Everyone in Ireland knew of the fabled place.

"Yes, indeed, but Niamh loved Oisin so much she did something very unusual. She invited him to return with her and live with her forever."

"And so he did," Trevor said, enjoying their conversation.

She put her hands in her pockets. "Of course, and he received all the gifts of that magical land: everlasting beauty, boundless health, and eternal happiness with the woman of his heart. For a while he was content to stay there in that far-off land with his true love, but after a time, he grew terribly sad. He missed his family, you see, and all of the places he'd once traveled with his friends."

Although he hadn't heard this tale before, he knew where it was headed. The Irish and their love tales were legendary, but they always ended in tragedy. It was like no one was fated to live together happily for all time. Oisin had given up everything to live in Tír na nÓg. What woman was enough? His mother would box his ears if she heard him say it that way, but she'd agree in the end that you couldn't pin all your happiness on one person. Trevor might not have been in love before—not the big L kind—and even he knew that.

"So she sent him back," Trevor said, since Aileen had paused like she was waiting for him to fill in the next part of the story, something the Irish often did when they told stories.

"Yes, on her very own horse," Aileen said, "but she told him with complete seriousness that he wasn't to put his feet on the ground of his former land, or he'd become mortal again, and they'd be separated forever."

Cue the tragedy, Trevor thought. The moron hadn't followed orders. He could hear his mother's voice in his head: *When someone smarter than you tells you something, you listen.* She'd used that line plenty on Trevor when he was younger, and he'd gone on to use it on other people. Sometimes they listened, and that included his siblings.

"But he didn't listen, did he?" Trevor said, grabbing another scone because what the hell. Who was counting?

"My mum would say it was just like a man," Aileen said, "but since I'm married to one of the best ones in the world, I can't say that."

The man he'd met earlier in the dining room had wanted to knock his block off, no surprise. "Your Cian clearly isn't Oisin," Trevor said, polishing off the scone and eyeing the last one. Should he? Oh, why not?

"No, he's not," Aileen said. "So Oisin crosses the sea on that beautiful white horse and returns to the land of his forefathers. Only nothing is familiar. His home is gone. His family and friends seem to have vanished from the face of the earth. With great sorrow, he travels the land, looking for them. When he comes across some men on the road, he asks after his people. Sadly, he discovers they're all long dead and buried."

"Because the time passes differently in fairy land," Trevor said.

"But Oisin didn't know it," Aileen said, shaking her finger at him.

Trevor wondered why in the hell Niamh hadn't told him. "Poor guy."

She nodded. "Prostrate with grief at the news, the poor man fell off his horse and became the old man Niamh had warned him he'd become. He died there, alone, on the land of his birth, separated from his true love for all time."

Because he couldn't follow simple instructions, he could almost hear his mom say. "It's a grand tale, Aileen. Thank you for telling it."

Beaming, she walked to the door, and he followed. "Don't think I didn't see you polish off all those scones.

Goodness, me. I know you're a giant of a fellow, but that's seven scones. It might be a record." She laughed. "Come now. I'll show you to Becca. It's getting late for me, and I need to be up early. We're baking bread tomorrow. You're going to be a happy man, let me tell you."

"If the bread is anything like your scones, I'll be in food heaven. All right, let's find Ms. O'Neill."

He felt a little weird saying her name like that, but Aileen didn't comment on it. She just handed him his room key and watched as he locked the door for good measure.

"Your Mr. Hargreaves is down the hall with the gray door in case you need him," she said.

"Good to know," he commented. Hargreaves was still a mystery in some ways. The man was a tad older than Uncle Arthur, yet he'd been with Aunt Clara since the late 1950s if Trevor recalled correctly. They were friends and companions, but Hargreaves took care of everything from driving his aunt's limo to making meals to arranging travel plans. His dry wit was an acquired taste, and he didn't say much in mixed company. Trevor had given up trying to talk to the man at dinner tonight. The butler had seemed uncomfortable to be joining them at the table, in fact, and had begged off early to get back to his reading. Arthur had teased him about the book he was reading, even suggesting it might be that Fifty Shades series that had been all the rage some years back. Hargreaves' icy stare had caused his aunt to fall into giggles.

"Anything else you like to eat?" Aileen asked as they walked back down the stairs to the main hall and then off to the right down another long hallway. The house looked large outside, but it felt even bigger inside.

"We don't have enough time for me to tell you all my favorites," he said, waggling his brows.

"Oh, you're a smooth talker, for sure," Aileen said. "I'm glad you and Becca formed a truce."

He was too, in fact, and not simply due to the promise of what the night had in store. Trevor had stayed in a lot of hotels around the world, and The Wild Irish Rose had something extra special going on.

They walked to the end of a brightly lit corridor and stopped at a dark-green door. "This is Becca's quarters. I'll let you do the knocking. See you in the morning."

"Thanks again, Aileen," he said, flashing her a smile as she left.

Standing in front of the door, he found he was oddly nervous. Unusual for him. He shook himself. There was nothing to be nervous about. They'd agreed to be Becca and Trevor and have a good time. Nothing more. Everything that awaited them at the end of his visit could go into a box and be shoved into a corner.

He knocked on the door and waited. When the door opened, he felt his breath stop. Becca had changed into a form-fitting green dress that made him long to have his hands on her. Her hair was freshly brushed, and a lock of it trailed over her right breast. There was a shine of pink gloss on the full lips he'd kissed earlier.

"You took your sweet time," she said, tapping her foot. "I almost fell asleep."

"Aileen was telling me a story."

She rolled her eyes. "Well, no wonder. Glory. When she gets going, there's no stopping her."

He met those wide blue eyes. Earlier, she'd gone all soft and sweet in his arms, but this was an assessing look.

"I thought you'd changed your mind," she said in a low voice.

Now he understood the reason for her pique. "Not at all. Can I come inside?"

She stood there like she was taking his measure again, and he heard Boru bark softly somewhere out of sight. "All right, but if I don't like the way things are going, you have to leave. I want your promise."

Something in her tone made him study her more closely. Had someone she'd invited to her room in the past done something untoward and then hurt her? She seemed oddly vulnerable under the hint of aggressiveness. "Of course. But I need your promise too."

She crossed her arms. "What is it?"

"If things aren't going the way I want, you'll let me leave. No tying me up or any weird psycho girl shit."

She laughed like he'd hoped and let him inside, locking the door behind them. Boru stood at the top of a flight of stairs in what looked like a sitting room. His tail wagged madly as they made their way up.

"How long have you had Boru?" Trevor asked as he stooped to rub the dog under the ears.

"Since he was a pup," she said, taking him into her sitting room.

He stopped at the edge, looking around and trying not to be too obvious. Like the rest of the house, it boasted an abundance of bold colors. The walls were a Tuscan yellow, and the plush purple velvet sofa boasted a hand-knitted teal throw and some embroidered pillows of cream Irish lace and orange silk. A landscape of what looked like a Moroccan city overlooking the sea hung over a marble fireplace, and he noted the painting of a wild desert at sunrise on the far wall. Large windows provided a view of the moonlit sea, the waves a lush, rolling white as the tide flowed in. There were lamps everywhere with velvet shades in deep purple, navy, and maroon. A leather-studded chest sat beside the sofa, clearly Moorish, and there was a red accent cabinet against the wall. Despite the array of colors, they worked together.

Being inside her room was like stepping back in time into a pirate's cabin in the best way possible, what with the view of the sea and the lush fabrics and furnishings around him.

"Are you into antiques?" he asked, trying to get his feet under him. She seemed more cautious now. Even in her own space, she was keeping her distance. Maybe she was trying to find her footing too.

"I mix and match," she said, crossing her hands over her stomach. "There are some fine new pieces on the market for a fraction of the cost. I mostly buy what I like. I figure, if you like something, what does it matter if it's new or old or by someone famous or not?"

"I feel the same way," he said. "Becca, we don't have to do this."

"What?" she asked immediately.

"Anything," he said, not sure how to classify it. "How about we have a drink? Or I can leave?"

She rushed to a caddy by the windows. "I can do a drink. Is whiskey okay? I noticed you liked Red Breast at dinner."

He nodded. "According to Aileen, you also noticed that I pocketed a couple of your delicious scones. Thank you for leaving some in my room."

"I thought you might like to have them around," she said, splashing whiskey in two crystal highballs and bringing them over.

Her hands were shaking, he realized. This was unexpected.

"I ate all the scones," he said, hoping to make her laugh.

She was taking a healthy drink when he said it and started to cough. "You did? My heavens! Did you eat the scones from dinner too?"

He grinned unabashedly. "I told you I like to eat."

"And you were starving," she said. "The Stag's Head really is a fine establishment. They were only treating you poorly...out of loyalty to me."

"I see. You have a lot of people on your side from what I can tell. But we're not supposed to talk about that. I know it's a gray line."

"No, you're right," she said, punching one of the pillows on the lush sofa. "Please sit down."

Boru was pacing as nervously as his mistress. "*Becca.*"

She finally stopped beating the poor cream pillow. "What?"

"We don't have to have sex. Tonight or any night." God help him, he made himself say it, and he wanted to kick himself when she quickly looked away.

She sat down with a thud, and Boru gave a worried whine. "Why ever not?"

Was she kidding?

This was not going to be a simple seduction, and they both knew it.

Chapter 8

Her plan wasn't going to be as easy as she'd thought. Becca stared into her whiskey, kicking herself for her nerves. Maybe she'd been caught up in the moment, but kissing him earlier had filled her with wonder. Her mind had gone blank and even her toes had curled. "Maybe you should just kiss me," she decided. "It was easier earlier. I feel like I should apologize. This can't be what you were imagining."

He sat down next to her and took the glass from her hand. Then he cupped her cheek, and she fell into those intent green eyes.

"I'm usually good at small talk," she found herself saying, and Boru gave a healthy bark in support.

Trevor's lips twitched. "This isn't exactly the usual forum for small talk. Besides, you said you were doing this because you liked my mind. I'm paraphrasing, but why should we limit ourselves to small talk? Oh, and you said that I wasn't bad to look at."

His teasing made her feel more grounded. "Your paraphrasing could use some work. Besides, you already know you're good-looking."

He shrugged as if it were simply a matter of fact, which it was.

"But you're not a preener. I personally can't stand men who preen."

"Me either," he said, dropping his hand but scooting closer to her. "I noticed you have artifacts and objects from all around the world. Of course, I didn't see a fake Sphinx anywhere. Where did you get them all from if you don't have time to travel?"

She didn't want to mention some of the objects were from her parents' travels before they died. That would invite questions that would lead to a discussion of her condition and, eventually, to him looking at her like she was mental.

"Online shopping is a wonderful invention. When my grandma was dying, she made me promise on her deathbed to make The Wild Irish Rose mine. She said every proprietress should remake it her own image. So I thought about it, and I felt that since most of our guests like to travel, they would like to be surrounded by international art alongside crafts native to Ireland. We have our folklore, but seriously, how much Irish lace and replicas of the Blarney Castle can one person take?"

"I personally like my blinking replica of Blarney Castle." He shifted a little so he was facing her and put his hand on her knee.

As a touch, it was gentle and unobtrusive. She decided she rather liked it. "So you went there and kissed the stone, I take it?"

He reared back and laughed. "Heck yeah, I did. Who doesn't want the gift of the gab? Also, it's not the easiest thing to do. Nowhere in America would you have a tourist attraction that requires a paid guide to hold people's legs while they stretch across a hole to kiss a wall. Talk about liability! Have you done it?"

Even if she could leave her land, would she visit Blarney Castle? No, there were dozens of other places that would precede it on her list. "I'm Irish. We're born with the gift of the gab. Clearly, you needed the gab rather badly to put your life at risk."

"I had plenty of gab before I kissed it," he said with a grin. "You seem to be doing fine in the department as well."

"It's in our blood," she said, looking down at the hand covering her knee. She wanted to lay her hand over his, but should she? Was it too bold?

"Are you good at telling stories? Aileen certainly knows how to spin a tale."

"Aye, I am," she said, finding it easier to relax into the sofa. Boru laid on her feet as if finally sensing she wasn't going anywhere. She wondered where Hatshep had gone off to. Well, she'd make an appearance if it suited her.

"What's your favorite Irish tale?" he asked her, rubbing her knee in a delicious way.

She gave in to temptation and let her hand fall onto the thigh he'd angled on the sofa so he could face her. "Oh, that's like asking me to pick my favorite star. But off the top of my head, I'd say the Pirate Queen."

His smile grew wicked. "Color me surprised. Grace O'Malley's story is one of my favorite tales too, but who doesn't like the idea of a female pirate? In fact, your chamber here reminded me of a pirate's cabin in some ways."

A tingle of pleasure shot up her spine. "When I was choosing Irish heroes and heroines to go with the rooms, I thought I should have one too. This is the Grace O'Malley Tower, but we don't publicize that online. I didn't want guests to ask to stay here."

He took the hand she had on his thigh. She held her breath for a second, waiting to see what he would do, but he simply held it, and she found her fingers curling around his. "I won't tell a soul. Your grandma would be proud of what you've created, Becca. I was thinking earlier that this is one of the most unique places I've ever stayed in, and trust me, I've stayed in a lot of hotels."

Oh, to travel like that. "What is your favorite place in the whole world?"

"That's like asking me about my favorite star," he said with a teasing grin.

"First one to come to mind."

"Honestly, it's Ireland," he said. "I came to Dublin with my brother Flynn for a pub-crawling weekend three years ago, and I fell in love with the place and the people."

She'd heard such stories before from other outsiders who'd made Ireland their adopted home. "Where were you living before?"

"San Francisco," he said. "My parents live in Napa Valley, and I went to school at Stanford. The main corporate headquarters for our family business is there, and it was easy to travel to wherever I wanted or needed to go."

"I've always wanted to visit San Francisco," she said. "Is it really as beautiful as it seems?"

"Yes," he said, "but it can't compete with all of Ireland's shades of green or the..."

When he trailed off, he looked almost sheepish. "The what?"

"You're going to think me a real sucker if I say it."

"The women?"

He laughed. "That too. No, the rainbows. My brothers tease me about it, but they're not unaffected. Of course, my sisters, Caitlyn and Michaela, gush like crazy over them. But they liked *My Little Pony* when they were kids."

She didn't know who this pony was, but she liked the way his voice filled with warmth as he talked about his family. "How many brothers and sisters do you have then?"

"We could compete with the Irish back in the day," he said, rubbing his thumb over the back of her palm. "Seven. Two girls and the rest boys. My twin brother, J.T., and I are in the middle, right after Connor and Quinn. Then it's Caitlyn, Flynn, and Michaela."

Good heavens. That was quite a big family.

"Of course, my mother is Irish American from Chicago and proud of her heritage. Her people came to Chicago during the potato famine like so many families did. Hearing her talk, her old neighborhood sounds a lot like mini-Ireland minus the green hills and rainbows. Coming here was like coming home for me in some ways."

What a surprising and lovely thing for him to say.

"Oh, forget I said that. My brothers would rag on me if they could hear me talking like that. Whenever they catch me at it, I always blame it on the water. I say it makes a man wax poetic. Like all that stuff about rainbows."

She let her fingers caress the hand holding hers. "I like to say it's in the mist. When I'm looking out that window and I see it come up across the sea, it feels like an invisible hand is grabbing my heart tightly and whispering about white horses coming out of that mist or other such grand sights."

He was looking at her with such seriousness, almost like he was studying her anew.

"We Irish have a good imagination for such things, I expect," she said, noticing how his eyes had turned a deeper shade of green, much like the hills right before the sun went down.

"I like your theory on the mist, and I like your imagination, Becca O'Neill."

Her heart started beating wildly in her chest. Was he going to kiss her? "I'm glad. I like your theory on the water. We have all kinds of water here in Ireland, everything from waterfalls to bubbling streams populated by the fairy people, so your theory has merit."

"Thanks for the vote of confidence," he said, his voice dropping an octave, much like it had when he'd kissed her before. The low, husky tone made her shiver. "Now how about I show you another one of my theories?"

Oh, suddenly she knew he wasn't talking about the Pythagorean theorem. "I'd love that."

"Come a little closer," he said, leaning his head toward her.

She did, watching how the golds in his eyes winked as she drew near. He took the hand he was holding and guided it over his shoulder, and she shifted until she was kneeling in front of him. His hand came around her waist.

"You're so beautiful," he said, drawing her closer until their bodies touched. "I like the way your hair curls and trails down your back, and I like the way your eyes widen or narrow depending on what I've said, but do you know what I'm really loving right now?"

Oh good Lord, he was making her breathless with this kind of talk. "Tell me."

"Your lips," he said, his mouth inches from hers. "They're the color of a rosy sky and so lush that all I want to do is kiss them until they darken to an even deeper rose."

Was there a sexy gift of the gab? If there was, she'd been missing it. She caressed his cheek. "I like the way your jaw feels like the Scots pine needles I've used for dyeing wool—soft yet deliciously prickly—and the way your voice drops lower and lower like the sun sinking into the sea."

He leaned his cheek against hers and rubbed it so she could feel more of those prickles. "I thought about shaving again for you."

She raised her other arm so she could link her hands

around his neck. "Oh no, you mustn't. I love the feel against my skin."

His sharp intake made her belly tighten. "Good, since I love your skin. Becca..."

Then he pressed his lips to hers. This time he was slower, and she was happy to follow his languid pace. Oh, good heavens, he could kiss, and the way he pulled her onto his lap...

His big body was warm and strong, and she loved the hard feel of his muscles. He changed the angle of their kisses, placing one on the corner of her mouth and then sucking on her bottom lip. He was so clever, this one, and she found herself eager to see how he'd kiss her next. Then he ran his tongue over her lips, and she nearly smiled with joy. *Yes*, she thought. *Kiss me like that.*

He slipped his tongue inside and circled hers, and soon they were playing with fire. She felt the hands at her waist brush up her sides and waited for them to cover her breasts. God, it had been so long since she'd been touched like this, and with him, it was a revelation. Urgency and desire were only one layer to what was coursing through her. There was also tenderness and enjoyment, and she simply wasn't in a rush.

She shifted in a way that brought his hands flush against her breasts, and the moan that fell from her lips seemed to vibrate from a deep place inside her. His hands caressed her, and she liked the way he held her breasts' weight as if getting their measure before starting to stroke her nipples through her dress and bra. She ran her fingers across the back of his neck, but it wasn't enough for her now. She wanted to touch the warm skin of his chest, so she snuck her hands between them and opened a button on his shirt.

He paused in kissing her and drew back to look at her. That look in his brilliant eyes, full of wanting, made her melt.

"You make me feel so... Never mind."

She wondered what he'd planned to say, but then he was shrugging out of his jacket and tossing it to the floor. She raised up on her knees and tugged her dress up and off as he worked on the buttons of his shirt. When he finally pulled it off, she was surprised to see a St. Christopher medal hanging from a chain around his neck.

"Goodness, you have a fine chest," she said, running her hands over the defined pectoral muscles. "I'm glad you have hair here. I've heard men from America usually wax it off."

His laugh was part snort. "Manscaping is for pussies. I figure the hair is there for a reason so why pay someone to burn you with wax and strip it off every few months. Forget I said that. How could I be talking about that when you're sitting here in your underwear. I'm a sucker for lace, by the way."

She'd thought the matching black lace bra and panties would bolster her confidence. "I'm glad you like it."

He ran his hand down her belly to her core, his eyes raking down her body and making her very aware of it. Trevor had a way of giving his full attention, and it made her heart race. This was foreplay, she thought, delicious, delicious foreplay.

His finger traced the edge of her belly right above the lace, and a wave of fire followed in its wake. "God, you're beautiful. I just can't seem to stop saying it."

"I won't tire of hearing it." She ran her hand over his chest, enjoying the way his muscles tightened in response to her touch. "You're beautiful too. In fact, you take my breath away."

He looked up and smiled at her. "You do the same to me. Come here, Becca O'Neill."

She boldly put her hands around his neck, savoring the shiver that ran through her when he traced the outline of her lacy bra. Oh, how she wanted to feel his hands there without anything between them. She reached behind her back for the hooks, but he stopped her.

"Wait," he whispered, his mouth against her breasts. "Let's try this."

He shocked her by kissing her there, black lace and all. Somehow it was more erotic. The pressure and warmth of his mouth inflamed her, and she arched into him, closing her eyes. She gave a delicious hum and edged closer as he shifted to her other breast.

Then she heard another hum, and this one wasn't from her. Trevor seemed to freeze against her, and then he shot back from her with a loud "Ugh!" and toppled off the cushions and onto the floor. Boru gave a bark, and Becca jumped back too, staring in shock at Buttercup, who stood behind the sofa, batting her long eyelashes.

"That thing!" Trevor cried, scrambling to his feet. "It licked my back. How the hell did it get in here?" Buttercup only cocked her head and gave another loud hum.

Good question. "I don't know how she got in here." She grabbed the teal throw to her chest. Buttercup hadn't figured out a way to open doors, had she? The alpaca had managed to unlock three different gate latches. Perhaps she was a genius in disguise.

"Shoo!" Trevor said when Buttercup walked around the sofa, advancing on him. "I mean it, Buttercup."

Becca stood, clutching the throw. "Buttercup, stop! Leave Trevor alone. No means no."

The alpaca emitted a stream of loud hums as if she were cussing Becca out for stealing her man or was outright jealous. Then she lurched at Trevor for another lick, and he ran around the sofa in an obvious panic. Boru gave a muffled bark and then lay back down on the floor.

"You're no help," Becca said, stepping over him.

"That animal isn't right in the head. Toss me my shirt, will you? I don't like the way she's looking at my chest. She's making me feel like a piece of meat."

"Oh, she won't eat you," Becca said, looking around for his shirt and not finding it. "I don't see your shirt."

"It was right there on the floor a moment ago," he said, not taking his eyes off Buttercup.

Hatshep, Becca thought. She scanned the room for the cat but didn't see her.

She donned her dress and then passed Trevor his jacket. "Put this on until I find your shirt. Buttercup, let's go. You don't belong in here."

When she moved for the animal's nape, Buttercup scampered past her and around the sofa, straight toward Trevor. He jumped, dropping his jacket.

"Jesus, Mary, Joseph, what's Buttercup doing in here?" Becca turned to see Aileen standing in the doorway. "The back door was open, and so was yours, and I got worried."

"I honestly don't know, Aileen," Becca said.

"It's sick in the head, that's why." Trevor ran around the sofa again, Buttercup right behind him.

"My heavens, what a fine-looking man you are, Trevor," Aileen said, humming much like Buttercup. "Becca, maybe we should have a spot of tea and watch this delightful show."

She found herself laughing. Trevor ducked as Buttercup went to lick him again.

"You both are as crazy as the alpaca." He darted out of the room with a shriek to evade the animal. "Sorry, Becca, but I'm out of here," he called, and then she heard him pounding down the stairs and slamming the door as he left.

Becca crossed her arms as she walked toward the stairs with Aileen, whose mirth was contagious. Sure enough, Buttercup stood at the top, staring forlornly down the steps.

"She has a real thing for your man there," Aileen said, shoulders shaking. "I'm so sorry we interrupted you. Even our dear Hatshep seems to want him in your bed."

Becca caught sight of white sleeves on the floor in her bedroom. "Hatshep, you'd better give me that shirt." She thought about Trevor running back to his room shirtless and laughed and laughed until tears streamed down her face and her chest hurt from it.

Hatshep finally sauntered out of her room with the shirt in her mouth, and then Boru appeared with Trevor's jacket.

"I'll say it again. Animals know the true measure of a man." Aileen put her arm around her shoulders. "Clearly, they want you to be with Trevor Merriam."

It certainly seemed that way, and it was yet another sign. They'd never taken to someone quite like this.

"While he's here, that's what I want too." Buttercup gave another pathetic hum and craned her head in the direction Trevor had left. Goodness, Buttercup really did have a crush on Trevor. Becca understood. She did too, it seemed.

"You might be wanting more, my dear," Aileen said. "My advice. Keep your heart open to what comes. You never know what magic might be afoot."

Aileen always did like a good story. Becca picked up Trevor's shirt and jacket, and his scent struck her hard in the belly. The truth was inescapable. She'd never been so affected.

Perhaps it *was* time to believe magic was afoot.

Chapter 9

Normally, breakfast was a meal Trevor looked forward to, especially in Ireland, but his good humor was being tested by a lovesick alpaca.

"Aileen told me she saw you shirtless in the house last night, running from Buttercup," his aunt was saying over their full Irish breakfast. "Said you were a right brawny fellow."

God help him, Aunt Clara was trying to pull an Irish accent. It sounded more like someone from New Delhi, India. He might have stayed with Becca if they could have herded Buttercup out, but Aileen's arrival had sealed his decision to leave. The interruption had been unwelcome, and he hoped they could get back on track. Like tonight. Her skin had been silky to the touch, and her mouth... The memory of her kisses had kept him up last night.

Still, although he didn't begrudge Aileen a good laugh over what she'd seen, he wished she hadn't said anything. "What can I say?" he joked with a clenched jaw. "The female sex finds me irresistible."

"What I can't figure out is how you ended up shirtless to begin with," Uncle Arthur said, stabbing his fork into his blood sausage. "You know, this stuff isn't bad at all."

"It's only a sausage, sir," Hargreaves said in a dry tone. "Of course, Master Trevor lost his garment to the alpaca when it tried to bite him. Isn't that right, sir?"

Hargreaves had opened his door last night as Trevor pounded down the hallway. The man had given him a regal nod before retreating back into his room.

He'd feared Hargreaves would tell all, but it turned out the butler had covered for him.

"Exactly," Trevor said, nodding to the man. "It got one chunk of my clothing, and it wouldn't let go. After repeated attempts, I ended up stripping it off."

"You seem to have inspired Buttercup to new heights of affection, Young Trevor," his uncle said. "Perhaps next time, you should use a stick to deter the animal from biting you."

Or a taser…

He was going to have to do something about that animal. Uncle Arthur's granddaughter, Jill Hale, had texted him this morning that she'd uploaded Aunt Clara's video of him running from Buttercup to YouTube, and it already had ten thousand hits. The damn thing was going viral. Of course, Jill thought it was all right that she'd referred to him as "an unidentified man," but the rest of his siblings save Connor had already seen the video, and he was getting ribbed right and left about his new girlfriend. God help him if any of his business associates saw it. His tough-as-nails reputation would be ruined. Running from an animal like that. Everyone might laugh, but they wouldn't understand. Buttercup had it in for him, and now the animal had learned to break into the inn. He turned his head and scanned the room just to make sure the alpaca hadn't appeared.

"Cian said he was changing the locks this morning." Aunt Clara patted his hand like he was a fraidy-cat. Great.

"Your virtue is safe," Uncle Arthur said with a snort.

His virtue. It was Becca's he'd been interested in last night. Things had been progressing nicely until that darn animal had shown up to interrupt everything, and he'd been too embarrassed after his flight from Becca's quarters to seek her out and apologize. She seemed to be of the same mind since she was conspicuously absent from the dining room this morning. Oh, hell, he was going to have to find her and think of something suitable to say. His choices weren't great if you asked him. *Your alpaca is a blight on peace. I was totally into you until your hairy farm animal tried to join us, and I'm not into that.*

Aileen was humming as she approached the table, and Trevor had the odd urge to slide under the table and hide. Maybe he would have if not for the steaming basket in her hands. "Trevor, dear. I thought you might need an extra serving of scones this morning."

Did he ever. "Thank you, Aileen." He was going to ignore the wide grin and the humorous gleam in her eyes.

"Would you care for a cup of...butter?" she asked and then laughed as she set extra butter on the table and sailed off.

Everyone laughed except him and Hargreaves, and he noticed the butler shaking his head after the woman. Who knew he would turn out to be such a pal?

"Clara and I are going to pop into town and check out the local museum," Uncle Arthur said, grabbing one of Trevor's fresh scones with a ghoulish grin. "You're welcome to join us."

He let his older uncle have his fun and didn't slap his hand for stealing a scone. There were plenty to go around, and he imagined he could wheedle Aileen into bringing another basket to his room. Someone should make up for Buttercup's harassment and Aileen's arrival, and if it was in scones, he was all for it, so long as the animal was prevented from future stalking.

"The local museum," he mused, thinking it over and then discarding the idea. It seemed prudent to keep Uncle Arthur and Aunt Clara in the dark about his plans for The Wild Irish Rose as long as possible, and the townspeople's attitude toward him might clue them in. "I have some work I need to look after. I'll catch you for cocktails later."

"Hargreaves?" his uncle asked.

"I loathe local museums, sir," he said, his face completely composed despite the bite of the comment. "They're usually trite and dusty."

Aunt Clara laughed. "Oh, Hargreaves. Dusty! You should come with us."

"No, thank you, madam. I plan on reading the history of Britain today after I drive you into town."

His uncle shook his head. "Missing your homeland, are you? We can stop in London on the way back if you'd like. Or heck, you can pop over there now, and we can meet up in Dublin and fly home together."

"But Hargreaves and I always travel together," Aunt Clara said, crossing her arms.

"My dear, perhaps he'd like to get away from you, err, us, for a while," Uncle Arthur said with a telling look.

Trevor almost laughed as Hargreaves picked his napkin off his lap and wiped his mouth as if the mere thought were unsanitary. "I'm perfectly fine here, sir. Madam, if it's all right, I'm going to head to my chambers now and meet you by the car in fifteen minutes."

"Fine," Aunt Clara said. "Be a fuddy-duddy. You know you can read at home."

This time Hargreaves snorted. "Then why do people covet the activity so on vacation, madam?" With that, he stood stiffly and bowed to the table.

"You have to give the man points for cleverness," Trevor said. "I mean, he's right. Why is a vacation read better than a regular read?"

"Oh, who cares?" his uncle said, tossing his napkin onto the table. "Clara, love, are you ready for your cultural activity in the village?"

"So long as it also involves some shopping," she said, taking a final sip of her orange juice. "I have presents I need to buy, after all."

"Christmas isn't for five months, for Pete's sake," his uncle said, standing up and holding out his hand to her.

"These aren't Christmas presents, dear," she said, taking his hand. "They're special treats from our trip here."

"Oh, for heaven's sake," he said gruffly, making Trevor fight laughter.

No one huffed and puffed like Uncle Arthur.

"Perhaps we can do something romantic too," she said, patting his weathered cheek.

"We did that this morning, dear," his uncle shot back, "and too much romance at our age—"

"Oh, do be quiet, Arthur," Aunt Clara said, crossing and kissing Trevor's cheek. "There are young ears listening."

Her wink was downright cheeky, and Trevor found himself winking back at her. What a pair they were, finding love at their age. He hoped he'd still want to be "romantic" when he reached those years.

"Don't wander around, Trevor," his uncle said, "or that alpaca might make you her love slave."

He was frowning as his uncle left. Love slave, his ass. But the thought brought back the need to apologize to Becca. Oh, hell, he liked her and wanted to hang out with her some more. He'd just have to buck up and do it.

"Aileen," he called when the woman drew near with more coffee. "Where would I find Becca?"

Her lips twitched. "In the dyeing room. If you go out back, it's the old detached kitchen. We've converted it, you see. Watch out for Buttercup, love."

He nodded and pocketed a few scones in his jacket before leaving. He'd have crumbs in the lining, but he honestly didn't care. Their scones were the finest he'd ever had. His phone buzzed in his other pocket, and he pulled it out. Wonderful, a text from his mother.

Saw the video. I knew you were special when you were born. Your father and I are so proud of your choice. We can't wait to meet Buttercup. Love you.

Love you, indeed. This meant his dad had seen the video now. And likely Connor too. He sighed. His older brother would take it as evidence he was loafing around. Well, he would deal with that if it happened. Right now, he needed to apologize to a lovely lady.

He didn't see Buttercup when he scanned the yard, thank God. The sunlight was rich in the bright-blue sky when he exited the back door, and the various shades of green called to mind dark limes and pale figs as he walked across the lawn to the stone building he guessed was the former kitchen. In old homes like this one, it was common for the original kitchen to have been built separately from the house, more due to the risk of fire than the heat they generated, unlike the Southern plantations his mother had made them visit on a family vacation to New Orleans one summer.

The bright-blue door was open, and when he caught sight of Becca, his mouth went dry. He stopped short. She was lifting what looked like a white shirt above her, studying it. Her body was a lush silhouette of feminine mystery with its graceful curves and lines. God, she was beautiful. Touching her last night had been pure magic, and he grew a little angry thinking about that alpaca interrupting them.

Then he heard a far-off hum, and all the hair on the back of his neck stood up straight. He craned his neck around, but he didn't see Buttercup. Maybe he'd imagined her call, but he increased his strides to the old kitchen just in case.

Becca lowered her arms slowly when he entered and closed the door behind him. Her chest seemed to rise with her breath, and he found his nostrils twitching at the raw plant essences in the room. Those earthly scents only added to his desire for her.

"You'll need to keep the door open," she said, all shades of awkwardness. "For ventilation."

He propped it back open, noticing all the windows were open too. It relieved him that she hadn't wanted the door closed because of him.

"I'm sorry I bolted on you last night," he said, coming closer. "I thought about sending you a note, but I didn't know the protocol for being chased away from a date by an alpaca." Best leave Aileen out of it.

Her lips twitched in the most enchanting way, and she held out the shirt she was holding. "I washed your shirt this morning as my own apology. But I didn't want to risk your beautiful jacket—that fine Italian wool must have cost a song—so I sent it to the cleaners in town. Trevor, I couldn't be more embarrassed."

"That makes two of us. So, how about we forget how the evening ended?"

"That sounds like a grand idea," she said, a smile cresting her face. "Must be hard to be so irresistible."

"That's exactly what I told Uncle Arthur when he teased me this morning."

She winced. "Yes, I'm sorry Aileen mentioned it, but she said she hadn't seen a chest that sexy since David Beckham modeled in his underwear."

"That's a compliment, I guess."

"I'm glad to see you have more shirts and jackets."

"I always bring enough. Where did you find my shirt, by the by?"

She made a face and crossed to the window. Leaning out, she hung it on a drying line covered in clothes pins, accessible from where she stood. "Buttercup has friends, it seems."

That news made him very afraid.

"Don't ask," she said.

He nodded. "So, this is where you dye wool."

"Yes, we did a new test yesterday and let it cool overnight," she said, gesturing to the various metal pots and pans that covered almost every available surface. "It's from our sheep mostly and some very unique wool from our Angora rabbits and... The alpacas you've met."

That beast was going to be a sweater or a scarf for someone. Too bad it wouldn't be dinner on the restaurant menu, ending his troubles. "Tell me more. I know nothing about wool except that it makes a great suit."

She laughed. "Do you *really* want to know? Because I'm warning you. I become very excited talking about this new enterprise of ours. I might talk your ear off, and that's saying a lot for someone who's Irish."

He didn't care so long as she kept smiling like she was, with stars in her eyes. "Talk away. As someone who's part of a large family company with lots of assets, I like to learn about new businesses." A shadow crossed her face for a moment, and he wanted to kick himself. "I'm sorry. I wasn't speaking about my family business that way, only that we have diverse interests." That didn't sound much better, and he winced. Her land was one of those interests, and suddenly, the heaviness of his mission hung in the air between them.

"Let me show you what's in our dyeing pots," she said, seeming to shake it off.

He followed her when she bustled over to the first in the large row of aluminum pots and pans. As he drew closer, he noticed they were all filled with different colors of water with odd bits floating on the top of some of them and what looked like yarn inside.

"Dyeing wool is like everything else," she said. "More science than art, as Aileen and I are learning. The colors you end up with are quite surprising sometimes. In fact, they go against what the naked eye sees in many cases.

Take this lavender bath here, for example. We thought it would be nice not only because I love the color and smell but because it has a natural antiseptic and can keep moths away from the sweaters and whatnot made with our yarn. But what color do you think we get when we dye the wool?"

He couldn't tell. Purple was too obvious, so he went with something else. "Blue?"

"Good try, but no," she said, taking a wooden spoon and stirring the water around until he could see the yarn. "Most of the time, we get a yellowish color."

The yarn sank back into the bath, but not before he noted it was more of a brown yellow to his eyes. Not an attractive tint to his mind.

"Now take our fern mixture here. They love our damp Irish weather. Aileen and I thought they'd make for a lovely dye, what with their poetic majesty and all. Can you imagine what color they produce?"

He tried to lean closer to the pot, but she stepped in front to block his view. "No cheating."

He found himself wanting to pull her into his arms right then, what with her pointing at him like a put-out school teacher. "Green, of course, but I'm guessing that's not the answer."

"Green is the hardest color to replicate in a dye. I've been beating my head against the wall trying to get the perfect one, and I still haven't mastered it. Aileen is beside herself as well. I mean, here we are in Ireland with greens all around us. People visit just to see the greens. Even this morning, your Aunt Clara told me she'd never seen so many shades of it, although your uncle says he's seen his fair share where he lives in Colorado. Oh, the way he talks about the Rocky Mountains made me want to..." The faraway look in her eyes washed away, replaced by something else. Sadness? "I'm getting carried away, aren't I?"

He didn't think so. In fact, it was another confirmation

of how much she wanted to see the world. Had she never thought to leave Aileen in charge? The woman seemed very capable, and while he didn't have Cian's measure yet, the man was always around, working hard along with the rest of them.

"Dare Valley where Uncle Arthur and Aunt Clara live is a beautiful town tucked away in the mountains. You'd like it. They have lovely shops on this quaint Main Street. I think there might even be a yarn shop."

He wasn't exactly sure, but if there wasn't one, there should be. This yarn thing was the kind of eclectic shop people in Dare Valley would like. He might ask J.T. about it. Then he discarded the idea. His brother was already laughing enough over his altercations with Buttercup. He didn't want to lose his Man Card for good.

"It sounds like a grand place. I wish..." Becca said, shaking her head as if to recenter herself. She picked up another wooden spoon and stirred the pot with the fern dye, her face in profile. "With our wild ferns here, what with the red stems and the spores, we're getting a red color for our wool." She lifted the spoon up to show him, then set it aside again. "It's simply fascinating. And we haven't even started talking about what happens when you add acid and play with the pH."

"I love it when you talk science," he murmured huskily, making a grab for her.

She only laughed and shuffled out of reach, facing him, mischief flashing in her eyes. "Did you know that red cabbage is a wonderful natural dye they used commonly during World War II?"

He stopped short, thinking about his Grandpa Noah and Grandma Anna as he often did when the war came up. "No, I didn't. My grandma had a victory garden in Chicago during the war. I wonder if she grew cabbage. I imagine she did, what with her being Irish-American. I'll have to ask my mom."

"Your face changes when you speak of your family," Becca said. "It's like the sun comes out inside you."

He was stunned speechless. No woman had ever noticed that about him. Usually they couldn't wait for him to get off the phone, and he'd never met anyone he'd wanted his family to embrace, but he could see her laughing with Caitlyn amidst her dyeing pots or showing Michaela her ferns. Those images gave him an odd feeling in his chest.

She lowered her eyes then. "Oh, don't mind me. I'm talking silly."

"No, I like the way you talk," he said, his voice pitching lower. "So what colors come from red cabbage? Not red?"

"Closer to pink in some cases, although we've gotten it a little darker if we use a bit more white vinegar and let the yarn rest in the dye longer, which is what Aileen and I are finding we prefer. But wouldn't you know, we can also get the most brilliant blues with some baking soda, the kind that make you want to take a walk outside after a nasty stretch of wet days."

Her eyes took on a dreamy quality again. She yearned to travel, he knew, but it seemed she also yearned for blue skies. He'd have to take her for a walk one of these days.

Then he remembered he would be leaving soon, and a flash of pain raced across his heart. He didn't want to leave this woman. The feeling was odd and unwelcome, and he brushed it aside.

"Aileen also managed a beautiful purple," she said, pointing to yet another dyeing pot. "We're sowing more cabbage now to harvest next spring so we can do some more experimenting. Chef Padraig wasn't happy when I purloined the last of our summer cabbage harvest, let me tell you, but I reminded him there were plenty of other plants he could use for salads and the like in the restaurant."

She spoke with a lovely tone of command at times, and he found it charming. She was the boss of a sizable small business, between the actual bed and breakfast and restaurant and this new enterprise. The running of things suited her, he thought. She was firm but fair, the kind of person he preferred to do business with. Then he stopped short.

No thinking about business, he reminded himself. Not now when she looked so beautiful in a flowing blue cotton dress with a white apron over the top of it.

"What about roses?" he asked. "This is The Wild Irish Rose, after all."

She grinned. "Lovely, magical shades of pinks, the kind that make you believe in fairies and unicorns. It's going to be our signature yarn if I have to beg the fairies myself for the perfect shades."

Laughter spurted out of him. Oh, he loved this side of her. "Show me more of your experiments," he told her, forgetting about the work he had waiting for him. Forgetting that Connor was likely pissed about the video and his general lack of progress.

She took him around the large kitchen, and he noted the initials carved in some of the stones with various dates and names from times past. There was a Johnny from 1888 and a Maureen from 1922, he saw. He wondered who they were but couldn't get a word in edgewise to ask her. She was too busy trying to explain something called a mordant, which bound the dyes they were using. She got very animated, telling him about plants that contained natural mordants like juniper (not only for venison, she joked) and oak galls (which he still wasn't clear on), and he had to bite the inside of his cheek to keep from smiling outright at her gushing enthusiasm.

She led him to a battered old desk. A few old, dog-eared books on natural plants and homemade dyeing lay on the surface. She gushed as she showed him charts of her various experiments, and he was impressed with the way she'd laid out her data, everything from the dye ingredients down to the time lapse in the dye pots. Then she started to explain the importance of using a pH-neutral soap, and she lost him. But he didn't care because she was so animated she was talking with her delicate hands, and sometimes, those hands came to rest on him as a way of both garnering his attention and sharing her delight.

By the time she wound down, he'd started eating one of the scones in his pocket, and she didn't even seem to notice, what with showing him her jars of alum salt and natural iron (from boiling old rusty nails, he was amused to discover) and various dried berries like elderberries, which apparently produced beautiful shades of pale gray.

She rushed over to another pot and held up her hands, almost as though she was throwing them up to the sun. "Isn't it wonderful what nature can do? It takes my breath away, the way the colors change from one process to the next. And when you make a sweater or a scarf—or even a pair of gloves—out of the yarn you dyed with your own hands, using your very own brain... Well, I feel as though I might simply float out of my body and out into the sky above us."

He could no longer fight the temptation to hold her. Reaching for her, he brought her to his body. Cupped her face and sought her gaze. The blue of her eyes made him think of the blues she'd shown him earlier, the ones that reminded her of a sky after a string of rainy days. Had she talked about floating out of her body? Because touching the velvety softness of her cheek made him feel like he was lifting out of his skin.

"Becca," he said.

Her hand rose to stroke his jaw, and she met his gaze head-on. "I like sharing all this with you."

Powerful words. He liked that, too, and how she looked in the sunlight soaking through the open windows and door. It picked up the reds and golds in her brown hair, the flecks of blue and green in her eyes. She'd shown him the beauty of color, and now he saw it everywhere. This woman was a beautiful miracle of excitement and heart, and he was falling fast here with no parachute to pull. Even scarier, he didn't want to pull the parachute and stop the fall.

"Share everything with me," he murmured, lowering his mouth until it was a hairsbreadth from her lips.

He felt her throat move, almost as if she'd had to digest his invitation. Then she pressed her mouth to his, and his heart sung in his chest. She was blue fire, gold fire, every color of fire in his arms, and all he wanted was to be consumed and reborn in it. He let his eyes close, losing himself in the feeling of her.

A loud cough punctuated his consciousness, and then she was springing back from him.

"Cian!" she cried, patting her dark hair back in place after his hands had tangled in it.

"You're needed back at the main house," the man said, staring Trevor down from the open doorway.

He returned the look, unflinching, noting Cian hadn't apologized for interrupting them. No, Trevor imagined he'd done that on purpose. In his place, Trevor might have been just as protective. He was with his own sisters even though they could take care of themselves.

"Will you show me the animals if you have time later?" he asked Becca. "Everything but the alpacas, of course."

She didn't laugh at his joke, only yanked on her apron as if to ensure it was back in its place. "I can't say just now. Thank you for letting me show you our dyes. Please feel free to look around on your own."

Since his work was done, Cian disappeared from the

doorway, Becca following in his wake. She started pulling on her apron, he noticed, as she reached the threshold. The pulse in her neck was visible as well. Was she nervous they'd been caught together? He didn't know what her relationship was with Cian, but if he was some sort of surrogate father, Trevor supposed she might be anxious about his opinion. He realized he didn't know anything about her family, except that her grandmother was gone. Had she siblings? Where were her parents, and why hadn't they taken over before her? He found he'd spoken the truth. He wanted her to share everything with him and vice versa.

"Will I see you again tonight?" he called before she escaped.

For a moment, he wasn't sure she'd heard him. But she stopped, her body angled in that same glorious silhouette he'd noticed as he approached her earlier.

"I'd very much like to," she said, taking a deep breath, almost a gulp of air, poor girl. Then she was gone, and he noticed how some of the vibrancy in the room had disappeared with her.

She was wrong about mordants and acid adding vibrancy to color.

It was her.

CHAPTER 10

BECCA WAS SITTING IN ONE OF HER FAVORITE PRIVATE rooms in the house with a pot of Barry's Tea. She didn't care what Aileen said—and the woman had very strong opinions on this topic, so much so they debated it once a month—Barry's was better than Lyons.

She'd needed some time for reflection after her surprise encounter with Trevor in the old kitchen. When she'd learned Aileen had told Trevor's aunt and uncle about seeing him shirtless in the house, fleeing Buttercup, she'd wanted to pull her hair out. She'd feared he'd be out of sorts with her. But Aileen was delighted Becca was getting along so well with the fine American fellow, what with all her talk of magic afoot. It certainly had been in the old kitchen. Aileen seemed to have forgotten all about Trevor's true purpose, and truthfully, Becca was starting to forget too.

Even more so after he'd listened to her so intently as she rambled on about dye and yarn. He'd seemed genuinely interested—in her, in what she did and loved. It had bolstered her spirits, which were already soaring from the excitement of her new discovery: it was easier to leave the main house for the old kitchen because she knew something special awaited her there.

Her excitement swung the scales in a happier favor, and the normal anxiety, while still present, only pressed at the edges of her mind. There was something to this new discovery. Perhaps if she were excited enough about what lay outside the main house, she would be able to more easily step toward it.

Maybe if she were excited enough about traveling to somewhere exotic, like seeing the ruins at Carthage...

The idea seemed crazy, and she let it fade from her mind, like a sailboat disappearing into the horizon. She would never be able to travel like that. It was a miracle she could even take a walk with Boru, and it was best if she didn't get her hopes up much beyond that. But it did make her consider the possibility she might work toward more accessible goals.

Her breath caught at the thought of being able to go to dinner at the home of the people who worked with her. No one asked her to tea, and certainly not for a meet-up in the local pub. It was a grace mostly, but sometimes she wished they'd ask her only so she'd have the illusion of being normal.

A knock sounded on the door, and she almost frowned at the interruption. "Yes?"

Cian poked his head inside. "Have a minute?"

She'd dreaded this talk. His disapproval stung, mostly because part of her knew he was right—she *was* flirting with danger. But it didn't feel that way when she was with Trevor. Could a man who'd listened to her love and dreams with so much eagerness still want to rip them away from her? She wanted to think Aileen was right, that she could change Trevor's mind, but she was afraid to find out.

"Always, Cian," she said, gesturing to the chair next to her on the sofa. "I'm sorry you interrupted me earlier."

"I'm not," he said, never one to mince words. "I know Aileen has this theory about animals only loving good people, but even bad people have dogs and cats."

"Oh, Cian," she said, trying not to be cross.

"Do you think I like to speak of such things? First, you're a grown woman of thirty-four, as Aileen keeps reminding me lately, and second, you haven't taken a fancy to anyone since Sven came around. Becca, I want you to be happy, but this man—whether he's good or bad is no matter. He has the job of trying to buy this very land we're standing on out from under you." He reached for her hand, which he clasped. "My dearest Becca, I see how you look at him and how you looked in his arms—although I hope that fades from this old mind. You're falling for him, and it's only going to cause you pain. I'd cut my own arm off before I let that happen. You know that."

She felt tears fill her eyes. Cian had been her lifeline for years. She'd clung to him from the moment he'd found her in that closet, crying for her mom and dad, who lay dead on the floor outside.

She'd seen everything, *everything*, and it had changed her entire world forever.

Cian had left Doctors Without Borders to take care of her, having promised her parents to do so if something ever happened to them. He'd brought her back to her grandmother, but her trauma had kept him near, the only link to parents now dead. Part of her knew he'd hoped to heal her as a doctor, and God knew, he'd done everything he could from researching her ailment to suggesting specialists when his treatments didn't bear fruit.

Whether he would have left if he hadn't fallen in love and married Aileen was immaterial. When she'd taken over for her grandmother, he'd closed his town medical practice, calling it retirement, and supported her in her every project.

"I only want what's best for you, love," Cian said, "even though Aileen tells me it's none of my affair. But

I promised your parents to look out for you, and I try my best. When I light a candle for them in church, I tell them how you've done them proud. The Wild Irish Rose was beautiful under your grandmother's hand, but under yours, my Becca, it's flourished beyond all my imaginings. You have a real gift, child, and I'll do everything I can to see you continue to flourish as well."

She wiped at the tears streaming down her face and laughed when Cian dug out a handkerchief and wiped his own eyes before handing it to her.

"Oh, Cian, you can't know..."

He squeezed her hand. "I know."

She blew her nose and wiped at more tears. "Oh, I'm *plobaireacht*."

"No," he said, kissing the back of her hand. "You're only feeling that grand heart of yours. In this moment, you remind me of your mother. She had a heart as large as the sun."

And it had been the death of her, Becca thought darkly. Even after all of these years, she still couldn't set aside her grief. How could two such generous people, who'd devoted their lives to healing, be killed for helping others?

Her mother and father had refused to hand over their medical supplies to a militia, and the men had retaliated by killing them. They'd almost killed Becca too.

How was any of it fair?

A memory from her first days back at the inn flickered to life. She'd spent most of her time in the closet that had been her grandmother's and was now hers, although much expanded now, wrapped up in a knitted blanket. Her grandmother had gone in there with her. Her stalwart love had helped ease some of the pain. *Life isn't fair, my dear, Becca. I only wish you'd discovered it when you were a little older and not quite so hard as you have.*

"Well, now that we're both plobaireacht," Cian said, sniffing for good measure, "I need to confess something weighing on my mind."

She took a sip of her tea, hoping to settle her nerves some. "All right, let's hear it."

"Aileen will likely bean me with a frying pan when she learns of it, and you may too, although I'm counting on that grand heart of yours."

Something about his tone snapped her out of the fog of emotion. "What did you do?"

He lifted a shoulder. "I thought it was a good idea at the time."

"*Cian.*"

"I was the one who let Buttercup inside your chambers," he said, his eyes on the floor.

"You did what!" she said, standing up. "But you scared Aileen at first even. Cian O'Shea, are you out of your ever-loving mind? What were you thinking?"

He snorted loudly. "I was thinking to interrupt you and the American who wants to buy this land out from under you. Truth be told, from the state of his undress, my timing was spot on."

"Are you thick?"

"In the head?" he asked with a smile. "Ask the missus."

He stood and put his hand on her arm. She didn't shrug it off. She'd never shrug him off.

"I know you mean well, Cian," she said. "I do."

"Fine, then, I've expiated my conscience so I can walk lighter the rest of the day. I'm here for you, regardless of what you do with the American. I'm behind you all the way."

Her heart warmed, and she kissed his cheek. "Yes, I know."

"And if you need me or any of our boys to rough him up, you say the word." He winked cheekily and then dashed for the door. "If you could find it in your heart not to tell

Aileen, I'd greatly appreciate it. I'll be kicked out of me own bed for days."

"You'd deserve it too," she said, laughing. "Okay, I won't tell her."

"You're an angel," he said with a wink. "I'm off to feed your furry rabbits. You might consider bringing one into the main house. The guests might like it. Aileen showed me this video on Facebook of people doing yoga with rabbits and goats the other day. I sometimes wonder..."

"Oh, off with you," she said, making a shooing motion with her hand.

He grinned and ducked out the door.

"That silly, interfering old..." Goodness, she loved him. Then she started to laugh. Well, at least Buttercup hadn't figured out how to get into the main house on her own. That was a relief.

Which meant tonight there would be no interruptions with Trevor.

Was that what she wanted?

Yes, she realized, she did want him to herself. She might be in for some heartache like Cian feared, but oh, to be with a man like that would be worth it. Aileen called Trevor a right fine thing, and Becca couldn't fault her assessment.

But that wasn't the real reason she felt drawn to him. He gave of himself so generously—he'd listened to her today, really listened, and his thoughtful commentary had soaked into her like the easy Irish rain into a lush landscape. She was all warm and glowing from Trevor's undivided attention. Now that was the kind of man one could...

She stopped her thoughts. No, this wasn't a forever kind of love, no matter how unique and compelling. He was the Oisin to her Niamh, which was why she'd placed him in that suite. He was like the rain—and it always stopped raining sometime.

It was important she remember that.

Chapter 11

ARTHUR HALE KNEW WHEN SOMETHING WAS UP.

He could all but sniff it in the pub. Of course, all Clara was sniffing was the foam on the beer she'd insisted on ordering. He'd told her she wasn't a beer girl. Big mistake. She'd told the chatty bartender *to pull her a nice one*. He'd almost choked and left her a widow. She'd only winked at him, the minx.

As he studied the patrons of the town pub, he could feel their regard. An old woman and an even older man wouldn't attract this kind of attention on their own merit, he imagined. It was like they were sizing things up. Trevor.

Had the townspeople heard about his interest in Becca? Arthur knew the young man hadn't lost his jacket and shirt because the alpaca had grabbed a hold of them. He wasn't born yesterday.

"Have you noticed, my dear, how everyone seems to be staring at us?" he whispered when they walked over to a booth and sat down. He was way too old to stand at a bar and drink.

"We are cute," she said, pulling on his cheek like he was a child.

"Stop that!" he hissed, rubbing it.

"That's not what you said this morning," she sang.

"Woman, you are out of control," he said, even though he appreciated the praise to his virility. At his age, most men were dead down there, while he was going through a Paris spring. Or an Indian summer. Who cared? It was incredible.

"I love this town and this country, Arthur," she said, smiling at one of the servers as he went by with a tray of brown bread and butter. He discovered he was hungry.

"I'm glad you do," he said. "I need some food, so waggle those silver brows at your young admirers and get a server over here pronto."

She laughed but did as he asked. In five seconds flat, the bustling man was taking their order. He could get used to this kind of treatment.

"You were talking about people staring at us, dear," she said, taking a huge drink of beer. "Now that I look around all spy-like, there does seem to be some extra speculation. It's the kind of attention I used to get at a gallery showing or a charity fundraiser in Manhattan. You know, where people are watching you but trying not to be obvious about it."

Exactly. "I think it's about Trevor."

She tapped his arm playfully. "Why ever would you say that?"

He harrumphed. "First, I still don't understand why he wasn't staying at The Wild Irish Rose to begin with. Second, he wasn't shirtless because the alpaca took a bite out of him."

The gales of her laughter reached every corner of the pub, and he wasn't surprised to see a few smiles. Clara did that to people. "Of course, he wasn't shirtless because of that. He was with Becca. In delico."

"In what? Woman, you need a dictionary. I think you mean *en flagrante delicto,* and if that were true, he'd have been missing his pants too." But he got pretty close, no doubt.

"Oh, Arthur, don't be a stick in the mud. Trevor doesn't seem to need our matchmaking efforts, but I'm sure as hell not going to leave." She gave a sharp cry of delight when the server brought a tray of steaming brown bread fresh out of the oven.

He couldn't blame her. After buttering the bread, he almost cried out too. It was earthy and delicious. He'd have to ask Margie to start making some in her bakery in Dare Valley. Or he could ask Hargreaves...

No, if he made such a request of Hargreaves, he'd likely owe the man a favor, and who knew what that might lead to?

"It is odd that Trevor was at the other inn when we arrived," she said, licking her lips in the most delicious way. "I didn't buy his story about staying close to the pub."

"And he didn't put up a fight about us coming to visit him, remember?" Arthur said. "I told you it was too easy." Maybe this was about more than his interest in Becca. In fact, why had he been in this sleepy Irish town to begin with? He'd only said he was taking a holiday. Right. And yet, he'd admitted he'd be working some.

Clara polished off her beer—God help him—and signaled to the bartender for another pull.

"Please, my dear," Arthur said. "Only make that motion of your hands when you're alone with me."

"You're an old rascal, but I love you. And fine, only with you. Now, what are you going to do? I can hear those clogs working in your mind."

He pulled his hair to make his point. "It's cogs, Clara. For Pete's sake."

"So? I speak just fine. Now, again, what are you planning to do?"

He inclined his chin to a hefty man in the corner talking with some other townspeople. Somehow Arthur knew they were talking about him and Clara. He'd lived in a small town most of his life. He had the radar.

"I'm going to do what I do best," he told her, cutting another piece of bread and buttering it. "Investigate."

She gave a long-suffering sigh he was getting to know all too well. "I was afraid of that."

***

When Trevor caught up with his uncle and aunt for cocktails later, he was unnerved to find Cian sitting in their front parlor like a guest for tea. Even more so because he caught the tail end of a question his uncle had just asked him. "...you think of our boy, Trevor?"

Good God.

"Hello, folks," he called out, hoping to avert disaster. "How was your trek into town?"

"I had beer!" his aunt called out, hefting up a mug filled with brown ale from her seat on the sofa. "And then Cian brought by his favorite beer after I told him how much I loved the one I had in town."

"Murphy's is a favorite, of course," the man was saying to his aunt with a smile—a smile! He hadn't known the man could stretch his lips like that so pleasantly. "But Elbow Lane in Cork City has one of the finest brews around if you ask me."

Trevor normally would have agreed, but he didn't want to give the man the satisfaction.

"Come and try some, Trevor," his aunt called. "You're glowering like my husband."

Uncle Arthur shook his head. "I'm not glowering, woman."

When Trevor reached her, she smiled and crooked her finger. He edged closer.

"I love to tease him," she said in a whisper. "I'm finding it's the secret to a happy marriage. In my first marriage, all I had were cautionary tales. Now I seem to have a treasure trove of good advice."

She *had* only been married a few weeks, happily this

time, thank God, and here she was dishing out marital advice. He found it downright charming.

The mug she was holding sloshed dangerously when she thrust it at him. "Here. Have some. You look like you need it."

"I was going to have a whiskey," he said, and then at her crestfallen expression, took the mug and drank. "Good."

"Good? Sit down. Trevor, you need to let the Irish brush off on you a little more. My boy, after drinking this, I can see why the Irish call it 'mother's milk.'"

He laughed. "That's Guinness, Aunt Clara."

"You can't tell her anything," his uncle said, patting her knee. "Still, my dear, if you like it that much, we should go to this Elbow Lane and Smokehouse. Cian says it's only about forty or so minutes away. He and Aileen would be happy to take us on their night off tomorrow."

"How lovely!" Aunt Clara said, pushing off the sofa. She bustled up over to Cian, who was sitting in an adjacent chair, and kissed him smartly on the cheek, making the man laugh.

To see Cian now was like looking at a different person. Well, a woman as lovely as Aileen wouldn't pick a rotten apple, he imagined. His demeanor with Trevor had to be unique, due to a beautiful woman he thought of like a daughter, no doubt.

"It's a date then," the man said. "You're welcome to join us, Trevor."

He considered the invitation for a moment. Was it an olive branch or a way of keeping his eye on Trevor? "Only if Becca would be able to join us. I'd hate for her to be left out of the party."

The man's eyes turned downright stormy. "She'll be covering for us on our night off. How kind of you to ask after her."

He said it like he was running a knife over the words.

"The one thing I've learned living in Ireland is that everyone is invited to the party," he bandied back. Surely someone could cover for her. He wondered again why Cian and Aileen didn't cover for Becca so she could go on holiday. Surely they were more than capable. Didn't they know how much she longed to travel?

Cian stared at him—a silent, weighing stare—before giving a loud hum and standing up. He sounded a lot like Buttercup, in fact. Trevor got a little queasy at the notion. He'd been so relieved the alpaca hadn't ambushed him on his walk to Honeysuckle Cottage.

"I need to go see if Aileen needs anything," Cian said. "Clara, I'll have someone put more of that beer in your room, if you'd like, for later."

"That would be lovely, Cian, thank you," she said, giving a cute little belch. "Oh, excuse me. I have to say, Cian, I never want to leave this place."

"Still, we must," Arthur said, rising and shaking Cian's hand. "Thank you for coming by. We look forward to tomorrow night."

"I'll be telling Aileen," he said, still smiling, much to Trevor's shock. "She'll be over the moon."

The moment Cian left, Uncle Arthur pinned him with a gaze. "What are you up to, Trevor?"

"What do you mean?" he asked, queasy now for a different reason.

"Arthur knows you lost your shirt with Becca last night," his aunt said. "He's sure you're up to no good too."

"Clara, get a hold of yourself. Usually you can drink like a fish."

"I'm fine, Arthur." She set her mug down with a thud. "Anything you want to tell us, Trevor? Cian doesn't seem to like you much, and that strikes me as odd, lovely gentleman that he is."

He weighed the situation. Best go with Cian not liking

him purely because of Becca. "You're right, Aunt. I was with Becca last night. Cian is being a little protective, is all."

"Protective?" Uncle Arthur asked. "Looked like there's more to it if you ask me."

"When was the last time you felt protective of a woman, Uncle?"

He snorted. "If you must know, 1959, when some smooth-talking Spaniard tried to sweet-talk your aunt right in front of me at a gallery opening in Soho."

His aunt cooed. "Oh, Arthur, you remember." She glanced at Trevor. "Fernando *was* rather dashing, although not as dashing as that one over there."

"Who?" his uncle joked, looking behind him.

"Haha," she said, kicking up her feet like a much younger woman. "Trevor, pour yourself a drink and tell us about your day. Did you get a lot accomplished?"

Not a lick. In fact, he'd had trouble concentrating on work, something unusual for him. All he could think of was how animated and beautiful Becca had been, talking about the various dye baths. The ongoing barrage of jokes from his family and others in Dare Valley courtesy of Jill's video hadn't improved his mood. His sister Caitlyn had even gone to the effort of Photoshopping a picture of his head with an alpaca's body standing next to Buttercup in a chapel—and sent it to his entire family, no less. Surely Connor had seen it, although his brother didn't check his personal email at work, too focused and committed to business, he said, like he wished the rest of them would be. Everyone had laughed at that comment, except Quinn, because he was nearly as uptight as Connor.

"Business is boring, Aunt," he said, kicking back. "Let's talk about something else."

"Are you planning on seeing the lovely Ms. O'Neill tonight?" his uncle asked straight out.

"Arthur!" Aunt Clara exclaimed.

His uncle pinned him with that all-knowing gaze again. "Are you?"

God, it was like being called on the carpet by his dad all over again. "Yes." He'd thought of little else.

"Be careful with her," Arthur said, causing a hitch in Trevor's breath. "She's got a soft heart, I expect."

He nodded in complete agreement, trying not to worry about it. Hell, at this point, his heart was in trouble too.

"But good choice," his uncle said, rising again and pouring two whiskeys. "As your matchmaker, I totally approve."

"Me too," his aunt said as his uncle brought the drinks over. "I'm feeling all warm and mushy today."

"It's the beer," Uncle Arthur said, handing Trevor a tumbler.

"Balderdash, to use your word," she said, picking up her mug and thrusting it into the air. "To love. Wherever we find it."

Trevor's hand felt heavy as he tried to lift his glass. *Love?* Good God, not that. There were stories about the power of toasting to things like love in Ireland. Such toasts had a way of coming true.

Then his mind flashed an image of Becca standing in the doorway, holding up what he now knew was his very own shirt, the one she'd washed herself. The memory of her curved silhouette stole his breath all over again.

His hand rose of its own accord, almost as if lifted by fairies, or so an Irish storyteller would say.

He drank to the toast.

Chapter 12

BECCA FOUND HERSELF EVADING THE DINING ROOM THAT evening, certain her growing feelings for Trevor would be visible on her face, both to the man in question and her guests.

Still, she could hear his laughter from the kitchen. It was a conversation of laughter, in fact—his low, rumbling laugh, his uncle's gravelly one, and Clara's bell-like tones. Whatever stories they'd gotten up to telling tonight had been highly humorous from the sound of it. He would be in good spirits, and oddly, she was too, simply from hearing him laugh.

Oh, she was as lovesick as Buttercup.

"Get out of the kitchen," Chef Padraig Buckley said, making her look over sharply. "We're serving the duck with juniper berries tonight, Becca, not the peppercorn cream sauce. *Merde alors*. You're no use to me tonight."

Sure enough, she looked down at the plate she was finishing and realized she'd mixed up the finishing sauce for the entree. "I'm so sorry, Chef." Fresh back from the Cordon Bleu and an award-winning restaurant in Paris, her chef tended to lace a little French in with his Irish, usually of the profane variety.

"Out, my lovely," he said, waving his cleaver. "You

can make up for it by bringing me one of your precious Angora rabbits. I have the perfect sauce for it."

The ongoing jokes about her giving up one of her prize Angoras hadn't abated, but it was all in good fun. "Never." She flashed him a smile and sailed out of the kitchen, only to run smack into Aileen.

"Goodness, girl, go back to your quarters and prepare yourself for that fine man in there. You're making right bags of everything tonight."

Bags, indeed. "Fine, then. I'll see you in the morning."

Aileen waggled her brows. "Not too early, I hope."

"Oh, Aileen," she said, mostly in exasperation, but she felt her cheeks flame. Everyone seemed to know she had a romance afoot. Scurrying off, she called Boru to her side as she swept into the main hall.

"Becca!"

Oh, the way Trevor called her name. She stopped short and turned around. Tonight he wore another suit in various shades of gunmetal gray, without a tie like usual, a decidedly sexy look on him. Oh, she had the loveliest wool to suit him, one she'd just dried from her dye bath of elderberry. She should knit him a sweater or a scarf to keep him warm on cold, rainy days. He could probably wear a scarf and still look manly. Then she realized how fanciful those thoughts were, what with the reason he was here.

She shouldn't knit him anything.

"I saw you walk by the dining room and excused myself," he said, crossing to her and taking her hands. "While I love my aunt and uncle and Hargreaves, it's you I'd rather be with. Are you still working or are you free now?"

His eagerness sent her heart racing like one of her Angoras. "Aileen and Chef Padraig sent me off just now. I was going back to my chambers."

"I thought we might take a walk," he said, staring into her eyes with a touch of suggestion.

Was he planning on kissing her? Oh, yes, he was—his

green eyes were filled with flecks of fiery gold tonight. She needed to find a dye to match that gold. "Goodness, you have beautiful eyes."

He snorted. "Imagining a dye bath, are you?"

"What?"

"You had that same look earlier today when you were showing me your colors," he said, taking her hand. "Come out with me. The moon is full, and I imagine your land reflects a million different colors at night."

The longing to see it all with him was great, but she started to sweat at the thought of leaving the house with him. She could walk alone with Boru in daylight, but even then, there were moments of sheer terror intermixed with her stalwart determination. Cian and Aileen were used to it, if they accompanied her. But she couldn't face the ocean of darkness outside, not even for Trevor. Her parents had died at night, and the horrors she'd seen had been under the veil of darkness.

"I'd rather have a drink with you in my chambers," she said, rubbing Boru's head when he nudged her, as if sensing her distress.

"Oh, come on," Trevor said, throwing his hand out toward the window in the main hall showing the moonlight flickering over the open sea. "Look at how beautiful it is out there tonight. Do you really want to pass that up?"

"Yes," she said, her tone hard because it had to be. "Feel free to go though. I'll be in my chambers when you come back."

He put his hands on her shoulders as she went to walk off. "What's the matter? You're white as a sheet and clearly upset. Did I say something wrong?"

"No, of course not," she said quickly. "I simply don't want to walk, is all. Today was long, and I only want to sit a spell."

He opened his mouth to say something, then stopped. "Okay, a drink with you it is."

She wanted to ask what he'd planned on saying, but fear kept her mute. She let him take her hand instead, trying to relax back into the rhythm of being with him. They walked back to her chambers, and at the door, he made a show of pointing at it.

"Are we safe from Buttercup? I'd hate for us to be interrupted again."

"Yes, it shouldn't be an issue. The cause was taken care of." Thinking about Cian's protectiveness made her feel another pulse of uncertainty.

"Becca," Trevor said, raising her hand to his lips. "It's only a drink."

After their meeting in the old kitchen, she knew better and so did he. They'd made a connection—and even if it came to ruin in the end, there was no ignoring or denying it. "Come on up." Hatshep raced out of her bedroom when she arrived at the top of the stairs. "Well, hello there. Are you here to say hello to Trevor?"

The white cat wove around Trevor's ankles and then seemed to speak to Boru, who emitted a loud woof. Both of them pranced off for her bedroom. Were they trying to make a suggestion? Aileen was right about her animals liking Trevor.

"Would you care for another whiskey?" she asked, knowing that he'd had one during dinner. "You're not much of a wine drinker, are you?"

He wandered over to the sofa. "I'll drink it, but whiskey and beer are my favorites."

"Aileen told me your aunt took a liking to Irish beer." Of course, the woman had also told her about their dinner outing tomorrow night and how Trevor had asked if she could join them. Her heart had cracked clean through. How she wished she could be the kind of woman who could accept the invitations of the man she fancied.

"Aunt Clara has what my family jokes is a superpower in drinking. I have it as well. I can drink anything and not be affected. A whiskey would be fine." He touched her knitting project lying across the sofa's arm. "Hey, this is really good. What are you making?"

"It's a jumper," she said, pouring them each a whiskey and bringing them over. "For your uncle." His eyes narrowed, and she rushed to assure him. "It's a rare thing I do for guests when they're as nice as your uncle and aunt. I didn't know you were related when I offered."

He surprised her by throwing back his head and laughing. "That put me in my place."

And yet, here she'd been thinking about knitting him something gray since he liked the color so well.

"I only meant—"

"I know what you meant," he said, clinking their glasses together. "So tell me about this sweater. Are you making him a traditional Irish one? The cream-colored wool would suggest it."

"Have a few Aran jumpers, do you?" she asked.

"Of course. I live here, and they do keep the cold out."

"They're meant to," she said, sitting down and gesturing to the sofa beside her. "There's a reason some call them a fisherman's jumper. Yes, I thought it would keep him warm back in Colorado. Plus, it's a traditional Irish handcraft, after all, although fewer and fewer are made by hand. I hope to change that, of course, with my new enterprise." She laughed. "Aileen says I'll need more sheep, and every time she says it, Cian gets red in the face. He and the sheep are still finding their way to an understanding. They've held up traffic on our road more than once and... Oh, I'm rambling on."

"I like it when you ramble," he said, taking her free hand and stroking it. "Do you have any other knitting projects I could see?"

She leaned back so as to take a better measure of him. "Why?"

"You love it so much, and I thought... Never mind." He lifted his whiskey and looked away.

"What?" she pressed, feeling the air of something new and fragile blossoming between them.

"I'd like to see something you've made, is all," he said. "I know quality when I see it, and the kind of wool you're making is quality. I only wondered what the finished product looked like."

He might have gotten all business on her, but his ears were a carmine red color. How sweet. "I'll be right back." She had the urge to kiss him for being so cute, and she gave in to the feeling and bussed his cheek as she left the room.

Boru and Hatshep were lying at the foot of her bed when she entered, and both looked at her and then at the door as if to inquire why she hadn't brought Trevor. In fact, that was a right fine idea, if you asked her. She could ask him into her bedroom under the guise of looking at her knitting, allowing her to become accustomed to him in her space.

"Good idea," she told them, and Boru barked softly. "Trevor! Why don't you come in here so I don't have to carry all of these things out?"

He appeared in the doorway and leaned against the frame, seemingly at ease. My, he cut a fine figure. Her mouth went dry.

"It's tidier this way," she said, feeling her face turn pink.

"Happy to be of help," he said, sauntering in. "I see your friends are making themselves at home."

She opened her closet door, and its loving comfort settled around her. "Oh, yes. They do that. You can... Sit on the bed, if you'd like. In fact, I knitted the blanket at the edge."

"This teal one?" she heard him exclaim. "You're kidding me."

The closet enveloped her in the lavender scent coming from the sachets she'd packed in the shelves and the drawers. This was her true haven, her sanctuary.

Then she realized the door to the bathroom was open, and she darted to close it.

"You have a Jack and Jill bathroom?" a deep male voice asked near her ear. "And a desk in your closet?"

She jumped when she felt his breath and turned around. "Ah... It has a wonderful view. There's a window, you see, and the view of the sea is spectacular. Cian thought adding the door to the bathroom from here was...humorous and fitting. I get to working or knitting, you see, and I lose track of everything around me."

She held her breath, hoping he would believe her. On Cian's say-so, her grandmother had hired someone to build this closet and make it bigger. The door to the bathroom had been a practical addition.

"You do get distracted," he murmured, but his brow was furrowed. Desperate to distract Trevor from the oddity, she lurched into the closet and tugged out one of her pride and joys, a pale violet infinity scarf done in the difficult nupp stitch.

"This is one of mine," she said, almost shoving it in his face. "It's made of these little bobbles, you see. The stitch has Estonian origins, and it's one of the most challenging you can knit."

He didn't look at her right away, his attention still fixed on her private space. "This is one of the biggest closets I've ever seen in Ireland. I mean, I thought I had a big walk-in closet. In fact, my Irish contractor ribbed me endlessly about it, even going so far as to ask if I planned on entertaining ladies in it." Then he laughed, low and husky, making her want to shiver.

"Have you?" she blurted out. "Oh, forget I said that."

He took the scarf from her hands and rubbed his thumbs over the stitching in a way that weakened her knees. Goodness, he was intoxicating. No one else could have excited her like this by merely touching her knitwork.

"This is stunning, Becca," he said, his eyes lowering for a scant moment before rising and pinning her with a heated gaze that reminded her of a flambéed sauce. "And no, I haven't used my closet for entertaining. Yet."

Fighting the urge to fan herself, she dove back to her shelves and looked for more projects to show him. She thrust out her favorite Irish jumper in the most beautiful midnight-blue yarn she'd ever come across. "Entrelac knit." Then she grabbed her teal duster that hit her mid-calf. "Brioche stitch." Her version of a poncho caught her eye, and she tossed it to him as she ventured deeper into her closet. "Fair Isle with two colors."

And on it went.

He followed her into the depths of the cedar closet, holding the precious pieces she'd made by her hand as if he couldn't bear to set them aside. She pulled out still more projects from her shelves and piled them on his outstretched arms, babbling on about knitting techniques from other places like Spain and Portugal and then droning on about the Irish Moss stitch and how it differed from the Andalusian stitch.

"*Becca!*"

She stopped herself from pulling out her next example, a honeycomb stitch. "What?"

"Where can I put all these?" he asked, his eyes a stormy gray-green she recognized as desire.

If it hadn't been for the tension emanating from him and her, she might have laughed. There he stood, all tall, dark man, holding a pile of her knitwear stacked up to his neck.

"On the bed," she said, her heartbeat so loud in her ears she could barely hear herself.

He disappeared. She took a moment to suck in a huge

amount of oxygen and rise from her knees. Goodness, when had she gotten on the floor? Strong hands closed around her shoulders, and Trevor pulled her against his chest. She met the wall of solid muscle and raised her head to look into his beautiful eyes. The heat in them had her insides softening, and then his mouth found hers.

His touch unraveled her, the power and force of it unknown to her—almost as though he was pulling apart the stitches composing her life with the intent to create something new and beautiful.

The hot, hard mouth on hers drove her to new heights of desire, and she found herself pressed against a wall of hand-knit clothes, the textures soft and cushy, a compelling contrast to the hard body moving sinuously against her. She opened her mouth when his tongue traced the seam of her lips, and she was lost in a heat and hunger she'd never imagined. A moan surged up from deep inside her, and his answering groan had her gripping the strong muscles of his biceps to keep anchored.

He shifted, pulling her down onto the white sheepskin rug on the floor beneath them. His big body covered her, and she luxuriated in that fine mouth of his making sweet magic on her own and the silky texture of his dark hair under her fingers. Soon he was lifting her shirt off and unhooking her bra, laying her back to feast on her with his heated eyes. He ran his hand from her throat to the valley of her hips in one long, steamy trail of sensation.

A smile crested his face. "You're beautiful." Then he lowered his mouth to her breast and sucked on a hard nipple. Desire shot through her system, this time with hooks, and she gave herself up to the sweet loving of his mouth. When he rose up and took off his jacket and shirt and the medal he wore, she simply watched, enjoying the proud specimen of manhood before her.

"Like what you see?" he asked, that now-familiar smile upon his mouth.

She nodded, enjoying the feeling of her tingling lips transforming into a smile in such a moment. The urge to touch him was strong, so she ran her hand over the planes of his chest down to his abdomen. His skin was a texture all its own, like a soft wool that was smooth to the touch yet memorably rough to the fingertips.

"You have a beautiful body," she whispered, the scent of lavender filling her senses.

"Thank you," he said, his voice a low timbre now. "Let me show you how it feels against yours."

Yes, please, she thought, and gave her mouth up when he kissed her again. Long and soft, hard and fast, he offered her a bouquet of kisses, and she eagerly took them all. When he slipped off the rest of her clothes and his own, she lifted a hand to his cheek, wanting to see those stormy green eyes again.

He raised his gaze as if sensing her need for that connection. "I can't wait to be inside you," he said, the brash words sending a rush of gooseflesh across her skin. "But there's a few things I really want to do first. Let me show you."

He wove her a pattern of what he had in mind with his mouth and hands, strokes and kisses and licks up her thighs and to her core, circling in tighter and tighter as she moaned and thrust against his mouth. A rush of heat broke forth in her belly, and then she was crying out under him, her hands flung out on the rug as she came over and over and over again.

He lightened the sensual onslaught and then rested his chin on her stomach as she settled into a hazy, erotic afterglow.

"My heavens, that was potent," she whispered, her mouth dry as if the heat had burned up everything inside her.

"It's about to get even more potent," he said, giving her a cheeky wink before sliding up her body and kissing her square on the mouth.

She cupped his neck to keep him there, savoring the way he rubbed his tongue against her own and nipped her bottom lip now and again. Kissing him was heady stuff indeed, and she knew she could go on kissing him like this forever. Her hand ran down his back, crossing the lines where his muscles rose and divided in perfect symmetry. He turned to nuzzle her neck, and she realized he was still waiting for some sign from her, a signal she was ready for the next pattern they were knitting together.

She pushed gently on his chest until their eyes met and said, "Come into me, Trevor."

He traced her cheek, his smile falling away to be replaced by an expression both deeper and more profound. She wasn't sure what that look meant exactly, but she could feel something changing between them. When he slipped on a condom and came inside her fully, she knew. It was a joining, the kind where body and spirit came together, the kind that opened up reservoirs in the heart.

The feel of him, so large and hot and hard, inside of her made her stretch out full length underneath him, almost as though her entire body was expanding from the power of their connection.

He thrust deep, and she moaned. "Look at me," he said, his voice a dark whisper.

Struggling under the waves of sensation, she finally met his gaze. In his eyes she saw a million stars, a new map in her universe. A fresh wave of tears filled her eyes, and she cupped his cheek as he lowered himself fully onto her.

"Trevor," she said, her voice all hushed and warm.

"Becca," he answered.

Slowly he thrust into her, almost as though he was still learning the shape and pattern of what they were creating. She gripped his hips in answer, doing her part to guide him, teach him, school him in what she wanted, what they both needed. He responded by pressing his palms into the floor beside her head and gliding his body in and out, his thrusts ever-increasing in their force and speed.

A new heat flashed in her belly, this time white-hot, and as she stared into the stars shining in his eyes, she gave herself up to the pleasure of their joining. Another explosion flashed through her, this time in concert with her heart, and she was flung into a new stratosphere. She heard him cry out and come inside her, pulsing, filling her. His head lowered to rest on her shoulder as though it belonged there.

She floated like she'd always imagined she would on the sea, her body encased in golden warmth, not only from the force of their connection, but from the heat radiating from his body. Peace filled her, a peace that defied all pleasure, and with it, she knew she'd been transformed.

When he finally raised his eyes, she knew he'd been transformed too.

The stars were still there, only now they were shining with the promise of a million lifetimes.

Chapter 13

No experience had ever cracked Trevor open like making love to Becca O'Neill.

Everything had started out fun and innocent. She'd asked him into her bedroom on what he knew was a bum reason. He'd thought it rather sweet that she was still unsure and embarrassed about having sex with him. This morning, in the old kitchen that had become her dyeing room, he'd felt his heart crack and then again in her closet. This, he knew, was the real Becca. The closet was a haven of sorts. Why else would she keep a desk in such a place? And, stranger yet, a door to the bathroom. Yet, surrounded by the clothes she'd made with her own hands, he could see the appeal of such a sanctuary.

When he'd looked at the first piece she'd handed him—a pale lavender scarf made of what looked like hundreds of bubbles—awe had overwhelmed him. And that had only been the beginning. Each piece she handed or tossed at him captured his imagination. Her beautiful accent, so soft and lilting, wove stories about the difference between stitches and patterns, making his head swim. Every pattern, every color, every texture blew his mind. Mere clothing these were not. She created art, and he wasn't sure she even knew it.

Like in the old kitchen with the dyeing baths, he fell under her spell. As clothes piled higher in his arms, the passion and joy she had for life cracked him anew, this time in his belly. Her passion inflamed his, her knitting explanations becoming foreplay. When he could no longer stand not touching her, he'd been struck with the problem of where to put all of her precious creations. When she'd suggested the bed, he'd almost drawn her in there along with him. But no... Their first time had to be in her sanctuary, surrounded by her precious creations.

With each touch, each kiss, each sigh, she'd rent crack after crack inside him, breaking away pieces of the man he'd been to make way for the man he would become. Bringing her to pleasure that first time had been sheer magic, and the pride that he could bring her to such heights had moved him. But when he came into her and looked into her eyes, he heard the whispers of those final cracks inside him and welcomed it as she'd welcomed him into her body, holding nothing back. In the end, he knew he'd fallen the rest of the way and was standing on new ground. But he wasn't alarmed by the changed landscape. No, there was a rightness to it, the kind of certainty he'd only felt a few times in his life.

"We should probably get up off this floor," she said, kissing his neck.

He pushed off his elbows, thankful he had the strength to move when moments before it had seemed impossible. "Are you cold?" he asked, looking around for something to wrap her in.

"With you as my own personal heater?" she asked, sitting up. "I couldn't possibly get a chill."

She ran her hand through her long, silky hair, and he was spellbound again. Her lips were lush and ruby-colored, and there was a lovely pink flush to her creamy white skin. He realized he wanted to make love to her all over again.

"I need some water," she said, moving to stand.

He managed to help her up, his legs feeling none too steady suddenly. She patted him on the cheek, a soft smile on her lips. He watched as she grabbed a thin purple wool robe and walked out. Taking a moment to collect himself, he turned and walked over to her desk to check out this view she'd mentioned. Sure enough, it was spectacular, what with the moonlight raining down on the powerful waves of the sea. The rhythm of it all washed over him, and he stepped back, admitting to himself one thing had changed for sure.

He couldn't take this place away from her, not for his job or his brother. Connor wouldn't like it, but Trevor would have to find another way to give his brother what he wanted.

The decision lightened something in him. Should he tell her? No, he decided. Talk of business might spoil this moment, and he didn't want to do that to her. In fact, he didn't want to do it to himself either. This was their night.

He left the closet after pulling on his pants and pocketing his St. Christopher medal, not wanting to lose it. Boru lifted his head and gave a quiet ruff, and Hatshep stretched languidly on the floor, almost like her mistress had. The clothes were on the bed still, and they'd have to find a place to park them because he planned on making love to her in that bed.

She wasn't in the living room, but he heard water running and followed the sound to a small kitchen. She was downing the contents of a glass, the line of her throat long and sexy in the soft light. When she finished it, she made a satisfied sound, and he felt a smile hover on his face.

"Thirsty?" he asked, stepping toward her with the intent to kiss her.

Although he couldn't say why, he knew it was important to touch her, to let her know how much things had changed for him. For them, he hoped. She jolted when he put his hand on her waist, and he knew he'd been right to do this. Her entire body went still, and as he nuzzled her neck, she placed a warm hand on his bare chest.

"I'd like to say it was the closet," he told her, "but what happened between us just now would have happened anywhere."

He caught the rise of her chest as she drew in a deep breath. She was finding her way too, he realized.

"Yes, you're right," she said, pouring another glass of water and handing it to him. "I...didn't expect you to say so, however."

However? "Why deny what happened?" Trevor didn't waver or adopt half-measures. Once he was in, he was all in. He'd always been like that about everything important in his life.

She was silent for a moment, and he drank the water, his throat also parched from their lovemaking.

"Let's stay in the moment," she said, nodding for emphasis. "Given the circumstances, that seems best."

She was right. He wasn't in a position to tell her how deeply he felt, or that he'd only just decided to alter his brother's business plan and his own role in it. He'd do better to wait until things were squared away.

"I'd very much like to make love to you again," he said, noting how her gaze flew to his. She was surprised. Had she expected him to leave? "In the bed this time, although we'll have to revisit the closet. I'm not going to be able to see one without having lustful thoughts."

Her chuckle was soft, and he knew she'd gotten past whatever uncertainty she'd been facing. "Me either."

He tossed back the rest of the water. God, he could drink a couple more glasses.

"Trevor," she said, fiddling with the tie to her robe.

He knew she needed him to stay away as she said whatever was weighing on her mind. "Yeah?"

Her blue eyes were somber, the slow smile on her face an interesting contrast. "Thank you. For listening to me drone on about my knitting...and for afterward."

"First, I love to hear you talk about your work." He crossed now and placed his hands on her shoulders, turning her to face him. "And second, you don't have to thank me for making love to you. It was a joy."

In all his years of having sex, he'd never thought of it as a joy, but it was with her. Another sign.

She leaned up and kissed him on the cheek. "It was grand for me as well."

She refilled both of their water glasses then walked to the doorway, turning and leaning her head against the wall. He took a mental picture of her, knowing he'd bring it to mind often to commemorate his first night with Becca. He'd remember the way her brown hair trailed over her breast and the white skin exposed as the robe gaped open to her belly. He'd remember the soft way she looked at him, almost as if soaking up his presence just as much as he was hers.

But mostly, he'd remember this as the moment he'd decided this first night with Becca O'Neill had the power to turn into a lifetime.

Chapter 14

A loud humming noise woke Becca out of a deep sleep. Trevor shrieked and pushed back into her on the bed, and she opened her eyes to see Buttercup's head resting on his pillow.

"How in the hell did it get in here?" he asked, pulling the sheet up almost as if it were a shield.

Becca's momentary jolt out of sleep turned into laughter. She couldn't help it. Trevor looked so put out. The alpaca straightened to its full height and cocked its head to the right, giving another loud hum. Surely Cian wouldn't have...

"That thing licked my face!" His voice was filled with outrage. "It didn't feel like you and woke me out of a dead sleep."

"Well, that's a relief," she said, swinging out of bed. After the way they'd explored each other's bodies, she now understood what people meant when they could recognize their lover in the dark. She knew the way and shape of him, the sound of his breathing and groans.

Buttercup wandered over to her as she reached for her robe. Becca took her by the halter to keep her from rushing Trevor. "How did you get in here again?" She didn't think Cian was the culprit this time. "Come on,

Buttercup. Trevor is about to have a heart attack, and I can't have the man dropping dead in my bed."

"If a man was ever to die though, it would be after last night," he said, holding up a pillow now as if it were a greater deterrent to Buttercup than a mere sheet.

"I'm glad you think so," she said, laughing. When he'd reached for her in the kitchen, kissing her so softly and deeply she'd almost cried, she'd known he was trying to tell her something profound, something words were yet too fragile to say. They'd found a balance making love to each other and laughing in between.

"Where are my clothes?" he asked, leaning over the side of the bed.

She didn't see a single stitch of them. Boru and Hatshep weren't around, but she wondered if they'd done the honors again, trying to keep Trevor naked in her bed. Oh, those dear animals.

"Your pets took my clothes again, didn't they?" He wrapped the sheet around himself and stood up. "I don't suppose I can make it all the way to my room like this and not be seen."

"It's half past seven," she said, noting the time. "People will be at breakfast. While I imagine it would improve many a person's day, seeing you in a state of undress, it might be better if I find you something to wear. Assuming I can't find your clothes from last night. Of course, you could wear something from my closet."

Her lips twitched at the very thought of him in one of her jumpers. The fit would be tight to be sure.

"You're enjoying this way too much," he said, "and here I'd gone to sleep with the intention of waking you up in the most delicious way this morning."

Her thighs clenched at the very thought. Good heavens, she was turning into a sex goddess. And she rather loved it. "Later for sure. I need to find you some clothes, and then I'm off to see about things."

Her list was long today, but she was eager to start the day. And boy was she ready for a big breakfast after last night.

"I'll just stay here," he said, frowning like a thwarted boy. "If I hadn't been such a king in bed last night, I'd be worried about my Man Card."

Laughing, she led Buttercup to the doorway. "I can attest your Man Card, as you call it, is fully loaded. And I promise I won't tell anyone about this. Except Aileen." Becca dashed out of the room, and Buttercup hummed. She heard something land on the floor and realized Trevor had thrown the pillow after her. Oh, how she liked that playful, cheeky side of his.

Boru and Hatshep were waiting for her in the sitting room. "All right, now. Don't the two of you have something to tell me?" Boru lowered his head, and Hatshep only stared back. "Where are Trevor's clothes?"

Hatshep seemed to give a sly smile before walking off, and Boru stretched out on the ground, resting his head on the floor as if plagued by a guilty conscience.

"You two are terrible," she said in a loud voice, aware Trevor might be listening. Then she patted Boru and whispered, "Good dog. Now, Buttercup, let's see about you."

The alpaca hummed the whole way down the stairs, as if her soul were being ripped out of her. "I know you like Trevor, and you have good taste, but you can't keep coming in here."

Becca would have to find out how it had happened this time. She closed the door to her quarters and then led the animal a few yards to the back door. Opening it, she gave the alpaca a shove, and the animal reluctantly took a few steps, allowing her to close the door.

"Now, about Trevor's clothes," she said, retracing her steps into her chambers. She needed to get dressed herself before she looked for his things, although she expected her two beautiful treasures weren't going to bring them out until they were good and ready.

She walked back into the bedroom and stopped short at the sight of Trevor grinning at her from her bed. Goodness, but that man had a fine chest.

"I've decided I'm looking at this all wrong," he said, rising up onto his knees and resting his elbows on them. "If your animals want me to be your exclusive sex slave and never leave your tower—so to speak—I'm all in."

Sex slave? Heavens, she was going to combust right here. "Some of us have to work." Then she realized he had work too, and she felt the floor fall out from under her almost like she was in an elevator.

His sensual grin softened, as if he knew her thoughts. "You forget the pros of having a sex slave, Becca."

"Because I've never had one before."

His grin flew back at her wording, and she wanted to smack herself. "As the slave to your every sexual fantasy and pleasure, I'm at your beck and call. You can manage breakfast with the guests and then pop back here and demand that I kiss your creamy little thighs."

Creamy little thighs? Oh, my. "Some of us need to be better grounded in reality. I can't just pop back here for sex."

He cocked his head to the right, studying her. "Why not?"

She didn't have a clue. "It's not responsible. I have tasks, things people count on me to do. Oh, why are we talking like this? I need to get dressed so I can fetch you clothes." She supposed she could have Aileen go fetch them, but the woman would laugh herself silly and rib Trevor terribly when she delivered them. Becca planned on telling Aileen—nothing got past the woman—but she'd spare Trevor the embarrassment.

Crossing to her closet, she walked in. "Sex slave. That man..." But she was flushed and breathless.

"You're thinking about it," Trevor called in a playful tone. "I know you are."

As she looked down at the rug they'd made love on, she realized she was, indeed.

***

Clara Merriam Hale had lived long enough to know when a woman was in love, and seeing Becca spring into the dining room where everyone was eating breakfast was like having a front-row seat.

And Trevor, the sweetheart, hadn't made an appearance yet. *Hmm...*

She elbowed Arthur, who was busy reading *The Irish Times* with a single-mindedness she imagined would never fade away. Since his retirement from his own newspaper, she hadn't known what to expect of him. He loathed golf, he'd told her. Had never had a true hobby outside of work, which wasn't a hobby so much as a passion. Cheekily, he'd asked her if matchmaking could be a hobby, and she'd smacked him in the chest in response. She loved smacking him around playfully, and since he typically barked out a laugh or gave an emphatic harrumph, she knew he loved it too.

"I'm going to talk to Becca today," Clara told Arthur, "and see if she can come with us tonight."

"Cian said she couldn't," Arthur said, turning the page dramatically. She knew it was because he loved the sound of the paper crinkling and crackling.

"Still, I imagine there's a way for her to come," Clara said. "Besides, Trevor wants her there, and I suspect Becca will want to spend more time with him too."

"My dear, you know plenty, but perhaps let them figure it out."

She lifted her cup of tea. "Did I just hear the so-called great matchmaker, Arthur Hale, say two young people should figure things out?"

"Yes, when it's going well," Arthur said, not looking up from his paper. "The woman is practically glowing, and you know what that means."

"No, what does *that* mean?" she asked to be contrary.

"It means, madam, that the young Trevor and Ms. O'Neill had relations last night," Hargreaves took the opportunity to interject from his usually quiet place at the table.

Arthur lowered his newspaper. "Hargreaves, never, ever say that word again. This isn't the Victorian era. Good God, don't any of us have a sense of propriety?"

Clara couldn't believe her ears. Arthur, propriety? She wouldn't have married him had he possessed a single bone of propriety in his body. "I'm off to talk to Becca."

"You should sit yourself down and have more tea," her husband said, resuming his perusal of Irish news.

She stood because a woman had to do what she wanted. "Hargreaves, look after him for me."

"Always, madam," her ever-loyal butler and companion said.

"I don't need looking after, for Pete's sake," Arthur balked as Clara walked off.

She wasn't going to remind him that he'd had a mild heart attack only a few months ago. Of course, he seemed as fit as a fiddle now. *Cosmo* said sex at any age helped keep a person young, and they were both glowing in that department, to use his phrase. But she still worried about his health from time to time. They'd finally found each other again after so long. Now she wanted them both to live past one hundred. One night she'd told him she'd already planned their twentieth anniversary party, and he'd gotten teary-eyed, the dear man. No wonder she loved him so.

Catching sight of Becca moving quickly across the open hall, nodding to the other guests, she took up the chase. She managed to intercept her when Aileen stopped her for a word. Clara felt bad about intruding, but she didn't want to miss her chance. Perhaps if Becca knew about the outing this early in the day, she would be able to find someone to fill in for her.

"My dears," she said, putting a hand on Becca's arm. "Sorry to interrupt, but I wanted to follow up on Cian's dinner invitation tonight and see if there's any way you could join us, Becca. Trevor isn't the only one who'd love that. Arthur and I would like to get to know you better." Hargreaves too, if he'd agreed to go, which he wouldn't.

The ever-present smile on Aileen's face fell, and Clara became aware of a sudden tension in Becca's body. In fact, the woman looked downright teary-eyed. Whatever was wrong?

"Oh, Clara, you're the kindest to ask our Becca here," Aileen said, putting her arm around the younger woman, almost protectively. "But you see, we have a deal about that, and we simply can't leave this beautiful place to just anyone. I hope you can understand. Clara, I need Becca's help in the kitchen, if you'll excuse my rudeness. Cian and I will see you later."

Clara noted that Becca hadn't said a word, and her face, which had been so bright and cheery earlier, seemed wooden.

She watched Aileen hustle Becca away, whispering almost secretively to her, and stayed there tapping her finger against her side. Something wasn't right.

She was going to find out what.

CHAPTER 15

TREVOR GLANCED AT HIS PHONE, GRIMACING WHEN HE SAW Connor's face on his screen. Even in casual clothes, his brother looked foreboding. Maybe it was time to stop ducking his calls.

"Hey, man, do you ever sleep?" he asked, not surprised his brother was calling so early. It was close to five o'clock in the morning on his end. "How's things there?"

"Shit," his brother said without any preamble. "Why have you been avoiding me? It's not like you, Trev."

Damn, he should have known Connor would be direct. "I'm tired of the alpaca jokes. Flynn overnighted me a plastic wedding ring from some toy store. And you should see the memes Michaela has drummed up. I can't wait until she leaves for the Amazon tomorrow. The one about me finding my softer side—"

"You're lollygagging, Trev, and I want results."

He thought of the decision he'd made after making love to Becca. It was the right one. He felt it down to his bones. But Connor wouldn't see it that way. Still, he said, "She's not going to sell, Con. I think we need to call this off and look for another way."

There was an ominous silence, and then Connor said, "Does this mean I need to send Quinn in?"

Good God, no, he almost barked back. Quinn was as tough as Connor in some ways. Delaying was his only option. "Look, it won't do us any good to bombard her, but I'm going to need more time. I'm telling you, Con, she's got a really great thing going here. Did you know she'd just bought a bunch of sheep, rabbits, and alpacas and started a new hand-crafted Irish yarn business?"

There was a pause, and Trevor knew he had him there. "No, I didn't, but our offer would offset any capital investment. She can find another piece of land and continue it there."

"What about the bed and breakfast?" Trev asked. "You do realize it's named one of the top three in Ireland, right?" Trevor had hunkered down and done his research, ordering room service instead of joining his family in the dining room for breakfast. But he'd drawn the line at looking deeper into Becca's background, wanting to hear personal details from her alone when she was ready.

"She can move the house," Connor barked. "You know there's always a solution when you throw enough money at it. I need that land, Trevor. I won't lose another cousin to the sea."

He cursed softly, hearing the quiver of repressed grief in his brother's voice. He didn't want to upset Connor, and he certainly wanted him to keep Patrick and other employees safe. No one should die like Corey and those men had.

But Becca's land wasn't the answer.

And so he had to find a new one. Still, he'd never gone behind his brother's back before, not on something this big, and that didn't sit well. But what choice did he have when his blockhead brother wouldn't see reason?

"I'm working hard on getting you what you need, Con," Trevor said, using words that were true.

"Fine," his brother said after clearing the emotion

from his voice. "I need to run. Tell Buttercup I've ordered monogrammed towels as your wedding present. Where are you registered, by the way?"

Trev barked out a laugh, and brief relief swept through him. God, he loved his brother, even if he wanted to smack him sometimes. They all knew Connor carried the heaviest responsibility in the family business, and it weighed on him. "Up yours, Con."

"Back at you," his brother said. "I've gotta run. Keep me posted."

"Only if I'm not out with my new girl," he said, but his laughter cut short when Becca flashed into his mind. She *was* his girl. Had been since he'd seen her in the old kitchen talking about her dyes. They'd sealed that truth last night as he stared into her liquid-blue eyes and made love to her ever so slowly, so slowly it was as if the entire world had stilled around them.

"Later, bro," Con said, clicking off.

He stared at the phone. "Yeah, later." Restless and ill at ease, he stalked over to the ever-present plate of scones in his suite. God bless Aileen. He munched on one and then another before deciding on his next move. Picking up his phone again, he eyed the time. It was close to six in Dare Valley, and while J.T. would bitch, he would pick up.

"What am I, a baker?" his brother asked, his voice hoarse with sleep. "You okay?"

He eyed another scone and shoved the plate away, his stomach suddenly a little queasy. "Would I be calling if I just wanted to chitchat?"

"Give me a minute," his brother said, muttering to Caroline, whom Trevor heard ask what was going on.

Crossing to the window, Trevor opened it and sucked in some fresh air. He was the negotiator, wasn't he? He'd figure out a way for everyone to have what they wanted, he told himself. He had to.

"All right," J.T. said, his focus evident now. "What's wrong?"

Trevor watched as the sea churned past the cliffs. He scanned the view, thinking about all the oil Becca was sitting on. He found he couldn't tap into his inner businessman today. All he could see was beauty, and the way her eyes lit up when she talked about this place and her new enterprise.

"What I'm about to ask your help with could really piss Connor off. Hell, it will piss off Quinn too, and maybe a few others." Would it upset his mom? God, he'd rather cut his own arm off than that.

And yet he'd do it for Becca.

"It must be big for you to risk that kind of a row," J.T. said. "You know I trust you. I'll always have your back. You've had mine a hell of a lot lately, remember?"

"Helping you with your ex wasn't fun, but this is different. You can back out after you hear what I need help with."

"Like I would," his brother said. "Give it to me straight."

Shit. Was he really going to say this? Yeah. "I need you to help me find another oil-rich property for Connor close to the one I'm supposed to buy. Somewhere he can still drill on land and keep Patrick and our employees safe."

The silence was deafening, and Trevor knew J.T. was putting things together. "She won't sell? Why won't Connor accept that?"

"Have you heard him talk about how important this is? He won't sanction any new offshore projects because of what happened to Corey. So, he's intent on making Merriam Oil & Gas the first company to drill on Irish land. You know it's never been done before."

"What am I missing here?" his brother asked.

He'd known his brother would ask. "I've fallen in love with the owner, Becca O'Neill."

"Shit," his brother said. "Seriously? You? I thought you weren't interested in looking for something long-term yet."

He hadn't been, but he wasn't fool enough to deny what he wanted. Once he made up his mind, there was no going back.

"Are you happy about it?" J.T. asked.

Last night had been one of the best nights of his life. "Yes. She's...smart and beautiful and funny, and I can see her fitting in with the family, laughing with Caitlyn and you and shit. God, I sound like an idiot."

"No," J.T. said. "Man, I'm so *freaking* happy for you! I was afraid... Oh, shit, now I'm going to get emotional."

"We're a fucking Hallmark card. Might as well tell me."

"I was afraid my divorce might have messed you up a little about marriage, and I hated that."

Trevor let out a deep sigh. "It did a little, I suppose, but I decided not to let your ex screw things up for any of us. Besides, Mom and Dad are so happy, and now you are with Caroline. And I want a family. Always have." A house with a wife and kids running around had always been in the back of his mind. But he'd thought it was still a ways off, even though he was turning thirty-six this year.

"I'm glad it's not the alpaca," his brother joked.

The jest lightened the mood, just as J.T. had intended. His brother knew him well. "Its head was lying on my pillow this morning. You should have seen me. I huddled on the bed while Becca corralled the animal and led it out. Not my finest moment."

"I like a woman who can handle herself, including an alpaca," J.T. said. "Uncle Arthur and Aunt Clara have been raving about their experience there. I assume Becca's a big part of it."

"She's a natural businesswoman, J.T., with tons of vision and heart." He fingered the rich texture of the window valance. "You should see what she's created here. It's her own universe, and she's expanding." He told his brother about her new business plan, and it felt cathartic to share it. As his twin, J.T. knew he wasn't a bullshitter.

"I can't wait to meet her," J.T. said. "But back to your problem with Connor. It's dicey, Trev."

"I know it," he said, pulling a nearby chair closer to the window so he could feel the breeze and smell the sea. "I hate this, but I've tried to tell Connor it's not going to happen. He won't hear it. Today he asked if he needed to send Quinn."

"Shit, that's...unusual."

Quinn was head of their European operations, stationed in London. "You know he doesn't close deals. If he comes, he'll pressure the hell out of her. I can't let that happen."

"Part of Connor's genius is that he doesn't take no for an answer and always finds a way. Like you, usually. And Quinn. And me before I left. It's a family trait from Dad."

It went back a couple generations to Grandpa Emmits, he knew, but right now, he wasn't proud of it.

"You're worried Con and Quinn might play a little dirty?" J.T. asked.

"We've done it before," he said. "Always within the law, but we often employ a take-no-prisoners strategy." All in the name of expanding the family's business interests, of course. They tried to make everyone happy or at least give them their due, but business was business.

"So you protect Becca and her land while we find a parcel equal to or better than what she's sitting on. Can you send me the scouting report on our Irish offshore claim?"

"I need to get it myself," he said. "Connor and his team did the upfront work after Corey died."

"Also very unusual. This is personal for him."

No kidding. “Hell, I’m only here because Becca turned Connor down first.”

“You’re always brought in for the tough deals. It’s what you excel at.” Right now, there was no tougher deal than the one he had to sell to his big brother. “I’m sorry to ask for your help, but I couldn’t trust anyone else. I know you wanted to put this behind you when you resigned from Merriam Oil & Gas.”

“I had a new dream with the art museum,” his brother said. “But I’m happy to help.”

“Thanks, man.”

“It’s what brothers are for,” J.T. said. “All right, send me what you have, and we’ll buckle down and find an adjacent tract of land.”

Trevor glanced out to sea. The view was beautiful and serene, and yet it was these very waters Connor now feared. Not the way to run a multi-billion-dollar business and take care of the thousands of employees who depended on Merriam Enterprises.

“Corey wouldn’t want things to go down like this,” J.T. said, “so you need to remember that when you’re feeling guilty.”

His twin knew him all too well. “You trying to win Best Brother of the Year or something?”

“Already done,” J.T. said. “Talk to you later.”

“Yeah,” he said. “You’re the best.”

“I know. Why else would I have shared a womb with you?”

He was laughing when he hung up. While he loved everyone in his family, he and J.T. had a special bond even he couldn’t fully understand. Okay, now he was really acting like a Hallmark card. Time to get down to business and find Connor a new tract of land.

After falling for Becca, there was no way he was going to let his brother take away what she held so dear.

CHAPTER 16

THE ONE PERSON BECCA HADN'T EXPECTED TO SEE AT DINner was Trevor. She smiled at the other guests as she wove through the tables to where he was sitting alone.

"What are you doing here?" she asked, trying not to look too conspicuous. The other guests didn't need to know she was having an *affaire de coeur* with someone staying with them. Besides, she didn't want it to hurt her or The Wild Irish Rose's reputation.

"I decided to let the older people enjoy themselves," he said, picking up his whiskey and toasting her. "Besides, I'd rather be here with you, and since you couldn't go, I thought I'd eat here."

She signaled to the nearby server and grabbed the water pitcher off his tray to pour Trevor another glass. After returning it to the server and sending the man off with a smile, she said, "But I can't eat with you."

He shrugged. "I still get to see you, and that's enough."

If she'd been holding the water pitcher, she would have dropped it for sure. That was enough? Yes, from the soft look he was giving her, she knew he meant it. "I'll try and finish up early."

The way he sipped his whiskey made her want to shiver. "That would be nice."

Nice? Yes, it would be. "I'll find you."

He gave a knowing smile, and she realized she'd better move away, or she'd implode right then and there. Goodness, what this man did to her. Composing herself, she nodded and left to see to her guests and check in with Chef Padraig, who'd topped himself tonight with the pan-roasted black bass and sorrel sauce. She'd had a plate earlier and almost swooned in sheer delight. This year she was hoping for a visit from the Michelin people because she and Chef both wanted a star. Two or three, in fact.

Everything seemed to be coming together.

When she searched for Trevor an hour later, she couldn't find him at first. He hadn't responded to her knock on his door, and he wasn't in any of the common rooms. Something made her go to the back door and look out, and that's when she saw his silhouette. He was standing at the edge of her cliffs.

Her heart seemed to leap after him, full of longing to be beside him, outside on a land she loved but rarely traveled. The feeling grew. Should she try and go to him? Oh, how she wanted to. The thought strangled her, and she found herself unable to breathe, her chest as tight as if someone were ringing her out like dye cloth.

Bending over at the waist like Cian had taught her, she sucked in air and waited for the sensation to pass. Boru laid his head against her thigh, but she was barely aware of him. She saw stars, the urge to pass out strong, but she gritted her teeth and kept breathing while tears streamed down her face. When she finally could breathe again, she raised herself back up.

Tears continued to stream down her face, and they didn't stop when she told them to this time. No, she was crying for herself—for the girl who'd lost her parents and a treasured freedom of feeling safe in the world. Then she realized she was also crying for the woman she was now, the one who longed to feel the warm arms of her man around her as they listened to the sea crash against the cliffs.

Anger burst forth inside her. She was tired of feeling like a prisoner. Her tingling hand rose to the doorknob, but she didn't have the strength to open it. Part of her was still terrified the dark would smother her again. Something horrible would happen. In the daytime, she could trick her mind into forgetting that feeling, into burying it down deep, but it had always refused her efforts at night, just as it did now. Instead, she tunneled her fingers in Boru's fur and waited for Trevor to return.

When she saw his dark shape returning to the main house, she busied herself by fussing with the flower arrangement in the main hall.

"Hey!" Trevor called from behind her. "I was hoping you'd come join me outside."

She schooled her face, praying the color had returned and all traces of tears were gone. "There were a few things to see to. Shall we..." She stopped herself from saying 'go to my rooms' because they were in a public place. Then she wondered if he'd prefer to go to his room for a change. She didn't dare, not when someone might notice and start talking.

When he simply took her arm and led her to her chambers, she was glad for it. Still, as they were walking up her stairs, she said, "It might be awkward if I were seen coming out of your suite." This morning, she'd been so careful to avoid suspicion. She'd brought a fresh stack of towels to his suite when she'd gone in to find him a new set of clothes. She'd even left the door cracked in case anyone walked by.

"I understand," he said, taking her hand and kissing it.

Oh, how she liked those small romantic touches. At the top of the stairs, she gave in to the urge and hugged him. Her heart was so full.

Cian's words about heartache filled her mind, a reminder she didn't need after her failure to step outside earlier. She didn't doubt him. There would be heartache when Trevor left, yes, but she would enjoy him for as long as she could. Love glowed inside her, and she longed to share it.

She led him to her bedroom, no pretense of an after-dinner drink on the table now. Shooing out Boru and Hatshep, she closed the door behind them.

"I thought we might have better luck keeping your clothing if I kicked them out," she said, tugging her top off.

He sat on the bed. "Good thought. Ever find my things?"

Her lips quirked. Apparently, he intended to sit there and watch her undress. "No, if you can imagine it."

"I have a feeling we'll be safe this time," he said, toeing off his shoes as she slid down her pants. "They must know by now that they don't have to steal my clothes to keep me here."

The hitch in her heart was almost like a flash of lightning.

"I plan to spend every night in your bed," he said, resting his hands on his open thighs. "Now, take the rest off and come here, Becca O'Neill."

She slid off her bra and panties and padded across the floor until she stood between his legs. He cupped her breasts, his brilliant green eyes still on hers.

"I plan to love you thoroughly tonight," he said, his voice husky.

Hadn't he done so last night? She stroked his jaw, loving the evening stubble. "Good. We're of the same mind then."

And so they were as the shadows of night shifted and stars fell outside the window. They supped on each other as if a feast of paradise lay before them. His groans became a music she craved, and his touch, so silky yet so reverent, inflamed her senses. Under him, she felt like a siren reborn, calling out to him from across what had been the lonely expanse of her heart. Now her heart was on fire, and it burned for him.

When he cuddled her close, his body heavy with sleep, he whispered, “Take a walk with me later.”

Those words didn’t create fear this time. Instead, hope surged in her heart. She could see herself walking beside him in the daylight, his warm hand curled around hers. In fact, she felt the same excitement she experienced thinking about walking to the old kitchen.

“Yes,” she heard herself say. And then again. “Yes.”

When he kissed her softly on the lips and nodded off to sleep, she lay awake listening to him breathe.

A miracle had just happened, and she wasn’t going to miss a moment of it.

CHAPTER 17

TREVOR LEFT BECCA THE NEXT MORNING FEELING LIKE A new man. He'd lived in Ireland long enough to believe in things like magic and destiny, and those special fates had arced between them last night. Of course, he'd never admit it to another soul, but in her arms, he'd found an oasis, the kind men had traveled across deserts for. Perhaps Ireland had finally fully rooted itself inside him here on her land, but he was thinking fanciful thoughts these days. One thought that was far from fanciful?

Becca had changed everything.

The urgency to find Connor a new tract of land pressed on him all the more. Once he did, he could usher his brother onto a new course, offsetting his grief and guilt. Everyone could rest assured their cousin, Patrick, would be safe, and Uncle Liam wouldn't have to worry about losing another son. He could clean the slate with Becca and tell her the Merriams would never make a play for her land, not now, not ever.

And then he could tell her that he wanted to stay with her on the very land he'd come to buy.

If she'd have him.

But the more he dug into the scouting report of the area, the more depressed he became. There simply weren't any other options. Becca owned four hundred acres, and according to the geothermal imaging and other data in the report, the perfect drilling point for the oil running from the sea floor to dry land was on the cliffs he'd walked last night.

Looking at Connor's Plan B, Trevor knew it was going to be a bitch and a time-suck. The land was littered with stone, making it hard to both drill and construct an on-land rig. The upfront investment on the land would mean less profit for Merriam Oil & Gas, something Connor seemed unusually keen to accept. But people's lives were at stake in his brother's mind, and this prevented it.

His hopes for an alternative looked to be impossible. What was he going to do? God, he couldn't wait to hear J.T.'s assessment.

Someone pounded on the door, and he shut his laptop. No one on staff was so obtrusive, and he knew who it was before he opened the door. Uncle Arthur was glowering beside a fierce-looking Aunt Clara. Hargreaves bowed to him and took off for his room down the hall.

"We should speak inside," he said, knowing what was coming. It had been a risk to leave them alone with Cian and Aileen for dinner, but he'd been honest with Becca. He *had* stayed because he wanted to be close to her.

"I assume you know why I'm here," his uncle said without preamble after closing the door.

"I could sock you," Aunt Clara said, "and I'm not a violent woman. If you hadn't been with Becca when we got home, I would have burst into your room and punched you, Trevor."

"If it would make you feel better, go ahead, Aunt," he said, opening his arms wide.

His uncle scoffed. "So this is why you were so eager to have us visit you. You needed an in here at The Wild Irish Rose. You used us."

Hearing him say it like that brought on the guilt. "Yes, and I'm sorry. Truly. Will you sit down and let me explain?"

His aunt crossed to him and did sock him in the chest like she'd threatened. She was surprisingly strong. "I'm so mad at you. How could you even think about buying this beautiful place? Then there's how you're acting with Becca—"

"Hold it right there," he interrupted immediately. "I am not with Becca to persuade her to sell. We were clear about that up front."

Uncle Arthur took his aunt's arm. "I told you he had more ethics than that. Come, sweetheart. Let's sit down and hear him out."

His aunt was still shooting daggers at him, but she took a seat beside her husband on the red sofa in the small living room. Trevor thought about ordering tea, but the very thought was ridiculous. This conversation was no tea party.

"Let me say up front that I don't plan on buying this land for Merriam Oil & Gas anymore," he said, sitting in the gold-studded chair across from them.

His aunt reached over and patted his knee. Of course, it was less of a comforting pat than the way an angry person swats a fly, but he'd take it. "Good."

"But Connor still wants it." He told them the reason and how it related to Corey's death.

Uncle Arthur looked out the window when he was through, almost as though searching for oil. "So your brother is afraid to drill out there."

He hated hearing it said like that, but it wasn't untrue. "Not for himself, perhaps, but for Corey's brother, Patrick, and our other employees. J.T. and I are trying to find him another alternative close by." He decided not to share his morning's findings.

His uncle popped in a red hot and offered one to everyone. Trevor took one, but Clara declined.

"I read in *The Irish Times* about how controversial offshore drilling is with the locals," his uncle said. "I can't imagine how controversial onshore drilling would be."

"Very," Trevor said simply. He decided not to bore them with talk of the Barryroe oil project, also off the Cork coast, or the recently abandoned projects in Druid and Drombeg which hadn't borne out—even though his uncle might have been curious.

"I thought something was wrong with Cian's attitude toward you," Uncle Arthur said, "so I might have asked some leading questions last night."

"By leading, he means he was a regular Tom Brokaw," Aunt Clara said, taking her husband's hand.

Uncle Arthur fingered a button on his shirt. "Of course, Cian had his own questions about you. In the end, I didn't have to probe much. Aileen was tipsy on beer and let loose the beans about Connor's offers. And yours. When Cian asked what you wanted the land for, I told him that we came into the situation blind. And I couldn't find any information when I looked on Clara's smartphone after we got home."

"Our offshore acquisition hasn't been public yet because Connor is trying to persuade the Irish government to allow him to drill on land—something they've never done before."

"So you could still drill offshore?" his uncle asked.

"I'm not involved in Connor's discussions with the government officials, but yes, I believe so."

"Connor just doesn't want to," Aunt Clara said. "What a pickle."

That was one word for it. "What did Cian want to know exactly?" he pressed.

"He wanted to know what you did for the company," his uncle said.

Trevor's gut tightened. "What did you say?"

His aunt swatted the air. "He told the truth, of course. Really, Trevor."

"Uncle," he said. "I need to know. What did you tell him?"

"I said you handled the toughest negotiations and acquisitions for Merriam Oil & Gas."

Shit. So far Becca hadn't asked him why he'd wanted to buy her land, and since she'd hung up on Connor, twice, he knew she hadn't asked him either. This new knowledge could change things. Oil drilling was controversial enough, but onshore drilling... He imagined Becca would have strong views about it. Many felt it would hurt tourism, and that would concern her, he imagined.

"And then Aileen asked if you *only* work on oil and gas issues," his aunt said, "because she knows Merriam Enterprises is into a lot of things. They thought you might want to create some posh hotel or something."

They did have a branch of luxury hotels, so that guess wasn't half bad. Well, he'd deal with the fallout. He imagined Becca knew something now.

"They weren't very happy last night or this morning—something you would have seen if you'd come down for breakfast." His aunt gave him a knowing look.

"I had some urgent business," he said. "I'm sorry I used you both."

"You'd better be," his uncle said, "and you sure as hell had better not do it again."

He made sure to meet Uncle Arthur's gaze. "I won't, sir."

The man harrumphed. "Let's circle back to the problem. Can you sell the offshore claim here?"

"Yes, but Connor still wants the oil."

"He won't drill offshore anymore?" his aunt asked.

"Since our cousin Corey died, Connor has sworn all of our new operations will only drill on land."

"What about all the offshore holdings you already have?" Aunt Clara asked.

"They'll continue because we can't afford to stop operation." He supposed Connor could sell them, but that would cause the board to riot. Offshore was half their oil business now.

"This sounds like a costly business decision," his uncle said, reaching into his pocket and pulling out more red hots. Trevor took another, knowing his uncle chewed on the candy like some NFL coaches chewed on gum. It was part of his thinking strategy.

"Building and maintaining an offshore rig is very expensive, so in some ways, Connor's plan might be better for business long-term," Trevor said cautiously, although he didn't believe his brother had made the decision for that reason.

"Less accidents and environmental spills too," his uncle added.

"Well, I think Connor's idea stinks," his aunt said, crossing her arms. "I don't want to see this place pockmarked with oil rigs. It's beautiful."

"I've tried to tell him that, but Connor is adamant, Aunt. To protect Becca's land, I need to give him an alternative."

"If I need to chain myself to something like those Greenpeace people do, I will," Aunt Clara said.

"Oh, for God's sake, Clara," his uncle said, crunching on his candy.

Trevor's lips twitched. "You could go to jail, you know." Part of him wanted to see how committed his aunt was to the cause.

She narrowed her eyes at him, sensing the challenge. "I figure Irish jails can't be that bad."

He barked out a laugh as his uncle grunted. "You might die before your parole comes up," Trevor pressed, raising his brows.

She gave a dark chuckle. "You reminded me of Grandpa Emmits just now. He was always one to take a joke too far."

"The apple doesn't fall far from the tree, Aunt," he said, wishing Grandpa Emmits, as his heirs all called him, was around so he could talk to Connor. After all, he'd founded the company after striking oil in Oklahoma. But he wondered if his brother would listen.

"Is it too early for a martini?" Aunt Clara asked.

He shrugged. God knew he needed one, and he had time before he was due to meet Becca for their walk. He rather hoped he'd find her in the old kitchen with her dyeing baths.

"I'll ask Hargreaves to bring some in for us," Aunt Clara said, pulling out her phone and texting her butler. Trevor wouldn't ask how he'd get the glasses... Or the olives. Probably had them stocked in the mini-bar in his room.

"They have people downstairs for that, my dear," Uncle Arthur said.

"Hargreaves likes to make them for me," she said. "Us. Now what can we do to help? You mentioned J.T. is working with you. That's good. He's one smart cookie."

But he couldn't summon the perfect property out of thin air, as it were. "No, you and Uncle Arthur should just enjoy yourselves. I'll figure this out. It's my mess."

"If you need me to talk to Connor—"

"Good God, no," he said, holding up his hands. Aunt Clara would only put his back up more.

"Oh, don't get your panties in a wad, like your uncle here would say. I'm only saying that you have allies if you need them. Right, Arthur?"

"Right," his uncle said. "Now let's talk about Becca.

You're sure she understands your position? She's in love with you, you know."

The very words seemed to lighten the air. "I'm in love with her too."

"Good," his uncle said, and Aunt Clara clapped, adding, "Bravo, boy."

He was oddly touched by their approval. "Trust me, I'm doing everything I can to protect her and this land she loves so much."

He begged off an hour later, postponing his call to J.T., and went off to look for Becca. There was no sign of her in any of the usual places, so he stopped to ask one of the staff if they'd seen her. They hadn't, which seemed strange. He pulled out his phone to call her, only to realize he didn't have her number. In fact, now that he thought about it, he'd never seen her with a phone. She was always around, talking to people in person. Giving her staff orders verbally rather than texting them.

He finally caught Aileen coming out of the kitchen. She moved her mouth like she'd just tasted something unpleasant. Well, he would handle that situation after he found Becca. He needed to set things straight with her right away.

"Aileen, I'm trying to find Becca," he said, stepping in front of her lest she try ignore him. "We were supposed to take a walk."

The woman stopped short, and shock rolled over her face. *"A walk?"*

Why did she sound so surprised? Perhaps Becca never took a break. He'd noticed she was always working, and he respected that. "Yes."

She looked down, fingering her hem, and was silent. In fact, she looked on the verge of tears. He didn't know what to do. Was she like this because they'd figured out why the Merriams wanted the property?

"I was so mad at you," Aileen said, "when Cian figured out why you wanted to buy our land. You want it for oil, don't you?"

He couldn't deny it. "I'll tell you what I can later, but I need to talk to Becca first. Please, Aileen."

Her silence made his chest tight. He stood there, helpless.

"She's in her chambers, stewing," she said finally. "Come with me. Normally, I wouldn't interfere like this, but if Becca was willing to take a walk with you before this happened, it's simply got to be done."

He'd never imagined a walk would be so monumental. "Thank you, Aileen. After I talk to Becca, I'd like to explain to you and Cian, if that's all right with Becca."

"Cian might still take a swing at you," she said. "I sent him off to the pub to cool off."

Trevor's knees grew weak. "He won't tell anyone in town, will he?"

It would be a PR disaster if news got out before they had a solid plan for moving forward.

Aileen drew up short and drilled her finger into his chest. "Don't be insulting my man. Even if Becca hadn't told us to keep our speculations private, he would have done so. He might want to take a punch at you, but he wouldn't put your aunt and uncle in an uncomfortable position in town."

Trevor hadn't thought about that. "I remember how it was when I first arrived."

"Day-old scones and no cleaning service would seem like a blessing compared to the ire of people in town. This is sacred land, Trevor Merriam, and you'd be wise to remember that."

"I know that, Aileen," he said, putting his hand on her arm. "I've fallen in love with this place as much as I have with Becca." It seemed right to tell her.

Tears sprang into her eyes, and he almost winced.

"I didn't mean to make you cry," he said, rubbing her shoulder.

She sniffed and wiped her face with her sleeve. "They're my tears, not yours. If I had a moment, I'd dash off to church and light a candle of thanksgiving. It's a grand thing, you being in love with Becca, Trevor. Cian and I have prayed for such a thing, but we'd lost... Never mind."

He didn't understand all she was telling him, but he was deeply moved. The old couple clearly cared for Becca like she was their own daughter.

"Come," she said, increasing her speed as she ushered him toward Becca's chamber door. "She won't like it, but if she takes me to task later, I'll tell her what was on my mind when I did it."

She opened the tower door and turned to look at him. Her gaze was direct, and he felt like a third grader being assessed by his teacher.

"I like you, Trevor Merriam. I have ever since Buttercup began to follow you around like a lovesick mule and Becca's animals started stealing your clothes. But if you hurt my Becca, I'll take Chef Padraig's cleaver to your private parts. Understand me?"

No one had ever threatened him with a cleaver before, and his balls shrunk. "I understand."

She patted him much like Aunt Clara had, a touch laced with affection and threat. "Then go up and explain yourself."

The door shut behind him, and he heard a soft bark. Looking up to the top of the stairs, he saw Becca sitting on the sofa with Boru by her side.

"I can explain," he said, his gaze searching her shuttered face.

"Don't bother."

CHAPTER 18

BECCA WASN'T SURPRISED TO HEAR TREVOR STOMPING UP the stairs. If he'd simply walked away, he wouldn't have been the man she knew him to be. Although maybe she didn't know him at all. She'd thought he saw the beauty in this place, just as she did, but he and his brother wanted to destroy it.

How did they plan to do it, anyway? Drilling on land was against Irish law. Did that mean they intended to achieve their ends through corruption? She didn't like that one bit. Even worse, how had they discovered oil on her land? Had they sneaked onto it in the dead of night and run tests? None of that sat well with her.

Her sanctuary had been violated in the worst way possible.

He came around the sofa and crossed his arms over his chest. "You're really going to tell me to feck off after what we've been to each other these past couple of days?"

He didn't often use Irish words, and it shook her that he should do so now. "Yes, I am. Feck off, you gobshite."

His mouth twisted. "I deserve that. Will you hear me out?"

Boru came around the sofa, Trevor's pants in his mouth. Hatshep followed in close order with his shirt.

They both laid the clothes they'd taken the other night at his feet and then plopped down in front of Becca, furry sentries if she'd ever seen them.

"My animals don't seem to want to keep you here any longer," she said, edging back against the cushions, hoping it would give her some space.

He shook his head. "I'd hate to think of what Buttercup would do to me. Becca O'Neill, you're going to listen to me if I have to talk until I'm blue in the face."

She shot up off the sofa. "Save it."

"No," he said, standing his ground.

"I'm done talking to you." She hated the way her voice broke. "I want you to leave here and never come back. I'm not listening to your offer. Ever! I don't care what I told you."

"I don't care about that anymore." When she tried to go around him, he caught her arm. "I love you, dammit! Doesn't that rank a conversation?"

He loved her? It couldn't be. Not if he intended to destroy her land for oil. "Please don't say things like that."

"*I love you*," he repeated, softening his tone.

She lifted her gaze to him, and he reached out and tentatively caressed her cheek. The gentle, familiar touch pinged her bruised heart. She wanted to believe him. He seemed to sense it because he stroked her skin before letting his hand fall away.

"I wouldn't say that unless I meant it. I've *never* said it to a woman before."

Oddly, that admission moved her. Hadn't she thought she loved him too? That was one reason why she'd been so injured by the news of what the Merriams planned to do. "Succinct, if you please." She sat back down, prepared to listen, but there was no way she was going to make it easy for him.

"Can I sit down?" he asked.

She gestured with a hand, and Boru let out a bark. "It's okay, boy."

Trevor took his place next to her, but he didn't crowd her, thankfully. "I'm sorry you're so upset, and I totally understand why."

She turned to him. "Do you? Answer me this. Did you make an offer for my land because of oil?"

He nodded. "But that's—"

"Then you understand nothing," she said, anger flushing her face. "You might live in Dublin, but you're not Irish. There is no way I would ever let anyone drill for oil on Ireland proper and destroy the beauty of our green hills. And the fact that you want to do that on *my land*... This is my home, my sanctuary, if that's not too fanciful for you. How did you even find oil? Did you send people out here without my permission?"

"No," he said, his voice laced with urgency. "We use geophysical imaging technologies. Honestly, it wasn't difficult. We'd bought an offshore oil tract connected directly to your land. Our data showed a line of oil stretching from out there to here. Becca, you're sitting on a whole bunch of crude oil."

The thought terrified her. Was the government thinking about changing the law? Surely his words suggested it. Would there be a long line of tough-as-nails businessmen lining up at her door, taking numbers like they did at the butcher? God help her. "Like I care about that. If I'd known your intentions from the beginning, I would *never* have let you stay here, even if your aunt and uncle are the kindest, dearest people. How could you use them like that?"

He sighed deeply. "I was wrong to do it, and I've apologized to them. Look, Connor sent me to complete a task after you turned him down. My job is to make deals, any way I know how, legally. My aunt and uncle just happened to want to visit me. I knew I was skating the line bringing them here, but I didn't think anyone would get hurt."

And yet she had been hurt. Deeply. If he could use his own flesh and blood, how could she trust him? Trevor had a job to do, and he apparently wasn't above using people to do it. "I don't like this side of you."

He put his hand on her knee, and she moved it off. "I can understand that. Sometimes I don't like it either, but I work in places around the world that call for tough action. Right now, I'm skating a line for you. Because I love you."

Did he *have* to say those words again? "I don't want you to skate any lines for me. I only wanted you to be honest, but it would seem that's impossible given your task here. I don't think we should have any more personal interaction. In fact, I want you to leave. Today. You are no longer welcome at The Wild Irish Rose." She wanted to cry. She'd never kicked a guest out, and it broke her heart that her first one would be him.

She stood and walked to the window, unable to bear being this close to him. Looking out at the sea usually comforted her, but for the first time she was afraid of it and all it contained. Oil brought ruin to places. It had been one of the causes of the civil war in Angola—the bloody, awful, brutal war that had ultimately claimed her parents as two of its victims. Oil brought troubles, and she wanted no part of it. And yet, how was she to stop it? Even if she blocked them from drilling on her land, they'd be out there, mucking up the sea. When he came up beside her, she thought about running for her room and locking him out, but it seemed cowardly.

"You might not like me skating the line, but I'm still doing it. Becca, I give you my word that I no longer plan to persuade you to sell us your land."

His voice was thick with emotion, and even Boru gave a whine behind them. "You just said it's your job and you always get your way. Why would you back off now?"

He turned her to look at him, his eyes blazing with emotion. "Because I love you, that's why. Would I rip out your very soul?"

Her tears welled up like a spring after a rain, and she pursed her lip to contain herself. No one had ever said such a thing to her before. It spoke to his knowledge of her. They'd only known each other a matter of days, and yet he saw her. "You sound like an Irishman."

"I sound like a man who's close to begging, and I don't like it." He dropped her arms. "Becca, I love you and everything about this place. I'm going against my duty as an officer of the company my family owns in a way I'd never imagined, and yet I know it's the right thing to do. Dammit, I don't want this to wreck what we're building together. Please, don't let it."

Her heart was an aching, pulsing mess in her chest. God, she didn't want things to be done between them either. If he loved her like he said, there had to be something here. "I want to trust you."

"When I give my word, I mean it." He took her hand and laid it over his heart. "I love you. I love this land of yours and everything on it, and I'm even starting to see the humor in your crazy alpaca chasing me around. I didn't expect to say this so soon, but when I make a decision, I'm all in. I thought I might stay here with you, in time, if you'll have me."

Stay with her? "What are you saying?"

He cupped her cheeks with his hands, gazing into her eyes. "It means I think I've found the person I want to make a home with and spend the rest of my life with. I know we've just met, but no one has ever touched me like you have, and that's why I know it's real."

She had known it too, hadn't she? What they shared was unique and singular, the kind of connection that only came around once in a lifetime.

"I plan to give you proof I keep my word," he continued. "And someday soon, I hope you'll say yes when I ask you to marry me."

Marriage? He had to be joking. Her knees felt weak, and they dipped a little before he grabbed her by the waist to steady her.

"I need to sit down," she said, seeing dancing stars in her vision.

He helped her to a chair and then leaned over her. "They always say to take deep breaths. I don't know why, but...breathe, dammit."

If she'd been in better condition, she might have laughed. Instead, she took deep breaths until she felt more level.

He tipped up her chin and studied her face. "Your color is better. Still chalk-white but not death warmed over."

Lovely. "Maybe I can name some yarn that. I'll sell out for sure."

His grunt was sufficient. She couldn't find much humor right now either.

"You hurt me," she whispered, "but more, I was afraid I didn't really know who you were. That the man I'd fallen in love with didn't exist."

His brows shot up at that. "You love me? You could have said it earlier. Becca, I sweated out my shirt."

He embraced her awkwardly, and she patted his back. "I've never felt this way before, or so fast. And I thought maybe—"

"I'd led you on or lied to you to get what I wanted," he finished, his mouth twisting. "That's why we had *that* conversation up front. I am not and never was interested in you as a means to an end. I was only interested."

The directness of his gaze was powerful. She believed him. "I'm glad we cleared that up. Trevor, this is a lot to take in."

"I know it. It was a lot for me, but I'm fast on my feet." He kissed her on the cheek sweetly. "So are you."

But would it be enough? He talked about loving her and her land, but he'd only been here for a few days. And he didn't know about her agoraphobia yet. Could she tell him?

All her old fears rose up.

She'd need to tell him, eventually, if he was as serious as he said. But she couldn't bear to do it yet. She'd never spoken about her condition to a soul save the specialists she'd worked with and her grandmother, Cian, and Aileen, and Sven, who turned on her—although she imagined others suspected but were too kind to say so. What if someone found out and used it against her? She'd read a story about an agoraphobic woman whose family put her in a sanitarium in order to take over their family estate. Trevor might be on her side, but Connor wasn't.

"Won't Connor be upset you've failed in your duty?"

"Yes," he said. "That's why I'm looking for an alternative, although honestly it's not looking very promising."

"You're still aiming to drill on Ireland proper?" she asked. She wasn't an environmentalist, but this didn't sit well with her. It would hurt tourism too, wouldn't it? What tourist wanted to come to an Ireland decorated with metal towers?

His jaw worked. "It's what my brother wants, and he calls the shots. I disagree with him on this one, but I understand why he's so adamant. Our cousin died recently on an offshore oil rig, and Connor swore our new operations would all be on land. He was closest to Corey, you see. They were best friends, and it hit him hard."

The poor man. "Did he have a family?"

"Yes," Trevor said, running his hand through his

hair. "A beautiful wife and two kids. And his brother is slated to run our Irish operations."

"Even after his brother's death?"

"He's always been brave," he said, grimacing. "He'll work on it even if it's offshore, but Connor is adamant. This acquisition has more emotional weight than any other project I've worked on."

Weight seemed a good word for it, and she felt her compassion rise for them all. "You feel guilty too. For your cousin's death."

"Yes, even though I know there was nothing I could have done. It was an earthquake on the ocean floor. A rarity. But losing him... Hell, I loved him too. He used to give me a chunk of his Dubble Bubble chewing gum when I was younger, and it made me feel grown up. Stupid."

He was leaning over her, so she reached up and stroked his back, needing to comfort him. "Not stupid. Losing someone you love hurts like hell. It...changes everything." Who knew better than she?

He pulled her out of her chair and into his arms, resting his head on her shoulder. "I've been trying to push it away, I guess. Man up. But Patrick's raring to go on this project, like it'll help him forget, and my mom's out there in Chicago with Corey's wife, trying to help out with her and the kids, and sometimes Connor's voice sounds...like it's killing him."

And he wanted to help, like any good brother would. Trevor hadn't just come here in the hopes of acquiring another piece of land. He was trying to help his brother heal and protect another family member from a terrible eventuality.

"Can you not find another country to drill on?" she asked, knowing it was a bit selfish of her. "You have to know how controversial such a thing is in Ireland."

"I do," Trevor said. "Connor made this decision alone."

But he had his duty. His job wasn't merely a job. He worked with and for his family. She understood that in her own way. It had always been the same for her with The Wild Irish Rose. "So what now?"

"I'm working on that, and I'll be happy when it's all behind me. I don't like being in this position. Not with you, and not with my brother."

But somehow she had won out in this war she hadn't known he was waging. Her heart grew warm as the realization flooded her. "If I have oil, more people will come, won't they?"

The look in his eyes gave her the answer before he spoke. "Yes," he finally said. "So far, the Irish government hasn't changed the law to allow onshore drilling. But Connor hopes to change that."

Panic raced through her. If he managed to open that hornet's nest, other companies would be able to drill by law. Would they use every means they could to force her off the land if she wouldn't go? Stars filled her vision again, and she fell back weakly in the chair. "They can't take my land from me. My home. They...can't."

The pounding in her heart grew until it was as though a great spotted woodpecker was drilling against her skull.

"Take it easy," he said, kneeling by her side and stroking her arm. "I'll be here. They won't take your home. I promise."

"How do we keep it safe? All the people who work here depend on me. My animals. My new enterprise. Cian and Aileen aren't the youngest..."

"Breathe, Becca," he said, his calm voice at odds with the flush of red on his cheeks. "We'll figure it out. Together."

They were words she'd dreamed of hearing but had lost hope would ever come. God, she wanted to believe him. She wanted to think he'd stay, even after he knew.

Relieved, she continued to let herself settle while he held her hand. Boru and Hatshep came closer, signaling a tentative peace with Trevor. Their loyalty never failed to fill her heart.

"Shall we go for our walk?" he asked, making her sit up straight. "Some fresh air might do us some good."

Anxiety raced through her like an unholy elixir. No, she needed to cocoon herself in her home, especially after learning the peril it was in from a shiny black substance in the ground.

"I'm a little light on my feet still," she said instead. "How about a nice pot of tea? I can call Aileen."

He kissed her cheek. "I'll make you up a pot myself. You sit there. You're still not back to your normal self."

As he left her, she wondered if she ever would be.

Last night, she'd thought his love might heal her, and a new hope had blossomed in her heart. Today, she felt certain her fear of going outside would never, ever go away, and the confines of her prison seemed even smaller and less tolerable now.

She was scared inside her own sanctuary.

CHAPTER 19

SITTING AT THE BREAKFAST TABLE WITH HIS FAMILY, TREVOR watched Becca wander through the tables in the dining room, smiling at guests, taking the time to hear about their plans for the day. She had been careful not to show any preference for him from the start, but it seemed there was more to it today. His lovely Irish lass, always so warm and welcoming, had a cold chill coming from her.

While their heated exchange had led to declarations of love, they'd made love on shaky ground last night. She seemed to have erected a wall between them, and while it wasn't unassailable, he didn't want anything like it to stand between them. Even her animals had given him the cold shoulder. Boru had wandered away when he'd rubbed the dog under the ears, and Hatshep had raised her tail in the air and sauntered away when he'd tried to pick her up.

"You're a mess this morning," his uncle said, kicking him under the table. "Give her time."

"She's processing things," Aunt Clara said, picking up her teacup. "It's good you aired things out. Now it needs to settle."

He was too impatient for that. If only they had more time together, he was certain they could restore the easiness between them. Aileen appeared in the dining room, holding a basket of fresh scones, and he immediately called her over.

"Are you needing more scones?" she asked, checking out the table.

He hadn't been able to eat more than one, a testament to how anxious he felt. "No, we're good. I wanted to see if you'd be able to cover for Becca for a few hours today. I wanted to take her for a drive."

The basket of scones tumbled onto the table, and Aileen gave a cry. "Oh, I'm so clumsy." She scooped up the scones before anyone at the table could help and then immediately stepped away. "I'm afraid we have some baking to see to today."

She wasn't looking him in the eye either. "That's fine. It was a last-minute idea. What about tomorrow?"

"Meeting with the maids, I'm afraid," she said, looking off in the direction of the kitchen. "I think Chef Padraig is calling me. *Oui*, Chef, I'm coming. Trevor, if something opens up, I'll let you know."

She dashed off, and he turned back to the table. His aunt and uncle and Hargreaves were all watching him. "I messed up pretty big."

"Then you fix it," Uncle Arthur said matter-of-factly.

"Maybe do something for Becca that doesn't involve her taking time away from the inn," Aunt Clara said, patting his hand from across the table. "She's a hard worker."

"It's something to respect," his uncle said. "She loves this place like I loved my newspaper. When you love what you do, it's not work."

Trevor hadn't thought of it that way. Maybe it was selfish of him to try to get her away. When he was working on something, he often gave it his full attention. The family needed him, and he was good at what he did. He liked being able to do what no one else could, but he'd never loved his job that way.

"If I may make a suggestion," Hargreaves said, clearing his throat.

The man didn't often converse at the table. There was a companionable silence about him, one he and Aunt Clara had mastered over the decades.

"Please, Hargreaves."

"You might help her with her new enterprise," Hargreaves said. "Running the bed and breakfast is a full-time job, and I've heard Aileen mention that Becca wishes she had more time to explore dye colors."

"That's brilliant, Hargreaves." He could look at branding or packaging or— Wait, he could help her find the perfect green dye for her yarn. Hadn't she mentioned they'd struggled with that? He'd call his sister, Caitlyn, and see if she had any ideas. She worked in another Merriam company, one focused on skincare and cosmetics, so at least her job was dye adjacent. He was fairly sure she had never hand-dyed wool before, and he certainly hadn't, but they were both smart people. They could figure out something.

"I'm going to take off," Trevor said, standing up, feeling he was on firmer ground now that he had a purpose. "Have fun on your trip to Waterford. Are you going, Hargreaves?"

The man nodded. "I have a keen interest in seeing how they make the crystal."

"Hargreaves has always thought it top-notch," his aunt said. "I'm looking forward to the tour."

"I'm not looking forward to the two-hour drive," his uncle griped.

"Hargreaves is driving," his aunt replied, giving her butler a smile. "It's been some time since he drove on the left side, but it's not the kind of thing a person forgets. Right, Hargreaves?"

"Indeed, madam," he said. "And I've asked the kitchen to pack us a lunch in case you grow hungry."

His aunt fairly beamed, so Trevor refrained from mentioning the abundance of restaurants in Waterford town proper. Then he had an idea. "I'd like to give you a special gift to make up for everything. Waterford Castle is a beautiful place. How about I arrange for you to stay there tonight? That way, you'll only have to drive up today." Four hours in one day might overtax them, and it was the least he could do.

"Oh, a castle!" Aunt Clara clapped her hands. "I'd love that."

"Seems crazy to pay for two hotel rooms," his uncle growled. "A man only has one body."

"Oh, Arthur, you are practical, and I love that about you." She laid her hand on his cheek. "Don't be practical just now."

His eyes softened. "Okay," he said, covering her hand. "If it makes you happy..."

"It does," she said, her voice laced with delight. "Thank you, Trevor."

"You're welcome," he said. "I'll make the reservation when I go upstairs. If you decide you want to spend another night, just have them add it to your reservation. It's a nice part of Ireland. You might want to do more sightseeing." He winked at his aunt, and she winked right back at him.

As he left the table, he was glad he'd set one thing to rights this morning.

***

"He's working overtime," Arthur said as he watched his nephew stride out of the dining room. The boy looked as jumpy as a jackrabbit.

"After what he pulled, he should be quick-stepping," Clara said. "Besides, even I know men like to fix things. And after seeing poor Aileen drop scones all over our table, it's pretty clear he has more quick-stepping to do."

"I believe it's high-stepping, madam," Hargreaves said

in his dry butler-knows-everything tone.

"Thank you, Hargreaves."

"If I corrected you like that, you'd box my ears," Arthur remarked, because he'd noticed more than once Hargreaves had some kind of eternal pass on correcting his mistress, as he called her. The butler's habit of calling her that in public was a sure way to confuse people, especially when they traveled, and Arthur had said as much to her. Clara had laughed so hard she'd cried, loving the idea of people thinking she'd brought both her husband and lover on vacation with her, and she almost eighty years old. He'd harrumphed plenty, but a smile had slipped through his grousing. He did so love to hear her laugh.

"You made a fine suggestion on how to win back Becca's full affection, Hargreaves," Clara said. "She wasn't herself this morning. It was plain as day."

Arthur had noticed it himself. Usually the woman snuck glances at their table when she hoped no one was looking, but not today. She'd been focused, too focused, almost like she was closing Trevor out.

"Broken trust is hard to repair, but it's doable. He'll find a way to ease her mind." Of course, Arthur still wasn't sure how Trevor's brother, Connor, was going to react to this whole situation. Connor was a hardheaded businessman, focused mostly on the bottom line. His second-in-command, Quinn, was equally serious but had a bigger touch of the Merriam charm. They made a fearsome pair, but they'd continued to steer his old friend Emmits' legacy in the right direction. As descendants, they weren't half bad. He almost laughed. He had to be old if he was calling young people descendants.

"You're off in your own little world," Clara said, pressing her fingernails into his hand. She was mostly gentle—until she wanted his attention. "You think we can leave Trevor alone for a day or two?"

Arthur chuckled. "What could possibly go wrong?"

CHAPTER 20

BECCA WAS GOING OVER THE NEW BATCH OF RESERVATIONS in her office when she heard a knock on the door.

"Come in."

She looked up from the computer, surprise rippling over her. The man Trevor and his family called Hargreaves stood in the threshold of her office. Of course, she knew his full name: Clifton Hargreaves. He'd put it on the reservation. "Good morning...ah, I'm embarrassed to ask this, but what should I call you?" He wasn't her butler, after all, but even Trevor called him by his surname.

"Hargreaves is fine, miss," he said, closing the door and then coming to stand in front of her desk in his regular dress of a black jacket, tie, and trousers with a crisp white shirt.

She wondered if he ever wore anything else. "Please, sit down."

"I prefer to stand," he said, his demeanor impeccably proper yet warm and welcoming too.

"What can I do for you? Aileen tells me you're off to Waterford today. Everyone says the tour of the House of Waterford is spectacular." Funny how being the owner of a bed and breakfast opened up her world. Hearing the guests tell their stories wasn't just the highlight of her day. It was her lifeline to the outside world.

"We are, indeed," he said, reaching inside his suit and drawing out an envelope. His face was inscrutable as he laid it on her desk. "I thought this might be of use to you, if I may be so bold."

Curiosity made her rip open the envelope at once. She drew out the paper. There were only three lines printed out in perfect cursive.

Dr. Andreas Poread

Doctor of Psychology

(212) 555-0177

As if the envelope had doused her with a sheet of cold water, Becca crossed her arms over herself. "I don't understand." He couldn't know. She looked up at him, her chest aching now at the horror of being exposed.

"Dr. Poread is one of the leading psychiatrists treating agoraphobia, miss," Hargreaves said, his words riveting her to her chair. "He understands that people suffering from the disorder are usually unable to leave their homes for help, so his practice is mostly over the phone. I thought he might be a resource for you. If I'm mistaken, please accept my sincerest apologies."

She pressed her hand to her mouth and turned her head away. Tears filled her eyes, and she barely had the presence of mind to open the bottom drawer of her desk where she kept the tissues. Inside, she was dying. He knew her shame. Her secret.

"You needn't worry about anyone else knowing, miss," he said, laying a finely ironed linen handkerchief in front of her.

"Oh, Hargreaves," she said through her tears. Pressing the handkerchief to her eyes, she inhaled jaggedly, the pain pouring out of her. It was terrible to have someone else know, but in another sense it was a relief someone *had* noticed—and had cared enough to offer a helping hand.

"It's quite all right, miss," he said, calm and unflappable as ever. "Take your time."

And so she went completely to pieces in front of him as he stood there, a silent witness to years of pent-up pain and frustration. When she was finished carrying on, she'd soaked his handkerchief and grown completely light-headed from the tears.

"How did you figure it out?" she finally asked him.

"A butler is trained to see everything, miss, and I noticed you rarely leave the house. When you do, it's with some trepidation. There were other clues, but they are unimportant. I knew someone who seemed to share your affliction. She didn't leave her house for some time. I grew concerned about her and did my research and found someone to help her. In the end, I realized she didn't leave the house not because she was afraid to do so, but because she felt she had no reason to."

Depression and not agoraphobia, then. While different, they ended up leading to the same situation: isolation.

"I thought perhaps Dr. Poread might not be known to you seeing as how he's American and living in New York."

She sniffed and shook her head. "In the beginning, Cian and my grandmother brought a few specialists to see me, but none of their treatments seemed to help. They could map my problem, as they say, but not fix it. They did suggest some breathing exercises that helped. As I grew older, I reached out to a few psychiatrists in Dublin and went through a series of treatments that didn't work."

She'd reached out to an anxiety coach in Galway

when she'd come across him in her ongoing research for new treatments, but he'd only suggested coping cards and muscle-relaxing exercises, neither of which had improved her condition.

"Cian is the one who's helped me the most," she told Hargreaves. "He's a medical doctor. Retired now."

"Cian is a good man," Hargreaves said, looking very much like a kind and gentle old English professor.

"He is, indeed." She fingered the handkerchief. "I'll have this laundered and returned to you."

He gave a slight bow and walked back to the door.

"Hargreaves?"

He turned to face her immediately, the move immaculately executed.

"You're a good man too."

His smile seemed to deepen, and he bowed again. "Thank you, miss. Good day."

As he left, she picked up the piece of paper and looked at the contact information. Should she try again with a professional? Hargreaves wouldn't have interceded unless he had faith the man could truly help her. She thought of all the places she wanted to go outside these walls. She thought of Trevor and how much she wanted to be a normal woman, loving him and living by his side.

Yes, she would call.

It was early in New York, but she could wait until the office opened. She looked the doctor up on her computer in the meantime and almost cried at some of the testimonials in his online reviews from other patients. Then she fussed with other paperwork, "fussed" being the operative word—she couldn't process anything other than the changing numbers on the clock. The moment his office opened, she picked up the phone and dialed.

"Dr. Poread's office." The voice had a crisp, slightly

nasal accent she'd heard in movies set in New York.

"I suffer from agoraphobia and would like to make an appointment with Dr. Poread over the phone. I...live in Ireland."

"Oh, Ireland. I've always wanted to go there."

"It's a grand place." But America was too, and wouldn't it be incredible to go there someday and see the Statue of Liberty and the Grand Canyon?

"Must be the luck of the Irish. We just had a cancellation. Otherwise, you'd have to wait two months."

It was another sign, and Becca was finally able to release a breath.

"How does next Wednesday at one sound? You're ahead of us, right?"

"Yes." It would be closing in on dinnertime, but Aileen and Cian would happily cover for her. "Thank you."

The woman took her information and then surprised her by asking more about Ireland. She ended the call with a sweet compliment about Becca's accent.

Becca set down the phone and fingered the paper and the handkerchief. One contained her hopes while the other had collected her tears.

From now on, she planned to have more of the former than the latter.

Chapter 21

After saying goodbye to his aunt and uncle and Hargreaves, Trevor closeted himself in his room. His first call should have been to J.T. about the land issue, but it was the middle of the night, and all he could think about was finding Becca the best green dye for her wool. Okay, he was evading the land issue a bit. As the sun rose high over the sea and morning turned to afternoon, he dug into the sometimes wacky, sometimes incredible world of hand-dyeing yarn. When it was eight in the morning in New York, he texted Caitlyn to see if she was awake. She promptly responded, so he called her.

"How's the alpaca lover?" she asked when she picked up.

"Get it out of your system," he said, leaning back, happy to hear her voice.

"Was it her eyes or her pretty little head that did it for you?"

"Haha. Listen, what do you know about dyeing wool?"

She snorted. "Other than the fact that's it really hard, not much. I don't go back that far down the clothing chain. Why?"

"The woman I love is starting her own hand-dyeing enterprise, raising animals and the like."

"Hence the alpaca. Wait! Did you say *the woman you love*?"

He knew he'd have to needle her to keep it quiet—it absolutely could not get back to Connor yet—but he couldn't contain himself. He wanted his family to know about Becca. Hell, he wanted them to meet her. "I did, and you're going to love her."

"Holy shit! Okay, fill me in. I want to know everything. How long has this been going on?"

He gave his sister the CliffsNotes version. "She says greens are the hardest to make," he told her, changing the subject back to his present project. "Do you know anyone I can talk to about plant dyes? Surely we employ an expert or two in the organic line, right?"

"Dozens," she said, making a humming noise. "Let me see what I can drum up for you. I'll talk to our French experts when I meet them for dinner tonight."

So she wasn't in New York. But who could keep track? Sometimes she was in New York or L.A. publicizing a new product line with various celebrities, but she preferred the City of Love. "You're in Paris?"

"Yes. Nowhere I'd rather be."

She'd loved the Madeline books as a kid and dressed up like the character for Halloween three years running. "Same time zone. Convenient."

"This will be fun for me," she said. "I'm looking into creating a line of perfume. I need something new creatively, and the perfume market keeps killing it. Did you know that nearly two million Americans spent more than five hundred dollars on perfume this year?"

"Quinn must love your new idea," he said. His brother was the one who approved new product lines and companies. Again, he remembered Connor's threat to have Quinn replace him. It wasn't normal.

"I haven't pitched him yet, so don't say anything. You know Quinn. You need a file so thick he grunts when he lifts it."

Indeed. "I won't say anything about it if you'll swear on our mother's life that you won't tell anyone about Becca."

"Does J.T. know?"

"You know he does, but he's the only one except you."

She made a delighted sound, like she'd just eaten a chocolate. "And you told me second. I'm feeling all squishy inside. If you were here, I'd kiss you."

"Funny."

"You'll have to settle for alpaca kisses instead. Or Becca's. Becca and Trevor sitting in the tree, k-i-s-s-i-n-g..."

He moved the phone from his ear as she sang, knowing better than to try to stop her. Sometimes it was hard to imagine she'd just turned thirty-two. "You done?" he asked when she finished.

"For now," she said, a smile in her voice. "I'm really happy for you. Tell Becca I can't wait to meet her. I'll get back to you on the green dye."

"You're a sweetheart. Talk to you soon."

"Love you."

"Love you too."

When he hung up, he puffed out his chest. He was already feeling better. Being proactive, that was the key. Liking the feeling, he put in a web search for green dyes to see what he could find out on his own. He had a couple hours until he could call J.T., but really, what was there to say? Becca's land was the best place for them to drill in Ireland. Every time he thought about it, worry edged itself under his ribcage like he'd swallowed the wishbone. Becca was right. She was sitting on a goldmine, and others were going to come calling, and they might not balk from using unsavory tactics.

Would she sell the property to him for safekeeping? He was in a better position than she was to keep it safe. No, she didn't trust him enough for that yet.

How did one go about protecting property in Ireland, anyway? He only knew of two types of protected land offhand: natural heritage sites and wildlife preserves. Could they use that to their advantage?

And yet, he found himself continuing his quest for the perfect green dye rather than searching for property laws and loopholes...

God, if his brothers could see him now.

He'd already made a page of notes on plants and vegetables that produced greens when he realized he needed to know which ones Becca had already tried. He left his room, wishing he could seek her out and suggest a walk, but he suspected she'd turn him down flat. The woman worked as much as he did, if not more, and while he respected that, he was planning on making some changes in his schedule to spend more time with her. He hoped she'd do the same.

Hatshep stared at him with her freaky green eyes as he entered the main hall. Maybe he needed to buy her a treat to bring her around. Hell, now he was bribing her animals. Ridiculous. He went to the rear door and headed out the back, making his way toward the old kitchen. Becca had shown him where she kept her logbook about the dye. He'd take a peek.

He heard a loud humming sound behind him and braced himself, knowing who it was. Then he smiled. At least someone at The Wild Irish Rose still appreciated him. He decided he needed a different perspective on his lovesick friend. Maybe it would soften Becca up if he formed a friendship with Buttercup. The alpaca was coming toward him, a spring in its step. He stood his ground and lifted out a hand, hoping to prevent her from licking him—it was a *her*, and he supposed it was time to start thinking of Buttercup that way. She stopped when she reached him, turning her head to look at his hand.

"Okay, let's be nice about this." He lowered his hand gently. "No licking."

The animal hummed, righting her head, and then padded forward. His muscles locked in response, but he stayed still, waiting to see what she would do. When she lowered her head and rested it on his shoulder, he almost laughed. "We're a right pair." He petted her neck, and she started a symphony of hums.

The sunshine was bright and the sea breeze cool and salty. All around him were shades of green, from spring greens to the deep moss variety. God, he loved this place. He was starting to think of it as his too. Hopefully, Becca would see it that way soon.

"I need to go now, Buttercup. You go back to your friends." He still didn't know why the other alpacas stayed inside the fence when this one didn't, but he knew the guests liked to visit them. He'd heard a young boy giggling like crazy at the fence the other day, laughing as a trio of alpacas tried to lick his face. In fact, there was a lot of laughter here, he realized.

"Your owner is one hell of a businesswoman," he told Buttercup, patting the alpaca's head one more time before heading in the direction of the old kitchen.

Glad no one was around, he opened the door. He'd hoped she didn't lock it. People often didn't lock up in the smaller towns outside of Dublin. He rather liked the thought of living somewhere people didn't have to lock their doors.

There was a strong earthy scent in the old kitchen, and he sniffed to make out more notes. He identified lavender, rose, and juniper—hard to miss that last one for someone who enjoyed the occasional gin and tonic.

Strands of wool were drying next to their individual dye bath stations. Some people preferred to keep a separate drying station, she'd told him, but she liked to keep the wool situated beside the bath from which it had emerged. He thought she had it right. There was something novel about seeing the final product alongside the dye in the water. Usually the water was darker, but not in all cases. The rusty yellow yarn next to the dye bath with the yellow onions looked largely the same to his eyes.

Heading over to her desk, he drew out what she called her dyeing book. She had it organized by color types, and he quickly found the section on green thanks to the tab she'd stuck to it.

"What are you doing in here?"

He straightened immediately at the accusing tone. Aileen shut the door behind her.

"Don't tell Becca, but I'm trying to find the formula for the best green. My sister Caitlyn's on the case too. She works in our family business with organic plants." He held up the record book. "I thought it might help us narrow our search if we knew what you and Becca had already tried." He made sure to smile, hoping she wouldn't throw him out of the old kitchen—or worse, tell Becca he was up to no good.

"You're looking to find a green color for my girl?" She gripped the bottom of her shirt so hard her knuckles turned white.

She wasn't mad, he realized. She was upset. "Yes. I hope that's okay. I wanted to do something special for her. She's so busy around here, and I know it's hard for her to get away."

Tears appeared in the woman's eyes, alarming him. Good Lord, was she that sentimental?

"I thought this might be just the thing given her schedule."

She turned around quickly and muffled a cry. His insides tightened at the sound. "It's only a dye, Aileen."

She only shook her head, wiping her nose with her sleeve as she turned to face him. "Oh, you dear man. You don't understand."

No, he sure as hell didn't.

She sniffed. "It's a grand thing, what you're doing for our Becca. I'm sorry I doubted you. I didn't think you were a dosser."

No, he hadn't been up to no good, and thank God she knew it.

"I'll leave you then," Aileen said, yet she stayed where she was, studying him.

He seemed rooted to the ground. What the hell was she looking at him like that for? "I meant what I told you. I love her."

"I believed you then, and I sure as heavens believe you now," she said, a smile lifting her face. "Why else would I be crying?"

He would never understand women. "Someday soon, when she's ready, I'd like to take Becca to meet my family. In California. If I gave you enough notice, would you and Cian be able to handle things here?"

Fresh tears spilled down her cheeks, and she shook her head from side to side. He waited, nerves dancing in his belly. She opened her mouth to speak before pressing a hand to it. It almost looked like she was physically stopping herself from saying something.

Before he could say anything, Aileen left, crying softly.

CHAPTER 22

BECCA WAS GOING OVER CHEF PADRAIG'S WEEKLY SPECIALS when Aileen entered her office. The woman's face was wet with tears, and she immediately stood.

"What's wrong?" she asked, coming around the desk.

Aileen pulled her into a tight hug, causing her breath to whoosh out of her lungs. "You need to tell him, Becca. Oh, my dear, you really need to tell that wonderful man."

Her heart thudded in her chest. She didn't have to ask who Aileen meant, and she certainly didn't have to ask what she was referring to.

"I can't tell you why I feel so strongly about this," Aileen said, "I only know you must." Then she took Becca's face in her hands, and everything inside Becca seemed to drop to the ground, almost as though her friend's very gaze had made her protective cloak fall away. There was no hiding from this look.

"I want to," Becca said, knowing it was the truth, "but I need a little more time. Aileen..." She gripped the woman's hands. "I had a miracle today."

As she revealed what Hargreaves had done for her—the tangible help he'd placed in her lap, so to speak—the older woman cried more tears. By the time she finished sharing the testimonials she'd read, they were both crying softly. Many of the patients said they'd tried everything, from medicine to various forms of therapy, and nothing had worked for them—until Dr. Poread. He specialized in helping people whose condition was as acute and long-term as Becca's.

There was no doctor like him in the Emerald Isle.

Aileen bundled her up like she was a human blanket and rocked her in place. "Oh, that dear, dear man," she whispered.

"I have hope again, Aileen," Becca said, her voice raw. "I feel as though this miracle came right when I needed it." Trevor and love had entered her life, and God or the Universe or whatever you wanted to call it had sent her the keys to her cage.

"My dearest Becca," Aileen said, kissing her cheek. "It's everything I've been praying for and more."

"So you see why I want to have a few appointments with Dr. Poread before I tell him. I want to be able to show Trevor I'm getting better, and if I wait, I can share our long-term treatment plan with him." Because she knew it would be a process, and should he decide to stay, it would affect him too.

It was the only way she thought he would be able to handle the news. To learn the woman he loved was condemned to this very narrow place in the world would be a shock.

"He would be happy to know you have new help, Becca," Aileen said. "He'll stand by you."

"I hope so."

"I know I should cajole you into telling him now, but this news is so grand, I simply can't manage it."

"It is grand, isn't it?" she said, wiping her tears, a smile on her face. She hadn't felt this spectacular in... well, forever.

"The grandest," Aileen said with a firm nod. "We must do something for Mr. Hargreaves."

Becca didn't point out that the man preferred the simple use of his surname. "I'm going to knit him something extra special." She could have it done by the time he returned from Waterford if she put in a few more hours. Arthur's sweater was half-finished, but she hadn't had much time to work on it since Trevor came to her rooms each night. She shivered. The very thought of him filled her with a wave of love and desire. Oh, to feel this hopeful again. It was a grand miracle, indeed.

She floated on clouds the rest of the day, and when dinner rolled around, even the guests noticed her happy mood. A couple from Boston commented on her contagious smile, and she simply said, "There was magic in the air." She forced herself not to look over to where Trevor was sitting, having dinner alone.

He'd been watching her too, she knew. Her insides seemed to be aware of his every look, and by the time dinner was through and she'd sent Chef Padraig off with a cheeky, "*Bonne soirée*," she was eager to find Trevor.

When she didn't find him in one of the public rooms of the inn, she looked outside the windows. He wasn't on the cliffs like he had been the other night, so she decided to head to her chamber and wait for him. This way she could start on Hargreaves' sweater.

As she walked back, she laughed because Boru seemed to have caught her grand mood. He pranced beside her, his tail wagging happily. Hatshep, too, rubbed her head against Becca's leg, purring softly as they arrived back in her tower. Yes, they knew she was happy, and they were happy too.

She wandered into the spare room where she kept her yarn. Scanning the shelves, she let inspiration touch her. Hargreaves would want something elegant and not too colorful. It struck her that a sweater wasn't the right gift at all. He had his butler's uniform, which he wore religiously, if his dress on vacation was any indication.

But he wore a coat, she expected, when he went outside. Which meant he would wear a scarf. That was perfect. Colorado was cold, after all.

She selected her newly dyed Angora wool of the palest gray-blue, dyed from elderberries. The color was rich yet not showy, and the texture was silky soft. And the stitch? Maybe Trinity? She examined the wool. What about Cat's Paw? He might like the small and large eyelets. Then she remembered the stitch was also called Crowns of Glory, which seemed perfect. He'd given her the most treasured of gifts, almost like he was bestowing her glory back to her, the glory of being a human being, one who could run through the green hills and face off against the wild wind from the sea, her hair blowing madly behind her.

She grabbed her favorite knitting needles for such a stitch and settled down on the sofa in the sitting room, too eager to make a pot of tea.

As the rows took shape, her mind cleared. She fell into the peaceful rhythm, knitting easily while Hatshep purred next to her on the couch. Halfway through, something made her look at the time. It was growing late, on toward midnight. Where was Trevor?

Her needles fell to her lap, and she wondered if he wasn't coming. Last night had been strained for both of them. Revealing their love for each other hadn't erased the tension between them, and that had broken her heart. Then she'd ignored him at breakfast and forced herself not to give him extra attention tonight. Had he felt slighted?

Was he staying away because of her?

She stood. No, that wouldn't do.

Perhaps he was waiting for an invitation? She hadn't given him one tonight, and perhaps she'd been in too grand a mood to realize he needed a push. Well, she would put that to rights immediately. She walked over to the house phone and dialed his room.

"Hello," he said, answering after only one ring.

"I want you to come to my rooms tonight," she said, her voice soft and a little unsure.

"Okay." He hung up, and she looked down at the phone before placing it in the receiver. Okay? That was all he had to say?

Her belly seemed to flop about like a restless sea, and Boru gave a high-pitched whine. "Oh, stop that. Everything is all right." She knew she was saying it to herself.

Crossing to the bar caddy, she poured them whiskies. Then she stared down at the amber liquid. She didn't want to have a drink with him. She wanted to make love with him. Immediately. Perhaps it was time she was bold enough to show him how much she wanted him.

When she heard the door click downstairs, she came around the sofa and leaned back against it. He paused at the top of the stairs, his eyes searching hers.

"I'm sorry you didn't know I wanted you here tonight," she said softly.

His chest lifted with a deep sigh. "I didn't see a sign from you at dinner, although you seemed happy. It didn't feel like it was because of me."

He paused as if waiting for her to fill in the answer, but she wasn't ready to tell him the cause.

"You've ignored me all day," he continued when she remained quiet. "I...didn't like it."

She looked down at her feet, Hatshep rubbing her head against her calf. "I'm sorry I hurt you. Last night was..." She trailed off, not knowing what to say.

He stayed where he was. "What?"

"I know we have a lot of outside things pulling at us, but I... I love you. I don't want it to be like this."

His mouth turned up. "Neither do I."

"I'd very much like to start over," she said, pushing off the sofa and standing tall under his searching gaze. "Forget about last night and all the misunderstandings and harsh words."

Boru walked over to him then and nudged his thigh as if trying to move him toward Becca. "Your animals have strong opinions. Seems I'm back in their good graces."

"They're loyal to me," she said. "Trevor, when I say I love you, I mean it."

His eyes were still an inscrutable green. "So do I. But I don't like you ignoring me. You had a smile for everyone but me tonight. I thought you were acting happy to piss me off."

"It's not so. But I'm sorry I made you feel that way. I don't want the guests to know about our connection. Not yet."

He nodded. "I normally wouldn't get so bent out of shape, but there was a moment tonight when you looked right past me, and I felt sure I'd lost you."

Lost her? Today she'd been given the possible keys to her future, one she hoped to share with him. "You haven't lost me. We're only just finding our way with each other, under less-than-ideal circumstances."

"But that's all done now," he said. "You believe me when I say that, right?"

Mostly, but she only nodded.

"Then come here," he said, holding out his arms to her.

She strode forward and wrapped her arms around him. He tunneled one of his hands in her long hair, the other spanning around her ribcage, as if seeking anchor.

"I love you," he whispered. "I know it hasn't been easy, but it's going to get better. Just hang in there with me, Becca. Let me show you how much I love you."

Hadn't she been thinking the very same thing? Maybe they both needed some reassurance tonight. "Come with me."

She took his hand and led him into her bedroom, closing the door on her beloved animals. Pausing only to shut the light off, she pulled him gently past the bed to the window seat overlooking her land. The stars were twinkling overhead, and she cracked open the window to let in the distant roar of the sea. For years, this was the closest she could handle to the outdoors, and it was both her greatest doorway and her saddest portal.

She undressed him slowly, brushing aside his hands when he went to help her remove the St. Christopher medal. Needing to give to him, she traced his skin and pushed him back onto the seat. Kneeling between his open legs, she took him in her mouth, stroking him until his hand cupped her neck, his body arching in response to her ministrations. When he finally came, she stroked his hip, trying to tell him how precious he was to her, how indispensable he'd become in such a short time.

When he reached for her, she stepped back and undressed in front of him. The act made her feel both vulnerable and powerful, all at the same time. This was how she imagined it would feel to stand on the cliffs outside, above the wild frenzy of the sea. When she finished, she moved into the open V of his legs and cupped his face in her hands. Their eyes met, and she held his gaze, letting him see into her heart, into her soul, and into places she had, until now, only traveled alone. She watched him swallow thickly. Noted there was no smile upon his face. She smoothed his hair off his forehead and leaned forward to kiss his lips, first lightly, and then with more pressure.

His hands came to rest on her waist, but he let her set the pace, sensing she needed to. Her tongue traced the seam of his lips while her hand trailed across the hard planes of his chest. She celebrated the beauty of his body in gentle touches and the delicate scrape of her fingernails along his thigh and back. With desire thrumming in every cell, she guided him back further on the window seat and climbed onto his lap. After grabbing a condom, she sheathed his arousal before setting herself onto him. She took every inch of him slowly inside her until she heard a part of her whisper, *Yes*.

As she began to rise and fall upon him, she heard the call of the sea outside. Her eyes closed, and she was swept away on wave after wave of sensation, aware of his breath, aware of his hands gripping her as power rose between them. She arched back, crying out, and felt molten fire explode in her belly. Everything pulsed and pulsed afterward, and she luxuriated in his hard body locking with the force of its desire for her.

She rested her face in the crook of his neck and whispered, "I love you."

He nuzzled her, the stubble of his jaw rubbing her skin ever so delightfully. "I love you too." Then an explosive breath gusted from his chest, and he seemed to relax, as if her assurances had finally done their job. He was content in her love, and she in his.

He lay back on the window seat after disposing of the condom, and she climbed back on top of him, not yet ready to be a separate being. Her eyes soaked in the view spread out before her. Everything felt possible, and she was lit with the moon and the stars in that moment. Nothing could have told her she wasn't part of the magic now.

She was the magic, and every wish would be granted on a night like this.

She compelled her mind to envision what she wanted most of all: her and Trevor holding hands, walking toward the cliffs. She imagined the feel of the sea's cool mist on her skin, the smell of the salt and moss filling her senses. But what was most vivid was the warmth of his hand and the love shining in his eyes when he gazed at her.

A star fell in that wide, dark expanse above the sea, and she made her wish. And in her still-fragile heart, she sent up prayers to all the stars still shining in the midnight-blue sky, willing the vision to come true.

Chapter 23

TREVOR AWOKE TO A COOL BREEZE WAFTING OVER HIS SKIN. Becca's warm body lay on top of him. Rolling to the side with her, he gathered her to him and looked out the window. The sunrise was glorious with ribbons of pinks and blue, the kind that made him think of her dye. God, what a night. He looked down at Becca, her hair covering half her face. Love filled his heart as he eased those tangled locks behind her ear. She was so beautiful, and last night, he'd discovered new reservoirs of love and desire with her. Caressing her face, he let a new, unexpected truth settle more deeply inside him.

This was where he belonged.

Propping himself up on an elbow, he let his eyes wander over the land. The sea was brilliant shades of gray and blue, and the stone and grass a feast of earthy roughness. He loved this woman, and he loved this land too.

His life would need to change to reflect that, and he let his mind spin with plans for the future. He could work from here and take the company plane from Cork City when he had to travel. But only when the need arose. He was sick of spending his life on the go, in hotel rooms and boardrooms, and he didn't like the idea of spending half his time away from Becca. If he needed to delegate some of his responsibilities, he would. Delegation had never been one of his strengths, but other people did it successfully. He would too.

He heard a loud humming and looked down to see Buttercup gazing up at him from below. He waved before he realized what he was doing. That silly animal. He'd even grown fond of it.

Settling back down, he tucked Becca close and savored the peace inside him. Who would have guessed he'd come on this mission only to discover the woman and home he'd always hoped to find someday? Bards sang to violin and Uilleann pipes about love's unexpected nature being part of its magic in pubs across Ireland, and he'd always enjoyed listening to their ballads, little expecting the magic of his adopted country would rub off on him.

She stirred and rubbed her head against his chest, reawakening all sorts of desire in him. Last night, she'd bared herself down to the bones of her soul. He'd let her take control—which had required him to be vulnerable too. They'd fallen asleep soundly afterward. Perhaps the rawness of it all and the release had finally ushered in a powerful sleep. He didn't know. It didn't matter. All he knew was that they were closer than ever before.

"What are you thinking about?"

Her voice was rough with sleep, and she rolled onto her back, keeping her hand on his thigh.

"You. Life. The big questions. You know. Nothing important."

She snorted out a laugh. "All that, and the sun's barely up. Have you always been an overachiever?"

"Yes," he said, leaning in and kissing her on the mouth. "I love you. I didn't say it enough last night."

Her blue eyes seemed as languid as the calm sea. "Last night wasn't about talking. It was about showing."

His mouth twitched. "You showed me just fine. Is it strange to say thank you?"

"I don't rightly know," she said, turning on her side and facing him. "It was a first for me."

He tucked her hair behind her ear again. "Me too."

"Trevor, I want this to work, what's between us. I just ask you to be patient with me."

Patient? What a funny word. "I can be a total bear sometimes, so I'll ask the same of you."

"That's not exactly what I meant," she said, her eyes falling away.

She had to be referring to the company's interest in her land. Until things were settled, the weight of it would be between them. How could it not be? "I know. Now, how about we stop talking and you let me do some showing?"

Her eyes flashed to his, and a slow smile spread across her face. "I'd like that."

He tugged her onto her stomach. "Let's make this memorable." Then he set his mouth to her neck, loving the feel of her back arching in response.

He loved her slowly, touching her skin as the cool breeze from the window feathered over them. Her breasts were sheer perfection, and her thighs a place of wonder. He lost himself in her sighs and moans and later, as the sun rose higher over the sea, her sharp cries of pleasure.

When he sank onto her, she stroked his back.

"I love you too."

He grunted and kissed her cheek, taking a moment longer to hold her, knowing she needed to rise and dress soon. They stayed that way for a moment, looking out the window, still joined together, until she turned in his arms.

"I need to go," she said.

Funny how those same words used to spill from his

lips so easily with other women, but he now dreaded hearing them from Becca. "I'd like to understand more of what you do here, the ins and outs of running the inn. How would I go about that?"

She cocked an eyebrow. "I could give you a tour, I suppose."

"Great." He kissed her swiftly. "I'll get dressed and meet you later then. Just call my room when you have time." He had some serious work to do.

"You should bring over a change of clothes," she said, disengaging from him. "Shower and shave here too, if you'd like."

"I'd like that." He took her hand when she stood, not wanting her to leave. "If there's anything I can help you with..."

Her brow wrinkled. "Like what?"

"This place." He shook her hand playfully. "I want to be of help to you, Becca. When you love someone, you support them. We need to think of how I can do that."

"You want to help me run The Wild Irish Rose?" she asked. "Oh, don't be silly. You have your own work." Crossing the room, she grabbed a robe hanging from a nearby chair.

He sat up on the window seat. "You run things just fine, but I'd like to help, if I can." Did she not understand? In his family, love and business were one and the same.

"Are you an award-winning chef in disguise? Oh, wait, I already have an award-winning chef. How about cleaning and polishing?"

He stared her down, knowing she was having a little fun with him. "I'm trying to be...a good partner."

Her hand fell away from her robe. "Is that what this is about? Oh, I see. Well, then..."

She spun around, hastily tying the robe now. He came up behind her and turned her to face him. There were tears in her eyes. "Why are you crying?"

"Only something in my eye," she said, trying to pull away from him.

"Becca..."

She stopped short. "I wasn't expecting you'd want to help. I'd given up hope thinking I'd ever find someone who wanted that, like my grandfather did with my grandmother. I've always considered myself lucky to have Aileen and Cian, but I never imagined..."

He tipped her chin up so he could look into her eyes. "Family and business are intertwined for me too." Again, he wondered about her parents. Her words implied she was alone, but he'd wait for her to tell him the full story. "While I don't intend to give up what I do, I want to help you here if I can. You know, I have some business acumen."

She worked her lips as if fighting a smile. "I'll keep it in mind."

Kissing her softly, he waited until she slumped against him. "You'd better get going before I make you late."

She ran her fingers down his chest in the most arousing way. "I should be okay. It's not like I have to commute."

He was chuckling as he tumbled her onto her bed.

After breakfast, she found him for the grand tour, going over everything from the food ordering for the restaurant to her online presence and reservation system. It was impressive. When they entered the kitchen, a burly black-haired man stopped chopping onions and stared him down. Trevor was amused when Chef Padraig picked up the cleaver while still looking at him.

"He's protective of you," Trevor said when they left.

"It's sweet of him," she said, glancing back the way they'd come. "We get along brilliantly. He's a core element of our success."

Trevor tucked that away. He'd have to win the man over. "Do you have time to show me the animals? I haven't checked out the rabbits or the sheep yet. I thought Buttercup might get jealous before, but now she's sure of my affection."

Instead of laughing, she clenched her hands. The change in her was clear as day. Why was she nervous suddenly?

"I've taken long enough for today," she said, forcing a smile. "Another time."

"Okay." He didn't understand what was going on in her head. Was she afraid to show him that part of her enterprise? Why? She'd been so happy to explain the dyeing process to him.

"You go on," he said. "I'll find a way to keep occupied." He needed to call J.T. and talk about the Connor situation. Avoiding it was folly. They had to figure out another way.

His entire future was riding on it.

CHAPTER 24

BECCA HEARD THE FRONT DOORBELL RING. AILEEN WAS overseeing the baking while she went over accounts. Pushing back from her chair, she strode out of her office. When she opened the door, a dark-haired woman stood beaming at her. She looked to be about Becca's age, and there was something familiar about her.

"Hello," the woman said, thrusting out her hand in a very American fashion. "I'm Caitlyn Merriam. I believe my brother and my aunt and uncle are staying here."

Goodness! Trevor's sister. "Ah, yes. Of course. Please come in."

Caitlyn took a few steps inside and seemed to bounce on the stone floor as she looked around. Her dress was a wild plum color and fell over her lean body like a second skin.

She clasped her hands and turned in a circle. "Oh, I love this place! Are you Becca?"

"How did you—"

"Trevor told me about you," she said, reaching a hand out and rubbing Becca's shoulder.

The touch was friendly, and Becca stood there in shock. What had Trevor told his sister? Had he spoken about her to the rest of his family?

"I can't wait to see Buttercup," she said, grinning now. "The video Aunt Clara took had all of us in stitches. I mean, if anyone was going to have a lovesick alpaca stalk him, it would be Trevor. He likes to think he's all tough and manly, but really, he's a sweetheart."

Becca had concluded the same thing, but she wasn't sure she should say so. "Do you live in Dublin too?"

"Not on your life. It's a great town, but not my style. I live in the Big Apple, like Flynn—another brother—and I go back and forth between New York and L.A., but I sneak off to Paris every chance I get. It's the best city in the world in my opinion."

She'd always wanted to visit Paris. Weave through the Louvre and marvel at the masterpieces. Meander along the side streets and across all those amazing bridges. Oh, to visit such a city. Maybe it would be possible with Dr. Poread's help. "Does everyone in your family like to travel, then?"

"Yes, mostly," she said. "Except Connor. He holes up at headquarters and rarely takes a night off. Hell, the man even sleeps there from time to time. He needs to get a life."

She couldn't agree more. "Are you planning on staying with us?"

"Yeah, I was hoping to. Flew to Cork City from Paris. It was a breeze. Rented a small little car to make sure I didn't get stuck. One time Trevor rented us a mid-size car in Spain, and we went down this street no bigger than an alley and got pinned between the walls. It took three hours to get us unwedged. Talk about awful. Have you ever been in the car for that much time with two of your knuckleheaded brothers?"

She didn't have any brothers, so she only shook her head.

"It's no picnic, let me tell you. J.T. is as bad as Trevor sometimes, and that's karma or something since they're twins. Man, are those scones I smell? Good heavens, I'm starving. Did I miss lunch? I read your restaurant closes at two, and I'm a little late."

Good heavens, the woman could talk. "I'm sure we can scare up a sandwich and some scones. Your brother is fond of them."

"He can eat," Caitlyn said, laughing. "Heck, we all can. So where is the moron?"

Should she say? "You might check his room. He's in our Oisin and Niamh suite."

"God bless you," Caitlyn said, sputtering laughter like a car backfiring. "Sorry, bad joke. That was a mouthful."

"It's an Irish myth," she said, trying not to laugh herself. "About ill-fated love."

Caitlyn waved a hand. "I don't believe in stuff like that. Only happily ever afters for me. I mean, I can binge-watch chick flicks like nobody's business. It drives my siblings insane, even my sister, Michaela. She's more into the Nature Channel than romantic comedies. So what room can you put me up in? I'm hoping to stay a few days unless Trev kicks me out."

"Ah, let me think. You probably don't want to stay in the Tristan and Isolde suite."

"Another pair of unhappy lovers? I think I saw the movie. James Franco was the hero, right? It was awful."

She'd thought the same. "I preferred him in *Milk*. We have a vacancy as of this morning in the Diarmuid and Grainne suite. It's not ready for occupancy yet, but I can put a rush on it."

"Did they have a happy romance?" Caitlyn asked, her green eyes dancing. "Because I just can't stay in a depressing room. It's bad energy, you know."

She didn't and refrained from disagreeing. "Yes, they lived happily in County Sligo— after some travails, of course."

"Then sign me up," Caitlyn said. "Okay, if you'll point

me in the right direction, I'll go see what my bro is up to. Oh, you beautiful creature. Come to mama."

Becca looked over her shoulder to see Boru prancing madly toward the woman. He gave a woof as she knelt down and hugged him.

"You like dogs," Becca said, smiling easily now.

"I love dogs," she said, making baby faces at the animal. "Mom wouldn't let us have pets growing up. Too many kids, she said. But I was crazy about my friends' pets, so I wasn't scarred for life."

"You're funny," Becca said, making Caitlyn glance up at her. "I mean, your brother is too, but he's—"

"Got a stick up his butt sometimes," she said, keeping a hand on Boru's neck as she rose to her feet. "Trust me, it's not even close to the big one Connor is sporting, and Quinn... Well, he's working on giving Con a run for his money in the stick department."

Good heavens. "I'll show you to Trevor's room and then find you some lunch."

Suddenly the woman was hugging her, and she stood stiffly, not used to such mad displays of affection.

"Oh, I'm so happy to meet you," Caitlyn said, leaning back and jostling her a little. "Okay, I'm backing off. I sometimes get a little carried away, but personally I like that about me. I mean if we can't be excited about life and express it, what the hell are we here for?"

The woman's enthusiasm was contagious. Becca had the urge to punch her fist in the air and say *hear, hear*, but since she *was* on duty, she contained it. "Caitlyn, I know all of you work in the family business. What is your area, if you don't mind my asking?"

She stretched out her arms. "I do fashion and skincare right now, but I'm in expansion mode. I'm looking into perfume. Like I was telling Trev, the market is insane. Okay, I'll talk your ear off if you don't point me in the right direction. Plus, my stomach is grumbling so loud I'm afraid they'll hear it in the next town."

"This way."

Caitlyn linked their arms as they walked—a charming and completely unaffected gesture. *This* was Trevor's sister? After talking to his brother, Connor, it was hard to imagine. Thank God all the Merriams didn't have sticks up their arses, like the woman had said. When they reached the hallway, Becca wondered if she should just point out Trevor's suite and leave Caitlyn to go the rest of the way.

"My God, I just love what you have going on here," the woman said, her head turning from side to side as if to take it all in. "Did you use an Irish decorator?"

"I did it all myself," she said, heat staining her cheeks.

Caitlyn stopped short. "You're kidding! Wow! You're mega talented. I mean Trev said... Oops, I'm shutting up now. My mouth needs a zipper, I swear."

What had Trevor told her? At the door, she felt nerves start to creep in. "I'll leave you two to catch up."

Caitlyn locked their arms, making it impossible for her to move. "Don't be silly." She pounded on the door, the sound reverberating across Becca's chest. "Open up, moron!"

Becca wanted to sink into the floor. Thank God, the other guests in this section of the inn were out.

The door sprung open, and Trevor stood there, his face blank. "You're kidding me! Go away, brat."

She launched herself at him. "Never. You're stuck with me forever."

He grunted and bear-hugged her. When Caitlyn started kissing his cheeks, he angled his head away. "Cut that out. Jesus, you're like a puppy sometimes."

"I just love you," the woman said, finally stepping back. "And Becca is awesome. Hell, this whole place is awesome. Your woman has mad skills, bro."

His woman? Becca's eyes flashed to Trevor's. He cocked his head as if daring her to disagree. "Excuse my sister. She's crazy but loveable. Like a Chihuahua."

"Please," Caitlyn said. "More like a Siberian husky."

"In your dreams," Trevor said. "Well, are you going to come in or what?"

Caitlyn struck a pose. "Yep. Becca, can you hang with us for while?"

Hang? Oh, my. "I should find you something to eat, and I was working on the accounts."

"Working woman," Caitlyn said, holding her fist out. "I'm with ya, girl."

Becca eyed the fist.

"She wants you to fist-bump her," Trevor said, his mouth twitching. "Like this."

The siblings demonstrated the move, and then Becca held her fist out to replicate it. Caitlyn mashed her knuckles eagerly, and Becca had to refrain from massaging her hand.

"Go on," Trevor said, putting his hand on her back and giving it a brief caress. "I'll take care of this crazy woman."

"Crazy woman? I'll have you know—"

Trevor pulled his sister inside and shut the door. Becca simply stood there, hearing Caitlyn's animated chatter but not the words. The woman was a tempest in a teapot, for sure, but Becca liked her. What a relief. While she hadn't asked much about his family, she'd feared the rest of his siblings might be like Connor. She shivered at the thought of that man. He was someone to fear. The kind of man you didn't want as an opponent. She'd known it over the phone. Taking off toward the stairs, she realized Caitlyn showing up was significant.

Someone in Trevor's family had wanted to meet her, and that meant they were in serious waters for sure.

Chapter 25

TREVOR DEPOSITED CAITLYN IN THE CLOSEST CHAIR, CROSSing his arms over his chest.

"Are you out of your mind coming here?" he asked.

She grinned without contrition. "Are you kidding? I *had* to come after you told me you'd found your dream girl. Besides, I had another good reason." She took an envelope out of her purse and handed it to him. "I think we have the green dye you want, from spinach leaves, no less, but I need some of Becca's wool to make sure. The dye will absorb and set differently depending on the type of wool that's used."

"I read that too, but got...carried away here." He opened the envelope and studied the dyed green wool, the shade of St. Patrick's Day if you asked him. "I like the green. Let's hope she does. Thank you."

"You're so going to pay for dinner tonight."

Like she didn't have her own money. "Hell, I'll pay for your entire stay here if you have the right dye."

She kicked back in the chair and crossed her ankles. "Aren't I a genius?"

"You're a brat," he said, throwing the envelope onto the sofa. "But I love you."

"Becca's wonderful from what I saw, Trev." Pressing

her hand to her heart, Caitlyn grinned. "I mean, you found a good one on the first try. After J.T.'s colossal screw-up with Sin City, I was afraid you might follow the same pattern. Thank God, you have better sense."

"Don't tell J.T. that." He dropped down into a seat next to her. "So you came here to check her out?"

"Damn skippy. I wasn't going to let another one of my brothers screw up his life."

He kicked at her feet playfully, and she stuck her tongue out at him. "You're a total sweetheart when you're not acting nutso."

"I blame it on the chemicals we use in our skincare lab. I'm probably inhaling particles that change my brain matter."

Trevor laughed. "Our products are all organic, moron."

"That's *your* name." She swung her leg playfully. "Oh, I like it here. There's something magical about this place. Did you know she decorated it all herself?" Suddenly she popped up and headed for the window. "These curtains. My God, I love the color and the fabric. Knotted velvet drapes are serious business."

He loved when she got like this. "You know you have more crazy facts rolling around in that brain of yours than should be legal."

"Please! You're thinking about Connor and Michaela. They're like alien fact babies. Okay, now, tell me everything. How did you find this place? Did you suggest it to Uncle Arthur and Aunt Clara and then come up yourself?"

She hadn't put their offshore operation in Cork together with this place, but why would she? Connor hadn't brought it to the board, which Caitlyn sat on, and he wouldn't have called her to bitch about Trevor's lack of progress. His stomach sunk. Shit. Leave it to Caitlyn, Ms. Spontaneous, to throw him off. Should he tell her the rest of the story? Hell, he'd told her about Becca, and that bespoke serious trust. But his decision to balk Connor's will was different. Even if she agreed with him, he didn't want to put her in a tough situation with the rest of the family.

"Let's leave it for another time," Trevor said. "What do you want to drink? I imagine Becca will send something up, but I've got a mini-bar and—"

"What aren't you telling me?" Caitlyn asked, coming over and gripping his arm. "Are you here on business? We have holdings in Cork, right?"

He looked away. Double shit. She was too sharp by far.

"Oh, my God. You are! I thought it was weird you were staying here and not in Dublin. Okay, you'd better tell me."

"Will you settle down? Jesus, Caitlyn. I'm trying to keep you out of a potentially awkward situation. Why won't you let me?"

"Because I know you, and when you get that constipated look on your face something is super wrong. What is it?"

Constipated look? "It's a big deal, Caitlyn. Only J.T. knows. I'll tell you if you insist, but be sure you want to know and can keep quiet about it."

"Does it concern Becca?" she asked, her dark brows furrowing.

"Yeah," he said, feeling that familiar sickness he experienced whenever he thought about Connor wanting her land. "Yeah, it does."

She socked him in the chest. "Well, tell me, you idiot. I love that woman because you do."

"I *do* love her, which is why I'm taking a stand against Connor for the first time in my life."

Caitlyn's eyes widened. "You'd better start at the beginning."

And so he did. For once, his sister kept her mouth shut until he finished, but he noted her mouth was getting progressively more scrunched as he spoke. When he got to the part about Corey, and how Connor was determined this new operation would be on land, she turned her head away and wiped at her eyes.

"This whole thing is horrible, Trev," she said when he finished, sitting down with a thunk. "Colossally horrible."

"Yeah." He hung his head. "What's worse is that I can't find another property that's anywhere near as good as Becca's."

"So what? You tell Connor you couldn't make the deal. She doesn't want to sell. Case closed."

"I already tried that." He shook his head. "Connor isn't himself, Caitlyn. He won't back down, and he threatened to send Quinn if I can't secure the deal."

"What? That's not his job."

"Exactly. Heck, I haven't let myself say the words, but I'm afraid they'll find a way to force her out."

She tapped her thigh with a fingernail, clearly thinking. "You've done it before."

Shrugging, he said, "Oil and gas is a dirty business. It was all legal, and everyone was well compensated." But not always ethical, he could admit now. Some people hadn't wanted to sell at first, sure, so they'd bought up the surrounding land and raised property taxes. Yeah, it had taken longer, but it had worked in the end. Developers did it all the time. The march of progress and all that...

"How can I help? Do you want me to talk to Connor? He should have run this through the board, and we all should have voted."

He agreed, and yet... "Con would eat you alive, especially since you don't work in his part of the business."

"But I'm on the board, and I'd do anything for you,"

she said, touching his arm. "I saw your face when you opened the door. You look at Becca like Dad looks at Mom. It made me...all emotional."

Hell, did she have to turn into a mush ball on him? "I love you bunches for saying you'd brave the lion, but no, I'm going to figure out another way with J.T."

"What if you tell Con how you feel about Becca?" she asked.

He snorted. "When have you ever known him to be sentimental? Besides, I'm afraid he'll call me a bunch of names and *still* send Quinn in."

"I see your point. Okay, I don't know diddly about this side of the business, but I'm a fast learner. Put me to work."

He pulled her out of her chair and into a hug. She wrapped her arms around him, nestling close. Yeah, she was a total sweetheart.

"Stick to what you do best. Now, tell me more about the green dye. Did you use a salt or vinegar fixative?"

Caitlyn dropped back into her chair. "Who are you and where did you put my brother?"

He couldn't help but laugh as he sat back down. She was right—this was a conversation he'd never imagined they would have. "A man can expand his knowledge, can't he?"

She didn't say anything, only grinned at him.

"You're an imp."

"And you're a moron."

"I'm glad you came." It was time to admit it.

She made a delighted sound. "'Bout time you said so. Now, about the green dyes we tested..."

And as she walked him through their experiments, he basked in the comfort of having another ally.

Chapter 26

Becca ran around the rest of the afternoon in a state of happy tension.

She'd seen Trevor and Caitlyn walking the grounds from the back windows, and while her heart had longed to join them, she'd enjoyed hearing their laughter drift in on the breeze. When she saw Aileen rush toward them, almost skipping in her exuberance, she'd pressed her hand over her mouth to keep from calling out to them. Caitlyn embraced the older woman, of course, and they hastened into the old kitchen together.

Hurt clogged her throat, the earlier happiness receding. Why was Aileen taking them to the dyeing baths? Becca wanted to be the one to explain everything. Had Trevor thought her too busy? Was Caitlyn too eager to wait?

Whatever the reason, she decided to leave them to it. Although she longed to join them, they hadn't asked for her company, and perhaps they had a reason for it. Instead, she headed to the kitchen to check on Chef Padraig and make herself a special plate of scones and tea. Back inside her office, she tried to add up the accounts, but in the end, she was unable to drown out all thoughts of their happy tour.

When she heard the front doorbell ring again, she almost called upon Cian to answer it. But he was working outside on the property today, and it was a silly fancy. She never had problems facing the walk-ins.

Opening the door, she stopped short at the tall, handsome man grinning at her on the other side. He was dressed in designer jeans and a gray T-shirt.

"We seem to be having a mini-family reunion here," he announced in an American accent, jingling a leather overnight bag. "I'm Flynn Merriam. I hope you have a room for me."

Another sibling? "Was I supposed to? I mean, Trevor and Caitlyn didn't mention they were expecting you."

"Typical," he said, shaking his shaggy sandy blond hair. "Thoughtless. I'm just playing with you. I came as a surprise. I was in Stockholm with a lady."

Stockholm? They must all travel. She'd ignore the lady comment. "You're most welcome, of course."

His grin was easy and charming, and she didn't doubt he attracted many a lady with it. "Please tell me you have a room. I hate bunking with Trevor. He snores."

She knew that was true.

"And Caitlyn would use her scissors on me if I even suggested it. Don't mess with her. She's fierce."

She'd seemed perfectly sweet to Becca.

"Where's Buttercup? I have to thank her for giving me some of the best laughs I've had in ages. Of course, now that I'm here, your alpaca might change her mind. The ladies seem to think I'm the better-looking brother."

Becca could see why—Flynn had a Calvin Klein model look about him, but it didn't appeal to her.

"Buttercup is outside, of course," she said. "I can show you to a room in the meantime. You don't have any problems with ill-fated lovers, do you?"

"No. Is that a trick question?"

"Your sister had reservations about staying in the Tristan and Isolde suite. I believe she feared it would possess unhappy energy."

Snorting, he said, "Sounds like her. I'm totally cool with ill-fated lovers. I figure love comes in all shapes and sizes."

She held back a snort of her own. "Follow me, Mr. Merriam?"

"Please, call me Flynn," he said, checking out the surroundings like Caitlyn had. "You have a beautiful place here...ah...I didn't catch your name."

"It's Becca O'Neill."

He held out a hand smoothly as they continued to walk up the stairs.

"I got the alert that Caitlyn was on her way here, and I thought I'd hop over and see what was going on. Aunt Clara's been so high on your place, and it's nice to see a couple siblings now and again. Don't tell them that though."

From his cheeky grin, she knew he wasn't serious. "I'll keep your regard for them in strict confidence."

"Oh, I love your accent. It's lighter than the ones in Dublin."

"Thank you. Your brother is in the Oisin and Niamh suite to your right while your sister is down this other hallway on the left in the Diarmuid and Grainne suite. You're in the West Wing."

"Terrific," he said, following her. "This is a big place. It used to be a manor or something, right?"

She nodded. "Yes, it's been in my family for four hundred years. We opened it as a bed and breakfast in the 1920s."

"It's wonderful," Flynn said. "I can see why it has five stars on Expedia."

It was hard not to beam. She'd worked hard for their reputation. "Thank you. Here we are." Opening the door, she handed him the key. "Do you need me to show you around?"

"Nah, I stay in hotels all the time when I'm traveling."

Oh, how she envied the Merriams. They traveled so much they were casual about it. Like most people would be about taking a walk. Like Becca was about crossing the inn. "What's your favorite place to visit?"

"Tough one. Right now, it's the south of Spain. God, there's nothing like Andalucía."

"Seville. Grenada. The wilds of the old Moorish empire."

His head darted back. "You know it."

"Yes." Her parents had taken her there on holiday once when she was a child. Heaven on earth. "Your brother and sister are outside. In the old kitchen."

She walked to the window and looked out. The door was still closed. What were they doing in there? "It's right there," she said, trying not to let him see her consternation.

"Great, I'll get settled and find them. Do you have any scones by chance? All the reviews mentioned them."

The corners of her mouth tipped up. So he ate like his brother. "We have some fresh out of the oven. I'll have someone send up a basket."

"Are my aunt and uncle around?" he asked, throwing his bag on a chair and opening it.

"They're still in Waterford, taking a tour. I'm not sure whether they will be back tonight." Trevor hadn't mentioned it, and she hadn't felt it was any of her business.

"Good for them. Touring around Ireland. It's a beautiful country."

"A grand one," she agreed, stepping into the hallway. "I'll leave you then."

He gave her a playful wink. "You've been a doll. Thanks."

Closing the door, she released a heavy sigh. Two siblings in one day? Flynn had called it a mini-family reunion. Well, it seemed so. She walked to the end of the hallway and looked out the bay window. They'd left the old kitchen at last. Caitlyn was dancing around Trevor, and he was holding his hands up like he was trying to keep her away from him.

Then Becca heard an unmistakable hum and watched as Buttercup pranced over to them. Caitlyn hugged the animal and started laughing when the alpaca rested her head fondly on Trevor's shoulder.

Becca's heart sped up at the sight. When had he stopped running from Buttercup? To her astonishment, he scratched the animal behind the ears, making Buttercup let loose a litany of hums. Caitlyn bent over, holding her stomach she was laughing so hard. Trevor just continued to smile, the kind of good-humored, confident smile that made her want to run her fingertips over his lips.

His gaze lifted, and she met his eyes from afar. He waved at her, and she almost stepped back, hoping he wouldn't ask her to join them. She would be fine to walk that far, but what if he asked her to tour the grounds with them? Instead, she waved, and both Merriams waved back.

Someone shouted something, and Trevor and Caitlyn both turned toward the sound. Flynn must have left his room as soon she'd left him, for he was striding toward them. Caitlyn ran and leaped up on him, and he caught her and kept right on walking with her in his arms. Trevor was shaking his head fondly as they approached him, and Flynn dropped Caitlyn with a dramatic flair in order to bear-hug Trevor. Their love and camaraderie was tangible. Oh how she wanted to join—

Trevor was happy, and she liked to see that.

Feeling as if she were intruding on a private moment, she made herself walk away and headed back downstairs to the kitchen for Flynn's scones. He could eat them when he returned. Aileen was laughing with Chef Padraig, tasting the charmoula sauce for the haddock special.

"Aileen, can I speak to you?" she called, picking up a basket and crossing to the trays of fresh-baked scones.

The woman smacked her lips and patted Chef on the back. "Delicious. It's going to sell out fast." She hustled over. "Yes, dear?"

"Trevor's brother, Flynn, just arrived, and he's a fine fellow."

"Oh, how wonderful!" Aileen cried. "How fine a fellow is he?"

Becca laughed. "He looks like a Calvin Klein model."

"Oh, no wonder he dates all the models then," she said, picking up a crock of butter and putting it on the plate Becca was arranging. "I can't wait to get a look at him."

"How did you know he dates models?"

"I've asked Trevor and Caitlyn about all the siblings except that Connor."

Becca felt that strange spurt of hurt and envy again. "Why did you take them to the old kitchen?"

Aileen waved her hand in the air. "Oh, Caitlyn got all excited, what with her interest in fashion. Didn't want to wait. You didn't mind, did you?"

"Of course not. I only wondered." She hated lying.

A warm hand touched her arm, and she looked up to see Aileen smiling at her. "They're here to meet you, my dear. They know how much Trevor loves you. Isn't it wonderful? Them coming here like they have?"

Her knees went a little weak. Had they truly come to meet her? "That's grand," she murmured.

"Yes, it is," Aileen said, "and if I could make a suggestion."

"Of course."

"I heard Trevor say his aunt and uncle and Hargreaves are driving back this evening. You might consider opening the Cellar and having them eat there."

The Cellar was for special events and would give the Merriams more privacy. "Good idea."

"Now for my next suggestion," Aileen said.

"The tasting menu?" It was common for the guests in the Cellar to enjoy Chef Padraig's eight-course meal.

"No, dear. *Join them.* Let them get to know you better. Cian and I can look after everything tonight. It would mean a great deal to Trevor."

"Isn't it presumptuous?" she asked, picking at the hem of her shirt. "Me going without him asking?"

"He doesn't know why you turned down his invitation to Cork City. He thinks you're too busy to take a moment for yourself. You'll need to show him otherwise."

"All right, I'll do it." She forced herself to leave the poor shirt alone and looked up at Aileen. "Thank you."

"You're most welcome, my dear." She kissed her cheek. "Now, I'm off to find this fine man and give him some of our prize scones."

Becca laughed as she watched her walk out of the kitchen. Crossing to Chef Padraig, she said, "I have some guests joining us in the Cellar last minute."

He muttered rapid-fire French swear words under his breath, but she didn't care.

Tonight was to be her first meal with some of Trevor's siblings, and she intended to make it a grand occasion.

***

Clara loved her husband, but if he told one more person how she'd bought *every* Waterford Crystal ornament known to man, she might have to kill him.

When she saw Becca coming toward them as they entered the main hall, she braced herself. "*Arthur*," she said. "Remember what we spoke about."

The odious man shot her a grin and tossed a red hot in his mouth. "Becca! My beautiful bride bought out the entire stock of Waterford Christmas ornaments. We're going to have to spend Christmas in Ireland from now on because no postal service on earth can ship them all. I don't care what Waterford House said. They'll never reach us in Colorado."

"We'd love to have you here for the holidays," the sweet woman said, embracing them warmly. "It would be ever so grand."

"Poor Hargreaves might drop dead from carrying them all," Arthur continued, crunching on his red hot, knowing full well he was getting her fired up.

"Not before you do, dear, if you don't stop yammering about my shopping," Clara said, giving him a warning elbow in the ribs.

"You'll have to tell me all about it," Becca said. "Every guest who has gone to Waterford has raved about the tour and the crystal. I'm so glad you had a wonderful time. How was Waterford Castle?"

"Haunted," Arthur barked.

"Beautiful," Clara said, shooting him a glare, which he ignored. "Don't listen to him. In fact, if you have a scone around, I'll stuff it in that big mouth of his."

He smirked, and she found herself smiling. God, he could be a boor, but she loved goading him.

"Trevor has a surprise for you," Becca said. "I hope you're ready for more fun."

"Fun? What did he do? Hire a circus?" Arthur extended a red hot to Becca. "It's an American cinnamon candy. I only give it to people I like."

She stared at it before accepting it. "Then thank you. I have dozens of things to prepare, but I'll see you at dinner. Don't spoil your supper. Chef Padraig and I have something special planned."

"Do you know where our boy is?" Arthur asked, warming Clara's heart with the phrase.

"He's outside. There's a pavilion close to the cliffs where people can take in the view comfortably. It's a favorite with guests who dislike heights."

"I'm not acrophobic," Clara said, eager to see what Trevor had in store for them.

"That's good," Becca said, her whole body stilling right before Clara's eyes. "It's a terrible thing to be afraid of something so severely. I'll leave you now."

As she hurried off, Clara stared after her. What had caused such a sudden change in the woman?

"Maybe she's afraid of heights," Arthur said.

"Well, it's none of our affair. Let's find our boy."

For all Arthur's joking, she knew Hargreaves was handling the things they'd brought home from Waterford. He'd been a downright dear like always, helping sort out which ornaments were for whom. Now that she had her very own family, she was already looking forward to Christmas.

For years, she'd dreaded the silent formal dinner with her now-deceased husband and the perfunctory exchanging of gifts. He'd always gotten her jewelry, and she suspected he'd shopped for her and for whatever woman he was carrying on with at the same time. But she hadn't let him ruin her love of diamonds or anything else sparkly. She wouldn't give that son of a bitch the satisfaction.

When they stepped outside, she heard the sound of laughter. Trevor's laughter. She'd missed the rascal, although his gift of a stay at the castle had been a luxurious treat, from the special champagne to chocolates he'd arranged to have for their room. She'd eaten every one of them with Arthur teasing her about preferring his red hots.

Grabbing Arthur's arm, she propelled him forward.

"See here, if I wanted to engage in speed walking, I would sign up for a group."

She continued to hurry him along, ignoring the token protest. The grass was a delicious green in the sunlight, reminding her of peridots. Had she brought that necklace?

She spotted the pavilion and noted Trevor wasn't alone. Other guests?

"Trevor!" she called out, pulling Arthur along.

"At least he's not talking with Buttercup," her husband said. "I saw that animal with its head on his shoulder the other day. Scandalous."

She snorted, watching as Trevor and his two companions stood. There was something about the jawline of the man—so reminiscent of her brother—and then she was running forward like a young girl, dragging Arthur with her. She'd only met the other children once before, at her wedding, but she hadn't forgotten the look of them.

"Clara! My God, woman, act your age."

She stopped short of launching herself at the handsome man who reminded her so much of her brother despite his longish sandy blond hair and casual T-shirt and jeans. "My goodness, Flynn." She extended her hand to the woman, who was beaming at her, resplendent in a beautiful plum dress, accentuating the long lines she'd gotten from her mother. "And Caitlyn. What a wonderful surprise! How did you..."

She gestured with her hand, so moved she was unable to speak.

Caitlyn hugged her. "Oh, Aunt Clara, it's so good to see you again. You were such a beautiful bride, but I wished we could have talked more."

She knew she was going to cry if she didn't pull herself together. The estrangement from her brother had hurt her deeply, and she'd grieved not knowing her nieces and nephews. But all of that had changed, thank God.

"Hello, Aunt," Flynn said, embracing her softly. "Are you as surprised as Trevor?"

"Yes," she said, pushing her soft hair from her forehead. "Goodness, you smell good. And you look so much like Shawn. I'm very sorry. I'm getting a little emotional."

Arthur put his arm around her and kissed her cheek. "No matter. It's always a special day when you get to see the younger generations. We didn't get to talk with these two much at the wedding. I believe you were off dancing that horrible line dance Jill staged."

Caitlyn hugged Arthur tightly and kissed his weathered cheek. "The Nae Nae. That was awesome."

"Awesome for you," he said, tousling her hair like she was a child. "I had nightmares on my very own honeymoon."

"Hello, Uncle Arthur," Flynn said, hugging him as well. "I've heard you're already on your second honeymoon. That's how I plan to roll too."

"When you have one foot in the grave like me, you have to space your honeymoons closer together."

Clara swatted him. "Oh, stop staying things like that. I told you we're both living to one hundred now that I've found you."

"Oh my God, that's so sweet," Caitlyn said, clutching her chest. "I might cry."

"Here's a handkerchief from Waterford Castle," Arthur said, not missing a beat. He pulled one from his pocket and handed it to her. "Clara bought two dozen of them in her shopping binge, God help us. So, Caitlyn, what brings you here? Was Trevor needing more family to rally the troops against Connor?"

Flynn's head jerked back. Trevor, who'd been smiling at the reunion, looked like his jaw had turned to stone.

"What's this?" Flynn asked.

Clara swatted Arthur again. "Now you've done it. For once, couldn't you have waited for an answer?"

"What's this about Connor?" Flynn asked, planting his feet in front of Trevor. His eyes darted to his sister. "Wait. Caitlyn knows, and I don't? Man, that *really* pisses me off."

"Hello, Uncle Arthur," Trevor said, rolling his eyes. "Aunt. I was planning on asking about your trip, but I need to deal with my brother here. Come on, Flynn. I'll tell you about it."

Caitlyn whistled as they watched the two men walk off. "Oh, Flynn is going to rip him a good one for keeping it a secret these past couple of hours. Hey, why don't we sit down? They might be a while. Flynn should be on our side about things, but no one likes this kind of a divide in our family."

Clara had become estranged from her brother over a business issue. It couldn't happen again. Not to these dear people. And not when she had finally found her way back to them. Of course, Shawn was still playing it cool, giving himself time to see if he could trust her. But J.T. and Trevor had both assured her they were tearing down their dad's remaining wall brick by brick, and that her marrying Arthur—whom Shawn admired—was doing the rest. Still, Shawn hadn't invited her and Arthur to visit him and Assumpta in their Napa home yet. Arthur told her to be patient. She was *trying*.

"Trevor will find a way to make it better," she said firmly. "I know it." Turning back to Caitlyn, who seemed preoccupied, she asked, "When did you arrive?"

"Earlier today. Trevor asked me for some help, and I used it as an excuse to visit. I had to meet Becca."

"And what did you think?" Arthur motioned for her to sit in one of the weathered chairs, and as soon as she did so, he sat beside her. Caitlyn took the empty seat on her other side.

Goodness, the view was incredible, but Clara looked back at Caitlyn because the presence of her niece here was the best view of all. In her brow line, she could see her mother.

"I love her! I mean, she's incredible. This place rocks, and her new hand-dyeing enterprise is freaking awesome. I've never bought yarn before—everything I do with fashion is a finished product—but I haven't even seen her work yet, and she's seriously making me consider taking up knitting."

"She's making me an Irish sweater," Arthur said, puffing out his chest.

"Oh, awesome! I can't wait to see it. Maybe she'd make me something."

He extended his legs like he was getting comfortable. "She only makes things for special guests, she said."

"I'm special," Caitlyn said, pointing to herself. "Is that a challenge, Uncle Arthur?"

"Are your ears clear, girl?" he spat back. "Take it however you want."

"You're so competitive sometimes," Clara said. "Now catch me up with you, Caitlyn."

She gave the young woman her full attention, soaking in her wit and her industriousness, as she spoke of her interest in the perfume industry. But Caitlyn broke off mid-sentence when Trevor and Flynn finally returned. Searching their faces, Clara couldn't tell what had transpired.

Flynn sat down in a free chair, and Caitlyn immediately kicked his crossed feet. "So?"

The boy took his time. She'd give him that. His cranky expression wasn't near as fearsome as her brother's when he got a bee in his bonnet.

"I don't like it," he simply said.

"What don't you like, Flynn?" Caitlyn glanced up at Trevor. "Clue me in. Are we busted?"

Trevor shook his head. "No, we have another ally in keeping this land safe."

"Hot damn," she said, rubbing her hands together, much like Clara wanted to do. "Good. I mean, this is going to be your home. Right, Trevor?"

Clara's heart simply melted when Trevor smiled.

As a woman who'd found love for the first time in the eve of her life, she knew how precious the feeling was.

CHAPTER 27

TREVOR HAD TO KICK CAITLYN OUT OF HIS ROOM SO HE could change for dinner.

Leave it to his sister to remind him that they all used to shuck off their clothes and go skinny-dipping in the pond on their property growing up. She playfully tugged on his pants, and he resorted to hauling her up bodily and depositing her outside his room as her gales of laughter filled the hallway.

What could he do but smile at that? He'd missed her laughter, the loon.

Flynn was off talking to his "lady," and they weren't due downstairs for dinner for another hour, so Trevor took the opportunity to check his texts once he'd changed. The first one made his balls shrivel. Connor had a way about him sometimes.

A family reunion? That's the update I get secondhand from Caitlyn's Facebook page when she posted a picture of The Wild Irish Rose. What in the hell are you doing? Trying to get Ms. O'Neill to like more Merriams so she'll be sympathetic and sell? Is this a new business strategy? Call me.

Shit.

The second text wasn't much better. It was from

Quinn, likely at Connor's beckoning.

Heard about the family reunion. Thinking about flying up. Call me.

Connor didn't have to replace him outright as his boots-on-the-ground negotiator. But he could send up Quinn. It would apply another crunch of pressure on him to do his job.

To Connor, he simply responded, *Everything is well in hand. My business strategies are pure genius. Don't be jealous.*

His reply to Quinn was more challenging. His brother ran their European operations from London, so he was only a short plane ride away. *You hate family reunions, remember? And you're still not sure about Aunt Clara. Don't come. You'll be a bear, and Flynn and I will have to pants you.*

Even though Quinn was three years older than Trevor, they'd all horsed around plenty growing up. He couldn't be sure how Quinn would respond to that crack about Aunt Clara, but it was on the money. He and Connor hadn't been as open to her return to the fold. Of the younger generation of Merriams, they were the most skeptical and closed off.

Connor replied, *Don't let me down. You know what's at stake.*

Quinn's response came moments later. *Pants me? Connor and I will kick your ass to kingdom come if you don't close this deal. I too am skeptical about the family involvement.*

He stared at his phone. God, he needed to call J.T. Stat.

His brother picked up his FaceTime call immediately, and Trevor had to school his features to look less panicked.

"Yo!" J.T. said.

"Hey! I wish you were closer. Caitlyn flew in from

Paris, and Flynn from Stockholm. We're having a ball." Minus the text threats and the developing family feud.

His brother grinned. "Damn, that sounds like fun. Makes me miss living in Rome, but only for the quick plane ride over. I should tell you that Caitlyn already texted me to say how much she loves Becca."

Of course she had. She'd even posted on Facebook, for God's sake. "Until today, she was the only other one I'd told about Becca. Flynn hopped over when Caitlyn did, sensing something was up. He knows everything now."

J.T. grimaced. "How'd he take it?"

"It wasn't easy for him, but he's not going to say anything."

His brother hadn't asked if there was anything he could do to help though. Flynn had thought staying neutral was the best course for him. Trevor hadn't tried to talk him out of it. After seeing Connor and Quinn's texts, he thought his brother pretty damn smart.

"Flynn is solid," J.T. said. "Look, I'm getting a little depressed over here about your lack of options. I think you're going to have to tell Connor about Becca."

He told his twin what he'd told Caitlyn. "I think Connor will call me fifty shades of unprofessional for falling for her. And still send Quinn in. Worse, he might suggest I use our relationship to get her to sell."

J.T. was silent. "I can see that. I talked to him yesterday. Some of it was catching up and some was my undercover attempt to see which way the wind was blowing. He's strung up pretty tight, tighter than I've ever seen him."

No shit.

"Con didn't ask outright," J.T. continued, "but he mentioned you might need my help closing the deal."

So Connor was planning on using J.T., perhaps, since Quinn was the nuclear option? He hung his head.

How had it come to this? He didn't feel like he could talk to his own brother. That he would be heard by him. "I hate this, J.T."

"I do too," his brother said darkly. "Do you need me to come see you? I know you have everything in hand, but if you think it'll help to have me around, I'll jump on a plane right now. You were always there for me during the divorce."

Trevor had certainly tried. He'd bolstered J.T. to keep fighting or cracked a joke when things had seemed hopeless. "This is nowhere near as bad as your divorce. The overall situation is crap, sure, but...I'm happy." He was hoping she'd join him and his siblings for a late-night drink after the restaurant closed. Sharing her with them, and them with her, made him happy in a way few things had.

"That's great to hear, man."

"Yeah. Look, I need to head out for dinner. But maybe it's time to expand our search. If we can find a better onshore location somewhere else, we might be able to convince Connor to sell the offshore tract here. Try something different altogether." He hadn't wanted to look at other countries, but what choice did they have? They weren't going to do better than the O'Neill land here in Ireland, and giving Connor something more attractive might be the only way to avert disaster.

"Am I wrong here, J.T.?" he asked, needing reassurance suddenly.

"No, you're not, given the situation. I'll start on other options while you're at dinner. Talk about pulling a rabbit out of my hat. A sizeable onshore oil field. Poof."

He sighed, knowing all too well it was a tall order. "Use your biggest wand, J.T."

"My wand is huge, bro. Have fun tonight. Wish I were there."

"Me too, man."

"Are you going to tell me you miss me?"

"No." Moron.

"I love you too. Say hi to everyone for me."

"You got it." Trevor signed off and stood gazing out the window.

His phone rang, and he looked down to see his mom calling to FaceTime him. He shook off his malaise and answered. "Hey."

"How did no one tell me three of my children were getting together at a beautiful bed and breakfast in the Irish countryside?"

"It was last minute. Caitlyn and Flynn flew in this afternoon. How are you?"

He didn't have to ask. At seventy-two, his mother didn't look her age, but the lines around her mouth were stark today.

"It's been hard," she said. "The children miss their dad, and they wake up crying. Sometimes from nightmares and other times from nothing at all. Olivia tries to be strong, but she's trying to take care of everyone else's needs. She wants to keep busy and shut it out. My presence here has been affecting that, no surprise."

"You were good to go to them, Mom," he said, his heart tightening. How did anyone recover from a sudden loss like that?

"Uncle Liam wasn't the right person. He's worried about Patrick now."

Great. Exactly what he wanted to hear today.

"I told him Connor is making everything safe so he needn't worry. You know me...I'm pretty good in tough situations."

"No one is better," he said, feeling like shit.

"In fact, I hope you know that I'm here for you if you need me."

All of the oxygen left his chest. Had Caitlyn let something slip? Or Flynn? "Why would you say that?" he asked cautiously.

"Three of my children got together on the spur of the moment, and you look troubled, honey, although you're trying to hide it."

He tried to breathe shallowly so she wouldn't hear. "Uncle Arthur and Aunt Clara are here and now two of my sibs. I'm having a blast."

"All right," she said. "I'll let it go. But you remember what I said, Trevor."

Great. Her mom-dar wasn't going to stop. "I know you'd drop everything if I needed you—I've always known that. It's why you're such a great mom."

She laughed. "You're so much like your father sometimes. Give everyone my love. Especially Clara. I keep telling Shawn we need to reach out to her and Arthur. You children seem to be rebuilding that bridge quite nicely, but it's time for us to put aside the past and do the same."

"How did Dad take that?" he asked.

"Like you did when I asked if you needed my help. Bye, honey."

She always got in the last word, much like Grandma Anna used to. "Bye."

When she clicked off, he started to pace. He felt like a noose was tightening on his neck, and he didn't like it one bit. Screw it. He was going to call Connor and tell him how he felt about Becca. No more of this pussyfooting around. His brother was going to find out anyway, and this wasn't how he wanted his life with Becca to start.

His brother picked up right away. "Tell me you finally got her to agree," he said without preamble.

"No," he said. "Look, Con, like I've told you repeatedly, she's not going to sell. But there's something else you need to know. I've fallen in love with her." There, he'd said it.

"I knew something was wrong!" His brother's laugh was almost sinister. "How could you, Trev? I expected better of you. I never imagined you'd let your family down, and over a piece of ass."

The first lash stung, but he'd expected it. "Okay, it's unprofessional, but I didn't plan this. And she's not a piece of ass. She's wonderful."

"*Right.* Seems J.T.'s bad choices with Sin City have rubbed off on you. This O'Neill woman is only screwing you to stop us from getting her land."

The second lash cut his flesh and had him seeing red. "Don't you dare talk about Becca or our brother like that again, damn you."

"No, damn *you*, Trev."

The emotion in his brother's voice stopped him cold.

"I gave Uncle Liam my word, Trev. At Corey's gravesite."

Oh, Jesus. "You've made this too personal, Connor. You're not hearing me."

"I'm sending Quinn," he said flatly. "You head back to Dublin and take the rest of the family with you. You're all acting like a bunch of jackasses on a holiday. Forget about the woman. Once we have her land, she won't want you anymore."

He sucked in a breath at the threat. "You don't mean that."

"This is business, Trevor. She'll sell to us, all right, if it's the last thing I do. Failure is not an option."

The man speaking to him was not the brother he'd known his whole life. Had grief ravaged him so? "Look, I have another solution I'm working on, one that will give you what you want. How many times have I pulled a rabbit out of the hat at the last minute? Con, give me a little more time. *Please.*" There was a long pause. He'd never begged his brother for anything in his entire life.

"Three days."

Connor hung up on him, and Trevor threw his phone aside, sick to his bones.

His brother's single-mindedness had turned into an obsession, and he would destroy Becca if he could.

He and J.T. had to find another tract of land.

His future with Becca was riding on it.

Chapter 28

Becca was adjusting the flower arrangement she'd created herself when she heard Aileen's laughter outside the Cellar door. She knocked the vase, and it wobbled. Nerves! All afternoon, they'd been tumbling through her stomach like stones skipping across a pond. She wanted the evening to be perfect, needed it. The table was set with their best dishes and flatware, and the linens had been dyed a pale gray from elderberries in their own vats.

"Oh, this place is so cool." Caitlyn came in, leading the Merriam party inside. "I love all the old stone and wooden beams. Hiya, Becca. Where have you been? Trevor told me all about your incredible hand-knit clothes. Girl, I need to see them."

She let out a shaky breath. *Hold it together. This is Trevor's family.* "I'll be happy to show you. Please, everyone! Come in. Chef Padraig has created a special feast for you tonight to celebrate Caitlyn and Flynn's visit."

"What about Clara and me?" Arthur said, pausing to kiss her on the cheek as he passed by. "Don't we rank a special meal?"

The wicked gleam in his eyes made her smile. "Anytime."

"Good to have someone finally acknowledge how special I am," Flynn said, flopping down in the end chair and reaching for the whiskey she'd set out. "I'm underappreciated in this family."

"Because you're a moron," Caitlyn said. "Oh, whiskey. Danger!"

"You're only saying that because you're a champagne junkie," Flynn said, popping the cork. "Trev? You drinking with me?"

She'd been watching him since he'd entered the room, taking in his strained jaw, his slightly too straight posture. Something was wrong. Was it her?

He locked gazes with her before smiling, but his face seemed drawn. "Damn straight."

"Count me in too," Clara said, coming over and putting her arm around Becca. "J.T., their brother, has been daring me to engage in a drink-off with Trevor here. He's immune to alcohol apparently, and proudly, I can drink like a fish."

"Trev's inhuman," Caitlyn said. "Aunt Clara, I would advise against this. No one in the family has topped Trev."

Trevor sat down and leaned his hands on the table as if testing its strength. "I like this place, Becca. Thanks for opening it up for us."

"You're welcome." She found herself flushing. Aileen poked her, and she looked over her shoulder to see her friend crane her head in the direction of the empty corner seat beside Trevor.

"You look a touch shook, dear," Aileen said in an undertone. "Now, pull it together and go sit by your man before someone takes the seat next to him."

Moment of truth time. She pushed her shoulders back and turned around, heading straight for Trevor, who was turning his highball glass in a circle, watching her. She pasted on a smile as she drew nearer.

"I thought I'd sit beside you for dinner," she said, her voice unsteady. "If you don't mind."

She worried from his demeanor that he *would* mind, but his eyes lit up, and his hand fell from the glass. "You're joining us?"

She cleared her throat. "I thought I'd take the night off to spend time with you and your family. If that's okay."

His hand covered hers and then slowly raised it to his lips for a sweet kiss. "You made my day." And she could tell he meant it. Whatever had been bothering him seemed to lose its hold, temporarily at least. He pulled her into the chair next to him, shifting until their thighs touched. He leaned close to her ear and whispered, "Thank you, babe."

Her heart blew open in her chest. Yes, this was the right decision.

"Becca? How are you in the drinking department?" Flynn gestured to the whiskey he was pouring for the table.

"Somewhere between a heavyweight and a lightweight, I suppose," she said. "Where is Hargreaves?" She'd hoped to see him tonight.

Clara made a rude sound. "He doesn't like to intrude on family occasions like this. He's so rigid about the butler rules sometimes."

"Would it be all right if I asked him to join us?" she asked.

Trevor snuck his hand around her waist. "I love the guy. Go ahead."

"It won't work," Arthur said, sniffing the whiskey Flynn had pushed across the table to him. "He doesn't break butler protocol. He only eats with us here in the mornings because Clara threatened to follow him to his separate table."

Flynn laughed. "I love that you have a butler, Aunt. It's so old-school."

She lifted her whiskey. "I'll show you old-school,

sonny. Like they say here in Ireland, *slainte*." Downing the entire contents of her glass, she smacked her lips.

"We're not doing shots, Clara," Arthur said, sipping his whiskey. "For heaven's sake. Have some decorum."

Flynn raised his glass and downed it. Trevor followed suit, giving Becca a wink.

Caitlyn lifted her glass, studying the liquid. "I can't do it."

Arthur patted her hand. "Good decision."

She loved how they were with one another, but it didn't feel right that Hargreaves was alone in his room.

"I'll be right back," Becca said, rising. "Aileen will bring in the first course shortly."

She rushed out of the Cellar and climbed the stairs to the main floor. She took the next steps two at a time and arrived breathless at Hargreaves' suite. Without stopping to think about how she should persuade him, only that she felt she must, she knocked on the door. When he opened it, his smile was warm and welcoming but still reserved.

He bowed. "Ms. O'Neill. What can I do for you?"

"Well, I hoped you might join us for dinner. I mean, I'm used to serving guests, but I'm sitting down with everyone for once, breaking a cardinal rule for me. But I knew it would mean a lot to Trevor and—"

"It's only natural you should join Trevor and his family given your relationship," Hargreaves said. "I still serve my mistress."

"But you're part of the family, Hargreaves," she said, wanting to put her hand on his arm in an entreaty but feeling it would be unwelcome.

"No, I'm not," he said, "and I know my place. But your place is by Trevor's side. I'm glad you've realized that."

Her throat grew thick. "I want to respect your feelings here, Hargreaves, but I know...well, what it feels like to be isolated, and I don't want that for you."

His smile cracked a fraction. "I don't feel isolated,

Becca. But I thank you for asking me to join you. Goodnight."

He was waiting for her to walk away so he could close the door. It would be rude to do it in her face, and he was never rude. "I made the appointment, Hargreaves."

"I'm glad, miss."

That was all she could hope for from him, she realized. He wouldn't bend. "We'll miss you. Have a pleasant night."

He nodded, and she walked off. The door closed quietly, shutting the older man up inside, and her heart clutched. Did he really want to be alone? All she'd wanted to do was wrap him up in a blanket she'd knitted and toast him.

Didn't he know his kindness had motivated her to change her life?

When she arrived back at the Cellar, she had to gather herself. The laughter emanating from the room boosted her mood, however, and she was finally able to walk in with a smile on her face. The first course lay untouched on the table.

"No luck?" Arthur asked. "I told you."

"Oh, don't be that way, Arthur," Clara said, tossing back another whiskey. "Hargreaves is Hargreaves, and I love him as he is."

"He completes her," Arthur joked.

Caitlyn laughed. "I want someone to say that to me someday."

Flynn groaned as Becca took her seat again. "Heaven help that guy."

"Hey! Don't be a jerk."

"You okay?" Trevor asked, his voice low by her ear. His warm fingers caressed her leg—a welcome reassurance.

"Yes," she said, scanning the table. "Oh, you shouldn't have waited for me. Please, everyone. Eat."

"What are we eating, Becca?" Caitlyn asked. She had a glass of champagne in front of her now, Becca was glad to see, beside the still-unfinished glass of whiskey.

She gestured to her plate. "This is our take on a crab cocktail with fresh tarragon, served with parsnip chips. I hope you enjoy it. If anyone doesn't like it, I can send for something else."

Trevor squeezed her leg. "It's wonderful, Becca."

Caitlyn scooped up the cocktail with her typical gusto, groaning as she chewed.

Flynn elbowed her. "Get a room, brat."

"Oh, stuff it. I intend to enjoy every bite of this." She scooped up another chip.

"It's delicious, Becca," Clara said. "Please tell Chef Padraig he's outdone himself."

She beamed, taking a chip in her hand. It was a little weird to eat like this, she realized—like it was an event in itself. Normally, she grabbed a bite in the kitchen or ate while going over business items in the office.

"Are you going to relax?" Trevor asked, still leaning toward her.

"Trying," she said between her teeth.

"Have some whiskey." He handed her his glass with a grin.

It felt more intimate that way, and she gave him a slow smile over the rim of the glass as she drank.

Flynn groaned then, and Caitlyn smacked him. "See, I told you this food was groan-worthy."

He leaned back in his chair and closed his eyes, chewing softly. "I'm going to need a moment here."

"Oh, pull it together," Arthur said. "I'm too old for food porn."

"Food porn," Clara said, barking out a laugh. "Where do you come up with these things?"

"I watched *The Food Network* the other night when I was jet-lagged." He waggled his eyebrows. "This is good, though. What did you call it, Caitlyn? Groan-worthy?"

"Oh, I just love you, Uncle Arthur," Caitlyn said, lifting her glass. "To family."

"My favorite toast," Arthur said, and Becca felt a surge of powerful warmth steal through her as everyone clicked their glasses.

She felt the power of the toast, like she was being enfolded into this big, beautiful family. Trevor took the opportunity to pull her even closer, and she didn't care that she was sitting partway off her chair.

The rest of the meal went off like clockwork, punctuated by laughter and stories, some outrageous, some dear. Flynn continued to tease Caitlyn about moaning over the food, only to turn around and do the same thing. Becca had never heard a family call one another so many names, brat and moron and silly head, so sweetly.

By the time the tray of desserts was served, Trevor and Clara were the only ones still drinking whiskey. Flynn had bowed out when he'd said he could feel the room wanting to spin. She hadn't known if he was serious. Caitlyn continued to sip champagne, and Arthur had long since asked for a black coffee.

She learned more about the rest of the Merriams from the questions Clara asked. Where was Michaela these days? The woman was on a superfood-seeking jungle trek through the Amazon, something Becca could scarcely imagine. Quinn sounded like a tougher version of Trevor, according to Caitlyn's assessment. He could be charming—he'd even been invited to Buckingham Palace once—but he could also stare you down like nobody's business. No one talked about Connor, and Becca wondered if it was a purposeful avoidance. Trevor had tensed up at his siblings' talk of Quinn, so they'd likely taken the hint not to continue.

Clara spoke about her grandfather, Emmits Merriam, who'd been Arthur's mentor back in the day, and she loved hearing both of them talk about this larger-than-life man who'd struck oil in Oklahoma and built an empire.

"Becca," Flynn said, running his spoon slowly through the sticky toffee pudding. "Tell us more about your new enterprise. Trev says you're raising animals for wool and then hand-dyeing it here."

"Her dyes are beautiful, Flynn," Caitlyn said. "Aileen took us on a tour."

Her sprits lifted like sails catching wind. "The Irish hand-dyed yarn market has been booming the past couple of years, and it struck me how our bed and breakfast might be a strong player. We have a solid online presence from former and repeat guests. Plus, our guest volume continues to increase, and many of our visitors are interested in Irish handcrafts or locally made yarn. You'd be amazed how many women knit or crochet. It's making a comeback as an art form, what with all the new yarn."

The whole table was staring at her, and she looked down in her lap, suddenly self-conscious.

"I'm sorry to have gone on like that," she said.

"Are you kidding?" Caitlyn said, standing up and leaning across the table to gently sock her shoulder. "That's how we talk at home. The more passion, the better. Right, Trev?"

She looked over to see him grinning at her, all admiration. "You can see why I'm totally in love with her."

"I thought you were in it for the alpaca," Arthur said, chuckling.

"Buttercup and I have come to an understanding," Trevor said, making her smile. "She knows there can be no one for me but this woman here."

"Oh, I love hearing you talk like that," Caitlyn said. "Mom is going to be so happy when you tell her."

Becca had to take a breath at that. The weight of what she still hadn't told Trevor bore down on her. He was talking about forever, and his sister was talking about their mother, and he still didn't know...

"Tell me more about raising the animals," Flynn said. "What does it entail and what are your profit projections?"

This was such an easy question, and she was eager to answer it and move the conversation along.

Flynn peppered her with more business questions as she picked at her dessert of buttery brioche. On some level, Becca knew it was both a test of her acumen and a vetting process.

"So you're a woman of means," Caitlyn said, toasting her. "Way to go, Becca. It's like our mom always tells us. You have to stand on your own. That's why we all have our own niche in the company. Except J.T. now. He's establishing a world-class art museum at the university Grandpa Emmits founded in Dare Valley."

"And he and my great-niece are doing a damn fine job of it, aren't they, Clara?" Arthur asked proudly.

"Yes," she said, laying her head against Arthur's shoulder.

"Are you falling asleep?" her husband asked her in disbelief. "Has the whiskey finally gotten to you?"

"No, only happily content," Clara said. "It's been a wonderful night. Trevor, my boy, I believe you and I are a draw in the drinking department."

"Seems so, Aunt," Trevor said, lifting his whiskey in a toast. "To being superhuman."

"Oh, to live forever," Clara said, her smile radiant. "So much family to enjoy now."

"We should leave these young people, my dear, before you fall asleep on my shoulder." Arthur kissed her forehead. "Becca, it was a beautiful meal."

The older generation stood to leave, and everyone hugged and kissed them. After they left, Flynn pushed back and kicked his legs out.

"You and J.T. weren't fooling," he said, looking at Trevor. "Aunt Clara's terrific. I can't believe she and Dad had a rift."

"Her first husband came between them. He was apparently a total jerk, and Dad didn't like him one bit." Caitlyn scrunched up her face. "Imagine being married to a prick like that."

"Now she's with Uncle Arthur," Trevor said. "Good hands."

"The best," Caitlyn said, finishing off her champagne. "I'm off to bed too. Becca, can you show me your knitwear tomorrow? I want to be properly enthusiastic, and right now all I want to do is snuggle in my bed and go to sleep."

"Come on, brat," Flynn said. "I'll make sure you reach your room."

She swatted at him as he lifted her out of her chair. "I'm sleepy, not drunk."

"I know." He turned and smiled at Becca with new warmth in his eyes. "Becca, thank you for a wonderful evening. The food was excellent and the company mostly top-notch."

"You're such a jerk," Caitlyn said, punching him. "Thank you, Becca. Everything was so wonderful. Night, Trev."

She kissed her brother on the cheek. Flynn lifted his hand in a wave that was at once lazy and jaunty, and Trev lifted his chin in acknowledgment. They both departed, leaving Trevor and Becca alone at the long, empty table.

"Do you have any idea how much I love you, Ms. O'Neill?" he finally asked, pulling her chair around until it faced him.

Then he leaned in and kissed her until she was breathless. "Goodness."

He cupped her cheek. "I'm glad you like them. It's... important to me. Family means everything."

"I want them to like me."

"Don't worry about that," he said, running his finger along her collarbone in the most enticing way. "That's a slam dunk."

What did that mean? But her curiosity gave way to thoughts of Connor and the tougher-than-Trevor brother, Quinn. She doubted *they* would be a slam dunk.

"You're thinking about Connor, and I'm starting to do the same," Trevor said, opening her legs and letting his hand trail up her thigh. "We need to stop that right now."

She lurched forward when his hand cupped her core. "We should go upstairs."

"Is someone coming down to clean up?" he asked, rubbing against her, lighting all sorts of fires.

Aileen would surely be off to bed, wouldn't she? It was nearly midnight. On occasions such as these, someone normally came down to clean up first thing in the morning. "I don't think so."

"Does the door have a lock?" he asked, pressing against her in a way that made her hips move in response.

Oh my, but he knew where to touch her. Their first time together had been sublime, and each time was better than the last. "Yes."

He swung out of his chair and hit the lock. When he returned, he pulled her onto his lap. "I've been thinking about taking you in here all night."

Is that what he'd been thinking when he'd looked at her like she was dessert? "You have?"

Pushing the dishes and flatware out of the way, he settled her onto the table. "I'm about to expand your horizons, Ms. O'Neill," he said, unzipping his pants and pulling at her clothes.

If only he knew how true that was...

CHAPTER 29

TREVOR SLIPPED OUT OF BECCA'S CLOSET, WHERE CAITLYN was on a fashion tear, oohing and aahing over Becca's knitwear. They'd been acting like total girls for about an hour, something that made him happy even if their chatter was like a foreign language. Becca was making time for his family, and he'd shown her in every way he knew how, until the sun was rising, how much that meant to him.

He slipped into the living room so he couldn't be overheard and dialed J.T. back in response to his text. God, he hoped his brother had found something he could use. "You're up early."

"I've been working all night after you texted me about your last call with Connor," J.T. said. "How do you feel about Croatia?"

"Fine beaches and nice people," Trevor said cautiously, wondering if Becca would be up for quick beach weekend sometime. "Why?"

"I talked to one of my most trusted sources about our problem, and he said he's been hearing about something potentially big in the Dinarides. It's been kept quiet by the locals because they're afraid of the Russians moving in on it and pulling their usual crap."

The Russians were both respected and feared in the oil and gas world. Lots of companies paid to grease the wheels, but many Russians also employed violence as part of their ongoing business strategy. "How big?"

"Not as big as the Irish projections, but close," J.T. said. "The high-risk nature of working in the Dinaric Alps will eat into some of our profit margin, but the government is behind the project, and it's on land. It's the best option I've come across. I know we can't guarantee Connor that we'll be awarded the land, but—"

"We're running out of time," he said.

"And Quinn will be on your doorstep in two days, God help you."

His heart was like a stone in his chest, the laughter coming from the closet in the other room adding to the weight. He had to handle this fast, and in a way that protected Becca and her interests.

"I was up early and have a few ideas about how to protect her land," Trevor said. "I haven't run it by Becca yet. I'm trying to rebuild some more trust here." Besides, he didn't want to mess up the fun she was having with his family. Flynn had managed to talk her into joining them for breakfast in the Cellar after running it past Aileen.

She'd surprised everyone, including herself, by calling Flynn a moron in response to his jokey request that she knit him some boxer shorts because he was packing some fine merchandise.

"All right," Trevor said. "Send me your numbers, and I'll write up the report. This will have to be the best pitch of my life." He hoped to Christ Connor would listen to him.

"Already started," J.T. said. "I have a better way with the written word than you do, man."

He got choked up. "You're writing my report? It's like that history report on the Ottoman Empire in fifth grade all over again."

"Mrs. Prequire had it in for you," J.T. said. "I couldn't let my twin flunk and risk him being held back."

No, J.T. had thought it unjust, swearing he'd make sure his brother aced the final report. There was no way they were going to be separated in school.

"Thanks for having my back then," Trevor said. "And now."

"More like your ass," J.T. shot back. "But regardless of the body part, I've got ya, bro. You sure you don't want me to talk to Connor with you when you pitch it?"

In a weak moment, sure, but he was a man and a professional. Mostly he was worried about letting Connor down. "It's my job. It will be fine. I'll do it tomorrow so I can have some practice time." He'd even make up a few Power Point slides.

"Positive thinking," J.T. said. "I like it. Okay, I'm going to hang up and flesh this out. Give me a few hours to get it to you."

"How certain are you that we can get our hands on this land in the Dinarides?" Trevor asked.

"I got an unofficial wink, which is by no means a guarantee," J.T. said. "In a fair fight, we beat the Russians every time."

But the fights weren't always fair, and they'd lost out before. "How fast do we need to move?"

"It's been kept quiet for a few weeks," J.T. said. "They just finished the final exploration and mapped the tract out with geothermal. It could have leaked, but I don't think so. Secrets are best kept when people are afraid they'll get screwed, and in this case, the locals have that fear. Big time."

Great. Another cesspool working environment. Connor would love that. More than once, he'd said he couldn't wait for the straightforwardness of Ireland. "Thanks, bro."

"You got it. See ya."

"Yeah, later," he said, hanging up.

The laughter in the closet hadn't faded, and Trevor felt a wet nose brush his hand. He looked down to see Boru staring up at him. The dog gave a woof and laid his head against Trevor's leg, as if comforting him.

"It's going to be fine," he said, stroking the dog's coat.

It had to be.

CHAPTER 30

FLYNN MERRIAM HAD BEEN FOLLOWING BECCA AROUND The Wild Irish Rose all afternoon. Trevor had peeled off from them hours ago, claiming he had some work to see to. Surely it had something to do with his brother's plans for her property, but she hadn't asked and there wasn't any time to dwell. Flynn reminded her of a determined rooster, pecking questions at her nonstop. But he'd already proven himself useful by suggesting a couple of technology upgrades to her online registration system and a new phone app to manage guest requests on the fly—connected to the kitchen, no less. Behind his Calvin Klein looks and shaggy hair beat the heart of a computer nerd. Who knew?

She'd continued to feed him scones, hoping for more morsels of brilliance, as he combed over her operations.

The trouble came when Flynn expressed an interest in seeing the rabbits. She'd only ventured out to the shed twice since they'd bought the rabbits. The first two times, she'd hyperventilated halfway there and had to squeeze her eyes shut and focus on her breathing before continuing. After only a peek at her new animals, Boru had led her back at a swift pace. And yet something had prevented her from denying Flynn's request outright. It occurred to her that if she walked to the shed where they kept the rabbits ahead of time, meeting Flynn there, no one would notice her discomfort.

She arranged everything with Flynn, but Cian insisted on accompanying her. "Are you sure you're up to this, Becca?" he asked. They stood by the back door, preparing to make the journey.

"If you're with me, I'll be grand." Even if she had to grit her teeth the whole way. "Your wrinkles are more pronounced when you stare so," she said, forcing a light tone. "In fact, your face might freeze that way."

The jest didn't make him smile. "I don't like this, Becca. It's a risk, making yourself walk out that far with them around. What if they see you?"

"Aileen is going to keep them occupied until we're there," she said, patting him on the arm. "This is important to me. I want to do this for Flynn." And she wanted to prove to herself that she could do it.

"We should have built the shed closer to the main house," he said, shaking his head.

"No, we shouldn't have. We didn't know if the rabbits would smell in the summertime. Plus, we didn't want guests to be uncomfortable with the presence of so great a warren."

"Or have them take the rabbits out of the cages and play with them like pets," he said. "I know, I know. All right. Let's go. Boru! Come."

The dog trotted over to her, his red leash in his mouth. Cian wrapped the end around her palm. She gripped it tightly, trying to smile.

"You focus on Boru here," Cian said. "I'll be right beside you."

Her heart was already racing as she turned to face the back door. She reached for it before Cian could. It was important that she do it. The door flew open with her firm push and banged against the stone, much like her heart beating in her chest. The land stretched out in front of her, like an endless carpet of green and sea and sky. There was so much of it, and she was so small in comparison. Something could happen to her out there. It was so far, and...

No, she was going to make it.

The breeze rushed over her face, and every hair on her body stood up, fear covering her like sticky spider webs.

Who was she kidding? She was vulnerable out there. God, she was going to hyperventilate again. Boru barked.

Breathe.

Another bark sounded from Boru, and he nudged her hard in the thigh with his nose. She looked down. His big brown eyes were staring at her, demanding attention. He barked again.

"Okay," she said, shaking like a leaf. "Let's go." It was now or never.

That first step outside was always the hardest. One. Two. Three. She continued to count. There were three hundred and eighty steps to the shed.

Best not think about that, she thought. *Just keep counting one at a time.*

Sweat pooled between her breasts, on her temples, and slid down her back. The hand holding Boru's leash grew damp. When she reached one hundred, Boru barked, and Cian whispered, "Way to go, love. Just a little bit farther."

Her gaze slid up past the grass punctuated by moss and stone. She saw the flat, empty stretch ahead, the shed punctuating it like an exclamation mark. Anxiety splashed over her like a wave. It was still so far away. She couldn't do this. Seeing stars, she stopped, her knees giving out.

Cian caught her as she was sinking to the ground. "I've got you, love. Hold onto me and Boru."

She placed one hand on the dog's back and the other around Cian's waist. Her lungs screamed for more oxygen as her heart pounded double-time in her chest.

"Breathe," Cian said, his voice as steady as his hands. "You can do this. You're a brave girl. Always have been."

That firmed up her muscles. Yes, she was brave. Down to her bones. She'd made it this far. She thought of Trevor and all the visions she'd had of them holding hands, walking about the land. She *would* do this.

"Let's continue," she said, forcing resolve into her voice.

One hundred and one. One hundred and two. Boru gave three consecutive barks and seemed to increase his speed. For a moment, it was like she was in a sled being pulled by a team of Alaskan huskies in the Arctic. Yes, she was a famous explorer, facing perilous conditions, but she continued her trek.

One hundred and nine. One hundred and ten.

She felt the reins around her hands as if they were a part of her. She heard Cian's steps along the stone and moss at her side. When the wind brushed her body, she squared off against it. *You're not going to stop me*, she thought.

At two hundred, the feeling of victory sparked to life inside her, so rare and precious, she almost wept. She increased her speed, everything quickening in anticipation. Boru started to prance, and then she was racing forward over the stones and shades of green under her feet, chugging like a steam engine.

In this moment, she felt certain nothing could hold her back.

"Three hundred and three," she called out loud, her mind calculating only fifty more steps to go. She kept her focus on the ground flashing under her feet, and then she saw the shadow of something. The shed! She raised her gaze and sank to the ground in relief.

Wrapping her arms around Boru's neck, she wept. Cian's hand stroked her hair, and she reached for his hand.

"Oh, you're a brave one. The grandest of us all, dear Becca."

His words were a hot blade cauterizing the pain in her heart. She'd made it. And this time, she was going to stay out here. See and hold her very own animals. Give Flynn his tour. Perhaps she would even dare to look up at the sky and the long horizon back to her home. She dreamed about the view of the main house from vistas on her land. Sometimes she looked at the pictures she'd had taken by a professional photographer, the ones she'd put on the website, and longed to see the glorious sight in person.

Today she could.

Today was a new beginning.

Cian left her, and she shakily rose to her feet, wiping away tears. He came back to her with a fat brown rabbit cradled in his arms, its nose twitching as it sniffed the air.

"Oh, you're a darling," she said, holding her hands out and letting Cian transfer the rabbit to her.

"This is Margaret the Hospitable," Cian told her, crushing her heart with his sentimentality. "I like to think you're a modern Margaret O'Carroll of Éile. Medieval queen. Patron of the arts. A builder. What say you?"

"You're going to make me cry again," she said, pressing her face into the bunny's soft fur to gather herself. "No queen surely, but I'll take the others." Oh, the grand plans she had for this land. She could feel her grandmother at her back and all her other ancestors who'd loved this land.

"I figured you'd like knowing I named some of the rabbits and sheep," he said, his grin downright fairy-like. "Not all, of course, but some of the animals aren't only animals."

No, they were both Irish enough to know the souls of special people resided in certain animals. "I love it."

He grinned. "Your party is coming. Seems Flynn wasn't the only one interested in the rabbits. The whole Merriam family is on its way. Even Clara and Arthur." She was turning her head before Cian's hand stopped her. "Let them come to you. Focus on me and Margaret and this grand dog." Boru barked, and she transferred the rabbit to one arm so she could stroke his head.

Yes, let them come. She was ready for them.

Their laughter reached her ears, and she smiled at their gaiety as her eyes tracked over all the rows of rabbits. Sixty rabbits required a lot of space, and God knew, she and Cian wanted them to have room. They multiplied quickly.

"How many rabbits do you have here?" Flynn boomed out as the Merriams reached them.

"My God, it's like *Alice in Wonderland* exploded all over the Irish countryside," Caitlyn called, rushing forward. "Oh, look at this one. Can I hold it?"

The furry gray rabbit was adorable, what with its pale nose twitching.

"I've got a rabbit in mind for you, Caitlyn," Cian said, crossing to one of the cages. "This is Osiris, and he's as dark as the Egyptian god he's named after and as calm as he is clever."

"Sounds like me," Trevor said, coming to stand beside Becca.

Their eyes locked, and his entire face was transformed by his ear-to-ear smile. Her chest grew warm, looking at him. Oh, to be this free, to be outside with him and on her land, surrounded by his family. This was her future.

No, she corrected. *This is your present*.

"I want a rabbit," Clara said, planting her feet on the ground. "Arthur?"

"I gave up everything rabbit-related in 1987 after watching *Fatal Attraction*," he said, popping a red hot in his mouth.

"Oh, yuck!" Caitlyn made a gagging sound. "That's so disgusting. I hated that movie."

"And you aren't even a man," Flynn said, tapping the side of his head. "That movie will mess with your mind. Becca, run me through things."

"Cian runs the show out here," she said, gazing at him fondly. "When we started this new enterprise, he said he'd care for the animals and work with some local farmers who have experience with the shearing. It's been a match made in heaven."

"You have a lot of space for them," Flynn said, stroking Caitlyn's rabbit. "More than I expected."

"If you're going to claim ethically sourced yarn, you need to meet certain conditions. We conform to the Responsible Wool Standard."

Trevor plunked a fluffy white rabbit down in Flynn's arms. "She's so sexy when she talks business."

"You can get a room later," Flynn said, stroking the rabbit's fur. "Tell me more about your operation, Becca. I think I'm getting in touch with my inner farmer."

Caitlyn laughed. "Yeah, you really strike me as Old MacDonald. Becca, you should start rabbit yoga out here."

"Cian already mentioned it," she said.

"I mean, seriously! There isn't a good yoga studio in town. Believe me, I checked. My muscles have been begging for it."

"Can't you just bend over in that down dog thing anywhere?" Arthur asked, chuckling under his breath. "Clara, dear, you're going to have fur all over you." She held two rabbits, one in each arm.

"All the more to pick off later, my dear," she said, grinning outright.

Flynn laughed. "Man, I want to still be having sex at eighty. You guys give me hope. Before I thought getting old sucked."

"It does," Arthur said, rubbing his hip dramatically. "But the sex is still good if you make it."

Becca laughed as she brought Flynn deeper into the shed. Cian joined them, pointing out various details only he would know, letting her answer questions more in her wheelhouse, including the fact that two rabbits needed to be sheared to make one sweater, for example.

Margaret the Hospitable snuggled against her chest, and Boru walked with them, stopping to sniff at some of the rabbits sniffing back at him from inside their cages. Becca liked the feel of the rabbit on her hands, but even Margaret's silky soft fur couldn't compare with the warmth of Trevor's hand on her back.

"We're still experimenting with the best cruelty-free methods of obtaining fur," she told Flynn, who was a human sponge for information. "We've done shearing so far, which combines both long and short hairs, not ideal. Cian has been thinking through brushing."

"What's that?" Flynn asked.

"Well, as you can see from my hands," she said, holding one up, "Angora hair comes off easily. If we brush each rabbit, we'll get only the long hairs, which is the best for what we want in our wool. Cian suggested we need to look into pet therapy. What if we brought rabbits into hospitals and hospices and had the patients brush them for therapy? It would help the people who are ill, and we'd have natural helpers in expressing more fur."

"That's genius," Flynn said. "Not everyone likes cats or dogs, right, but rabbits for pet therapy? Perfect. Like Caitlyn said, they use them in yoga. Surely that's a sales angle."

She loved Flynn's open-mindedness. Before coming

here, he likely had never considered the ins and outs of yarn production, but here he was asking questions and suggesting ideas for further growth. "I'm reconsidering the yoga studio, Cian. It *would* bring more people to The Wild Irish Rose." They could convert the old barn after making some improvements perhaps.

"Maybe Aileen could become an instructor," Cian said, stretching his arms up overhead like he was doing some crazy yoga pose. "I wouldn't mind her getting more limber."

"Oh, you're terrible," she said, laughing. "Arthur is rubbing off on you."

"Arthur should rub off on everyone, my dear," Cian said. "He's taking a second honeymoon directly after his first at eighty."

"Enough said." Trevor met and held Cian's gaze as they all stopped. "Right, Cian?"

Her friend only took a moment to regard him before answering, "Right."

As an olive branch, it wasn't much, but her heart melted anyway. Whatever Cian's remaining concerns might be, he'd softened with the arrival of Trevor's family. Aileen had confessed he'd been downright humbled at the way they'd opened their arms to Becca.

"Okay, how much for a pair of, say, rabbit mittens?" Flynn asked. "Of this quality."

She did the calculation in her head. "Only Angora? About two hundred and thirty Euros."

"That's two hundred and sixty dollars," Flynn said, whistling. "Nice. But you need more rabbits, Becca. If you only made mittens, that would be fifteen thousand per year. Chump change given all the work you're putting in."

"What?"

"He means it's small potatoes," Trevor said. "Flynn, leave the woman be. She's only just starting. Plenty of time for expansion."

"Yes, but think about the market potential," Flynn said. "Ask Caitlyn about the luxury fur market. That's her jam. Seriously, Becca. You need a capital investor, and I just might be it."

A capital investor? She clutched the rabbit in reflex, and it squirmed. "Sorry, Margaret. Oh, Flynn..."

"No, I'm serious here," Flynn said. "Caitlyn loves what she's been seeing, and so do I—although we bring two different lenses to this. She's in love with your final product, and I'm in love with your original product. Seriously, are you open to me thinking up some ideas and putting them down on paper?"

She looked at Cian, whose face was unreadable, and then at Trevor. There was a slight smile on his lips. "Flynn doesn't talk about capital investment unless he's dead serious. And in case you're wondering if it's because I'm in love with you, don't."

"No, I'd want to do this if I met you on the street," Flynn said. "You have a good thing going on here, and the luxury market is ridiculous. Again, ask Caitlyn."

"I will," she said, her head swimming. Did she want to expand that much? She hadn't thought much beyond her dyeing in the old kitchen, but that didn't mean she couldn't think bigger, dream bigger. It was how she'd gotten to where she was now. "Let's join the others."

Cian picked up her cue. "I need to talk to Becca about some business. Why don't you head back to the main house? Aileen will have some scones and tea. We'll see you in a bit."

Trevor kissed her cheek, and the rabbit lurched into his arms. "Seems Margaret knows a good thing when she sees it."

Becca was laughing when she heard the *chop chop chop* of a helicopter approaching. Her entire body locked in place. Her mind flashed back to the large sleek black helicopters she'd seen in the war zones of her childhood.

They'd brought soldiers and death and ferried the wounded off after disaster. That repetitive mechanical cranking sound had been present the night her parents had been shot and killed.

Danger.

Everything went cold and clammy as she started to tremble like the vibrations that were even now coming closer, getting louder. Something bad was going to happen. She fisted her hands together at her sides, squeezing her eyes shut as her heartbeat surged in her chest.

"That's a helicopter," Flynn remarked. "That's weird."

"Trevor and Flynn, why don't you go see what it is?" Cian suggested.

Someone's hand was on her back, but she couldn't move. She'd become a wall of stone. The sound reverberated in her ears, making her head hurt.

"Becca," she heard Trevor say, his warm hands on her arms. "What's wrong?"

"You and your brother should leave," Cian said. "Now."

The pulsing was screaming overhead, and she could hear the blades whooshing. She sank to her knees, covering her ears, wanting to hide.

"Becca!" Trevor called. He sounded panicked, but no more so than she felt. The sound was screaming in her eardrums now, the ground beneath her shaking.

Someone put both hands on her shoulders. "Make it stop!" she shouted.

"I have you, girl," Cian called, pulling her against his chest. "Go and wave that wanker off."

"What's wrong with her?" Flynn asked.

"She's afraid of helicopters," she heard Cian say.

Her mind flashed to another day when a helicopter had hovered overhead. A barrage of bullets had struck their house. Wood and concrete had flown through the air, hitting her body and face in the closet where she was hiding. Through the blistered holes in the wood, she'd seen her mom and dad lying on the floor.

They didn't move when she screamed their names. Then blood had started to trail across the floor toward her. She'd crawled back into the corner of the closet, but the wetness had finally reached her, making her shake uncontrollably.

"Becca," Trevor said, urgent by her ears. "Let me help."

She was shaking too hard to reach out to him. She couldn't reach out. Her arms wouldn't move.

"Go! Wave the eejit off. It's the only way you can help her."

Trevor squeezed her hand and ran out of the enclosure.

"She needs a doctor," she heard Flynn say.

"I'm a doctor!" Cian shouted, his arms fisting around her. "I have you, Becca. Hold onto me."

The shed shuddered with the force of the helicopter. It was like the entire earth was rumbling under her. She pressed her face into Cian's chest and held on, the sound growing louder. "Make it stop. Please."

"Hang on, Becca. Just hang on." Cian kissed her head, squeezing her with all his might.

Heart beating, lungs screaming for air, she felt her muscles lock in place. Cian was rocking her, and she gripped his shirt to hang on, needing an anchor.

"Let me take you back to the house," Cian said. "Boru will be—"

"No!" she shouted. Danger was out there. She had to stay here.

"Okay, we'll take a moment," Cian said, his voice breaking. "As long as you need."

"Oh, Becca!" She heard Caitlyn and then slender arms were wrapping around her from behind. Boru was whining, his paw laid on her leg.

She kept her eyes closed, the dark her only comfort.

If she couldn't see, she couldn't be afraid. If she couldn't see, she could tell herself she was safe.

But today it was only lies.

Chapter 31

THE LOOK IN HER EYES WOULD STAY WITH HIM FOREVER. Sheer terror.

Trevor rushed outside to see a black helicopter landing a short distance from the shed. The Merriam name and logo were on the door, and he cursed. It could only mean one thing. His brother had lied about the three days.

"Oh shit, is that Quinn and Connor?" Flynn asked, joining him.

Both of them? Sure enough, the door opened, and he watched as their older brothers descended from the helicopter. He ran toward the cockpit, his thoughts flying to Becca. "Shut it down!"

A pilot he recognized as Quinn's regular waved at him. He knocked on the window. "Shut it off!"

A heavy hand gripped his shoulder, and he turned to see Connor there, frowning at him. The judgment in his eyes wasn't nearly as horrible as the fear in Becca's gaze. "Come on."

He shook his brother off, banging on the glass again. "Kill it."

The pilot finally shook his head, pointing to his headphones. Trevor made a slicing motion to his neck. If he could have climbed in the helicopter, he would have killed the engine himself.

"He's taking off," Connor yelled at him. "Let's go."

He planted his feet. "No! I need him to stop the noise." Becca was crouched on the floor like a frightened animal. "Tell him to cut the engine, Con. I mean it. We have someone with a fear of helicopters in there. Tell him!"

His brother walked back to the door and stuck his head in to convey the message, thank God. Quinn was talking to Flynn out of range of the chopper, decked out in one of his fancy gray London-tailored suits. Shit. He was so screwed. If Con had flown all the way from California—and picked up Quinn along the way—he was in for the ass chewing of a lifetime.

But all he could think of was Becca. What could he do to help her? He'd only walked out because she'd wrapped herself around Cian like a vine, and it had seemed of paramount importance to stop the noise.

The engine died, and the rotors slowed. He put his hand against the side of the chopper, trying to gather himself. He wanted to kick the thing into the sea after seeing what it had done to Becca.

He rounded on Connor. "You said I had three days, damn you! And then you show up in a fucking chopper? Couldn't you and Quinn drive up like normal people—for once in your goddamn life? Do you have any idea what you've done?"

He tried to walk around Connor to the shed, but his brother slapped him back. "Are you kidding me? You're jumping on *my* ass? After Quinn got a call that we're in the running for an oil tract in Croatia? Fuck you!"

"Fuck you, Con!" He shoved him back. "I was going to tell you tomorrow. Why do you think I asked for the extra time?" Done in by a leak. Talk about bad luck.

Running past him, he entered the shed. Uncle Arthur had his arm around Aunt Clara.

"What's wrong with Becca, Trevor?" she asked, her brow line stark.

"She's afraid of helicopters," he said, still in shock at the speed with which things had happened. How did one develop such a specific phobia? Then he thought about kids who feared vacuum cleaners and huddled in corners. Who could account for fear? All he wanted was to help her.

"Get Aileen," he said, and his uncle nodded.

The woman was like a mother to her. Surely she would be of help. Cian had jumped into action immediately, like he'd had some experience helping allay her fear. But how often did helicopters show up in this part of Ireland? It seemed crazy.

His aunt firmed her shoulders and said, "We'll get her right away."

But there was no need. He caught sight of her running toward the shed. So she'd heard the helicopter and known enough to come on her own.

Quinn was headed his way as well, his loose-legged stride like a cowboy in the Old West. Trevor knew what it meant. He was about to get fucked up.

"Not now!" He pointed at his brother and disappeared farther into the shed.

When he reached Becca, his heart seized up in his chest. Cian had Becca in his arms, and Caitlyn was hugging her from behind, flanking his woman. Boru lifted his head and stared at him, giving a pained whine. His heart rose up in his chest, and he felt tears fill his eyes. God! How could something do this to her? She was one of the strongest women he'd ever met.

"What can I do?" he asked, his voice raw.

Cian raised his head, and there were tears in his eyes. "Can you bring Aileen to our girl?"

Jesus, he was going to lose it. "She's coming right now."

Cian closed his eyes as if offering up a prayer. "Good. Can you go get my car then? It's a red Volkswagen Golf. Corner of the parking lot. Keys under the seat. Drive it straight up here. We need to get Becca back to the house."

He nodded and turned around, only to run directly into the hard frame of Connor. "That's the owner of this place?"

"Get out of here, Con," Caitlyn said, her cheeks wet with tears.

"We need to talk," his brother said to him. "Right now."

Did his brother not see Becca huddled on the ground like that? Did he even care? No, his brother had called her a "piece of ass." She was nothing to him. Irrational anger burned a hole in his gut, and he pushed his finger into his brother's chest. "Get out of here! I don't want you to see her like this."

Grabbing his brother's arm, he hauled him back a few steps before Connor shoved him. "What's wrong with you?"

"I need you to get out of here right now," he said, his voice hard. "Your helicopter messed Becca up."

"Where is she?" Aileen asked, her face white.

"Down the row and to the right," he said.

"I'll show you," Flynn said. Quinn had trailed him into the warren, and he turned to look at him and said, "I say this with love, but you and Con need to leave."

The brothers drew up in their suits. "You grounded our chopper. Where are we supposed to go?"

"I don't care," Trevor said, "but get the hell out of my way."

He dashed past them, running out of the shed. The parking lot was on the other side of the house, and he was breathing hard by the time he reached Cian's car. He fumbled for the keys under the seat and punched them into the ignition. He hadn't been in a car this old for ages, but he started it just fine and punched the gas, heading to the edge of the lot and then onto the flats. Aunt Clara and Uncle Arthur were walking back to the house, and even though they lifted their hands in greeting, he kept his hands on the steering wheel. Every fiber of his being was anxious to get back to her. To help her. To comfort her. He was single-minded in his approach.

At the shed, he put the car in park and left the engine idling. The pilot was walking around the now-silent helicopter. Trevor still couldn't take it all in. Minutes ago, everything had been fine, and then his brothers had shown up in the helicopter, and now Becca was having some sort of an episode.

He ran to the shed, passing Quinn and Connor, who were arguing with Flynn.

Becca was still shaking when he arrived. Aileen was on the floor beside her, along with Caitlyn, God bless her. The older woman was singing to Becca. His throat stopped up, and he couldn't breathe. She looked like a crumpled piece of paper, not anything like the woman he knew.

"The car's outside," he rasped out.

Cian stood up, but remained hunched over Aileen and Becca. Caitlyn unwound and hurried over to him. Still crying, she hugged him and whispered in his ear. "What's wrong with her?"

He put his arm around her and kissed her hair. "We'll fix it." He moved toward Becca. "Honey, I've got the car outside."

Her limbs were shaking so hard he was afraid the bones would shatter.

"Come on, *acushla*," Aileen said, lifting Becca to her feet slowly.

Boru whined and put his nose on her leg, like he

was lending his strength. "Let me help, Aileen," Trevor said, stepping forward and lifting Becca into his arms.

She latched her arms around his neck, gripping so tightly he couldn't breathe.

"Oh, Trevor. Don't let me...go," she said, the words a choked plea.

"I won't. Ever."

He hadn't even noticed the older couple preceding them out of the building, but when he reached the car, Cian was already standing by the now-open back door. "Lay her inside. Aileen, get in before her."

"I know the way of it," the woman said, ducking her head and sliding across the back seat. "Give her to me."

Trevor kissed Becca's pale cheek, his heart breaking as Cian peeled her hands from around his neck.

"Get in the front with me, Trevor," Cian said after he lowered Becca gently into the back.

"That's the woman you're 'in love with'?" Connor asked, almost a scoff. "She's crazy."

"*Shut up,* Con," Flynn said in a hard tone.

He thought about lunging toward his brother. Punching him repeatedly in the face. But Becca needed him. Instead, he met Connor's eyes as he walked to the passenger door. He shook his head once. Flynn tucked Caitlyn close as she pressed herself to his side, crying. But Connor and Quinn continued to look impervious to it all. He almost hated them in that moment.

Shutting the door gently, he didn't bother with a seatbelt. Cian put the car in drive, but the seatbelt indicator started to chime as they drove back to the main house. *Beep. Beep.* Trevor slapped on the belt quickly, anything to stop the noise. He would have ripped the guts out of the car to make it stop. Aileen was singing to Becca, the words in Gaelic, a song he didn't recognize.

At the house, Cian opened the back door. He bent to pick up Becca, only to step back and gesture to Trevor.

He didn't need an invitation to see to her. He leaned in and picked her up, her frame slight and shaking and more vulnerable than any human form he'd ever seen.

Aileen stayed by his side, almost like she was one of those medics who wheeled patients through the emergency room on stretchers. A few guests stopped short as he blew into the main hall. He headed to Becca's chambers, Cian throwing open the door for him. He took the stairs two at a time, Aileen and Cian right behind him.

When he reached the bedroom, Aileen called out to him. "In the closet."

He turned, Becca in his arms. "What? Why?"

The older woman opened the door. "Bring her in here, son."

He followed her, not understanding but trusting she knew better. Aileen pulled out a featherbed from a chest, and he watched as she prepared it. When she pointed to it, his muscles seized up. He didn't want to put Becca on the floor. In a freaking closet. She was too precious for that.

But then she moaned and leaned out of his arms, as if seeking the haven Aileen had created. He laid her down, his heart in ashes at his feet.

"You can trust me with her," Aileen whispered, lying down next to Becca, who'd curled into the fetal position. "You go on now."

This was over a helicopter?

He wandered out of the closet and closed the door, dazed. Cian was sitting on the bed. He stood uneasily, weaving on his feet. "She lost her parents when she was thirteen in Angola."

Merriam Oil & Gas worked there. He'd visited many times. The conflict in the nineties had been horrible, he'd heard.

"Why was she even there?"

"They were doctors in *Médecins* Sans Frontières. I was too. They were killed in an assault, and it changed her."

My God! He rocked back on his heels. Why hadn't she said? "And the helicopter?"

"Was overhead," Cian said, putting his hand over his mouth a moment before adding, "She was in the closet. Her parents used to put her there when there was danger or fighting around."

Oh, Jesus, no.

"She's agoraphobic," Cian said. "Has been since I brought her back here to her grandmother."

The words rolled over him, and he sunk onto his haunches. Agoraphobic? He racked his mind. Didn't that mean she was afraid to leave her house? "Why didn't she tell me?"

"She doesn't tell anyone," Cian said, his voice shaking. "Not even Chef Padraig. She's made her whole world here. So when you and your brother came here, trying to take her land, it stirred everything up again."

He turned to stone. "No."

She couldn't leave her home.

He'd tried to take it away from her, and now his brothers had come to finish the job.

Chapter 32

Arthur hadn't seen Connor and Quinn in years—their schedules had kept them from the wedding—and this certainly wasn't the way he'd wished to remake their acquaintance.

Both men stood in the living room of Honeysuckle Cottage, looking inscrutable in their gray suits while Caitlyn cried softly in Flynn's arms. He and Clara were seated on the sofa, too wiped out to stand with the rest of them. They'd come here at Arthur's suggestion after seeing Trevor, Cian, and Aileen take Becca inside.

"Pull yourself together, Caitlyn," Connor said, putting Arthur on the defensive.

"She's upset," he barked. "It's understandable."

"Who's that afraid of a helicopter?" Connor scoffed. "It's ridiculous."

"It's certainly an unusual fear," Quinn said. Flynn stared at his brothers in a way that told Arthur the affable young man could be serious when the situation required it.

"Fear isn't rational," Clara said, her eyes filled with challenge. "Also, this is a bed and breakfast with guests. Why would you bring a helicopter unannounced anyway? It's inconsiderate."

And walking the line of trespassing, Arthur imagined, although he didn't know much about Irish laws.

"It was faster," Quinn said with a Gallic shrug.

"We needed to speak to Trevor urgently," Connor said. "It's a business matter. Flynn, go get him."

Flynn transferred Caitlyn to Clara, which was what a good brother did in Arthur's opinion. "*Go get him?* Are you kidding? Who am I? Your assistant? Besides, he's with Becca, and she needs him."

Connor's face turned red as Flynn turned to him. "Don't throw Ms. O'Neill's name in my face. She's the reason he's blowing this deal."

The words were almost spat out, and Arthur weighed the wisdom of saying something.

"He loves her!" Caitlyn said, freeing herself from Clara. "We all do. She's a special person, and she has an incredible thing going here. It would be a travesty to drill for oil in this place, Con."

Connor's head spun her way, and his neck popped in the silent room. "You know about Trev's business here?"

She crossed and poked him in the chest. "Yes, and you're wrong to do it."

"Caitlyn, you'd best stay out of it," Quinn said, glowering like a Dickens ghost.

The front door blew open, and Trevor ate up the distance separating him and Connor and grabbed him by the lapels. "What in the hell is wrong with you?"

"What the hell is wrong with *you*?" Connor asked, rancor in every word.

"As an officer of this company, your behavior is totally unacceptable, Trevor, and I'm relieving you of duty," Quinn said, pulling on his cufflinks.

Cufflinks? His Grandfather Emmits wouldn't have been caught dead in cufflinks.

Trevor looked ready to punch Quinn in the face. "The hell you—"

"How's Becca, Trevor?" Arthur asked, hoping to avert violence.

Trevor threw his hands up. "Finally, someone asks the million-dollar question. She's lying on her closet floor in the fetal position with Aileen."

"Oh, Trev," Caitlyn said, crossing to him and wrapping her arms around him. "It's so terrible. She just kept shaking. I've never seen anyone so afraid."

"And you're going to blow a multi-billion-dollar deal for a woman who reacts like that to a mere helicopter?" Connor asked. "What's gotten into you? Have you forgotten what happened to Corey?"

Trevor lunged at him, and Quinn stepped in the way. "Stop this! Trev, you're totally out of line."

"Out of line?" Trevor asked, pushing Quinn in the chest. "Me? You said I had three days."

"That was before the Croatian ambassador to Britain pulled me aside at a party last night and told me he and the rest of the government were looking forward to Merriam Oil & Gas coming to his country. You went behind my back."

"*Our* backs!" Connor said, coming around Quinn and getting in Trevor's face. "You had no right to make this kind of business decision without talking to the board."

"Like the call you made about forgoing future offshore projects?" Trevor asked. "You didn't ask the board about drilling in Ireland, Con. Besides, like I told you earlier, I was planning on talking to you about it tomorrow."

Connor's eyes were flinty, and Arthur could feel the chill in them across the room. "I'm the chief executive officer of Merriam Enterprises. I don't have to run things by the board. You, however, do."

"That's bullshit," Trev said. "You made an emotional, unilateral decision based on Corey's death, and it's a big one for Merriam Oil & Gas."

"*Trevor*," Quinn said.

"No, this needs to be said." He put his hands on his hips. "We all loved Corey, and I know you loved him best. God knows, I want to protect Patrick and every other employee. But deciding we aren't going to drill off shore anymore is crazy. That's half of our oil business. The accident in Indonesia was a fluke. There was nothing we could do about that underwater earthquake."

"Trev," Flynn said, a warning in his tone. "Take it easy."

"What happened to Corey wasn't your fault, Con, or anyone else's. And I'm sick to death of you putting it on me."

The room was as silent as a wake, and Arthur realized even he was holding his breath. God, he hated to see brothers in discord like this, but he knew they had to get it off their chests.

"Are you done?" Connor asked, venom in his voice.

"That's all you're going to say?" Trevor asked, pushing his brother in the chest. "When you call the woman I want to marry a piece of ass?"

Caitlyn gasped. "Connor, how could you?"

But their brother only remained silent.

"Don't you dare go all ice on me." Trevor had always respected his brother, but right now he wanted to grab him by the jacket and shake him. "Talk to me. Say something, dammit."

"You're fired," Connor said.

Now Clara and Caitlyn both gasped. Arthur felt a hitch in his heart.

"Now, Con, don't be rash here," Flynn said, nudging Quinn, likely hoping for an ally. "Right, Quinn? This is a horrible misunderstanding and bad things have been said. Let's sit down like adults and work it out. I'm not saying Trev went about things the right way, but he's not wrong about offshore drilling. It's a big decision to discard one of our most profitable business models, and it's something that should have gone to the board."

"Is that what you think?" Connor asked, glancing at his brother like he was a flea he'd like to flick off. "If you feel like that, Flynn, you know where the door is."

Flynn shook his head. "You're serious."

Quinn turned and faced Connor. "Things are escalating here, and we need to stop before we say anything more. Connor and I will find somewhere nearby to stay while we all cool down."

Trevor snarled, "No, if he wants to treat his own brothers like this, I'm done. You want to fire me, fine, but you're still wrong. Oh, and you'll never get this property so long as I draw breath."

"Stop it!" Caitlyn cried, stepping between the two men. "We're family. This isn't how we treat each other. Con, say something. Please."

"Tell *him*," Trev said, inclining his chin Connor's way. "I guess it's a good thing J.T. already resigned because he agrees with me on this one."

"I thought someone helped you with the Croatian deal," Connor said. "The minute Quinn called me, I was on a plane this way. Thanks for clarifying that point. It will make it easier when I call J.T. later."

"Stop it!" Caitlyn shouted again. "Connor, what's gotten into you? Why are you acting like this?"

"I'm acting like the chief officer of the company," he told her. "Since you feel like I'm wrong, too, Caitlyn, you know what you can do."

Her sharp intake could be heard throughout the room.

"Please stop this," Clara finally said, her eyes wet with unshed tears. "My grandfather is rolling over in his grave, hearing you talk to each other like this over the business he started."

"And yet, Aunt," Connor said with a cold smile, "you

became estranged from this family because of a business matter."

Arthur put his arms around Clara. "Watch yourself, boy."

"No, he's right," Clara said, patting him reassuringly on the chest. "And I regretted that for nearly sixty years, Connor. You can never know how much."

Arthur had had enough bullshit. "A good leader listens to the people he works with, the ones he trusts. He certainly doesn't fire a brother and threaten two other siblings with termination because they disagree with him."

Connor smiled. "I thought I could trust my brother. I thought he cared about this family. I was wrong."

"Let's go," Quinn said, walking to the front door. "Trev, I'll be in touch."

Trevor flicked his hand up like an angry Italian might. "Whatever. I'm done. Just don't come after Becca or her land, or I'll have to punch you straight in that pretty face, Con."

"I'll have this land," Connor said, "and I'll use her crazy stunt today to take it from her."

Trevor lunged for him, but Flynn stepped in the way. "Don't! Let him go. It's not worth it."

Connor gazed at Trevor long and hard before he and Quinn opened the front door and walked out. Arthur patted Clara on the back. Her muscles were rigid with tension.

"It's going to be all right," he whispered close to her ear. How, he had no idea, but he'd try to make it so for their sake, and hers.

"It's so terrible," she whispered back, turning her face into his chest.

"Connor has lost his mind," Flynn said, storming in a straight line while Caitlyn sat down, her face white with shock. "I've never seen him like this," she said.

"If he comes for Becca, he's dead to me," Trevor said, his voice harsh.

"Quinn and I will talk to him," Flynn said, running a hand through his hair. "I still can't take it all in."

"I can't believe he fired you or talked about Becca like that," Caitlyn said, extending her hand to Trevor. "I'm so sorry."

He cleared his throat. "Don't be. He's not acting like the brother I know. I don't want to work with him anymore if this is the way he does business. I need to call J.T. Then I should check on Becca."

"Is there anything we can do to help her, Trevor?" Arthur asked.

Trevor's throat worked before he said, "I...don't know. She's agoraphobic."

Caitlyn surged out of her seat. "What?"

"And I was going to take away her home," Trevor said, his voice almost rueful.

That sweet, enthusiastic woman was agoraphobic? Arthur couldn't believe it. "Are you certain?"

"Cian told me." He pinched the bridge of his nose. "Christ, I... She didn't tell me. Why didn't she tell me?"

Caitlyn put her arm around him. "Maybe she was embarrassed."

"She didn't trust me," Trevor said. "And how could she? I came here for her land, and now Connor and Quinn have followed me here."

"And she can't leave," Flynn said. "God, I'm sorry, Trev. So sorry."

"Me too." He walked to the door. "I don't want my beef with Con to mess things up for any of you. If you want to leave, I won't take it personally."

"Leave?" Caitlyn asked. "What do you mean? I'm with you on this, Trev. All the way. I love Becca. And Con isn't thinking straight."

"Even if it means losing your job?" he asked, and Arthur had to admire his guts for asking.

She swallowed thickly. "Like you said...I don't like

this side of him. It was like talking to a different person. I mean, he can be cold, but... He's never been cruel."

"What about you?" Trevor asked, turning to Flynn.

The other man took a deep breath. "I figure there's power in numbers. After seeing Connor today, I agree he's making emotionally unsound decisions. I mean... He told me where the door was. Are you kidding me?"

Arthur could hear the hurt in the younger man's tone. God, what a horrible day. He'd never expected to see the Merriam children at odds like this.

Flynn punched the air. "Even if you resign your position—"

"He fired me, Flynn," Trevor interrupted.

"You're still on the board," Flynn said. "You still own part of the company like the rest of us. He can't kick you or any of us off the board."

"Maybe I should resign from the board like J.T. did," Trevor said sadly. "God!"

Caitlyn poked him in the chest. "No, you should not! J.T. resigned to protect the family from his ex-wife, and that was the only reason. You're a Merriam. You worked hard like the rest of us to make this company great. I will not hear of you leaving it. Do you hear me? I couldn't take it, Trev."

Her voice broke, and Trevor pulled her into a hug. "Hey, it's okay. Don't cry."

"It's not okay," she said. "This is horrible. I'm going to call Mom."

Arthur thought that was a good plan. Assumpta Weatherby Merriam was a force of nature. He'd always admired her, both as a woman and an educator. But he kept his mouth shut. He hadn't reached eighty years without learning when it was best not to butt in.

"You call Mom," Trev said. "I'll call J.T. I'm sorry you've been caught in the middle of things. Both of you."

"It's not your fault," Flynn said. "Con crossed so many

lines. Of course, I'm not saying you're in the clear either. This Croatian deal—"

"Was an alternative I thought I had to put to Con," Trevor said, opening his arms like a white flag.

"That makes me feel a little better," Flynn said.

"I wouldn't make a deal like that on my own," Trevor said. "But it bothers the shit out of me that Con and Quinn thought I would. And to call Becca those names... Okay, enough of this. I need to call J.T. before Con sets the dogs on him or something."

His shoulders were stooped as he walked to the front door and opened it. Buttercup hummed in the shade at the front of the house. It had a mournful tone to it. "As long as Becca and her land is safe, I don't care what else happens."

"You have our support on that," Caitlyn said.

"One hundred percent," Flynn said. "I'll even pinky swear if it would make you feel better."

His mouth tipped up on the side, and he walked to Buttercup and stroked the animal's neck. She leaned her head on his shoulder. "Thank you."

"You have our help too," Arthur called out. Although it wasn't his place to interfere, he'd do what he could to help the boy. "In whatever way you need. I might be retired, but I could write an Op-Ed for *The Irish Times* about the possibility that onshore drilling might be on its way to Ireland. Rouse some public outrage. It's a highly controversial subject in this country."

"I know it is," Trevor said, "and I've told Connor the same. I appreciate the support. Really." He glanced back in the direction of the house, his gaze pinning on Becca's tower. His whole face scrunched for a moment before he turned his head back toward them and said, "Everything has to be about Becca now."

Watching the man walk off, Arthur's only silver lining was that Trevor Merriam, one-time cynic, had learned what it truly meant to love someone.

Chapter 33

Once her off-the-charts heart rate finally settled, Becca found herself pulling away from Aileen in shame.

Her cheeks turned red, and she wanted to cry. Trevor had found out about her condition in the worst possible way—and so had his entire family. How could she ever face them again?

"Is the helicopter still here?" she asked Aileen, whose singing tapered off.

"Yes, love," she said, "but Trevor's grounded it for now. Oh, Becca, I'm so sorry this happened. And when you were doing so well."

She had felt more empowered than ever, what with the new psychiatrist, the steadying power of Trevor's love, and her new enterprise. How foolish she'd been to think her nightmare over. She looked toward the closet door. The steps to the threshold seemed endless, and her heart sped up at the mere thought of trying to leave it.

"Don't rush things," Aileen said, wrapping the blanket more securely around Becca. "You can stay in here as long as you need. There's no shame in it. Who would have imagined someone would land a helicopter here?"

And yet Trevor's brothers had done just that. She'd seen the Merriam logo on the black body as Trevor carried her out to Cian's car. The two men in crisp gray suits standing beside Flynn were unmistakably Merriams, but they'd seemed so much colder than the rest. They were here about the land. Connor hadn't listened to Trevor. Her breath hitched. Was everything still in danger?

"I need to see Trevor," she said, sitting up and gripping her knees. He'd have questions surely, but she'd simply have to reach deep and answer them, no matter how much it hurt. Why had she thought love and some doctor could fix her? What a fantasy.

"Are you sure you're ready to see him, love?" Aileen asked.

She wasn't, but that didn't matter. "I need to ask more about why his brothers are here."

"For the land, I expect," Aileen said. "Should I leave you alone with Trevor?"

"I'll be fine. Let's get me up to the desk, at least." Meeting him in her closet was bad enough, but she wasn't going to do it on the floor. She didn't want to see the pity in his gaze.

Her muscles were as jiggly as an undercooked pudding, but she made it to the chair. The window was in her peripheral vision, but she couldn't face looking out yet. "All right, Aileen. Thanks for finding him."

"Once I do, I'll wait outside your chambers, my dear," Aileen said, kissing her head.

"No, you take care of the guests," she said. "We have a full house. Are Trevor's brothers planning to stay here? Oh, you couldn't know." Aileen hadn't left her side. "I'll ask Trevor."

"I'll be back to check on you," Aileen said. "Do you want to call the new psychiatrist about what happened?"

"I don't imagine he takes emergencies," Becca said. "Besides, I'm a new patient."

"We could try," Aileen asked, wringing her hands.

She was silent for a beat. "Maybe later. Let me...face one thing at a time." That was the only way she knew how to move forward after an episode like this. It was so easy to get overwhelmed at times like these.

"Of course," she said, backing out of the closet.

"Thank you, Aileen." She gripped the edge of the desk, trying to take strength from the solidity of it beneath her fingers.

"Oh, love, it's what family does for each other. You'll be right as rain in no time, you'll see."

She wasn't so sure. The last time she'd had an attack this bad had been when a local transformer had blown, killing all the power for twenty square miles. The boom had sounded like a bomb, and everything had gone dark in its wake. She'd fallen to the floor immediately and crawled toward the nearest wall like her parents had taught her when they were living in Angola. She'd scraped off the tops of her fingernails against the stone wall. Cian had found her like that, huddled in the corner, with his flashlight. She'd been in the closet for eight weeks after that. Her heart broke, wondering how long she'd be condemned here this time.

Trevor walked in, his face haggard, and the rest of her heart broke into tiny pieces. This was what she'd done to him.

"I'm sorry," she whispered as he came near her desk. "I didn't want you to find out like this. See me like this."

He rested his hands on the surface, gazing at her. "Don't worry about me seeing you like this. Oh, baby, why didn't you tell me?"

She inhaled a shaky breath before saying, "I was hoping a new treatment I was starting next week would help. And I was afraid to tell you."

Nodding, he looked down. "Did you think I would use it against you to get the land?"

"At first, but not after you promised me you weren't interested in my land. I did wonder if Connor might try something. Trevor, are your brothers here for it?"

His breath was almost a growl in his throat. "Yes and no. They discovered I'd found another tract of land in Croatia without telling them—something I was planning to do tomorrow. They decided to come see about the situation and dress me down in person. Becca, I love you and plan to protect you and your land from them. I think they understand that now."

And it had broken his heart. "Oh, Trevor," she said, resting her head in her palms. "I don't want you to fight your family for me. Trevor, I know how much they mean to you."

"Becca—"

"No, I mean it," she said, touching his hand. "He can't force me to sell, although he can try. This is my fight." Even if it meant fighting him from her closet.

Trevor worried his lips. "He's gone off the deep end over Corey's death. He said he'd use what happened today as ammunition. Christ, you have no idea how that makes me feel. Becca, I brought this to your doorstep. What happened today was my fault, and look what it did to you. Please, let me help you."

Connor was going to use her episode against her? She grew sick at the very thought. Could he prove she was unfit to own The Wild Irish Rose? "I have an uncle who's estranged from me who might help Connor prove I'm crazy."

"You're not crazy!" His words were emphatic. "You're agoraphobic. Cian told me. Plus, your business has been increasing every year since you took over. No judge would buy that you're crazy."

But people could be paid to lie, couldn't they? "Has your brother used tactics like that before to make people sell?"

Trevor's jaw ticked. "Nothing illegal, but yes, we've found ways to make things happen in our favor."

Not reassuring. "My uncle was angry when my grandmother left this land to me, not him. Of course, he didn't want to run The Wild Rose, just sell the land off and get rich. He's the only way I see Connor coming at me. I'm square with the tax man, and the community is behind me—even if I don't venture into town."

"Other family members will be talking to Con about backing off. Caitlyn and Flynn are squarely behind us. They're still officers in the company and board members, although Con told them they could walk if they wanted to question him. If he and Quinn remain resolute, I'll have someone keep an eye on your uncle. Becca, I won't let anything happen to you or this land. Do you believe me?"

She didn't need to consider it. She simply reached for his hand and said, "Yes."

"Good. I was afraid...good."

Emotion clogged her throat, but she said, "We need to hire a wildlife expert immediately to see if we have any species on the property that would help us become a protected area. It's a long shot, and I don't know much about it, but Cian has seen an Irish hare before, and it's an endangered species."

"What about historical preservation?" Trevor asked. "Surely this house is old enough."

"There are lots of houses this old and older," she said, tapping her foot on the ground, nerves still dancing through her. "I looked into it briefly when I took over after my grandmother died. Being in the EU adds extra layers to Irish historical and cultural preservation. It seemed complicated and not worth the effort or the legal expense of checking into it."

"Perhaps we need to reconsider that just in case," Trevor said. "I have a lawyer I use in Dublin I'd trust to look into it."

He was acting like a partner, one who had an equal stake in the outcome, and she had to force back tears. "Thank you. Trevor, I..."

Leaning forward, he pushed a lock of hair behind her ear. "What?"

It was now or never. "If you're set on helping me, I'll willingly accept it. I'm smart enough to know I can't fight your brother alone. But about us...after seeing me today and learning what's wrong with me, we need to be clear that you're only helping me as a friend. Of course, if you want some type of...consulting fee, I'm happy to oblige."

His face darkened like a thundercloud. "Are you trying to piss me off?"

"No, I'm being practical." She released his hand and folded hers prayer-style on top of the desk. "I have a serious condition that precludes me from leaving this place, and for that reason, I think it's time for us both to see things for what they are. This could never work long-term although it's been...grand." Heart-wrenching, soul-inspiring, and lovely was more like.

"You're still pissing me off."

She couldn't let that stop her. "I thought this new psychiatrist Hargreaves suggested would be able to help me." She had to swallow a thick lump before continuing. "But after my reaction today, I have to conclude I may never get better, and you deserve someone normal, someone who can leave this house without having a panic attack. Or finding refuge in this closet for weeks on end. Weeks, Trevor."

His verdant green eyes continued to gaze at her, and she noticed they were wet in the corners. His heart was breaking too, she knew, but that didn't change the fact that she was right.

"Do you know why I put you in the Oisin and Niamh suite? Because you're Oisin and I'm Niamh. Trevor, this is my world, one I'm bound to, in my own way. If you stayed, you'd miss your family and everything the world has to offer. We'd both end up unhappy."

His jaw was granite now.

"I'm sorry," she whispered, pressing her hands into her lap to contain her riotous emotions.

He lifted up her chin. "My turn."

No, she wanted to say, but that wasn't fair. She owed him the freedom to speak his mind. "All right."

His chest lifted as he took a deep breath. "Does your inability to leave this closet or this house stop you from being able to *love* me?"

She gasped at his directness.

"Well, does it?" he pressed, coming around the desk and sinking onto a knee in front of her.

"That's not the point," she said, trying to push her chair back to escape his body heat and presence. "I told you. You deserve someone normal."

"What's normal anyway?" he asked. "Becca, I want an answer. Does you being agoraphobic stop you from loving me?"

"Don't make me say it."

He pulled her chair closer and put his hands on her knees. "Does it?"

"You know it doesn't." He was going to be stubborn. Well, he couldn't do stubborn like an Irish woman could. "That's not what I'm saying. Short-term, this was good. Doable. Long-term, it's impossible."

"Why?"

Was he going to break her heart all over again and make her tell him?

"Tell me, Becca."

"Do you really want a wife you can't take on a honeymoon or even a date?" She bit her lip before continuing. "Who can't take your children to school or the doctor or even a football game should they decide to play? Trevor, I may never be able to leave this place, and that's something I live with every day. I won't condemn you and any children we might have to that kind of death sentence."

He sat back on his heels. "Loving you isn't a death sentence. It's a joy, a goddamn miracle. So maybe you can't leave this place. Big effing deal. It's pretty damn great here, if you ask me." Something flashed in his eyes. "Ah! I get it. You decorated this place with things from around the world because you were bringing the world to you. The restaurant. The music on the weekends. Everything you've done has been to create a world here because you can't visit the one outside these walls." He pulled her forward and kissed her on the lips. "Becca, you're brilliant."

Warmth shot through her heart. No one had ever understood her so well, and without her saying a word. "You're missing the point."

"No, I'm not." He stood and pulled his St. Christopher medal out and took it off before placing it around her neck. "Oisin and Niamh. No offense, but that's total bullshit. This is our story."

"What are you doing?" she asked, pushing his hands away.

"I'm giving this to you," he said, pulling her hair out of the way. "Stop fighting me."

"I don't want your necklace," she protested.

"Honey, I'm a man. We don't wear necklaces. And I'm not taking no for an answer." He gave a victorious *ah-ha*, and she felt the medal fall onto her chest. The weight of it seemed to rest on her heart, and she could feel tears welling up inside her at the gesture. It was the first tangible thing he'd given her, and she felt the weight of that.

"I never told you about this medallion or why I wear it." He sat on the edge of the desk and looked at her. "My

Grandma Anna sent it to my Grandpa Noah when he was fighting in WWII in Europe. My grandpa was best friends with her brother, but he died in the war. They started writing each other letters afterward, and she sent her St. Christopher medal to Grandpa to keep him safe. My mom gave it to me to wear when I started to travel to some dangerous places, saying it made her feel better. But this medal has a lot more significance. It's a symbol of love and courage in the face of great adversity."

Tears streamed down her face.

"It strikes me that we need a better model for our relationship than Oisin and Niamh, so I'm going to tell you what happened next. My Grandpa Noah returned from the war with PTSD, and he tried to talk Grandma out of marrying right away. Said he wanted to make sure he was going to be normal, to use your word."

She could do nothing but reach for a tissue to blot her tears. Oh, he told a story well, and it was hitting all the marks.

"When Grandma Anna heard his plans, she was pissed, to use my word. She loved him, they were going to get married, and that was that."

His full-blown grin shocked her. How could he grin at a time like this?

"Did I mention my Grandma Anna has a strong dose of Irish in her and grew up in Chicago's Irish neighborhood?" He pointed to himself. "That blood flows in these veins, Becca. Anyway, Grandpa Noah would always tell us kids Grandma Anna's tireless love saved him."

Oh, Trevor.

"I've always imagined that's what love is," he said, reaching for her hand and pressing it against his massive chest where his heart beat steadily. "Becca, I love you like that, but if you think I'm going to let your agoraphobia keep me away, you don't know me at all. I'm here, Becca.

All the way. In the closet. In your chambers. In this house."

She didn't want the tears to flow, but they ran down her face anyway, as unstoppable as Irish rain.

"Wherever you are," he said, raising her hand from his chest to his lips. "That's where I want to be. For always."

He stood and put his hands on his hips, towering over her.

"Get used to it."

Then he headed to the closet door. Since she didn't know what to say to him, she didn't stop him. Her chest was tight from grief, yet his words had surrounded her—a warm, protective halo she didn't want to leave. When he'd said *for always*, he'd meant it. She needed to regroup.

He turned, saying, "I'll get going on the wildlife expert and call my lawyer about the historical preservation. Do you want a pot of tea? Some scones? I expect Caitlyn and Aunt Clara will want to check on you. Oh, and my Uncle Arthur volunteered to write an Op-Ed for *The Irish Times* on onshore oil exploration to stir up public opinion."

"He did?" she sputtered.

"It's like Uncle Arthur said to J.T. a while back. When family is in trouble, you circle the wagons."

She imagined that must be some Old West saying, but she understood the sentiment.

"You're *my family* now." His voice was as steady as his gaze. "Get that through your thick Irish skull."

She stared at the doorway after he left, conflicting emotions bouncing around inside her. He'd gone against members of his own family for her. Surely that would cause a deep rift between him and his siblings. How was she to bear that? Besides which, she couldn't be sure her agoraphobia would improve. He might not want to be realistic about a future with her, but she had to be. How could she be a true wife if she couldn't leave The Wild Rose?

Still, she couldn't help touching the medal he'd placed around her neck and pray his tireless love could save her.

CHAPTER 34

AFTER LEAVING BECCA, TREVOR HEADED TO HIS ROOM AND called J.T. again. His brother insisted on flying to Ireland at once—Caroline was staying to help her sister, Natalie, with her new baby boy. He didn't object. Instead, he asked him to bring the letters Grandpa Noah and Grandma Anna had written to each other during the war. Their mom had given them to J.T. for Caroline to read, and now it was Becca's turn.

Oisin and Niamh. What crap. He wasn't going to live out some dark Irish fairy tale.

He'd be grateful to see his brother. There was a come-to-Jesus meeting brewing between Connor and Quinn and the rest of them, and while J.T. was no longer working with the company or serving on the board, it affected him too. Too bad Michaela couldn't make it, being in the Amazon and out of sight.

He heard a discreet knock at the door and rose to answer it. Caitlyn stood in the hallway, her face pallid. "How's Becca?"

"Calmer, I suppose," he said, letting her precede him inside before shutting the door.

She placed her hand on his chest. "Are *you* going to be okay? Your whole world was turned upside down today."

He still hadn't found his footing, but his head was clear despite it all. "I love her. As for Connor, he's wrong all the way. Am I thrilled he fired me? No, but if he's embracing dirty tactics, maybe it's for the best."

"It's not," she said, leading him over to the sofa in the sitting room. "For anyone. I talked to Mom. She's super upset. Said she'd talk to Dad and then regroup."

So the family telephone game had started. "What about me? Why haven't I gotten a call?"

Caitlyn smiled mirthlessly. "I told her to give you a while. Said you'd had a day. She was sorry to hear about Becca's condition. For both of you."

Leave it to Mom, he thought.

"Thanks for calling her. I don't want to be the cause of a feud in the family."

"She knows that." Caitlyn lifted her head heavenward. "We all know that. I told her how Con acted. You've always done your job, and it was wrong of him and Quinn to treat you like that. If we can't trust each other after all this time, what the hell do we have left?"

Nothing, and that cut him to the bone. "Where's Flynn?"

"He asked Quinn to meet at the pub. He hopes they can hammer out something reasonable. Otherwise, it's going to be a standoff."

Flynn knew which way the wind was blowing. This one would come to blows—he suspected there was no avoiding that. "J.T. is coming. Caroline's staying to help with her new nephew."

"I hoped he would." Caitlyn popped up like she couldn't sit still any longer. "He should be here too. I hate that he's not on the board anymore. He's a Merriam."

"He was protecting the family from his ex-wife. Didn't see another choice." And that made him want to beat Connor up all over again. He'd attacked J.T. too, after all, and over a mistake J.T. had long since copped to making.

"I'm going to see Becca," she said, bouncing on her heels. "Anything I should know? Say?"

He lifted the collar of his shirt aside. "I gave her my St. Christopher's medal. Told her the story about Grandpa Noah and Grandma Anna. J.T. is bringing their letters."

"Oh, Trev, you're such a sweetheart." She shook her head. "I feel so bad for Becca. Agoraphobia is a little like PTSD in some ways. I looked it up after I left Uncle Arthur and Aunt Clara."

He would need to do his research too, after he addressed a few of the items on his to-do list. "She wants to push me aside," Trevor said, pressing his hand to his forehead as pain shot through his skull. "I told her I wouldn't let her." Something niggled at him. "She mentioned Hargreaves had given her the name of a new psychiatrist. I need to go talk to him. You go to Becca. She'll be happy to see you."

His sister hugged him hard before heading to the door. "She's worth fighting for, Trev."

"I know." He went to her, poking her nose like he used to when she was little. "You're an angel."

"Some days," she said, kissing him on the cheek and heading toward the stairs.

Trevor left the door open to his stupid Oisin and Niamh suite—he was going to have to mentally rename it to something like Lovers Across An Open Sea in honor of Grandpa Noah and Grandma Anna, perhaps—and crossed the short distance to Hargreaves' room. Knocking, he waited until the man opened the door. Ever presentable, the butler folded his arms behind his back.

"I wanted to thank you," Trevor began, "for giving Becca the name of a new psychiatrist. I imagine you're aware of today's events."

"Unfortunately, yes," he said. "Mistress Clara called me. She's quite upset, as is Mr. Hale."

And at their age, stress couldn't be good. The way Connor had talked to Aunt Clara had totally been out of line. Thank God, the old girl had handled herself.

"How is it you knew about Becca's agoraphobia when I didn't?" He felt like shit for having missed all the signs. Looking back on recent events—like her avoidance of the outdoors, or the way Aileen had stared at him in the old kitchen, or even Becca's refusal to go to dinner in Cork City—so many things made sense now. Why hadn't he guessed?

"As I told Becca, I knew someone who didn't leave the house for some time, and I grew concerned enough to research various possible ailments. That wasn't her problem, I concluded in the end, but I had found her the best specialist in the country in case."

Trevor started to speak, only for his voice to fail him. He cleared his throat, then said, "You're resourceful, Hargreaves. There are no words to express my full gratitude, but if there's anything I can ever do to help you..."

Hargreaves remained completely unflappable, his smile as polite as ever. "When it comes to family, it's my job to help, sir."

Family. Yes, Becca was family now. Hargreaves had known that, and he was humbled all over again.

"She's a fine woman, sir." He bowed.

"She sure as hell is." Extending his hand, he waited until Hargreaves shook it. The clasp was brief and perfunctory, but Trevor could tell it was meaningful to them both. "I have more fires to put out, so I'll let you get back to your reading."

He nodded, and Trevor took his cue to leave. Weaving his way back through the main hall, he stopped Cian, who'd just come in the front door. He looked harried. Tired.

"What can I do to help you and Aileen?" Trevor asked.

"I'm not an expert on running a bed and breakfast, but I have two hands, and it looks like I'm about to have plenty of time. Put me to work."

The man ran his hand through his silver hair. "You're no longer a guest of The Wild Rose."

Trevor almost took a step back in shock. "What?"

"Do you need help moving your bags out of your room?" Cian asked.

Something tickled the back of his neck. Had he offended Cian in some way? He'd thought they finally understood each other. "What do you mean? Where am I moving to, Cian?"

"To Becca's chambers, of course." He made a rude noise as if Trevor were slow. "You belong there."

Crap. He was going to get emotional. First, Hargreaves and now this man. He was like Becca's father, and Trevor knew what this meant—he had earned the man's full approval at last. For the second time in five minutes, he held out his hand.

Cian clasped it hard. They shared a timeless look, the kind of understanding and appreciation between a father and the man his daughter loved.

"Shouldn't we ask Becca? She had some serious opinions about being with me now that I know about her condition."

Cian snorted. "She's always had opinions. In this case she's wrong, and I'll tell her so if she objects."

Trevor had another ally. He was going to need it.

"Looks like I'm moving."

CHAPTER 35

CRACKING HIS KNUCKLES, ARTHUR SURVEYED THE ROUGH draft Op-Ed he'd written for *The Irish Times*. Damn, it felt good to do something in a crisis. He had to be honest with himself, it also felt good to write: to weave words, to express facts and opinions, to raise questions.

"You're sounding pretty pleased with yourself from all the grunting and groaning over there," Clara said from the couch. "You about done?"

He surveyed the stack of Wild Irish Rose stationery he'd written on. The pretty rose symbol in the corner had given him fits at first, but he'd forgotten all about it after finishing the first page. "I feel alive, and it's a damn fine feeling."

"You didn't look dead before to me," Clara said, still holding her damn phone.

What in the world was she doing on it? Texting, likely. She'd been unusually quiet, and he'd given her space to settle. Still, she might need some prodding. "You going to see Becca? I wonder where Caitlyn and Flynn went off to."

"Caitlyn is learning how to knit with Becca. Talk about a good way to keep that poor woman occupied. Caitlyn texted to say she still hasn't left the closet. It's heartbreaking."

He pushed his papers aside. “She’s strong, and she’s made it this far.”

“I keep telling myself that,” Clara said, setting her phone down. “And yet, there’s no denying the family is in crisis. Flynn is trying to talk some sense into Quinn at the pub. J.T. is on his way. Caroline will stay with Natalie and the new baby.”

“Good,” Arthur said, sitting back in his chair. “The whole lot of them need to hash things out.”

“Yes,” Clara said, laying her head against the sofa. “I don’t want them to...”

When she broke off, Arthur rounded the sofa and took her in his arms. “What happened between you and their father is different, and it’s over.” His mind had gone there too—he’d tried to mediate the feud between Clara and her brother all those years ago, to no avail. Neither of them wanted to see something like that happen to the kids. “Don’t let the past creep into this. This is their issue, and they have to work it out.”

After seeing the hard line Connor had taken earlier, bolstered by plenty of attitude about Becca, Arthur knew warm fuzzies weren’t going to work, not when everyone had their blood worked up, but it wasn’t his business. He’d drafted the Op-Ed because he would protect Becca’s land if called upon to do so. It would be ready to go if Connor tried something funny. What kind of a man didn’t honor a woman’s wish not to sell? A ruthless one, he feared. Emmits Merriam had been tough, ambitious even, but never ruthless. But worse, what kind of a man didn’t embrace the woman his brother loved with open arms? A cynical, broken one. Not an easy thing to fix.

“I hate this,” Clara said, leaning on his chest. “I feel like I should be doing more to help.”

He stroked her long white hair. “You’re here. Maybe you should go to Becca and learn how to knit too.”

She laughed brokenly. “You angling for more sweaters?”

"You think you could knit a straight row?" he asked, hoping his teasing would comfort her.

"Who knows? I've surprised myself a lot lately." Sitting up, she said, "I think it's time I went over there. What are you going to do?"

He thought about it. "I'm going to find Cian and see if they need some help. With Becca..." He didn't know how best to cast her situation.

"I'll text Hargreaves and have him meet you in the main hall," she said. "The least we can do is to help out with the running of things."

"I can wash dishes," he said, rolling his sleeves back.

"I'm sure that's covered, Arthur, but you're a dear to say so."

Trevor and Becca didn't need any matchmaking right now—they'd done an admirable job of finding each other on their own—but they were going to need help keeping Connor from going after her land. His heart ached at the thought of how Emmits would react to this kind of family friction. In some ways, he was glad his friend wasn't alive to see it.

Arthur didn't want to go against a Merriam, but he would go to battle if Trevor made a war cry.

***

Becca had known what Caitlyn was about, swinging by to breezily ask if she'd teach her how to knit. As if she weren't sitting in a closet, unable to leave.

Becca soon realized the distraction would be good for them both. She was high-strung from the attack, her symptoms worse than they'd been in ages, and Caitlyn's brothers were having a row, and she was in the middle of it.

When Clara arrived with a gin and tonic in her hands, requesting a knitting lesson as well, she arranged them on the floor of her closet near the window, where the natural light was best, and equipped them both with medium-sized wood needles and thread. Her worries seemed to evaporate as she showed them how to hold the needles and make a simple slip knot.

Clara was a natural, they discovered, but Caitlyn had trouble holding the needles at first, and all three of them ended up laughing hysterically as she cursed up a storm. By the time Trevor appeared in the doorway, she felt more herself.

Cian was behind him, and he popped in his head. "A knitting lesson? What a grand idea."

It was grand, but she could no longer pretend nothing was wrong. She was shirking her duties, her role as innkeeper. "How's everything for dinner? Is the staff—"

"We have more help than we need, love." Cian clasped Trevor's shoulder. "Your man here has been helping, and Arthur and Hargreaves have been pitching in too. Aileen is ordering everyone about."

"She's got everything in hand," Trevor said lightly, but Becca knew they were trying to keep her from fretting.

"I'm sorry I'm not out there," she said. "I sent Chef a message, but if he needs—"

"He's sending up a tasting of tonight's specials for you to see if there's anything you'd like to add," Cian said. "Becca, we've done this before. Nothing will suffer."

But it was her place and her responsibility. Guilt was always her companion in this sanctuary.

"Don't focus on the negative," Trevor said, forcing a smile. "Keep your spirits up. That's the best remedy, Aileen tells me. When you're ready, you'll come downstairs. In the meantime," he added, speaking quickly, "Cian and I moved my things in here. We've checked a walk-in guest into my old suite. Well, we need to be off."

Moved his things in?

"Wait," she called as the men disappeared, much like she imagined they'd meant to do.

Trevor reappeared. "Yes?"

Caitlyn and Clara kept their heads down, focusing on their knitting, but she knew they were listening eagerly.

"Did you not hear what I said earlier?" She was purposefully vague, not wanting to hash their troubles out in front of the women.

His cheek moved like he was biting it on the inside. "And I said what I said. It so happens Cian agrees with me."

She dropped her knitting needles. "He does?"

Crossing to her, he leaned down and kissed her sweetly on the cheek. "He does. I'll be back in a while. Lots to do." And to punctuate his point, he picked up Hatshep, something he'd never done.

First Buttercup, now Hatshep. She'd make an animal lover of him yet.

Her infernal cat curled into him, stretching like she was lying in the sun.

"See. Hatshep agrees too. Have fun, ladies."

With that power move, he left.

The darn man.

"He seems to have outmaneuvered you, my dear." Clara handed her the knitting needles she'd dropped. "Take it from an old woman who was alone for much of her life. You don't push love like that away when it comes knocking on your door."

"Even if the door he had to knock on was her closet?"

"If he loves you, he'll knock on any door," Clara said. "Trust me, when you get to my age, you think about these things. If Arthur had to go to a nursing home, God forbid, I would knock on his door every day."

That left her speechless.

"If Trevor can't get in, he'll knock it down, he's that

stubborn," Caitlyn said. "Oh, and my mom wanted me to tell you that she can't wait to meet you."

"J.T., Trevor's twin brother, also said he's excited to meet the woman who's finally made his brother wax poetic," Clara got in while she was making yet another perfect slip knot.

"J.T.'s coming to the inn," Caitlyn said. "You're going to love him. Caroline had to stay behind, but she's so nice. I mean, his first wife was a total bitch. Trevor called her Sin City. We thought Trev might never want to marry anyone after seeing what that she-devil did to our brother."

Hearing that made her feel deflated. She'd thought she was right to push him away—that it would be best for him—but everyone else thought otherwise.

"J.T.'s also bringing the letters Grandpa Noah and Grandma Anna wrote each other during the war," Caitlyn said. "They're going to make you swoon. Until you read them, you can't imagine what they were up against. I mean, imagine falling in love with someone who might die any day in the war. Grandma Anna had the bravest, biggest heart ever, Grandpa Noah used to say."

What had Trevor said about them? Her tireless love had healed the man suffering from PTSD. Oh, to trust in such a love.

She reached up and clutched the medal he'd placed around her neck, looking at the closet door. Maybe it was time to image herself leaving this place and resuming her life. Yes, that was it. She vowed it wasn't going to take her weeks this time.

She had a new motivation, and his name was Trevor Merriam.

CHAPTER 36

TREVOR OFFERED CHEF PADRAIG HIS ASSISTANCE WITH ANYthing from cutting vegetables to taking out plates to the guests.

"I can see what Becca sees in you," the dark-haired man said, "but I do not need your help cutting vegetables. *Merde, alors.*"

Since he knew French, he replied, "*Très bien, parce que je suis maladroit dans la cuisine.*"

A trace of a smile appeared on the man's face, little more than a lifting of his lips, before he pointed to the door and said, "*Allez!*"

Trevor didn't mind being ordered out, especially after confessing he was clumsy in the kitchen. Flynn was sitting alone, drinking from a full tumbler of whiskey, when he appeared in the dining room. He took the seat across from him.

"That bad?" he asked.

"Yeah." He shoved his glass toward Trevor, who took a drink. "They're giving 'pigheaded' new meaning. Oh, and Quinn wants to know when he can have his chopper back. He and Connor don't see any reason to hang around."

A server brought him a highball glass and poured

him his own whiskey, leaving the bottle. Apparently word was out that everyone had had a bad day. "If they think I'm going to let the pilot turn on that helicopter and freak Becca out again, they have another thing coming."

"That's what I thought," Flynn said. "It's not like Quinn doesn't have more of them. How about I hire someone to tow it off the property? It's an eyesore. Besides, my rabbit friends can't be happy to have it so close to their shed. Cian came by before you left the kitchen. He said they were still shaking like crazy when he visited them earlier."

The older man hadn't mentioned it. Probably wise or he might have lost it on his older brothers for scaring Becca *and* her animals.

"We probably won't find someone to tow a helicopter until tomorrow since it's after work hours around here," Trevor said, downing his whiskey. "J.T. is on his way."

"So I heard," Flynn said with a heavy sigh. "Mom is flying out of Chicago too, apparently. Dad has a Merriam plane picking her up. Caitlyn's call stirred the nest."

No doubt. "Is she flying into Cork City?"

"Yeah," Flynn said. "I told her I'd pick her up."

"Thanks. I don't want to leave Becca right now." Trevor poured them both more whiskey. "I'm not sure if it's a good or bad thing that Mom is coming."

"Mom's outraged," Flynn said. "Caitlyn tried to call Dad, but he's not answering. I think he's weighing both sides or trying to keep out of it. He was really adamant about us handling company business on our own after he retired."

But this wasn't only company business, and they all knew it.

Uncle Arthur and Cian walked over to their table and wearily sat down. Another server brought more whiskey glasses straight away, and Flynn poured drinks all around.

"The women are still up with Becca," Uncle Arthur said, his wrinkles pronounced from fatigue. "Should we eat without them?"

"Chef is sending up dinner for them," Cian said. "I need to help Aileen, but you should all eat now."

After he left, Trevor looked at Arthur. "Where's Hargreaves?"

"Greeting guests at the door," the older man said, craning his neck in that direction. "Let's order. I don't have much of an appetite, but I know the body needs fuel. How did it go with Quinn?"

"Not good," Flynn answered, turning his glass in a circle.

They ate dinner mostly in silence, and Trevor asked Aileen twice if he could do more to help. She was firm about him staying put. When the restaurant settled down, Cian joined them for another drink.

"Everything seemed to go off well with dinner," Trevor said.

"We've done this a few times," he said, lifting the whiskey Trevor had poured him. "*Slainte*. It's good to have the extra help. Hargreaves and Chef are speaking French and having a brandy in the kitchen. The guests loved him."

"You can keep him if you'd like," Uncle Arthur joked, although he looked ready to fall asleep.

Trevor waited until his uncle had finished half his drink before rising and stretching. "I'm going up to Becca and plan to send the women out. Flynn, can you take Caitlyn? She might need a shoulder."

"And she'll want to know about my talk with Quinn," Flynn said, standing up.

"I guess it's time to stop the knitting party," Arthur said, leaning heavily on the back of his chair when he stood.

Upon entering Becca's bedroom, Trevor noticed his

suitcases were gone. Had she ordered them out? "Cian, do you know what Becca did with my clothes?"

"Clara had Hargreaves put them away on the sly," Arthur answered, his mouth tipping up. "He commandeered a few storage shelves and placed the empty cases under the bed."

On the sly? He was going to have to find a way to thank all of them for helping.

Uncle Arthur opened the closet door after tapping softly on it. Aileen had joined the party, and all four women were sitting on the floor in a circle. Aunt Clara had the makings of a scarf in her lap, and she was knitting with surprising speed and skill while Hatshep lay on her leg. Caitlyn was going slower, but her brows were pinched in a concentration he'd seen before. She was bound and determined to succeed, and so she would. Boru was snoring softly behind Becca.

"I knew you'd be useful at some point, Clara," Uncle Arthur called. "Come on. We need to get to bed. I'm pooped, and I can't do without you."

When she lifted her head, there was a fire in her eyes that went beyond the fatigue. "If I must. Arthur, you're going to have more sweaters, scarves, and hats than you can shake a stick at. I'm really good at this. See?" She held up the delicate mustard-colored rows like they were the Holy Grail itself.

"You're a marvel." He leaned close to Trevor. "Go and help your aunt up. She's been sitting too long."

"I've got this," Flynn said, waltzing into the closet. "You'll have to make something for me, Aunt. Come dance with me." He gently lifted her from the floor, holding her close for balance, and then started to sway with her in his arms. She leaned against him, chuckling softly. An affronted Hatshep hustled under Becca's hanging clothes, disappearing while Boru whined and padded out of view behind the desk.

"Unhand my woman, you upstart." Arthur was smiling though, and so were the rest of them.

Including Becca, who finally met Trevor's eyes. She was relaxed, he could see. Before, every muscle in her body had been stiff with tension.

Flynn passed Aunt Clara to their uncle and proceeded to replicate his dance moves with Aileen, who laughed gaily on her way to Cian. Both of the older couples said goodnight before leaving.

Caitlyn rose to her feet as Flynn approached her, already waving him off. "Keep away, moron. Every time you dance with me, you step on my toes."

"It's because your feet are so big," he quipped, holding out his hand. "Come on."

Before leaving the closet, Caitlyn leaned down and hugged Becca warmly. Trevor got choked up, seeing that. A real friendship was developing between them.

"I'll see you in the morning, Becca," Caitlyn said.

Trevor hugged her close, a couple of hanging sweaters swaying around them. "Thanks, kiddo."

"There's no cause for thanks." She kissed his cheek. "Love you."

"Love you too," he said and then lifted his chin to Flynn.

"No kiss?" his brother asked with a laugh.

"Out with you," Caitlyn said, pushing him ahead of her.

The two of them tussled playfully on their way out, but moments later, the closet was silent. Trevor walked forward and sat down Indian-style across from Becca. She looked as though she was on the verge of giving him *her opinions* again, so he headed her off. "Before you say anything, let me tell you that I'm not leaving. So, why don't you tell me how you normally make yourself comfortable in here, and we can go to bed. I'm pooped." He'd thought Uncle Arthur's word choice inspired.

"Pooped?" she asked.

"Knackered." Her understanding of his slang was so good, he didn't often need to translate it for her.

"Well, if you're going to be stubborn—"

"I am," he said, yawning and stretching his chest for show.

"You can sleep in my bed," she said. "You don't have to sleep in here."

"I sleep with you," he said, staring her down. "Deal with it."

She reached into the cedar chest under one of the hanging racks and pulled out a pillow and the small folded mattress he'd seen Aileen remove earlier. There was no way they were both going to fit on there. He rolled off the floor and walked out of the closet. Now he understood the Jack and Jill bathroom. Taking her down comforter off the bed, he grabbed a pillow. Returning, he stopped short at the sight of her staring up at him from the floor, tears in her eyes.

"I know you want to do this, but you really don't have to."

Her hoarse voice tore at his heart. "Do what? I sleep where you sleep and plan to do so for the rest of our lives." He sounded a little gruff about it, but he couldn't help that. He was trying to keep it together.

"We'll talk about that again later," she said, gesturing him inside. "Put that here."

"We'll fold ourselves up like tacos," he said, hoping to coax a smile from her.

"We don't do tacos in Ireland," she said, rolling her eyes.

He started to undress, and he heard her sharp intake of breath. Ignoring her, he stripped down the whole way. She was trying to divert her eyes, but he caught her secret glances. Yeah, she might have her opinions, but she hadn't stopped loving him or wanting him. When she started telling him he should back off, he'd do well to remember that.

"I'd very much like to make love to you, if you're not too knackered," he said, kneeling before her after she'd stopped punching her pillow.

He drew her hair back over her shoulders as she lifted her gaze to his. And waited. And waited.

Her face bunched up for a fraction of a second, but then she closed her eyes and took a deep breath. "I'd like that."

The words were his salvation. He helped her undress. The lights in the closet were on full blaze, and he said, "Do you sleep with the lights on?"

"I dim them," she said, tunneling her face in his chest. "I'm so ashamed. I don't want you to see me like this."

"I love seeing you," he said, taking her hand and lifting it to his mouth. "I'll always see you. Whatever happens. Whatever comes."

She pressed her cheek to his, gathering herself. When she steadied, he rose and dimmed the lights. Lying down beside her, he wrapped his hand around her waist and leaned in to kiss her. Her lips were soft and warm, and he kept it gentle. Tonight was about cherishing her. Tonight was about showing her he loved her unconditionally.

Her skin was smooth as silk as he ran his hands over her. He laid her back and set his mouth to roam over her curves, her soft places, the places that made her tense and arch under him, the ones that made her cry out in pleasure.

After the first few peaks, he put on a condom and slid inside her. Reaching for her hands, he drew them overhead and looked down at her. Her blue eyes were open, fixed on him. Starlight shone in her eyes, just as it had on other nights, and he allowed himself to relax—if only a little. Whatever else, he could trust what she felt. Now, she needed to trust him.

"I love you," he whispered, sliding forward inch by delicious inch.

He wasn't sure she'd respond. Perhaps she'd make him wait while she considered the wisdom of sharing her heart with him.

When she finally whispered the words back, he groaned and lowered his head to her shoulder, undone by the steadiness in her voice.

She might be unsure about them and their future.

But she wasn't uncertain about the love they had for each other.

He took her home with those thoughts rolling through his mind, igniting his heart, knowing the only true home for either of them was in each other's arms.

CHAPTER 37

BECCA AWOKE ON THE FLOOR THE NEXT MORNING WRAPped in warm maleness.

Trevor seemed to be all over her, wrapped up in that makeshift taco he'd joked about. Boru was still snoring, but Hatshep was on the windowsill, looking out.

That window would be her only view of the outside world for a while. How long this time? God, she couldn't take it, thinking about having visitors in her closet and sleeping with Trevor on the floor. Was she to have a knitting class every day? Not that she didn't love teaching the others or seeing Clara and Caitlyn take to it so, but she couldn't let day after day pass without doing anything. She had duties to see to and new dyes to fashion.

This time she *had* to get better faster.

She didn't know how that was going to happen, but she couldn't continue going through the same motions, hoping for a different outcome. If she stayed in here another day, she'd likely be in the closet for another eight weeks. She knew it.

She'd never tried to leave the closet right away. Her fingernails bit into her palms at the very thought. But it wouldn't be easy to leave it eight weeks from now either.

She had to steel herself to take the first steps. Count them one at a time. Ignore her pounding heart and drenched skin and light-headedness. Once out, she would have to keep steeling herself, one step at a time.

What did she have to lose?

One look told her that. He was lying beside her. Yes, Trevor Merriam had professed endless love for her. Slept on the closet floor. Folded his family around her. But this kind of living would peck away at anyone's spirit. It had hers. His would be no different.

She rolled away carefully. Thankfully, Trevor slept soundly. Boru stirred and Hatshep appeared in front of her, those wise eyes staring into her. She felt almost entranced, as if her cat was reminding her of her strength.

I am not a victim.

In that moment, she decided she wasn't going to give up on this new psychiatrist before she even talked to him. No, quitting wasn't an option. If Trevor wouldn't quit on her, she wouldn't quit on herself.

She donned some navy pants and a white tank top. Fitted some sandals on her feet. The closet door became her focus. All she had to do was walk to it. It couldn't be more than twelve steps. She could do this.

Looking down at her feet, she made them move. One.

Her heart started racing as she took the next. Two.

Her head went light, but she stepped forward. Three.

Four.

Five.

Six.

Boru nudged her leg when she stopped, her chest feeling like a crushed metal can. Sweat burned her eyes as she looked at the door. The sides reminded her of a long box. The image of a coffin popped into her mind, and she saw her parents lying on the floor dead. She shook herself. No, she didn't want to think those thoughts. Her parents were in heaven, and she wasn't a little girl anymore. She was a grown woman, and she wasn't going to let that image or the past hold her back any longer.

Seven.

Eight.

There was that magic switch in her energy, the kind that came from knowing she'd covered the worst of it. Only five more steps to go. She could do this. She made her feet move.

Nine.

Ten.

Panting, she could see the grains of wood in the doorframe. She focused on them.

Eleven.

Twelve.

She touched the frame with her right hand, the other hand pressing into a fist over her mouth. Crying softly, she surveyed her bedroom. She'd done it. She'd made it out of the closet. Oh, God.

Her knees felt weak, and then she heard, "You're the bravest woman in the whole world."

She couldn't look at him or break her focus. Even though she could feel his strength, only hers could propel her forward completely.

Boru gave a bark, encouraging her to go on. Hatshep made figure eights around her ankles, making her focus again on her feet. Right, they were only feet. They were designed to walk, each toe, bone, and tendon working in perfect harmony.

She calculated the number of steps to the sofa in her sitting room. Twenty-five, give or take. Steeling herself, she sucked in fresh air and took the first step, keeping her eyes on the floor. Hatshep padded ahead of her, leading the way. Boru stayed by her side, barking softly as if to cheer milestones like her eighth step, her tenth step. She was crying now, heart beating out of her chest, sweat burning her eyes.

"Sixteen, seventeen, eighteen, nineteen," she said aloud, her feet tingling.

She felt like she was outside her body as she took the remaining steps, falling onto the back of her beloved purple sofa. Large, warm arms enfolded her in an embrace, and she distantly felt Trevor turn her in his arms.

"You did it!" His voice was hoarse. "Oh, Becca! Look at you. I love you so much."

She loved him too, but she couldn't get the words out. She started weeping, everything crashing inside her. Perhaps it needed to. This was a breakdown, a break*through*, and she couldn't hold back the tears any more than a dam could hold back a flash flood. She thought of her parents and all she'd lost, all the years of lonely isolation, thinking she wasn't normal and never would be, fearing there would never be a man to love her like this one did.

Emotion ravaged her, swept her over and under until it thrust her up again. Exhausted, floating now on the warm light of release, she felt hollow yet whole at the same time.

She wasn't cured. She knew that.

But she'd overcome, and that was a triumph.

Chapter 38

Trevor's mother arrived like a sirocco, demanding an immediate family meeting on a neutral site. Assumpta Merriam was a force of nature, and her will was not to be denied. To Trevor, it came as a relief. Although he doubted this matter could be resolved so easily, if anyone could do it, surely she could. If nothing else, he was happy she was here with him. He'd told Becca he wanted her to hold off on introductions until after the impromptu meeting, hoping tensions would be alleviated. If not, Connor and Quinn sure as hell weren't getting close to her.

J.T. flew in shortly after their mother, and they barely had time to exchange a quick, relieved greeting before the family meeting. Arthur and Clara wished them luck, and they drove to the town meeting hall, which Cian had secured for their use.

And now they waited together—Assumpta Merriam standing sentinel at the window while four of her children sat around the table, a tray of tea and biscuits between them.

"Mom looks tired," Caitlyn whispered to Trevor. "And mad. *Really* mad. As bad as that time she caught all of us in that mud pit when we were kids."

"She looks madder to me," Trevor said, shifting in his chair. "I can't believe Connor and Quinn are late."

"I can," Flynn said, cracking his neck. "They're playing corporate games with Mom. Big mistake."

Making people wait to show power and strength was a common business tactic. But it was less effective when used on family, particularly on their mother, who knew precisely what they were attempting.

"She looks fierce," J.T. said, also in a low voice, "and sad. If she hadn't looked so sad, I would have made her let me change clothes at least."

"You look fine, J.T.," their mother said from across the room, turning her head and staring at them. "And so far I agree with everything you've said. I *am* madder than that time with the mud pit, and Con and Quinn made a real mistake making me wait to talk to them."

Caitlyn's eyes turned to saucers, and Flynn cleared his throat.

"I have super-sonic mom hearing, remember?" she said, turning back to the window. "And eyes in the back of my head."

No shit.

Caitlyn grimaced and poured everyone tea, rising to take a cup to their mom. She took it and patted their sister's shoulder. "It's going to be okay, honey."

Trevor wondered if she was saying that to herself as much as Caitlyn. Hard footsteps—ass-kicking ones—sounded in the hall and then Connor and Quinn stalked in, decked out in full suit and tie action like they were meeting with hostile strikers demanding better wages.

"You made me wait," their mother said flatly, leaning back against the window. "Not a good way to start, boys. Sit down."

Connor raised his brows before saying, "Hello, Mother."

She pushed off the windowsill. "Don't 'mother' me.

How do you think I felt to have to up and leave Corey's wife and children and fly across the pond so I could force my own children to talk to each other?"

"We were working it out, Mom," Quinn said, crossing and kissing her cheek. "They weren't listening."

She crossed her arms, giving him the patented mom stare. "Don't kid a kidder, Quinn Anthony Merriam. And don't you dare try and *handle* me. You're forgetting. I've been married to a Merriam for fifty years this June, and I know all the tricks. Sit down."

Quinn was working his jaw like Mom had just knocked him back, but he sat down. Connor took his time unbuttoning his jacket before dragging out a chair loudly and sitting across from Trevor. He stared at him, and Trevor stared right back. *Don't be such a dick*, he wanted to say but held his tongue. His mom wouldn't appreciate his interference.

Mom came over and stood at the head chair, which everyone wisely had left vacant for her. "When your father handed over the company, he knew there would be some ups and downs between you all, areas where the personal and the business would mix like oil and water. This seems to be one of them. But if you think I'm not going to find a way to make this into the best damn salad dressing ever, you're mistaken. So it's like I told you when you were kids... We can do this easy, or we can do this hard. Think before you start talking because I can tell you right now that this family and how we love and respect each other is *the* most important thing we need to remember right now. Not some piece of land or business deal. Got me?"

Mom's crisp Midwest tone left no room for interpretation, and Trevor nodded, learning long ago that she liked seeing the positive response.

"Now we're going to talk business," Assumpta said. "Normally, I don't involve myself with these things, but

I made the mistake of not intervening between your father and Clara decades ago, and I've lived with that estrangement, wondering if I could have helped bridge the peace. I told your father that, and he understands why I'm here. You will also remember that Grandma Anna's mother allowed grief to create a rift with her only daughter, and that is not going to happen here."

Whoa. Mom wasn't pulling any punches today, and Connor shifted in his seat. Trevor hadn't known the rift between Clara and their father had weighed on her, but she'd talked some about never seeing her own grandmother. His gut sunk. What would it be like to never speak to one of his siblings ever again? He didn't want to find out. For all the issues he'd had with Connor over the years, he loved his brother.

"Con, before you think I'm only doing this from an emotional angle, I've been advising your father since we met."

Trevor had always loved the story of how his parents had met. Both of them had been students at the University of Chicago—his father, an economics major; his mother, a teaching major. Grandpa Noah had invited their dad to the house for dinner, something he did with his more interesting history students, and the couple had immediately hit it off. Trevor had always wondered if his grandpa had had an inkling about the couple being a good match, but Grandpa Noah had never given him a straight answer. Trevor thought again about the medallion he'd given Becca and realized he needed to share that with his mother. He'd wait for the right moment.

"Good business is common sense most of the time," their mom said, finally grabbing her seat, which Trevor jumped up to help pull out for her since he was closest. "Thank you, sweetheart."

Con's smug stare screamed *ass-kisser*, and Trevor

had to pull his gaze away from his brother or his rage would show on his face.

"What I understand is pretty straightforward," she said, crossing her hands prayer-style. "From the get-go, Becca O'Neill didn't want to sell her land. Is that correct?"

When Connor remained silent, Trevor responded, "Yes, Con made the first attempts and then sent me to see if I could persuade her."

"He *persuaded* her, all right, only not in our favor," Con said, his tone insulting.

Trev lunged across the table and grabbed him by the jacket. "Stop talking about my future wife like that. Or me for that matter."

Their mom was on her feet in an instant. "Stop this! Trevor, I understand you being upset, but let go of your brother. And Con, I've heard the kind of language you've used to talk about the woman Trevor loves, and it cuts me to the bone."

"I apologize for that," his brother said, "but you have to understand. I didn't know this woman—"

"But you know me," Trevor interrupted. "You should know I wouldn't fall for someone unless it was the real thing."

J.T. cleared his throat before saying, "Perhaps I'm to blame here. My past might have colored the situation. I put this family through hell, and I'm sorry for it."

Connor stared at him as if waiting to see if Trevor was going to call him out. He thought about it for a second before discarding the idea. He wanted peace, not war, with his brother.

"You've apologized enough for that, honey," their mom said, "and your heart was in the right place. It's not your fault she threatened this family, but I can see your point. From now on, though, no one in this family is going to second-guess another person's love interest—unless they have a criminal record or something."

The joke fell flat.

"Is that clear?"

"As crystal," Connor said. "Again, I apologize."

Releasing a long breath, Trevor said, "Apology accepted."

Connor folded his hands together. "Now if we're done with the personal side of the stiuation, let's get to the heart of the matter. Trevor lied to me and Quinn and then went behind our backs to make another deal. I was right to fire him. He was more than unprofessional. He was disloyal."

Trevor couldn't hold his tongue. "I'm not saying I went about things in the right way, but I figured you might let up if I found another tract to develop. I hate making this personal, but we're there. Con, since Corey died, you've been running on emotion. You kept talking about keeping Patrick safe and how you'd promised Uncle Liam you wouldn't put him on an offshore project."

Tears flashed in his mother's eyes, and he had to look away.

"You overrode Becca's two refusals, plus my assessment—as an officer in this company—that not only would she not sell, but that we were going to have problems with her community."

Quinn tapped the table, and Trevor caught his measure. So, Quinn hadn't known that last part. He continued, "I want everyone to be safe too, but I was trying to protect Becca while also giving Connor what he wanted. Perhaps not the exact thing, but let's face it, pursuing onshore drilling in Ireland is bad business and so is canceling all our future offshore business plans due to one accident." Mom put her hand on Trevor's arm, almost a warning to be gentle. Like that was going to work.

Connor shot out of his chair. "That *one* accident killed several of our employees, including my best friend. You were out of line to go around me."

His throat was thick as he responded honestly, "I was, Con, and I'm sorry. But your grief has twisted you up so much I...didn't feel like I knew the man I was talking to anymore."

Shoving his chair back, Connor started to walk out of the room.

"Connor!" their mom called. "Please stop and listen to me."

He halted but didn't turn around. Trevor noticed Caitlyn was silently crying at the end of the table, and he reached inside his pants pocket and passed down a Waterford handkerchief from Aunt Clara. She blew her nose, and the sound echoed throughout the room.

"Connor, I talked to Olivia about this before my plane left," their mom continued. "She knew I was upset after Caitlyn called me. I felt it was right to tell her. She wanted me to tell you Corey would never have wanted you to change the way the company operates. He knew the risks. Everyone does. They'd talked enough about it, especially after having Max and Joseph."

Trevor's throat clogged as an image flashed into his head of Corey wearing a red hard hat with Merriam Oil & Gas on it. Corey had said his next post was going to be back in San Francisco, working in their renewable energy department, something he believed was the way of the future. How sad that wish wouldn't come to pass.

"Honey, I know you miss him," his mom continued. "We all do to our core, but a decision that has such big implications for the company should go to the board."

Trevor heard J.T.'s sigh gust out. Quinn lowered his head. Mom had a way of cutting through the crap, as she liked to say. But this kind of truth telling always hurt.

"If Patrick still wants to head up a project," she said, "he knows the risk too. I understand your promise to Uncle Liam, but I'm not sure he wants it. Did he ask it of you?"

Connor remained quiet.

"My brother worked with your father on engineering projects around the world before retiring. He understands the dangers of the work, but being a parent, of course, he wouldn't want another child to die. No parent does."

She rose and walked to where Connor stood, his entire body as cold and unmoving as a block of ice. She put her hand on his back and rubbed it, something Trevor remembered her doing when Connor had come home from school angry that he'd gotten an A- on a test. She'd always said he was so hard on himself, and Trevor still didn't fully understand why.

"Con," Mom said softly. "I know you're hurting, but striking out at your brothers and sisters isn't the way. Pushing this woman to sell her land when she clearly doesn't want to isn't the way. Perhaps it's my fault for naming you Connor. You remember it means strong-willed in Irish, don't you? Even in the womb, you always wanted your way, if the amount of times you kicked me was any indication." She laughed, but the sound was forced.

His oldest brother sure as hell was living up to his name, wasn't he? But Quinn sure as hell *wasn't*. His name meant wise and reasonable. Mom had named them all intentionally since she'd been named after a Catholic feast day, something she'd always bemoaned. J.T.'s first name was Julian, and the youthful attribution had always seemed fitting for his idealistic twin. It also alluded to a clan of Roman emperors, which J.T. thought serendipitous given he'd lived in Rome for a decade before moving to Dare Valley. Flynn meant the son of the red-haired one, and their mother had indeed been a redhead before going gray. Caitlyn's name couldn't be more apt; she *was* pure of heart. And Michaela was the feminine of Michael, which meant gift of God, which was how his mother had characterized getting pregnant for the sixth time with such a beautiful girl.

Trevor's name had always seemed to fit. Prudent in business he was, but now he remembered it also meant a large farm or estate. Chills touched his spine. Had his mother known on some weird Irish level that he would come to live with Becca on her land one day? He was oddly touched by the thought.

"Please, Connor. Come sit back down. I know this isn't easy, but walking out won't fix anything."

The way her voice wavered made Trevor cough. She was usually so strong.

"Don't make me tie you to your chair," she said, poking him teasingly. "Please, Con. I know you're upset, but do this for me. Come sit back down so we can sort things out."

He straightened to his full height. Then he walked back to his chair and sat down. Mom did the same, reaching for Trevor's hand and then Connor's, which he reluctantly gave her. Man, she wasn't going to make them hold hands, was she? Trevor squirmed in his seat.

"Now let's talk about this firing and resignation," she said. "Does anyone want to undo that?"

He waited for Connor to speak.

"I want to apologize," J.T. said. "I helped Trevor because I agreed with him regarding the situation and wanted to help—and because he's never gone apeshit over a girl like this."

Their mom's mouth tipped up in a lopsided smile. "Thank you for saying that, J.T."

"I'm sorry for everything too," Caitlyn said, "but I don't like the thought of pressuring people who turn us down on Merriam business. It's not how I want us to do business."

"I agree," Flynn said. "And I'm apologizing too."

"Con, I know you're still mad," Caitlyn said, "but you need to know how important this is to Trevor."

Trevor glanced her way, and her mouth tipped up into a half-smile that mirrored their mom's.

"He looks at Becca the way Dad looks at Mom," she said roughly. "Maybe if you'd seen that, you wouldn't have... Never mind. For that, I'd do anything to help him."

Connor didn't say anything, but Quinn's gaze had turned downright studious.

"Now I really can't wait to meet Becca," Mom said. "All right, let's talk some more about Flynn and Caitlyn. Are you really going to fire them too, Con? Sorry to pick on you, kid, but you're not saying much here."

"I need to know I can trust them moving forward," Connor said after a moment of silence. "I need to know something like this won't happen again."

"Back at you, Con," Caitlyn said. "Are you going to stop being a dick? Because I'm retaining my right to call you on it."

His jaw ticked before he said, "I'll try to keep my dick-factor to a minimum from now on. All right, I apologize for acting rashly regarding Flynn's and your involvement, but I hope you can see my side."

"I do," Caitlyn said, pushing back from her chair and coming over to where he was sitting. She kneeled down next to him. "I know you miss Corey like crazy, more than any of us probably, but how are we supposed to reach you if you won't talk to us? It scares me how you shut down, Con. It always has."

He swallowed thickly before tracing her cheek. "I'm sorry, Caity girl."

She pushed him in the chest. "You know I hate that name, Connor Bomber."

Trevor was glad Caitlyn had found a way to lighten the mood in the room with childhood nicknames because they all sure as hell needed a break. The makings of a smile finally touched Connor's mouth, and Trevor knew the worst was behind them. He breathed a sigh of relief, and his twin elbowed him as if to agree.

"We good?" Flynn asked, standing and holding out his hand.

Connor rose and took his hand. "Yeah."

"Great, then to make up for all my emotional turmoil, I'm going to need a hundred million for a new project I have in mind," Flynn said, making them all laugh, including Connor, although his was more of a chuckle.

"New ideas still go through me," Quinn said, leaning back in his chair, his mouth twitching. "But I admire your pluck."

Flynn shrugged. "I had to give it a shot. Although to be honest, I plan on investing in Becca's new enterprise with my own money. You should hear her talk business. She's going to fit in perfectly with this family."

Quinn lifted his chin in Trevor's direction, and it was a peace offering. He lifted his chin in response.

"I wouldn't expect anything less from Trev," Quinn said. "I mean J.T. found Caroline, and she likes to gush about paintings and shit. It must be a twin thing."

And it was Quinn's way of telling Trevor he approved of Becca.

J.T. put his arm around Trevor's shoulder and jostled him. "You're just jealous of our crazy bond. Have been since we were born."

"I wouldn't have shared a womb with anyone, man," Quinn responded.

"No one would have shared one with you anyway," Caitlyn said, standing and hugging him from behind. "You always kick when you sleep."

"It was one time," he protested, throwing up his hands. "She never forgets anything."

"Oh, and Quinnie boy," Caitlyn said as she resumed her seat. "I plan on asking for a hundred million for the new project I've been working on too."

He shook his head. "So long as you have a report and a convincing investment presentation, I'll consider it."

She flashed a smile. "Soon. It's going to rock your socks."

"She's not lying, Quinn," Trevor said. And then, because it was past time for him and Connor to speak directly to each other, he turned to his brother and said, "Connor, I need to hear from you directly that you won't go after Becca's land. If you still want me out, that's your call."

"If Ms. O'Neill doesn't want to sell, that's her right." Connor crossed his arms. "As for firing you... Do you plan on going around me again?"

Trevor wanted to grind his teeth. "You planning on not listening to me again?"

Their mother cleared her throat, and Trevor knew it was a warning to play nice. Tell that to Connor.

"I was out of line, and I apologize," his older brother said, his eyes like cold steel. "It would be a shame for the company to lose your skills over this."

"Oh, Connor, talk like a normal human being," Caitlyn said, slapping him on the shoulder. "He's still a Merriam employee and you love him like a brother, right?"

Leave it to Caitlyn.

"Yes to both," Connor said, although his mouth was still tight. "Good enough?"

That was the best he could expect from him. Trevor extended his hand, and Connor took it. "Yeah, we're good."

"Whew! That's a relief." Caitlyn hugged her mom. "How did you handle all of us growing up, Mom?"

"Day by day, honey," her mom said, shaking her head in bemusement.

"So when are we going to meet Becca?" J.T. asked.

Trevor thought about the way she'd forced herself

to walk out of the closet this morning, one excruciating step at a time. She didn't just make him happy. She inspired the hell out of him. They'd had breakfast in her sitting room, and he'd kissed her goodbye before going downstairs to collect his mom. She'd been knitting the remainder of Hargreaves' scarf when he'd left. "Let me talk to her first. I know she's eager to meet you all too."

"Trev, I'm sorry about the helicopter and all that," Quinn said. "If I'd known about her condition, I'd have never—"

"I know," he said, his mind flashing to that moment. "I'm having it towed today. Didn't see another way."

His brother laughed. "I call that an innovative solution. May be the first time a helicopter's ever been towed. Can I ask how she is?"

He wondered how much he should share. Becca was a private person, and he respected that. "Better. She's tough, as tough as Mom here, if not more so."

"It's not possible," J.T. said, standing and coming over and putting his hands on their mom's shoulders. "No one is tougher than our mother. Except Rocky Balboa maybe."

"Rocky Balboa isn't in my league, kiddo," their mom said, standing and leaning against J.T. affectionately. "All right, any last words?"

She'd always asked that same question after refereeing one of their fights when they were kids. Like she'd done in the past, she looked at each of them in turn, almost like she was framing them in a camera for a picture.

"I need some scones," Caitlyn said when Mom reached her.

"We'll get you some stat," Mom said. "Flynn?"

"I need a steak, medium rare, with *beurre blanc* sauce, and some really good bread and butter." Their brother rubbed his stomach for emphasis.

"I see where we're going here," Mom said. "J.T.?"

His smile was fast. "Nothing, except thanks for being our mom."

She teared up at that. "You're welcome. I'm glad I didn't cause WWIII by coming here, but I decided I couldn't sit this one out. I love you all too much. Okay, Trev?"

He reached for her hand. "What J.T. said. Oh, and Con, I won't be able to travel as much for work, what with Becca and all. I'll want to spend more time at home with her."

"We'll talk," Con said, not missing a beat.

"Plus, Buttercup would pine away without him," Caitlyn said, laughing.

"Buttercup, huh? I can't wait to meet this mythical animal capable of making my brave son run across the yard." Their mom threw her head back and laughed. "I confess I watched that over and over again when I needed some cheering up."

It was the first mention of her own grief, and Trevor leaned in and hugged her. She gripped him tightly before pushing back and slapping him playfully. "Okay, if we're all good, I could use a steak too. Anyone know where we could find one at this time of day?"

Trevor eyed his watch, noting it was close to noon. "I don't know about the pub in town, but we could check it out. Or I can see what Chef Padraig has for lunch at The Wild Irish Rose. Quinn? Connor? You plan on staying there with the rest of us? I can call Aileen and set it up."

He'd checked on their availability when he'd made the arrangements for his mom and J.T. Becca had told him she was okay with having Connor and Quinn stay at the inn as guests so long as they worked things out.

His mom patted him on the back as if to praise him for holding out an olive branch. Quinn and Connor shared a look—one that could have passed for the kind of silent communication Trevor had with his twin.

"That would be great," Quinn said. "I've been hearing about these incredible scones they serve."

"I ate a whole bunch the first day she finally agreed to let me check in," Trevor said, smiling. "On my first visit, she grabbed the basket of scones away from me before I could try any when she figured out who I was."

"I love her even more," Mom said. "That's something I would have done."

"I know," he said, nodding.

They shared a look, and she linked her arm through his. "To The Wild Irish Rose then."

And to my Becca, he thought.

CHAPTER 39

BECCA'S LIVING ROOM FILLED UP WITH THE MERRIAM family as the day went on, and she was mostly okay with it.

Trevor's mother embraced her warmly and said, "You can't know how happy I am to meet you, Becca. Welcome to the family. And please call me Assumpta. You know I'm from an Irish neighborhood in Chicago, right? My mother was a Sims before she married, and her people were from Sligo."

"It's wonderful to meet you too," she said. Then, not wanting to give his mother the wrong impression, she added, "but we're still talking things through."

She waved a hand. "You'll work them out. I'll admit I'm partial, but he's a keeper. Oh, look at your cat. She's a Persian, isn't she? What's her name?"

"Hatshep, after Hatshepsut," she replied, watching as her beloved cat approached the man standing at the edge of room, twining around his ankles.

"This is Quinn," Assumpta said. "He's a keeper too."

The man met her gaze before leaning down and picking up Hatshep, who stretched luxuriously in his arms. This was Connor's ally? Maybe it was the Irish in her, but she trusted Hatshep's judgment enough to take her behavior as a sign that all that was in the past.

"I'm happy to meet you under better circumstances, Becca," he said, crossing and holding out his hand. "I'm deeply sorry for what happened. More than you could know."

He seemed genuinely contrite. She shook his hand. "Thank you. Please, make yourself at home."

"Yeah, Quinnie boy," Caitlyn said. "Come see my knitting project. It's ambitious, but that suits me. If you're extra nice to me about my new venture, I'll knit you a sweater."

He winked at Becca before saying, "I can buy my own sweater, Caity girl. But show me your knitting."

The two of them huddled in the corner, bickering sweetly. Becca scanned the rest of the room. Flynn was playing tug-of-war with Boru with a dog toy, laughing with that easy way of his when Arthur noted that he'd lose a tooth or two if anyone did that to him. Clara was laughing as well, talking to J.T.—who did remind her a lot of Trevor, although they were fraternal twins—but Becca had caught her watching Assumpta earlier. She was still longing for a full reconciliation, Becca knew.

Trevor walked in from the kitchen with more drinks. He seemed completely relaxed, and after he'd briefed her on his family meeting, some of her lingering tension had leaked away too. The Merriams had been knitted back together, and for all of them, she was glad. For her and her land here...she was beyond relieved.

"Who needs more scones?" Aileen called, carrying in a steaming basket. "Oh, isn't this a grand party? Trevor, I talked to the butcher in town, and he's sending out his best steaks for dinner tonight."

He kissed her warmly on the cheek. "You're a love. Thank you."

"Yeah, thank you," Flynn called. "From me and my

stomach. Aileen, dear, I need a scone."

"Right away, you fine thing," Aileen said. "Assumpta, you have some handsome sons, if you don't mind me saying so."

"They take after their father," she said. "I hope he'll fly over and join us. He wants to meet you very much, Becca."

Mr. Merriam too? Some of Becca's tension came tumbling back. Perhaps it was time for her and Trevor to have that talk. "Maybe he should wait."

Assumpta ushered her aside. "I'm a frank woman, and I hope being Irish, you'll appreciate it. I can't begin to understand what it must be like to be agoraphobic, but J.T. told me he'd brought you the letters my mom and dad wrote each other during the war. I hope you'll read them and let me tell you more about my parents. I see you're wearing the St. Christopher medal my mother gave him during the war to keep him safe and strong."

Her throat closed up, and all she could do was nod, thinking about how the medal, which she'd treasured because it was Trevor's, signified something more to her now: the kind of love that could transform and heal.

"You think I'll be able to be the kind of wife Trevor deserves?"

A wrinkle appeared between her brows. "Does your agoraphobia prevent you from loving my son with everything you are? Because that's what marriage is."

Trevor had said the same. Perhaps this practical side came from his mother. "Of course it doesn't. What about children? Can I be a good mother, with a condition like this?"

"I don't see why not, do you? You've made adjustments—successfully, I might add—to run your business. Did anyone think you were incapable of doing so because you were agoraphobic?"

She'd feared as much in the beginning, but she'd

overcome her doubts. "My grandmother never wavered in thinking I could. I wanted to run this inn more than I wanted anything else." And now she wanted Trevor. She give anything to be with him, but she feared she'd become a burden to him in the end. Was she underestimating herself?

"I'll leave you with one last thing," Assumpta said, wrapping an arm around her shoulders as they surveyed the room. "My dad was scared to marry my mom because he didn't feel fully cured from his war trauma. She was having none of it, let me tell you, and eventually she showed him they were stronger together than they were apart. When you love like that, why ever would you choose to be apart? Besides, children can be helpers too. When I was little, I'd jump on my father's back. He'd tense, but I'd be laughing, and soon the memories would retreat again. So you see, when you have family to help, you're never alone."

Looking around the room, Becca could easily see that. They'd only made peace hours ago, but they'd truly forgiven each other. They loved each other, that much was clear.

"Think on it." She kissed Becca's cheek. "Okay, I need to have me one of these scones. I'll talk to you later, sweetie."

With that, she was off, and Becca walked over to the sofa because her knees were weak. My God, no wonder that woman had managed to mediate peace between her children!

Someone cleared their throat behind her, and she spun around, caught off guard. Before her stood Connor Merriam, his face as wooden as one of the African masks that hung in the West Wing's hallway.

"Ms. O'Neill? May I speak to you for a moment?"

She stopped short, not knowing where to take him. She hadn't been able to leave her chambers yet. The bedroom was the empty space accessible to her at the moment, and she was reluctant to talk to him there.

"Hey, Con!" Caitlyn called. "Come see my knitting project. I'm measuring Quinn for a sweater, and if you're good, I'll measure you too."

"In a minute, Caity girl," he said, a smile appearing and then retreating as he looked back at Becca.

She felt frozen, but she made herself move. "Follow me." Her bedroom wasn't ideal, but they could talk in the hallway and not be overheard if they spoke softly.

Trevor glanced their way, and she made herself nod at him. She had to do this alone. The family feud had started with Connor, and it was time to end her part in it. Plus, it was almost an Irish fairy tale, her meeting Trevor as she had. The fates didn't always send you what you expected. Many times, they knew better.

In the hallway, she stopped and crossed her arms, waiting for him to speak.

His jaw was tense, and he unbuttoned his suit jacket before saying, "I owe you an apology, Ms. O'Neill. I shouldn't have pressed after you turned down my offer. It's only, I'm used to getting my way, and if the offer is large enough, most people..."

He trailed off, and Becca watched as he looked off. Boru trotted into the hallway and took up sentry duty by her side. She hadn't expected an apology from Connor, but she could respect it.

"I'm deeply sorry about your cousin and the accident," she decided to say. If he could be gracious, so could she.

"Thank you." He coughed. "It was a tragedy, the worst of its kind since I took over from my father as the company's president."

His torment was so obvious Boru padded toward him and nudged his clenched fist with his nose.

"You have a good dog here," he said, rubbing Boru

under the ears. "I hope you won't hold my actions against me. For what I said to Trevor, I'm...deeply ashamed. He's—"

She waited while he took his time clearing his throat.

"He's a good brother and a valuable asset to our company. I might have disagreed with Trevor over this, but I still want him to be happy, and it seems you make him so. Caitlyn was right. I saw it the moment I walked in. He does look at you like Dad does our mom. I... welcome to the family."

Oh, good heavens. Her throat hurt, his words were so unexpected. "Thank you." Her reply came out more as a rasp.

He nodded. "If you'll excuse me, I hear your scones are excellent."

With that, he walked away from her. She rested her hand on Boru's head, stroking it softly. Well, today seemed to be a day of surprises.

Trevor appeared in the hall. "Everything okay?"

She nodded. "Yes."

He traced her face. "What did he say, if you don't mind me asking?"

"He apologized, said you were a good brother and a valuable asset to the company. Then he welcomed me to the family."

Trevor scratched his head. "I'll be damned."

"We need to talk, you know."

He put his hand to his ear. "What? I can't hear you. I gotta run and see Caitlyn's knitting project. She's gathering measurements for everyone's Christmas presents. How does everyone coming here sound? I thought an Irish Christmas might be nice." He dashed off with a wicked smile.

She let him go.

An Irish Christmas did sound lovely, at that.

***

Clara found herself itching to move around the room, but instead her feet seemed to be made of clay. Seeing Assumpta Merriam like this...

Well, it might as well have been yesterday when they'd parted despite the fact that the passing of time had left them with gray hair and a few wrinkles. They hadn't spoken much at her wedding to Arthur, although Assumpta and Shawn had both offered their congratulations. But it was time to forge a new path. She knew it.

"Get on with it, Clara," Arthur leaned down and whispered in her ear. "No more dillydallying."

She poked him, and he jumped. "You're a pain sometimes, but you're right."

"I tell you that every day, my love." He winked. "Call me if you need me. I'll come to your rescue if she takes a bite out of you."

Assumpta Merriam wouldn't take a bite out of her, she knew, but she didn't know if the woman still held a grudge against her. It was high time she found out. She could feel all the Merriam children watching her progress as she crossed the room.

"Clara," Assumpta said, moving toward her. "You beat me. I was coming to you, but I got delayed talking to Becca. Isn't she wonderful? I'm so happy for Trevor."

"They're both wonderful. It's been a joy to get to know Trevor, Assumpta. And J.T., of course, and Caitlyn and Flynn. They're terrific children. I imagine Quinn and Connor are as well, although I haven't had the opportunity to get to know them yet."

Hopefully she would after today. Caitlyn had filled her in on the situation when she'd come to the cottage to tell them the family was congregating in Becca's chambers. She'd raised her eyes heavenward, only to hear the tearing of paper. Arthur had ripped up his Op-Ed, a relieved smile on his face.

"I expect there will be a lot of opportunities for us all to get reacquainted," Assumpta said. "I know there's a lot of water under the bridge, Clara, but I want you to know, I'm past it. Shall we start over?"

She appreciated her frankness. "I'm sorry for what happened all those years ago. I was married to a total ass, but he was my husband, and I let my hurt turn into pride, something I deeply regret. Does Shawn feel the same as you?" She had to ask.

Assumpta's face softened. "His hurt turned into pride too, but I'm not sure he'd admit it out loud. He regrets things too, Clara. More than you can know. But he's really grateful for the help you've given our boys."

Clara's diamonds were tinkling softly, and she realized her hands were shaking. "I hope to do whatever I can for the rest of them. I missed their childhood because of my own stubbornness. I don't plan to miss any more time." Flynn and Caitlyn had told her that she and Arthur would be welcome to visit any time. She was going to take them up on it.

"Caitlyn mentioned we have Hargreaves to thank for Becca's new psychiatrist," Assumpta said, winking at someone from across the room. "I'd hoped he'd be here so I could thank him."

Hargreaves had suggested that Becca contact the man? That was news to her. "He never accepts invitations to family celebrations. He's an old-fashioned butler that way. I'm going to check in with him so I'll pass along your regards."

"Thank you," she said. "Well, I'd better get in line for Caitlyn's measurements. When that girl gets something in her mind, there's no stopping her. She gets that from me. I'll see you later, Clara."

Clara thought it a Merriam trait, but she figured a child could get such a trait from both parents. Assumpta walked off, and Clara smoothed her hands down her dress. She felt Arthur's eyes on her, and she turned and smiled at him. He blew her a kiss, a romantic gesture for him. He certainly had his moments. She could sure use a real kiss, but first she needed to see Hargreaves.

When she arrived at his door, he immediately opened it. Bowing, he asked, "What can I do for you, madam?"

His private quarters had always been off-limits, and she'd respected that. Living in someone else's home couldn't be easy, so he'd had to carve out his own space. She hadn't expected him to invite her in.

"Assumpta Merriam sends her regards," she told him. "She'd hoped you would join us."

He gave her that bland stare of his. "Please give her my regards, madam."

She hadn't expected anything else. "Hargreaves, she mentioned we have you to thank for Becca's new psychiatrist. How did that come about?" The man was resourceful, she knew that better than anyone, but this seemed beyond the call of duty.

"I've had his name for some years," he responded, his uncommonly polite yet warm smile fixed on his thin lips.

"Whatever for?" she asked.

He paused as if he were considering whether—and how—to respond. Goodness, prying information out of the man was like pulling teeth.

"*Hargreaves*."

"Yes, madam, I had acquired the doctor's name when I thought you might be in need of his services."

That stopped her cold.

"I concluded his were not the services you needed in the end," he finished.

She stared at him. "Why ever would I need his services? Hargreaves, really."

"You didn't leave the house for some time, madam," he said in that same even voice. "At the time, I suspected you might share Ms. O'Neill's affliction."

He did? She'd never known. "I was depressed, Hargreaves. Not agoraphobic."

"I realized that in the end, madam."

Standing there, they looked at each other. He'd been her constant companion since she was twenty years old, hired by Clara herself when her father had told her he'd give her a butler for her birthday. They'd been in London, and she'd thought it might be fun. Who hadn't seen *My Man Godfrey* and loved the movie?

Hargreaves had turned out to be a lot more than her butler. He'd been her steadfast friend, the only person she could count on until recently, when Arthur and the Merriams had come back into her life.

"Thank you, Hargreaves. For taking care of things above and beyond anything I could ever imagine. What would I do without you?"

His mouth twisted, almost a sly smile for him. "Good thing you'll never have to find out, madam. Is that all?"

Yes, you silly man. He wasn't into emotional scenes, as he called them. And yet, the man listened to opera. Still waters, if you asked her, but she never pressed. He hadn't pressed her.

"Becca finished your scarf today, and I think it's wonderful." Take that, you silly man. A scarf was pure love.

"I can't wait to see it," he said, bowing. "It's good you've taken to knitting. Those Colorado winters are cold, and Master Arthur does like his sweaters."

They shared a conspiratorial look. "He does, indeed. If you'd like, I can knit you something as well."

He paused and then bowed grandly, as if receiving the Queen herself. "I would be honored, madam."

A concession for sure, and one that bespoke of their unacknowledged friendship. "Well, good night, Hargreaves."

"Good night, madam."

She walked down the hall, filled with the promise of new adventures with her old and new partners in crime and a whole fleet of Merriam children.

No, she sure as hell wasn't depressed anymore.

Chapter 40

Trevor stood at the door to Becca's chambers the next afternoon, J.T. and Caitlyn beside him.

"You ready?" J.T. asked, socking him in the shoulder.

The engagement ring he'd picked out after flying Dublin's finest jeweler down to Cork City this morning was in his pocket, and Aileen, Caitlyn, his mother, and Aunt Clara had all helped him make his selection. The emerald was the same dark green as the Irish hills behind Becca's land, one he hoped to walk with her someday. In his other hand was the wool he and Caitlyn had dyed secretly with Aileen's help in the old kitchen. It was the perfect Kelly green, and Aileen assured Trevor that Becca was going to love it.

"Make sure to be romantic," Caitlyn was saying, "Get down on your knee and tell her how much you love her—"

"I can manage that," Trevor said.

"Good, because some guys' proposals are so dumb. This guy I knew pretended to have a vehicle breakdown on the highway at rush hour, and when he and his girlfriend got out to change the tire, he proposed with all the cars watching. Talk about ridiculous! I mean who wants a proposal in a traffic jam? Some guys really need a woman's input."

"You've given me something better than mere input," he said, kissing her cheek. "You developed the perfect green dye."

"You can tell her it was mostly you if it helps seal the deal," Caitlyn said. "Okay, go! What are you waiting for?"

J.T. laughed, and they shared a glance reminiscent of the one they'd shared on their graduation day from Stanford. Life was about to change, and they both knew it. "You're going to rock this. Man, I'm so happy for you."

Be happy for me when she agrees, he wanted to say, but Caitlyn would only call him a Negative Nancy. Even if she didn't agree to marry him today, he'd ask her again.

He opened the door and tucked the wool behind his back. "Wish me luck."

Caitlyn socked him in the chest. "You don't need it. She's a goner where you're concerned. But tell her I won't take no for an answer."

He could well imagine it, and he found himself smiling as he walked up the stairs. Boru and Hatshep were standing there at the top, as if waiting for him. "You'd better not take my clothes out of here after this."

Boru barked, wagging his tail, and Hatshep rubbed her head against his calf. Okay, they were on his side. Whew.

"Hey!" he called out, stepping into the sitting room. "I was hoping I would find you."

"Where else would I be?" she asked from the sofa. She looked to be knitting the last of Arthur's sweater.

He knew she was mad at herself for not being able to leave her chambers yet. After his family had left to go to bed last night, she'd tried to go downstairs. She'd gotten halfway down before sitting on the step beneath her, eyes clenched, breathing like she was asthmatic. He'd sat beside her and pulled her into his arms. "You got halfway down, babe. It's still progress." She hadn't said a word.

"What do you have behind your back?" she asked as Trevor rounded the sofa and sat next to her. Boru barreled after him.

"It's a secret," he said, "for the moment. Can you set your knitting aside please?"

She made the last loop and then placed it on the coffee table. "Are you ready to talk?"

His stomach went queasy. The way she'd said that made him fear she wanted to talk about why they couldn't be together long-term. Not a great way to start off a proposal. "Let me go first."

"I'd rather—"

"*Please.*"

Her mouth twitched as if she were deciding. Then she stood up. "I need to call Cian about something first. Be right back."

With that, she was off, heading toward the bedroom. He leaned back so she wouldn't see the wool. Looking around for a good hiding place, he realized he could tuck it behind the pillow for the time being.

She was only gone for a few moments, but it felt like an eternity of solitude.

"Okay, I'm back," she said cheerily enough, picking up Hatshep as she sat beside him again.

The Persian stared at him and then hopped off Becca's lap, nudging the pillow where Trevor had hidden the wool. Was that a sign of where he'd do best to start? He decided to let the cat pull the wool out. She dragged it onto Becca's lap.

Thanks for the assist, Hatshep.

"What's this? Oh my goodness, it's beautiful! The finest green I've ever come across."

She was holding it up, pulling apart the strands and studying it like a scientist might a new particle or something. He puffed out his chest. "I wanted to do something special for you. Something to show you how much I love you and believe in you."

Her eyes flashed to his. "You did this?"

"Well, Caitlyn and one of her plant experts helped, but I did a lot of research on the best green dyes. We have a recipe for you. Caitlyn partially came here to test it on your wool, and it's composed of—"

"Oh, tell me later," she said, launching herself at him and planting kisses up and down his entire face so sweetly he clutched her to him. Hatshep gave a meow and jumped off the sofa, followed by a bark from Boru. "You wonderful man! It's the best present I've ever received."

She was soft and sweet in his arms, and he brought her against his chest and savored the moment before pressing back. "It's the first of many, I hope." He untangled himself and got on one knee, pulling out the jewelry box and flicking it open with his thumb.

"Becca O'Neill," he said, his gaze steady on her shocked face. "I love you. I can't imagine living without you. I told you I want to marry you, but now I'm asking you. Before you give your answer, let me tell you why you should take a chance on us."

"Trevor, I—"

"Please, Becca, let me speak. This is...important for me to say."

She nodded, and he reached for her hands.

"Becca, I knew I loved you the first time I saw you in the old kitchen, sunlight streaming over you, and you told me all about the wool you'd dyed with your own hands." He squeezed them. "I want to be your partner in every single way. And this condition you think is a reason for us to be apart? I'll be behind you all the way, helping you get where you want to go. I only ask that you let me share your life."

Tears were running down her face, and she gripped his hand.

"I promise you that we'll face whatever comes to both of us. Together."

She took a deep breath, but she was smiling, and that had to be a good thing, right?

"Go look out the window," she said, throwing him off balance.

The window? Why in the hell would he look out the window?

"I'm proposing here." He jiggled the box in case she'd forgotten.

"I know you are," she said, kissing him on the cheek, "and quite sweetly. Did Caitlyn help you with the ring? It's brilliant, by the way."

He could feel frustration rising. "I had a little help, sure. Becca, are you going to answer me?"

She gave him a look. "Are you going to go to the window?"

"Fine, I'll go to the window." Nerves clawed at his guts. "You know, I was trying to be romantic. Caitlyn told me some guys need help, and here I thought I'd done a good job." He charged to the window. "It's a fine sunny day out. Calm sea. Not a breath of wind."

Her heard her chuckle and turned around. "Are you laughing at me?"

"Keep looking," she said, her mouth twitching.

He swung his head back and scanned the yard. Then he heard a familiar hum and looked down. Standing directly under the window was Buttercup, and a sign hung around her neck. He squinted in the sunlight to make it out.

Will you marry me?

Rocking back on his heels, he put his hands on his waist. Then he spun around to face her. "Did Flynn put you up to this or something?" Surely his brother would know better than to play such a prank on the day he knew Trevor planned to propose. Wait, did she think *Trevor* had made the sign?

"Becca," he said with new urgency, "I didn't make that sign." That was on par with the guy proposing in rush hour traffic.

This time she fell back laughing on the sofa. "I know you didn't make the sign, Trevor." Her eyes were dancing when they met his. "I did."

"You did?" His mouth parted for a moment as shock rolled over him. "But why? If this is your idea of a joke, let me be clear. I do not want to marry Buttercup. I want to marry you."

She stood and walked to him. "It's not Buttercup who's asking to marry you with that sign. It's me. I thought you might need a little encouragement since I put up such a fuss the other day. That's why I wanted to go first."

Oh, thank God. "You should have insisted on it," he said, his face breaking into a smile.

"I liked hearing what you had to say," she said, touching his arm.

"What changed your mind?" he asked.

"If you'll let me get a word in, I'll tell you, Trevor Merriam."

He shut up.

***

Becca touched Trevor's strong jaw, her heart filling with the warmth of her love for him. "It was a million things, both big and small. It was the way you slept beside me in the closet when I was at my worst, and the way you walked behind me as I forced myself to leave it."

He cupped her face, his eyes alight with love. "I'll always be there."

"I know," she said, putting her hand over his heart. "When you came here at first, I couldn't reconcile the man you were with your mission, but I soon learned you were everything I'd ever dreamed of finding in a partner. Steadfast. Fair. Easy on the eyes. Charming. Supportive. And loyal."

She reached inside her shirt and brought out the St. Christopher's medal he'd placed around her neck.

"When you gave me this and told me about your Grandpa Noah and Grandma Anna, I started to dream about us making it as husband and wife. When you were asleep last night, I snuck out here and read the letters they wrote during the war, and something Anna said really stuck with me."

He swallowed thickly. "What was it?"

"She said she was tired of letting fear run her life. She was just going to love your Grandfather Noah, not knowing what would happen or what would come of it. She only knew her love for him couldn't be stopped. Not by a war. Not by anything. I realized that's how I love you."

"Oh, baby," he said, stroking her cheek.

"Trevor, I don't know how well I'll become or if I'll ever be cured, but I won't give up. I'll try this new psychiatrist, and if he doesn't help, we'll find someone else. But I promise you... I'm never going to let it stop me from loving you or any children we have, and I'll never let my fear stop me from becoming more and living a better life. And yes, I want to share my life with you."

She held out her hand. "So let's make this official. Then we can see if I can make it out of my chambers because I very much feel like celebrating with your family."

He slid the ring onto her finger, and it didn't surprise her at all that it was a perfect fit.

He was the perfect fit for her, and she looked out across the sea, imagining the stars she'd seen that night they'd made love on the window seat. Her mind conjured up the same dream, of the two of them holding hands and walking out toward the cliffs with their children running ahead of them, the sunlight streaming down on them all, the scent of wild roses fragrant in the air.

She willed it to happen, and being Irish and believing in magic, she knew it would come true.

Because true love created miracles.

Epilogue

ANOTHER ENGAGEMENT IN THE BAG, ARTHUR THOUGHT, as he and Clara returned to Honeysuckle Cottage.

"We did fine work here, Clara," he said, glancing up at the midnight Irish sky filled with stars. "I'm going to miss this place."

"We'll be back," she said, taking his hand and pulling him inside. She was a determined woman sometimes.

He kissed her slowly, and she sighed in his arms. Yes, they'd celebrated the new engagement with her family, and he'd had more than a few whiskeys, but he felt young and vital again. "It's like I've drunk from the fountain of youth."

She had the audacity to laugh, but that's why he loved her so. "We're each other's fountains of youth, you idiot. I thought you knew that."

He did, but she could only handle a few compliments a day. "So where to after this, my love? Back to Dare Valley?" Goodness, he missed his family there, but his granddaughter Jill kept him up on all the news with her infernal texts and emoticons. Sometimes he was downright afraid the entire English language would be replaced by a string of smiley faces and other symbols, like some technology-inspired cuneiform. He hoped he'd be dead before that ever happened.

Clara linked her arms around his neck. "I figure we go home for a spell and then head to the south of France."

Forgoing kissing her, he asked, "Whatever for? Do they have a crystal factory there or something?"

Her hard look only made him grin. "No, you silly man. Caitlyn plans to pitch her new perfume enterprise to Quinn soon, and if all goes well—"

"Which it will." He'd seen that girl in action. No man in his right mind could turn down her brains and enthusiasm.

"Exactly, so I figure we fly out there after she settles in. Becca has inspired Caitlyn to go to the source of her product."

"And that is?" he asked.

Her sigh gusted out, and she got that very female look on her face, one he knew meant romance. *"Flowers."*

Oh, brother.

***

Caitlyn surveyed the rosewood double door to Quinn's office.

Even though his assistant had told her she could go in, she needed a minute to compose herself. She wanted this bad, and she had to get her way.

"What are you waiting for?" Michaela asked, popping out of her seat and grabbing her by the shoulders. "This is a walk in the park."

"A piece of cake," she echoed, grateful her sister had agreed to accompany her to the Big Bad Wolf's office. "My report is solid."

"It's better than solid," Michaela said, pushing her toward the door. "Not only do you have the product plan, but you have a crazy ingenious marketing plan. How could Quinnie boy say no?"

Because it wasn't Quinnie boy on the other side of the door. It was Quinn Merriam, M.B.A, Esquire, and total badass vice president of Merriam Enterprises, only second to the number one badass, Connor Merriam. They didn't eat children for breakfast, but they'd made more than one person lose their lunch from nerves. She was determined not to go that route.

But she wanted this new challenge. Craved it. Dreamed about it. Was slightly obsessed by it.

"Okay, I'm going in." She stormed to the door and yanked one side open.

Quinn immediately looked up from the papers arranged in perfect angles on his desk. "Don't pull the hinges off."

Great. What an opening salvo. She closed the door softly and crossed the room in her Manolo Blahnik Hangisi Floral Lace Crystal-Toe Pumps, the heels a subtle advertisement for her new venture, as was the moonflower pin on her navy suit jacket's lapel.

"Let's get this started," Quinn said, coming around his desk. "I'm running a little behind today."

She almost rolled her eyes, but she was a Merriam employee right now and not his sister. "I'll do my best to be short and sweet."

They walked over to his oval side table, a notable exception to the crisp geometric appearance of the rest of his office. Modern art hung on the walls and the London sky outside the large floor-to-ceiling window was foggy, obscuring his breathtaking view of the Thames. Good, she didn't need the distraction.

She slid her report in front of him. "I know you've probably read it."

"Seriously?" he asked.

Was that an eye roll from the Big Bad Wolf?

"I always read the report, Caitlyn. Let me make sure I understand the high points. You *think* there's a market for a boutique perfume from farm to vanity table, so to speak."

Clever way to put it, bro.

"I don't just think it," she said, folding her trembling hands in her lap. "I know it. Let me tell you why. Every market is trying to show a connection to local farms, whether by marketing stories about the farmers who make their products or telling the customer where something was raised—with organic materials, no less. Currently, there are few companies marketing pure plant essences, and they haven't been selling them as high-end perfume."

"Yes, as an essence," he said, sitting back. "I read your report. Why do you think you can sell a perfume that's organic?"

"Because I'm going to up the magic factor," she said, knowing he wouldn't like that word. "Hear me out. It's one thing to have a spectacular perfume. It's another to create something that women crave, and do you know what that is?"

"I'd like to think I do," he said, "but go ahead and tell me."

"They want a fantasy," she said, drawing out that last word. "Most perfume marketing campaigns use beautiful women who are actresses or famous models to target women. I think that's effective in only certain cases where a woman *believes* she can be as desirable as the woman in the ad. I mean, seriously. Take Charlize Theron in the Dior ads. How many women do you know think they can be that beautiful and sexy?"

His lips twitched. "I'm listening."

"But use one of the world's most compelling men," she continued, "the kind of man every woman wants to be with, the kind of exemplary man who seems to love all women simply because they're women?"

"Such a male paragon exists? Let me guess. It's Flynn, right?"

She almost laughed. "In his dreams probably. But the research I've done suggests I've landed on the perfect candidate."

"Is he an athlete?" he asked.

"No. Too violent for some women." She hadn't included this part in her report, and she knew she'd hooked his interest.

"Let me guess again. A celebrated actor?"

"Too fake in the end. People know they're being paid to act." That tidbit from the research polls had surprised her, although it did cast some light on why people paid such attention to reality TV stars, God help her.

"Caitlyn, who are we talking about here?"

She tried to keep the glee out of her voice. "A musician. One of the world's most popular stars who swings back and forth between country and mainstream. An All-American who's the ultimate boy next door, yet you feel yourself melt when he sings and looks straight at you with those gray-blue eyes."

His brows winged up. "Gray-blue eyes, huh?"

"You get the picture," she said, clearing her throat. Okay, maybe she was falling into the fantasy herself a little, but that's why she knew it would work. Michaela agreed, and even Flynn had claimed he'd do the guy if he were a girl. "The numbers don't lie."

She pulled out the bottom piece of paper under her report, something else she hadn't included. He picked it up, his eyes widening in surprise.

"He hits *all* demographics," she said, driving her point home. "From teenage girls to retirees. All the states and the big markets around the world, including Asia, which isn't always an easy market to navigate."

She let the words settle as he scanned the table she'd prepared.

"Quinn, he's an international male phenomenon."

He tapped the table. "You still haven't told me who he is. I don't have time for more guessing games, Caitlyn."

Oh, he could be so stuffy sometimes. "Beau Masters."

"Beau Masters? *That's* the man every woman around the world wants?"

She nodded. Was he kidding? "And he's single, which preserves the fantasy."

"What if his marital status changes?" he asked.

"Wouldn't matter," she said, hoping she didn't come off as a lovesick teenager. "Women would still fantasize about being with him."

"And you think he'll agree to be the spokesperson for our campaign?" he asked.

"Currently, his agent and business manager, who is his mother, has been shopping around for the right brand, but according to the reports I've read, Mr. Masters has been picky. He's looking for something new, something elegant, something relatable."

"And you think a farm-to-vanity table perfume is just the ticket?"

"His father was an alcoholic who died in a car wreck, so that rules out beer commercials and cars. No way he's going to do insurance or pharmaceuticals. Too narrow an audience. Cologne is saturated with hot models, but this angle? No one is doing it."

"That's the part that worries me," Quinn said. "There might be a reason."

"Look, I've hired consultants who've worked with two of the major perfume houses, and they agree this will work. Plus, I'm going to hire someone special to make our perfume, someone fresh to the larger international market."

"And who's that?" Quinn steepled his hands.

"In a second. I'll be using flowers from France in

the beginning since it'll give us a marketing boost, but the scent will be completely new because our mixer is an Egyptian who trained in both French and ancient ways dating back to the Pharaohs."

Her brother's brows shot up. Yeah, he was intrigued.

"He's been creating some of the best perfume around at a boutique company. Couple that with the other aspects of my plan, natural flowers and Beau Masters, and we're a slam dunk for big-time success."

"The Egyptian will take the job?"

"I'm told he'll be open to an offer since his current employer is content to remain small. He loves France and speaks the language fluently. Did you know they've found perfume in Egyptian tombs with the same strength as anything you'll find in a department store? And that's like four thousand years old."

"Most of our customers don't live that long," Quinn said, pushing the report back at her. "It's comforting to think our product would outlive them, I guess, but we need them to buy more than one ounce of perfume and use it in this lifetime to make a profit."

She was losing him. "Let me do things right. Hire the right people to pull it off. Secure Beau Masters. That's not negotiable."

His eyes went flat. Time to talk turkey. "Run me through the numbers."

These she had memorized. And dammit, she was thorough. In fact, when she finished presenting the capital outlay numbers, coupled with the expected profits minus employee compensation and marketing expenses, he was smiling at her.

"You did your homework," he said.

Damn right. "So what's it going to be?"

He tapped his hand on the table once, like it was a gavel punctuating his decision. "I'll give you thirty million to start, and you need to land Beau Masters since he's the make-or-break piece of your marketing campaign."

Since she knew how tenacious and persuasive she could be, that condition didn't bother her a bit. As for the money... She hadn't expected one hundred million upfront—but you always shoot for the moon, their dad liked to say. She let her feet do her dancing under the table. "Thank you."

He rose. "Keep me updated."

Her brother loved progress reports like some people liked Haagen-Dazs ice cream. "Of course."

She left, knowing he never did a sibling chitchat or after-meeting hug.

Michaela hugged her the moment she closed the door. "He said yes! I can see it on your face. Now what?"

She had to convince the world's most compelling man to believe in her.

Dear Reader,

This new series and the Merriam family have totally captured my heart, and we're only on book one. Hah! And Arthur, Clara, and Hargreaves continue to keep me in stitches with their antics. I'm so happy Arthur talked me into letting him be in this new series after our Dare Valley series ended. What would we do without him?

Certainly, we have a lot of excitement ahead. Caitlyn and Beau's story, LOVE AMONG LAVENDER, is turning out to be swoon-worthy and so funny. He's a good guy trying to get his bad boy on, and in Caitlyn's opinion, he's awful at it. And in her French farmhouse, no less, where she's creating her new perfume with a mysterious master blender. Beau needs to get on track as her celebrity spokesperson, and who better to help than Arthur and Clara? Except they're matchmakers with minds of their own. What trouble could they all get up to while creating this fabulous perfume? Honestly, a lot!

Dare River fans will be happy to know that our favorite hero, Rye Crenshaw, is trying to talk me into letting him make a cameo in this book. After all, he was the original bad boy country music star. We'll see.

I can't tell you how much fun I'm having researching flowers, scents, the process of perfume making, and Provence—one of my favorite places ever. I know you're going to love it too.

Thanks again for embracing this wonderful new family, The Merriams, and for spending time with all of us.

Lots of love,

Ava

P.S. Arthur and Clara and the rest of the Merriam kids would love to hear what you thought of this book and the series, so please leave a review. Big hug and thanks.

P.P.S. I did the best I could with all things Irish in this book, so if I missed something, let me just say, oops. Also thanks to Kathy Kennedy for sharing some of her favorite things and insights about Ireland with me.

About the Author

International Bestselling Author Ava Miles joined the ranks of beloved storytellers with her powerful messages of healing, mystery, and magic. Millions of readers have discovered her fiction and nonfiction books, praised by *USA TODAY* and *Publisher's Weekly*. *Women's World Magazine* has selected a few of her novels for their book clubs while Southwest Airlines featured the #1 National Bestseller NORA ROBERTS LAND (the name used with Ms. Roberts' blessing) in its in-flight entertainment. Ava's books have been chosen as Best Books of the Year and Top Editor's Picks and are translated into multiple languages.

CPSIA information can be obtained
at www.ICGtesting.com
Printed in the USA
LVHW111120010621
689012LV00022B/298